ALL
FALL
DOWN

Also by Tom Bale

SEE HOW THEY RUN

SINS OF THE FATHER writing as David Harrison

EACH LITTLE LIE

SKIN AND BONES

TERROR'S REACH

BLOOD FALLS

THE CATCH

ALL FALL DOWN

TOM BALE

Bookouture

Published by Bookouture

An imprint of StoryFire Ltd.
23 Sussex Road, Ickenham, UB10 8PN
United Kingdom

www.bookouture.com

ISBN: 978-1-78681-055-7
ebook ISBN: 978-1-78681-054-0

For Emily & Dan; James & Lizzie and Theo

ONE

It began with a sound like someone knocking. Rob couldn't place it at first: he'd had a fair bit to drink and was in a mellow, reflective mood. With his family growing up and moving on, days like these had to be savoured.

There were a couple of different conversations in progress, and music playing on Evan's portable speaker. The barbecue was fizzing and spitting with the last of the burgers, destined never to be eaten. Rob, sitting on the left-hand side of the terrace, looked over his right shoulder. Was it someone at the front door, or the gate at the side of the house?

The next knock was harder, with the flabby echo of timber yielding beneath the blows: a fence panel. But the neighbours on one side were out, and the others weren't the sort who'd object to a Sunday afternoon barbecue. So where…?

Rob gestured to his son. Evan and his girlfriend Livvy were intertwined on the swing seat; a quick tap on his phone and the music stopped. There was a moment of frozen silence before something thudded into the rear fence.

Wendy Turner frowned at her husband. 'What was that?'

Rob stood up and moved to the edge of the terrace. He was a tall man, nearly six two, but even he couldn't see much beyond the fence. The house backed on to a large wild meadow, some of it privately owned and enclosed for horses. The rest was common land with access to a network of trails that criss-crossed the fields south of Petersfield; as a consequence most of the residents along here had opted for high fences for privacy as well as security.

'Has one of the horses got out?' Evan began to extricate himself from the swing seat, but Rob waved him back down.

'I'll check.'

Later he would try to remember if there had been a note of caution in his voice. He jogged down the steps and was crossing the lawn, curious to see what sort of animal it was, when he heard a loud groan that could only have come from a human being.

Rob was close enough to locate the sound now: the third panel of seven. Someone – a man – was breathing in short, desperate gasps, bumping and knocking against the fence. Rob tracked him moving left to right, towards the gate.

And it was unbolted. Evan and Livvy had been on the common not half an hour before, tossing a Frisbee back and forth.

'Rob?' His wife's voice was uncertain, maybe even fearful.

'It's okay.' He had no idea if that was true, but he strode forward as the handle juddered against the latch. Rob quickly pressed his shoulder to the gate, holding it shut. He could feel the man's weight against it, heavy and insistent.

There was a moment when Rob could have thrown the bolts home and kept the intruder at bay, but instead he did the opposite. . . his decision swayed by a simple whispered plea.

'Help me.'

TWO

Wendy shouted something – it might have been, 'Rob, don't!' – but it was too late: he'd whipped the gate open.

Taken by surprise, the man stumbled in and collapsed at Rob's feet. Several of his fingers looked pulpy and misshapen, which was perhaps why he didn't try to break his fall. His long grey hair was matted with blood, as well as leaves and twigs and what might have been dirt or something worse. The smell coming off him was foul: a stench of ingrained sweat, bodily waste and decay.

As Rob recoiled, there was a high-pitched scream from Georgia. His fifteen-year-old daughter had been on a sun lounger in an alcove beside the terrace. As she leapt up and fled indoors, Wendy looked set to go after her, but Rob yelled, 'Get the first aid kit! Evan, call 999, ambulance and police!'

Gasping, the man struggled on to his elbows and knees. Thin strands of drool hung from his mouth as he tried to speak. He wore filthy jeans and a tatty blue fleece with a large tear across the back. Beneath it was a grimy t-shirt, stained with blood and pus from what looked like a network of slashes to the skin.

On one foot he wore a cheap trainer flapping open at the toes; the other foot was bare, and crusted with blood around a small circular wound to the top and bottom. Having spent his working life on building sites, where he'd witnessed a fair number of accidents, Rob knew it was a puncture mark: exactly as if someone had driven a nail through the man's foot.

Torture was the word that popped into his mind. This man wasn't just in terrible pain, but in fear of his life – that much was clear from the way he went on scrabbling over the grass. He was making a noise in his throat but couldn't control his breathing enough to form words.

'You're safe, you're safe here,' Rob told him. But when he reached out, the man flinched, his back arching in panic; he coughed up a gout of blood and collapsed once again, his body still except for one leg, juddering against the grass.

Rob tried feeling for a pulse, but his first aid skills were severely limited. Wendy, thankfully, was a lot more capable, and now she came running towards him, holding the emergency medical kit.

Evan was speaking urgently on the phone, and Livvy had gone inside after Georgia. Rob checked the gate. He couldn't see anyone on the common, but his view was restricted to a narrow slice of land. On the soft, springy turf it would be all too easy for someone to creep up on them.

Wendy gasped at the sight of the man's wounds. She dropped to her knees, then had to turn away, one hand over her mouth as she retched. Rob understood her reaction: up close the sweet, cloying odour of rotting flesh was overpowering.

'I don't know how much we can do for him,' he said. 'He needs a hospital.'

Wendy swallowed heavily. 'Let's get him in the recovery position, at least.'

Together they rolled the man on to his side, his head lolling in a way that reminded Rob of a landed fish. An unnatural, feverish heat radiated from his skin. His face was so bruised and swollen that it was difficult to put an age on him. Late fifties, if Rob had to guess.

Wendy bent forward to detect a breath. 'He's still with us, just about.' Straightening up, she took a gulp of less tainted air and shook her head. 'He must be in agony.'

Rob started to get up. 'You all right here?'

'What?'

With a nod at the common, he said, 'Whoever did this could still be out there.'

Rob listened to her objections – it might be dangerous; he should leave it to the police – but knew he had to do *something*.

'Just a quick look,' he promised, and without waiting for a response he moved through the gateway, ready to react at the first hint of an ambush.

But there was no one in sight. In the woods on the far side of the meadow, a light breeze stirred the treetops. Birds chirped listlessly; from far off he could hear the low rumble of traffic and the whine of a lawnmower.

Rob wondered if his son's music had attracted the man to their property – homing in on people who could come to his aid – but already, at the back of his mind, a much less welcome theory was forming.

He took a few steps towards the nearest footpath, checking the ground for signs of blood. Wendy shouted his name, and he realised that he'd drifted out of sight.

'It's fine,' he called. 'Won't be a minute.'

She's right: let the police handle this, he thought. But another voice didn't welcome that idea. Not if there was any chance that his other theory could be right.

Was this some kind of message?

A warning?

THREE

With his thoughts in turmoil, Rob made for slightly higher ground, passing the wire fence of a grassy paddock where two palomino mares grazed contentedly. He crossed a couple of paths that had been worn to dirt by regular use, but found no blood, no evidence of the man's route to their home.

At the top of the rise he stopped to scan the tree line beyond the meadow. There was still no one to be seen, and yet Rob had the feeling he was being watched. The sun was a dazzling white disc, and for a moment his vision blurred; he felt the first twinge of a tension headache and knew this was pointless: *I ought to be back with my family—*

An unnatural shape drew his attention, obscured from view by a large clump of gorse. Shielding his eyes from the sun, he trotted down the slope and saw that it was a boy – or a young man – hunched over in an odd position, one knee jutting forward.

He was sitting on a bike, Rob realised; a small, wiry figure, wearing a black t-shirt and long khaki shorts.

'Hey!' As Rob moved closer, the boy rolled back a couple of feet. There was a surliness about his posture that Rob, as a father of two young men, knew all too well. 'Can I ask you something? Hey!'

No response. The boy stared at him from behind the bushes. Rob caught a glimpse of a pale face, a mop of dark, scruffy hair. Something about his gaze seemed to radiate hostility.

'Were you here a few minutes ago? A guy in a blue fleece, he's badly hurt. Did you see where he came from?'

Still nothing. They were about fifty feet apart. Fuming, Rob said, 'This is important. Has anyone been along—?' He broke off as the boy's head jerked up, reacting to something.

Distant sirens, pulsing slowly towards them. The sound distracted him for a moment, and that was all it took for the boy to race away. Rob dashed forward but caught his toe on a root; stumbling, he managed to regain his balance as the bike went sailing into the trees.

Chasing him would be futile. Once in the woods, the boy had any number of routes to follow – and even if Rob were to catch him, what then? Rob might consider it his public duty to restrain a potential witness, but wasn't he just as likely to be prosecuted for assault as thanked for his efforts?

A sudden wave of dizziness had him doubled up, his heart thumping like crazy. Hearing a shout, he quickly stood and put on a reassuring smile. Evan was sprinting towards him in huge strides, virtually floating above the grass. He was a natural athlete, not quite as tall as his dad but leaner and faster; he made Rob feel like an old man.

'Paramedics are here.' Evan caught his glance at the trees and said, 'Who were you shouting at?'

'A lad on a bike. Thought he might have seen something.' Rob blew out a sigh. 'He just took off.'

'If it was a kid, you probably scared him to death.'

'Not a child. A teenager, or your sort of age.'

Staring at the trees, a patch of shadows caught Rob's notice. Was the young man still in there, watching them?

'Can't really blame him for not wanting to get involved.' Evan placed a hand on his shoulder. 'You need to come back and rest.'

'I won't keel over, don't worry.' To prove it, Rob set a brisk pace. 'How's Georgia?'

'Fine. Livvy's with her.'

'We need to be careful. This could bring back all kinds of. . .'

'Yeah, except she's tougher than any of us. Stop stressing, Dad. It's all under control.'

Rob couldn't help but give a rueful smile. Evan and his girlfriend had returned from their second year at university with an air of confidence that implied they had adult life completely sussed, and couldn't understand why the older generation had made such a fuss about the challenges of independence.

Reaching the gate, Rob waved his son through and took one last look at the woods. Evan was probably right, but something about the boy's reaction troubled him just the same.

What did you see? he wondered.

What do you know?

FOUR

Back in the garden, a couple of paramedics were tending to the injured man, who was already hooked up to a drip and had an oxygen mask covering his face. Wendy was being led back towards the house by a stocky, middle-aged policeman.

On the terrace a female officer was in conversation with Livvy, who had a protective arm around Georgia. The sight prompted a twinge of guilt; just for a moment, when the man blundered into the garden, Rob had forgotten his daughter was there.

Evan hurried past the activity on the lawn, but Rob paused to ask, 'Is he going to be all right?'

One of the paramedics was preparing an injection of some sort; she offered Rob a quick, professional smile. 'Too early to say. But we'll do our best.'

This brief exchange had alerted the policeman to their presence. Under scrutiny, Rob realised how hot and dishevelled he must look, which perhaps explained why the officer's expression seemed to harden slightly.

'This is Rob,' Wendy said, 'and my son, Evan.'

The cop spared Evan no more than a glance before his focus returned to Rob. 'Mr Turner, I'm PC Clark. My colleague, PC Jardine, is speaking to. . . your daughter, is it?'

Rob nodded. 'And my son's girlfriend, Livvy.'

'And where had you been?' PC Clark indicated the open gate.

'Just went to check the common, see if there was any clue as to. . .' Rob trailed off, aware of how defensive his tone had become.

'And was there?'

'Not that I could see.'

'How long were you gone?'

'Three or four minutes. I tried to speak to this lad on a bike, but he was too far away, and then I heard the sirens, and Evan came to get me—'

'Whoa, whoa.' Clark had his hands up, as if to stop traffic. 'Let's rewind a fraction. Your wife tells me you were having a barbecue.' He looked round, pointedly confirming the presence of the still-smoking grill. 'So the whole family were here, yes?'

'Everyone but Josh.' Wendy saw the man's confusion and tried to clarify. 'Evan's twin brother. He's not yet back from university.'

'It was just the five of us.' Rob must have sounded brusque, because Wendy flashed a warning glance: *Don't get tetchy.*

After recording the full details of everyone present, PC Clark asked Rob to describe what had happened. From Wendy's frown, Rob gathered that she'd already given the policeman an account.

He wants to see if our stories tally.

Rob tried to compose himself. 'There isn't much to tell you. We were just out here, enjoying the sunshine, when something banged on the fence.'

As he ran through the sequence of events, he watched the paramedics carefully lift the unconscious man on to a trolley stretcher. PC Jardine accompanied them out past the side of the house, signalling to Clark as she left.

After a nod in response, the policeman said, 'Is the gentleman known to you at all, sir?'

'Never seen him before in my life,' Rob said forcefully, even while a sly voice in his head whispered: *You should have taken a closer look, this could be a warning—*

'Sure about that?'

Rob, swallowing heavily, said, 'Positive.'

Clark held his gaze for a long moment, before switching his attention to Wendy. Shifting her weight from one foot to the other, she said, 'It's not easy to be sure – with all the blood on his face, I mean – but I don't think so.'

The policeman jotted a few notes, then said, 'In due course my colleagues will need to take full statements. And for the meantime, that end of the garden is out of bounds.'

He moved away, surveying the ground carefully before each step. At an offer of refreshments, he turned and smiled for the first time.

'Tea with milk and one, please.'

Rob followed Wendy into the living room. Georgia was on the sofa between Evan and Livvy but leaning forward, as if uncomfortable with their proximity. Livvy was saying, '. . . I'm sure he'll be fine once they get him to hospital.'

'Exactly,' Wendy added. 'It's nothing to worry about, darling. Honestly.'

'But what happened to him?' Georgia looked from Wendy to Rob. 'Why did he come here?'

Because of me.

Rob turned his shudder into a shrug. 'There wasn't any particular reason. Maybe he heard the music and knew there'd be people in the garden who could help?'

Georgia considered this explanation, then went back to staring at the floor. With a nod of thanks to Livvy and Evan, Rob joined Wendy in the kitchen. 'Okay?' he asked.

She shook her head. Her jaw was tight, a muscle twitching in her cheek. For a moment Rob interpreted it as anger, but then she threw her arms around him and let out a sob.

'The state he was in, Rob. The *cruelty* of what was done to him. . .'

'I know.' He hesitated for a moment before holding her tight. 'I'll make tea. You go and sit with the others.'

'No, I'd rather keep busy.' She eased herself away from him, tore off a sheet of kitchen roll and blew her nose. 'That's a good point, about the music.'

'It's the only thing I can think of.' He turned quickly to the window. PC Clark was at the gate, gazing out over the common. 'Interesting that he asked us both to describe what happened.'

'I suppose he had to.' Wendy put a couple of coffee mugs on the unit and then paused. 'But we don't have anything to hide, do we?'

Rob spun to face her, unsure if that was an allegation. 'What you said about the blood on his face – it sounded like you were contradicting me.'

'Not really. Anyway, your tone was getting a bit aggressive.'

'Because he was glaring at me like I'm the prime suspect.'

Wendy exhaled loudly. 'Look at it from his point of view. He responds to a call about a badly injured man in our garden. We say it's nothing to do with us, and he's, what, just supposed to accept it?' She mimed tugging a forelock. *Right you are then, sir, I'll be on my way. . .*

The bad Cockney accent made him grin, which helped defuse the tension. She was right, of course. The police would naturally consider the possibility that the householders were responsible for the attack – and it probably hadn't helped that Clark's first sight of Rob had been when he'd returned from the common, red-faced and sweating.

He fetched the milk and handed it over as a kind of peace offering, but was thrown by her next question. 'Do you think it's worth calling Dawn?'

'And ruin her Sunday evening? That's not fair.'

'No, all right, then. I just thought – if they are suspicious of us – she might put in a word on our behalf.'

Rob thought this a foolish idea, but he answered with a shrug. To be in the clear, what they really needed was for the police to identify whoever had tortured that man half to death.

But what if the answer caused more problems than it solved?

Evan and Livvy accepted coffees, and even Georgia agreed to have a hot chocolate. They'd put a DVD on, some kind of slushy romantic comedy to lighten the mood.

Outside, PC Clark was mooching along the flower beds, and eagerly changed course to collect his tea. No sooner had he taken a sip than his radio bleeped.

With a look of weary resignation, he retreated across the lawn to speak in private. Rob and Wendy tried not to show an interest as he listened, made a couple of muttered comments, then lowered the radio and turned back to the terrace.

'Cardiac arrest en route to the hospital. Never regained consciousness.' He tutted, perhaps because his afternoon had become a lot more complicated. 'Potentially, this is a murder enquiry now.'

FIVE

By six o'clock Russell Drive was jammed with vehicles, most of them bearing the livery of Hampshire Constabulary. It was one of those summer evenings that feels cooler indoors than out, prompting Wendy to fetch a cardigan.

'I think I've seen Dawn's car,' she called from the stairs. 'Did you contact her?'

'Not me, no.' Rob tried not to scowl when, a moment later, the doorbell rang.

Detective Sergeant Dawn Avery was on the step, wearing black leggings and a white t-shirt; still slim, but unmistakably pregnant. Rob greeted her with a brief, careful hug after she and Wendy had shared a longer embrace.

'Lovely to see you,' Wendy exclaimed. 'How many weeks is it now?'

'Twenty-eight.' Dawn rested a hand on her belly. 'This is supposed to be the "blooming" stage, but I just feel knackered all the time.'

'It's because there's no rest with the second one. Is Leo all right?'

'Yeah, he's good. Tim's on bedtime story duty tonight.' She grinned at Rob. 'He was disappointed you couldn't make the bike ride.'

'Petworth and back?' Rob said in mock horror. 'I like cycling, but not that much.' And then he thought: *Maybe if I'd known what lay in store for us today. . .*

After a little more small talk, Wendy said, 'We did wonder if you'd be assigned to this.'

'Actually, I'm not. DS Husein knew we were friends because I recommended your guys to quote for a central heating system.' Looking slightly embarrassed, she added, 'The fool went for someone cheaper, and he's had them back twice to fix leaks.'

'Oh, well.' It wasn't the first time he'd heard something like this. Rob was just grateful that Tim and Dawn, like many of their friends, had done their bit to promote his business after its troubles.

They moved into the living room, which offered a perfect view of the activity taking place on the lawn. There seemed to be at least a dozen officers in attendance, including a team from the Scientific Services Department, clad in the ominous white suits that Rob recognised from many a TV drama.

'It's actually a mercy for you that the victim died en route to hospital,' Dawn told them. 'If his death had occurred on the lawn, the body wouldn't have been moved till a full forensic examination had been conducted.'

Spotting DS Husein, Dawn went out for a chat, leaving Wendy to offer Rob an encouraging smile. 'Makes such a difference to have a friendly face, doesn't it?'

'Absolutely,' Rob agreed, though he wasn't sure how convincing he sounded.

They'd come to know Dawn well in the ten years she'd been with Tim, who was one of Rob's oldest friends. To begin with it had been slightly awkward, because they'd been similarly close to Tim's first wife, Jill. That marriage had foundered on a disagreement over children – to Tim's dismay, Jill was always adamant she didn't want them – and Rob and Wendy had never seen him as happy as when Dawn announced she was pregnant with Leo. Now there was a second baby on the way, and Tim seemed undaunted at the idea of becoming a parent again in his late forties. Rob couldn't imagine anything worse.

He stood and watched Dawn and the other detective in conversation. There were frequent gestures towards the common, and once or twice, when DS Husein glanced back at the house, Rob had to steel himself not to duck out of sight.

Dawn moved on to greet a couple of her colleagues: a spot of workplace banter, judging by the wide smiles and her playful attempt to slap the head of a short, thickset man in an Iron Maiden t-shirt. It reminded Rob that, as horrific as this afternoon's events had been, to the officers here this was simply another job.

Returning to the house, Dawn accepted a glass of cranberry juice, and told them that attempts would be made to search at least part of the common before darkness fell.

'Poor DS Husein got lumbered as Deputy SIO, and he has actions up to his eyeballs. It's a tough ask to gather enough bodies on a Sunday evening – I only got spared because I have to be in London for a trial tomorrow.'

The other priority, she told them, was house-to-house enquiries. 'Far more likely to catch people at home on a Sunday night than we will in the morning.'

Rob perked up at this. 'Do you think he was seen, making his way here?'

'It's possible, though we've had no other reports that fit the bill.'

Without intending to blurt it out, Rob said, 'And are we being considered as suspects?'

Dawn gave him a sideways glance. 'Why'd you say that?'

'Just the impression we had. The first officer on the scene, PC Clark—'

'Ah, you don't want to worry about Don.' Her smile was brief, and slightly unconvincing. 'Though that's not to say there aren't. . . formalities.'

'Of course,' Wendy said. 'You can't simply take what we say at face val—'

She broke off as DS Husein appeared in the doorway. Now Dawn's expression grew warmer, and contained a hint of relief.

'Just the man to put your minds at rest,' she declared, but Rob couldn't help adding the word that she seemed to omit.

Hopefully.

Detective Sergeant Husein was a slim, graceful man in his late twenties – that was the minimum age Rob assumed he had to be, given his rank – but with his soft brown eyes and clean-shaven skin he could have passed for a decade younger. He was one of the few people present who was formally dressed, in a well-fitting grey suit, which made him look like a schoolboy at a family christening.

He nodded in greeting, his gaze seeming to linger on Dawn's glass.

'Would you like some juice?' Wendy asked.

'Yes, please. I usually end up drinking gallons of tea and coffee, but I don't really like the stuff.'

With a teasing smile, Dawn said, 'Shahid prefers a beaker of squash with a bendy straw, don't you?'

'Forget the straw. A sippy cup is even better.' He raised his eyebrows at Rob. 'There's a running joke that I look about twelve.'

Wendy returned with the drink, and Husein sat forward on the sofa, notebook at the ready.

'We plan to start the search this evening. There's a chance of rain overnight, but I'm hoping the forecasts are wrong.' His eyebrows twitched. 'First I want to check that you're sure he came from the common?'

Rob said, 'Well, we didn't see or hear him till he was at the fence, so no, we're not a hundred per cent.'

'There's a path a few doors down,' Wendy added. 'In theory he could have cut through there from the road. Or even come from one of the other gardens.'

'But across the common is the likeliest route, isn't it?' Dawn asked.

They agreed that it was, and Husein said, 'What we have found are a couple of bloodstains on the far side of your fence, consistent with him brushing against the panels.' He stared into his glass. 'Are you certain you didn't recognise him?'

Rob glanced at Wendy, then immediately wished he hadn't. It might suggest that they were colluding.

'Definitely not,' she said, and Rob nodded in agreement.

Dawn offered Husein a wry smile. 'Never mind, Shahid. Job would be boring if the answers were there on a plate.'

SIX

When Husein's phone buzzed, he took his time checking the display. As they waited for him to continue, Rob was conscious of Wendy's rigid posture. Her hands were clasped together, fingers writhing. It made him realise he was working too hard to appear relaxed, when it was clear he was anything but.

'If you didn't know him,' Husein said, 'and we'll take it for now that he didn't know you, we've got some ten or eleven houses along here. . .' He tapped his pen against his teeth. 'What we need to determine is whether there was any specific reason for coming to your house.'

'It's probably random,' Dawn added, as if to reassure them. 'But we can't afford to overlook anything that could have governed his choice.'

'We get that,' Rob said. 'What occurred to me is that we had music playing, so he'd have known there were people here.'

'If there was no one in the neighbours' gardens, it could be that simple.' Husein shared a glance with Dawn, who shrugged.

'Did the man say anything to you?' she asked.

'Um, yeah, just "Help me".'

'In English?' Husein queried. 'And nothing else?'

'I think he was trying to say more, but couldn't get the words out. And I've only just realised this, but he might have had an accent.'

'What type?' Dawn asked.

'I couldn't say for sure. His voice was quite thick, guttural – could have been Scottish, or maybe the north-east.'

'So not Eastern European?' Husein had a hopeful edge to his voice.

'I don't think so, but I can't be certain. I'm sorry.'

Husein waved away the apology, and Wendy said, 'Did he not have any ID on him?'

There was a hesitation. Rob guessed the detective would deliberately withhold information, not least because he'd want their answers to be as unbiased as possible. But after a glance at Dawn, Husein shook his head. 'Not a thing.'

'That's a bit strange, isn't it?' Wendy said.

'It gets worse. From the preliminary examination of the body, we've discovered some. . . unusual wounds.'

'Unusual?' Rob felt a coldness spreading along his spine.

'In a couple of places his skin had been excised. He has several tattoos, quite conventional ones. Our theory is that his attackers might have removed other, more distinctive tattoos that could have assisted with identification.'

Wendy made a noise in her throat. Dawn reached over and grasped her arm. 'Sorry, that was more detail than you needed.'

'Yes, forgive me.' Husein looked embarrassed. 'And it is only a theory at this stage. His fingerprints are intact, and of course we'll be able to take his DNA.'

Dawn chimed in: 'To me, it says his attackers know he won't show up on our databases, which could point to him being foreign. Checking abroad can take a lot longer, whereas a description of unusual tattoos often gets a quick result. Friends, workmates – someone's going to recognise them and come forward.'

'On the subject of identification,' Husein said, 'I'm afraid we'll need to take fingerprints and a DNA sample of everyone present. It's a simple swab, not invasive at all.'

Rob looked to Wendy, half expecting her to object on Georgia's behalf. But her expression was calm, almost blank. 'Fine with us,' she said.

'Great.' Husein finished his juice, then asked them to run through the sequence of events once more. Rob described how the man had gone on trying to move, even after he'd collapsed in their garden.

'It was as if he was being chased, that was the impression I had.'

'And what gave you that impression, exactly?'

'Well. . . his fear, I suppose. The desperation. And with those injuries, the logical explanation was that someone was after him.'

'But you didn't see anyone? PC Clark said you went out on the common?'

'That's right. I had a quick scout round, but there was no one in sight – other than some kid on a bike.'

Husein frowned. 'Tell me about him.'

'I did mention it to PC Clark. A young lad, maybe late teens, twentyish. He was quite a distance away.'

'And which direction was he moving in?'

'He wasn't. He was sitting on the bike, sort of hidden by the bushes. I called out, asking if he'd seen anyone, but he didn't answer. Soon as I moved towards him, he took off.'

Husein sent a questioning look at Dawn, who said, 'Could be a useful witness, if nothing else. Perhaps he'd spotted the victim and was too scared to approach.'

Rob sighed. 'If I'd ignored him, I suppose he might have hung around.'

'Not necessarily,' Husein said. 'But we need to be on the lookout for him. Can you give me a description?'

'Quite a small build, I think. Pale skin, thick dark hair. He was wearing khaki shorts and a black t-shirt.'

'He didn't speak at all?'

'No. Just looked at me.' *Glared* was the word Rob wanted to use, but he thought it might sound too emotive.

Husein's phone buzzed again. This time, with a murmured apology, he slipped out of the room.

Dawn gave them an encouraging smile. 'You're doing great. I can't see there's much more we need to know.'

Wendy's relief was obvious. 'When do you think you'll be done here?'

'That depends on the search, and what – if anything – it yields.'

Wendy's eyes were glistening. 'It's awful to think the poor man's family may never know what happened to him.'

'Early days.' Dawn gave a sombre smile. 'Hopefully we'll get to the bottom of this.'

'But it's not certain, is it?' Rob asked. 'If you're unable to identify him, and you don't find out where he came from, then the case could go unsolved?'

'Neat endings are for the movies, Rob. I'd be a fool to try and predict the outcome here, but I will admit that we don't have a lot to go on.'

'So whoever did this. . .' Wendy's voice almost cracked. 'They might get away with it?'

Reluctantly, Dawn nodded. 'They might.'

SEVEN

You cheated us, you fucker, you were in on it all along—

The crash that jolted Rob from his nightmare could have been someone kicking down the front door. He was half out of bed before he understood that he was reacting to the long, fading reverberation of a thunderclap.

Resting back, he savoured the relief as he listened to the rain drumming on the roof. It was almost two a.m. and he was surprised to have slept at all. He'd gone to bed earlier than usual, only to lie awake, brooding, for what felt like hours.

The evening had been predictably subdued. First there was the experience of being fingerprinted and swabbed for DNA, which had left Rob feeling more like a suspect than a witness. Afterwards they'd milled about like visitors in their own home, watching as the detailed search got underway, the forensic staff inching on to the common as the evening light slowly dimmed.

No one felt like eating – apart from Evan, who grazed on cereal and toast before he and Livvy decamped to his bedroom. Georgia also vanished, insisting that she was *fine*, which meant that Wendy was reduced to messaging her on Snapchat every half an hour.

Dawn Avery phoned with an update at ten o'clock. There had been no progress on identifying the victim, though they were leaning towards the possibility that he was a migrant farm worker.

'I've not come across it personally, but we've all heard of cases where these men are kept in appalling conditions and worked like slaves.'

'But why would they torture him, if they needed him to work?'

'Could be punishment. The gang masters and traffickers are as vile as any human beings you'll ever meet.'

Rob made no comment. He wanted to believe in her theory, though it meant fighting a tendency to doubt that such things could go on here, in sleepy Hampshire.

Then again, he also wanted to believe that no one he knew could have been responsible for such brutality.

The next call had come within seconds of speaking to Dawn; a man this time, greeting Rob with the hearty tones of a trusted friend.

'Heard about your uninvited guest at the barbie!' A snort of laughter, while Rob tried to place the voice on his mental database. 'Didn't do much for the ambience, eh? Snuffing it on the lawn!'

Rob was running through current and former employees, distant acquaintances, friends of friends. 'Sorry, who is this?'

'Roger El—, —*aily M*—' the man mumbled, skidding over the words as if deliberately trying to obscure them. 'Chap was Romanian, I hear, illegal as they come. Did he threaten you and the family? Must have been a real fright. How old's your youngest again?'

Rob ignored the onslaught of what he now grasped was pure speculation. He had to push hard before the man conceded that he was calling on behalf of a national tabloid.

'We have nothing to say,' Rob growled, and, as he cut the call: 'Wanker!' After that he warned Evan and Georgia to be on their guard, particularly when they went online.

The late evening news included a brief report of a murder enquiry, launched after police were called 'to an address in Petersfield, where a man's body was discovered'. The report was accompanied by a map of the area but no live images, and no word of any witnesses.

Now Rob mulled over the possibility that other residents could have seen the man stumbling across the common, and yet no one had gone to his aid.

But say I'd spotted him from an upstairs window, would I have rushed out to help?

His honest response: maybe not. In fact, if he could rewind to the moment when he'd heard someone bumping against the fence, he wasn't sure if, this time, he would open the gate.

He seized on that idea with a leap of excitement. They couldn't have known he would let the man in. It was just too messy, too haphazard to be a warning – not to mention way too extreme.

Far more likely to be random, just as Dawn had said.

'Please, God,' he whispered.

After a flash of lightning, Rob counted seven or eight seconds before the thunder followed. Beside him, Wendy shifted and groaned softly. 'Rob?'

'Mm. Sorry if I woke you.'

'I don't think you did.' She listened for a moment. 'God, that weather!'

'I know.'

When she turned over, he thought that was it. But then she whispered, 'Shall we spoon?'

He couldn't help but frown. 'Sure? I thought. . .'

'Don't be silly.' She wriggled back a little as he moved forwards. 'If it feels right.'

And it did, Rob couldn't deny that. For a minute or so he focused on the simple pleasure of holding her close. . . until she said, 'I just wish we knew what this was about.'

'Mm.'

'Or when it's going to be over.'

'I guess not until after the inquest.'

He felt her stomach contract as she gasped. 'That could be months away. And we'll be called as witnesses.'

'I know.' For a moment he pictured them meeting outside a courthouse, smartly dressed and struggling to make small talk.

'And what about Norfolk?' she asked.

'We should still go, unless—' He swallowed. 'Unless you've changed your mind?'

After a hesitation, she said, 'Let's not talk about that now. What I meant was, do you think it'll be all right to leave the house unoccupied?'

'I don't see why not. Be bloody ironic to cancel, after all the stress getting Josh to agree, but he'll be glad if he's let off the hook.'

And so will I, Rob was thinking, but Wendy said, 'No, you're right. We need to go.'

Her tone was weary, perhaps because she knew it wouldn't be like the holidays of old. Feeling encouraged by her suggestion to cuddle up, Rob let his hand caress Wendy's arm, her belly, but after a second or two her yawn was an unmistakable signal.

'Sleepy now,' she whispered.

'Good,' he said, and told a little white lie: 'Me too.'

A few more minutes passed, and sleep wouldn't come. Rob eased out of bed, used the main bathroom so as not to disturb her, then crept along to the landing window. From here there was a view over the common, and once his eyes had adjusted to the dark he could distinguish the soft glow of the grass, the vague sense of a large open space. Earlier there had been a uniformed officer guarding the taped-off area. If he was still out there, he'd be getting soaked.

Trying to shrug off a feeling of unease, Rob went into Josh's bedroom and checked the road. There was a patrol car parked at the kerb, but he couldn't tell if anyone was inside.

He knew his imagination was getting the better of him, spooked by the thunder and by the images that had inhabited his dream: something about that kid on the bike, then a building site with gaping holes like graves; torrential rain mixing with blood on the ground.

At the doorway he paused, contemplating the bare mattress and empty shelves, and was beset by a rush of sadness at all the years that had slipped past, all the uncherished milestones and modest delights that he'd taken for granted. As toddlers the twins had been such a handful that Rob had often longed for them to be older, little realising it was his own life he was urging away.

He was heading back to bed when he heard the soft clatter of the letterbox. Frowning, he descended the stairs and saw the envelope at once: a stark white square on the mat.

Ignoring it, he hurried through to the dining room and whipped the curtain aside. But the street outside was empty. No one in the police car, either, by the look of it.

Rob waited, listening to the greasy thud of his heartbeat. Of course, it might be nothing more than a note from a kindly neighbour, who had observed the police activity and assumed the worst.

He returned to the hall and picked up the envelope. Inside was a small sheet of notepaper. Rob's hands shook as he read the brief message it contained.

WE KNOW WHAT YOU DID

EIGHT

The first test was a simple one. Straightforward, but not without risk.

You had to start a fire in a shop.

It was a test that required creativity and courage. The target was a department store in a large, ugly shopping mall. There was CCTV everywhere. There were security guards. There was the likelihood of an effective sprinkler system and the possibility of what the media sometimes call 'have-a-go' heroes.

You had to wear disguises. That part was fun. Some frivolity was allowed, but it remained a serious business. Great care had to be taken to avoid leaving the merest trace of DNA on any of the equipment.

You started several fires. You used a variety of incendiary devices, some made from fireworks, and one that involved a simple, pungent accelerant and a timber-based manual ignition method, courtesy of Swan Vesta. The most ingenious was a domestic iron, modified to overheat, which was surreptitiously plugged into the mains at a socket near an unattended counter.

All but one of the fires took hold. They burned for almost an hour, at a conservative estimate – by that stage you were gone. The mall was evacuated successfully, and reopened late the next day. The store itself was closed for almost a week. Repairs were costed at over three hundred thousand pounds, but that no doubt included an element of exaggeration for insurance purposes.

No one was hurt, but that wasn't the objective.

Not this time.

Nevertheless, the media followed the story for several weeks, hysterically at first. They whipped up fear and suspicion; they encouraged racism and intolerance while pretending to do the opposite. Proclaiming that this would be the first of many such attacks, they claimed that it was 'a savage assault on *our very way of life.*'

Shopping.

The police were thrilled. The politicians were ecstatic. What a perfect opportunity to justify more oppression, more surveillance. All this from half a dozen lowly fires in a drab provincial department store, ten minutes before closing time on a rainy Wednesday.

The excitement came from what they perceived as the motives for the attack.

They thought you did it because of religion.

They thought you did it because of culture.

They thought you did it because of ideology.

You did it because I told you to.

NINE

Wendy woke to the sound of a car pulling up outside, and another driving away. *Monday morning*, she thought, and then remembered why it was busy outside.

She checked her phone for messages. She'd texted Josh a couple of times last night, but he hadn't replied.

It was just after six, a while yet till the alarm. Beside her, Rob was snoring, not loudly but with a lack of rhythm that often kept her awake. He barely stirred as she pulled on a robe and checked the window.

A couple of police officers were chatting on the pavement, while forensic staff unloaded equipment from a van. Weak sunshine filtered through the clouds, sparkling on puddles in the road. Wendy hurried downstairs and opened the door before anyone could ring the bell.

'We'd have used the side gate, don't worry.' The officer who greeted her was about twenty-five, with pale blue eyes and a cheeky grin.

'I'll put the kettle on. Would bacon sandwiches be of interest to anyone?'

His colleague exclaimed: 'Oh my word, yes. You're a lifesaver!'

A fine compliment, Wendy thought as she turned away – except she wasn't a lifesaver at all. Her first aid skills hadn't been equal to the task the day before, and while it might have been that the man was simply beyond saving at that point, the thought plagued her that there was something else she should have done.

She busied herself in the kitchen, reflecting on the fears that had gripped her in the middle of the night. With the calming effect of daylight, it was easier to believe that life could soon get back to normal.

There were footsteps along the side of the house, and the young policeman came in to help with the teas and coffees, various preferences for milk and sugar scribbled on an old lottery ticket.

Once he'd taken the tray outside, Wendy tended to the bacon on the grill and checked her phone again. Rob trudged in, pale and bleary eyed, and immediately guessed what she was fretting over. 'Anything from the Lost Son?'

'No. I'll have to get Evan to call him. I don't want him worrying.'

'*Josh*, worry about *us*? Not in this universe!'

His laughter was harsh and, to Wendy's ears, a little unkind. She turned back to the unit, and was cutting up the soft rolls left over from the barbecue when suddenly Rob was behind her, his arms encircling her waist. Startled, she reared up, almost butting his chin.

'Jesus!' He let go and stumbled away.

'Sorry. You made me jump.'

'Normal service is resumed, then?' he muttered.

That was unfair, but Wendy let it pass. She didn't want an argument when the garden was full of strangers. Gesturing at the grill, she said, 'Can you take over while I have a shower?'

'Ought to start a catering business,' Rob grumbled, but he seemed just as eager to forget the spat. 'We'll tell them it's, what, two quid a bap?'

'Ever the entrepreneur,' she said with a concilia
'Don't forget to offer them ketchup.'

He pretended to look aghast. 'Brown sauce. It has
sauce with bacon.'

*

In the shower, Wendy tried to calm herself in preparation for the day ahead. She worked for an adult social care charity in Winchester, alongside a small, dedicated band of people, all committed to helping others. That said, she wasn't yet sure if she wanted to tell any of them about yesterday's tragedy. Some contrary part of her character recoiled at the thought of being on the receiving end of their sympathy and concern – especially as she felt it was undeserved.

I didn't do anything to save him.

Her reaction to Rob's touch also troubled her. Last night she had been grateful for the comfort of bodily contact; this morning it was an unwelcome reminder of how vulnerable she felt. From Rob's point of view it made her behaviour annoyingly inconsistent, and she wouldn't disagree with that. How could she, when her feelings about him changed from one minute to the next?

She was on the landing when a faint electronic *blurp* from Georgia's room gave Wendy an excuse to knock gently. The girl was barely visible beneath her duvet; just a spray of light brown hair over the pillow. . . and the trailing wire of an iPhone charger.

'Who's messaging you at this time of the morning?'

'Nth,' was the only reply. Then the duvet was pushed down and Georgia rolled on to her back, eyes open, phone in hand.

'This isn't because of yesterday?' Wendy asked.

'People wanna know we're okay.'

'But your dad said not to mention it—'

'It wasn't me!' A surly glance at her phone, which this time had trilled: Wendy knew this meant an incoming message on a different app. 'There's a kid whose dad is mates with one of the police, and he told someone else, who put it on Twitter.'

'Okay. Sorry.' Wendy leaned over and kissed her forehead. 'No matter what happens, your dad and I will always keep you safe, you know that?'

Georgia nodded, still trying to look blasé, but her eyes were shining with tears. Wendy spared her by getting busy, snatching up a wet towel, hooking a discarded bra on the handle of the wardrobe; huffing as a mother should at the state of the room.

She said, 'Evan and Livvy were planning on a picnic, if you wanted to go with them?'

'Nah. I'm meeting Amber and Paige.'

Wendy detected a note of pride in Georgia's voice. Amber was somewhere between an acquaintance and a friend, but Paige was a girl she'd previously only envied – and perhaps also feared – from afar. One of the school's queen bees.

In today's prurient world, Wendy shouldn't have been surprised that the drama had enhanced Georgia's status. And while the girl fiercely – and rightly – guarded the secret of her past life, an event like this was no doubt viewed as safer territory to exploit.

'All right,' Wendy said, 'but just be careful what you say—'

'*Mu*-um, I'm not a moron. I *know*!' Shoving the phone to the edge of the bed, Georgia grabbed the duvet and vanished beneath it.

TEN

Rob had woken with a start and immediately thought: *The letter.* He'd buried it among some paperwork in his study before coming back to bed, then lain awake, worrying himself into a frenzy until sheer exhaustion knocked him out.

WE KNOW WHAT YOU DID.

That phrase haunted him as he descended the stairs. Should he tell DS Husein? Should he risk the consequences, whatever they may be?

His mood was made bleaker still by Wendy's reaction when he tried to embrace her. Perhaps it was his own fault for assuming the tenderness they'd shared during the night would carry over to the light of day.

DS Husein arrived in time to cast an envious glance at the tray of bacon butties, and feigned disapproval: 'Spoil them like this and they'll start to expect it.'

'Blame Wendy. It's her mission on earth to keep people well fed. Do you want one?'

Husein declined, ascertaining from Rob's expression that there were none spare, then had a thought: 'I might have to confiscate PC Jarrod's breakfast on the grounds that he already has high cholesterol.'

When Rob told him about the phone call from the journalist, Husein said, 'You did the right thing, but I can't promise there won't be more attempts like that. Some of these people stop at nothing, believe me.'

The detective went on to ask when would be a convenient time for the family to give their formal statements. With a watery sense of dread, Rob said, 'Early evening is best for me, if that's okay? I've got a lot on today.'

Like finding out who sent that note.

He was munching on his bacon roll when Wendy came down with the news that Georgia was awake, and in unusually good spirits. 'I think this has given her a bit of extra street cred.'

'As long as she doesn't say too much—'

'She knows that. Don't worry.'

They talked about work, and whether either of them could spare time to pop back during the day. Wendy didn't like the idea of leaving the house empty.

Rob shrugged. 'I'll see how I get on, maybe reschedule a few things.'

'Really? As if you haven't already crammed in a fortnight's worth of jobs for this week?'

It was an accusation Rob couldn't deny – though he would argue that necessity had forced him to push his workload to an unreasonable level over the past few years. After a period of rapid growth, his plumbing and heating business had suffered badly as a result of the economic downturn from 2008 onwards. As a result, Rob made the fateful decision to form a partnership with a man named Iain Kelly.

At first the enlarged business had seemed to be back on a sound footing, but gradually the financial situation worsened again, and of course the banks weren't prepared to help. Rob was in the process of seeking support elsewhere when he found out why they were in trouble: Iain Kelly had been siphoning off money to feed a gambling habit and pacify a couple of mistresses. He'd also traded on the firm's reputation – Rob's reputation, in effect – to borrow from a range of friends and associates, all of whom were left out of pocket when Kelly fled to Spain, holing up in a luxury villa which he'd purchased in a girlfriend's name.

For months Rob had teetered on the brink of bankruptcy. In a tragic irony, only the death of his father – just two years after his mother had succumbed to cancer – had staved off financial ruin. Rob had used his share of their estate, some sixty thousand pounds, to clear many of the debts. It left him extremely bitter that his parents' legacy had, in effect, been squandered to satisfy another man's creditors, and he had felt little sorrow when he heard, a year or so later, that Kelly had been killed in a water-skiing accident. To Rob, it seemed like nothing less than divine justice.

Husein came in, asked if they could spare a moment and introduced them to the senior investigating officer. Detective Inspector Sandra Powell was a tall, plump woman in her forties with blonde highlights and a cheerful Black Country accent.

'Post-mortem's getting fast-tracked today,' she told them. 'Hopefully that'll give us something useful.'

Rob asked if any witnesses had come to light, and Husein shook his head. 'So far it's just your elusive boy on a bike.'

There seemed to be a slight edge to his voice, Rob thought. Certainly DI Powell was watching him a little too intensely.

'Would you recognise him if you saw him again?' she asked.

'If he was wearing the same clothes, maybe.'

'Well, I've recorded an appeal for TV and radio news, so maybe that'll prick his conscience.'

After thanking them for their co-operation, she headed out to the garden with Husein in tow. Rob shut the back door, and said, 'I still can't shake off the idea that they suspect me of something.'

'Hmm. I suppose if you hadn't run out on the common. . .' Wendy faltered as she registered the displeasure on his face. 'I don't blame you, because you were worried about who might be out there. But if you'd stayed in the garden with the rest of us, there wouldn't be any loose ends to pull at, would there?'

She had a point, so Rob only nodded. Wendy put the TV on in time for the local bulletin, which led with a report on migrants discovered aboard a ship in Southampton. That reminded him of Husein's theory about a farm labourer, possibly trafficked to work illegally in the UK.

Their story came next: a brief, dry description of a badly injured man, pronounced dead on arrival at hospital. A shot of the common showed crime-scene tape fluttering in the early morning breeze. Their garden was off camera, but a cut to Russell Drive put the location beyond doubt. It was followed by the appeal from DI Powell, which appeared to have been filmed in the car park of Heath Pond, a large nature reserve only a couple of minutes' walk away.

Looking at ease in front of the camera, the detective explained that they were keen to speak to anyone who was in the area yesterday, between two and five p.m. 'Even if you don't think you noticed anything untoward, we would still like you to get in touch.'

Rob imagined being that young man on the bike and hearing Powell's appeal. Would he, as a teenager, have picked up a phone to the cops, or told his parents that he might be a potential witness?

Not a chance.

DS Husein brought a warning that a few media representatives were out by the main road and would no doubt be prowling through the town today.

'They wanted to know about you, but Sandy deflected them, did that piece to camera instead.' He sniffed, as if slightly put out that his boss had seized the limelight.

With a glance at Rob, Wendy asked, 'What does DI Powell think of all this?'

'Oh, you've got nothing to worry about,' Husein said astutely. 'She's already on her way back to the office.' Their surprise must have shown, for he went on: 'Job's a lot more desk-bound these days. I probably spend more time looking for suspects on Facebook than I do pounding the streets.'

'Really?'

'A slight exaggeration, but not much. People live their lives online, so often that's the best way to find out what they're up to.'

'But not this poor guy in our garden?' Rob said.

'I doubt it, somehow. And we won't know that till we get him identified.'

He left them to it, and Wendy treated Rob to a smile. 'See? Nothing to worry about.'

Before leaving, he retrieved the note and slipped it into his pocket. He'd been fretting over an appropriate farewell, but Wendy surprised him by initiating a hug. He must have reacted awkwardly, because she said, 'We can still hold each other, for goodness' sake.'

'Glad to hear it.' He squeezed her tightly for a second, wanting her to know he wasn't being flippant: this meant a lot to him.

He left the house, half expecting flashbulbs to pop in his face, but the street was quiet. He'd reached the driver's door of his battered eight-year-old Land Rover when the neighbour opposite, Philip Denning, just happened to emerge from his house at the same time. Phil did something in the City and was, by his own account, tremendously good at it. Now he called out: 'Rob, are you—?'

'Just off to work, Philip. Gotta hurry.'

Ignoring another question, Rob started the engine and drove out. There were several unfamiliar cars parked close to the junction with the main road, one of them occupied by a young blonde woman with an iPad on her lap. No sign of the TV crew, though, and no one to accost Rob as he turned left on to Sussex Road.

He drove only a short distance before pulling up at the kerb to make a couple of calls. One was to rearrange an interview scheduled for this morning, while the other caused him a moment or two of doubt.

No, got to do this.

'Steve, mate, just wondered – any idea where Jason and his crew are working right now?'

ELEVEN

Rob was resigned to heavy traffic on the route to Chichester, and he wasn't disappointed. It was just after nine when he reached the northern outskirts of the city and turned east in the direction of the Goodwood estate. Another half a mile, and he pulled across the road into a lay-by overlooking a new development of executive homes.

Construction was in the early stages: the majority of the site was a sea of mud. Excavators rolled to and fro between vast mounds of subsoil, and a couple of men were directing the movement of a concrete mixer. Rob got out of the car, aware of a tight knot of tension in his stomach. There were trees growing parallel to the road, and he used them for cover as he moved closer to the site. Almost at once he made out the imposing figure of Jason Dennehy, standing among a cluster of men inspecting a newly dug trench.

Of all the building trades, Rob regarded groundwork as the most demanding. It was the one on which the other trades were dependent for scheduling, and there were few options for inside work when the conditions turned nasty. It therefore took a particular type of individual who chose to endure years of backbreaking physical toil in all conditions: not the kind of person you wanted as an enemy.

And Jason Dennehy looked the part of a tough guy, no question. He was well over six feet tall, broad and muscular and completely bald, with piercing blue eyes and tattoos that adorned at least a quarter of his body. Now in his mid-thirties, he'd met Rob more than a decade ago, when he was still just a jobbing labourer, but his determination and work ethic meant he'd quickly become a successful contractor with half a dozen men on his payroll.

Prior to the labouring job, however, there had been a misspent youth of shoplifting, robbery and assault. After spending his twenty-first birthday behind bars, Jason had made a concerted effort to clean up his act, but it was common knowledge that he'd continued to fraternise with some dubious characters from his past.

Rob watched him for several minutes. At one point Jason broke away from the other men to make a phone call, but even then he was only a few yards from them. Rob saw no prospect of getting him on his own, or of having a discreet conversation.

Whether it was common sense or cowardice, Rob understood that he wasn't going to do it. Despite the note through the door, he still felt too uncertain. And never mind that the trench was an unsettling reminder of his nightmares, no doubt inspired by the wisecracks he'd heard over the years (though rarely said to Dennehy's face) about how this was the perfect job for disposing of bodies.

Rob felt lousy as he returned to the car, annoyed with himself and with life in general. On the drive back to Petersfield he found himself brooding, yet again, on the state of his marriage.

He'd first met Wendy nearly thirty years ago, when he was an apprentice to a large plumbing firm in Worthing. He'd been a bit of a tearaway as a kid, indifferent at school and interested only in tinkering with motorbikes and hanging out with his brothers – the elder one an electronics engineer, the younger one a mechanic. Wendy, two years his junior, had excelled at school, then followed her vocation to become a social worker.

At first Rob had felt sure that he could only be a passing fancy, a chance for her to experience muscles, grease and instant gratification before she found a partner with a suitably prestigious white collar career. But the relationship had grown serious, and in 1991 they married and immediately began to try for a baby. Heartbreak followed, with several false alarms and a suspected early miscarriage. The stress led to a brief separation, but they were soon reconciled, having agreed to lower their expectations where children were concerned, and also consider the possibility of fostering or even adoption. Within a year or so, Wendy had fallen pregnant with the twins, and for the next two decades there was barely a wobble. As a result, Rob had taken it for granted that they would remain together for the rest of their lives.

Then came the bombshell: Wendy didn't see it that way.

Rob decided to call in at home en route to the office. He found Evan and Livvy putting a picnic together, and asked if Georgia was about.

'In town with her friends,' Evan said.

'Is she? Good.' Rob drifted to the window. The back gate was open, a couple of figures in white crouching just beyond it. There was no sign of Husein or anyone else that he knew. No one he could talk to about the note.

He followed his son outside, casting his usual critical eye over Evan's ancient VW Polo. 'Enjoy your picnic – and drive carefully, all right?' As he headed for his own car, he noticed that one of the neighbours was pruning a rose bush at a convenient angle to observe the Turner household.

Irritated, Rob backed out faster than was sensible, cutting diagonally on to a driveway across the street. His view was obscured by the police van, which meant he didn't see the young couple walking along the pavement until he'd nearly hit them.

He stamped on the brake, then saw in the mirror that he'd caused them to break their stride. They were about Evan's age, the boy in jeans and the girl in a floaty dress. She was blonde, and not dissimilar to the woman he'd passed this morning, working on her iPad. The boy made a vague gesture of protest and Rob lifted a hand in apology, then accelerated away, irked by his own poor driving when he'd only just urged his son to take care.

It was stupid to let inquisitive neighbours get to him. Like it or not, he and his family were going to be in the spotlight for a while. They had no choice but to tolerate it.

His office was on the first floor of a two-storey building in Lavant Street, midway between the High Street and the railway station. The ground floor was occupied by a soft furnishings store, and there was a separate entrance at the side which served three different office suites, two of them occupied by a firm of accountants.

Cerys Chaplin sat at the main desk, next to a window that offered a rather unprepossessing view of the car park. Rob used a smaller desk in the corner, while the remaining desk was kept clear for the teams to fill out timesheets and requisitions, or else just sit and rest between jobs.

From the moment he'd employed her, Rob had worried how Cerys would fare in what was still an absurdly male-dominated industry. But to his relief, she had proved adept at handling the crude and often downright filthy banter that was part and parcel of any tough working environment.

In fact, Cerys had turned out to be a godsend. He'd employed her just prior to Iain Kelly's departure – and it was thanks to her keen eye and administrative skills that he'd been able to piece together and record the extent of his former partner's dishonesty.

'The applicant's in a panic,' she told Rob when he apologised again for today's scheduling change. 'He assumed it meant rejection, but I've promised him you can do Wednesday at two.'

'I take it I'm free then?'

'You are, don't worry.' She handed him a sheaf of papers. 'A few things to sign, some estimates to review – oh, and there were a couple of personal calls for you, but they wouldn't say who—' She examined him more closely. 'Are you all right?'

'Yeah, it's just. . .' Rob shrugged, then realised he spent too long in this woman's company to keep it from her. 'We, er, had a bit of an incident yesterday.'

He told her the full story, and warned that the calls were probably from journalists trying to approach him via the business – the logo and website address were, after all, emblazoned on the side of his Land Rover.

Cerys was shocked. She was a short, slightly heavy woman with a round face and thin painted eyebrows that gave her a look of wry surprise. Now she rose from her chair, arms opening as if to embrace him, only to settle for patting his elbow.

'What a hideous thing to witness. You shouldn't have come in at all today.' The eyebrows twitched in sympathy. 'And there's really no clue as to who is behind it, or why it happened. . .?'

Rob shook his head. There was a moment when he was sorely tempted to reveal his suspicions about Jason and show her the letter. But that seemed like a step too far.

He felt guilty enough about what he was keeping from Wendy; confiding in Cerys would only make things worse.

TWELVE

On Monday evening it was six o'clock before they opened a bottle of wine, which in Wendy's view showed admirable restraint.

She'd been uncharacteristically subdued at work, prompting so many enquiries about her wellbeing that she'd invented the tale of a nagging toothache. Her manager immediately insisted she get an emergency appointment and leave early.

Wendy felt ashamed of the deception, but it meant she was home in good time to give her formal witness statement to the police. Afterwards, when she compared notes with Rob, they agreed that there had been nothing untoward or inconsistent in their respective accounts.

'So it should be over, really, from our point of view,' she'd said.

'I hope so,' Rob agreed, though he didn't sound particularly confident.

It turned out that he had confided in Cerys, after learning that the media were trying to contact him through the business. With that in mind, they discussed whether their wider families should be told of the incident. Wendy saw no reason to alarm her parents, who had retired to France, but Rob said he was inclined to call his younger brother, Sam.

'Only because he lives close, so he might hear something. I wasn't going to bother with Paul.'

From his grimace, Wendy knew to maintain a diplomatic silence. Rob's elder brother lived with his third wife in Carlisle and had barely spoken to them for years. She knew it pained

Rob that the three siblings were not closer, though he and his younger brother met up every few weeks to hear the latest on Sam's custody battle with his ex-wife.

It was probably inevitable that some of their family and friends would hear of the tragedy and wonder why they'd said nothing about it; a few might even take offence, but if they did. . . *well, tough luck*, Wendy thought.

This was their way of dealing with what had happened. Privacy, discretion, silence.

And generous measures of wine.

Both of the local TV news programmes featured the story, their reports typically dry and factual. An inquest had been opened and adjourned, pending the outcome of police enquiries. The post-mortem indicated that the man had died as a result of multiple injuries, though the police spokesman was 'not prepared to release any more specific information at this stage'.

'Perhaps because they don't know anything,' Rob suggested. Earlier, DS Husein had advised that the search of the common had yielded nothing of value.

Better news was that the garden was now theirs again. The evening wasn't as warm as the previous one, but it was still pleasant enough to sit on the terrace. Wendy wanted to talk about Georgia, and the extent to which she might be traumatised by this experience. No more than the rest of them, was Rob's opinion.

'But she's starting from a different baseline. She's more vulnerable than we are.'

'Really? Evan reckons she's tougher than the lot of us.'

'I'd like to think so. But what if that's just a façade?'

Rob had no answer there. What they could agree was that the incident had inadvertently boosted their daughter's social standing. After returning to give her statement, she'd rejoined her friends in town and was spending the night at Amber's. Wendy had gladly given assent: despite plenty of encouragement Georgia rarely invited any friends for sleepovers, and she was almost never invited to others.

At twenty past seven Evan trooped out with a rucksack on his shoulder. 'Thought we'd stay over at Liv's.'

'Mum and Dad want to see me,' Livvy added, as if she felt obliged to justify the decision. 'I think they're a bit worried, what with. . .'

'Of course.' Wendy smiled, but she sensed that Rob was put out by it.

After kissing her goodbye, Evan said, 'Oh – Josh texted earlier. I told him about yesterday and he said he hopes we're okay.'

Rob snorted. 'That's a first. Can I see the message?'

Wendy thought he was probably joking, but Evan baulked. 'I think I deleted it.'

'Right,' said Rob, scornfully.

After they'd gone, Wendy said, 'I daresay he was "interpreting" it.'

'Fabricating, more like – so we don't think badly of his brother.'

'In that case, we can forgive him the deception, can't we?'

Rob gave a grudging shrug, and they sat in silence for a moment. So far this evening he'd been uptight, twitchy, but now there was a distinct shift in his mood. A quick glance told her what had just occurred to him: they were alone in the house.

Rescue came in the form of a visitor, Dawn Avery, looking drained after a long day in London. Her court case had been delayed by a late-arriving witness, then suspended when a member of the jury was taken ill. 'If there's a more inefficient use of time and money than the British justice system, I'd hate to see it.'

Wendy smiled, and persuaded her to accept a small glass of wine, 'for medicinal purposes'. She'd grown to like Dawn a lot, having initially had to overcome a sense of disloyalty to Tim's first wife, Jill, who'd been reliant on Wendy in the aftermath of the split. Jill suffered badly from endometriosis, and her reluctance to have children was based partly on a warning that she might struggle to carry a baby to term. Tim seemed to brush that off as an excuse, and Wendy, who'd had her own difficulties with regard to conception, felt he could have been a lot more understanding.

Back on the terrace, Dawn gave them an update on the post-mortem. 'There was actually some doubt at first as to whether the man had been attacked. Some of his injuries, like the cuts and bruising, could be explained away as accidents, and even the knife wounds and, er, incisions, could have been self-inflicted. At a push.'

Rob let out a gulp of incredulous laughter. 'You're saying he did all that to himself?'

Wendy began, 'I can't believe that—' before Rob snapped: 'And who was he running from?'

Dawn shifted in her seat. 'To be fair, we have no evidence that he was running from anyone. We haven't been able to pick up a trail, and there aren't any witnesses who saw him before he reached your property.'

'So what—?' Rob broke off as Dawn raised an index finger.

'That's how it looked *at first*. But then we found the likeliest cause of death – massive internal bleeding, which would have caused organ failure. He'd been beaten quite savagely, and skilfully, to a point that would almost inevitably prove fatal.'

Wendy felt a bizarre mix of shock, sorrow and guilty relief. 'So there's no way I could have saved him?'

'I'm afraid not.'

'He didn't kick himself to death, then?' Rob's sarcasm had a bitter sting, which Dawn pretended not to notice.

'Very unlikely. The kidneys were targeted, so unless he was repeatedly throwing himself backwards against a blunt

object. . .' She took a sip of wine. 'Remember that we're operating on the balance of probabilities. Without CCTV to show
us what happened, there's nearly always a range of scenarios.
All we can do is home in on the most plausible, which in this
case is that someone attacked him, probably kicking him until
he lost consciousness, and then perhaps left him for dead.'

Wendy asked, 'When did that happen, do you think?'

'No more than a couple of hours before he died.'

'So he can't have got far from where the beating took place?'

'No, and that's a puzzle. If it was close by, there ought to have
been some sign of it. He was missing a shoe when he came in,
and we haven't even found that.'

'Unless he was thrown out of a car?' Rob ventured, and Dawn
nodded glumly.

'That may well be it, and then we're really in trouble.' She
described how the man had been in extremely poor health to
begin with. 'Heart disease, cirrhosis of the liver, and signs of heavy
drug use. I'd bet money that he's been homeless for several years
at least, prior to whatever happened here.'

'Are there still no clues to his identity?' Wendy asked.

'Not so far. His teeth were in a terrible state, though there was
some evidence of dentistry carried out in his adolescence, which
the pathologist thought was British.'

'What about the theory that he was a migrant worker?' Rob
asked.

'It's an avenue we're still exploring, but I'd say there's less
confidence in that idea than there was last night.'

Rob looked almost stricken by this news. 'So where, uh, where
does that leave us?'

'You?' Dawn frowned. 'Well, I know it's been a horrible
shock, but hopefully now you can put it behind you. For
us, though. . .' She shrugged. 'We'll go on combing through the
missing persons reports, and it may be that the case will be added

to the bureau's website, though that's pretty much a last-ditch attempt at identification. . .'

'And then?' Wendy asked, picking up on the air of hopelessness.

Dawn spread her hands. 'Like I said before, it's possible that this is a mystery we'll never solve.'

THIRTEEN

Rob slept badly on Monday night. A keen wind was blowing, causing the roof to creak and rattle; sounds he'd once regarded as benign, even cosy, now laced his dreams with anxiety. At one point the house was besieged by shadowy figures; at a safe distance the boy on the bike watched impassively, ignoring Rob's plea to fetch help.

Dawn Avery's warning that there might be no resolution had cast a shadow over the evening. Rob, though, had decided that it was essential to rule out Jason Dennehy's involvement. He'd sent the man a text, but hadn't had a reply when he went to bed.

At about two fifteen he was woken by a noise that seemed different to the rest – more deliberate – though of course it had faded before he was properly awake.

He sat up, groggily. The house had an alarm system, installed by the previous owners. The internal movement sensors often malfunctioned, so Rob tended not to activate them at night. But the magnetic contacts on the doors and windows ought to be operating, giving them some warning if an intruder broke in.

Fetching a cricket bat from Evan's room, he looked in on the other bedrooms and made sure all the windows were shut. Then he went downstairs, pausing every couple of steps. The wind blew in gusts, causing a low-pitched moan as it pushed against the roof.

Rob prowled from room to room, but there was nothing out of place. Then, as he was entering the kitchen, he heard it again – a loud clattering noise, like someone falling against the fence.

Exactly what he'd heard yesterday afternoon.

After peering, uselessly, into the gloom, he unlocked the doors and stepped on to the terrace. He was wearing nothing but his boxer shorts, but the wind that buffeted him didn't feel cold at all; the air was rich with the scent of honeysuckle and – he didn't think he was imagining it – a tang of the sea.

The garden seemed to be deserted, though there was some kind of small animal snuffling in the bushes to his right. Then, during a sudden lull in the wind, he heard a high-pitched creak and caught movement straight ahead.

The gate was swinging open.

His first reaction was to raise the bat. Heart racing, he turned and checked all around. He remembered locking the gate after the police had left, and no one had come out here during the evening. Had someone climbed the fence and then opened the gate to get out?

Before it could slam again, Rob hurried across the lawn and trapped the gate with his foot. There were clouds scudding across the moon, dimming its pale light and turning the acres of open ground into a silvery alien landscape, dotted with mysterious clumps of shadow. To Rob's fevered imagination, the hissing of the wind in the trees sounded like voices, whispering in collusion against him.

There was nothing to see, so he shut the gate and pushed the bolts home. Then, as he turned towards the house, he heard a shriek.

Wendy.

He sprinted across the garden and saw her in the living room, looking terrified.

'Are you okay?'

'I panicked because you were gone. And then I saw the door open. . .'

'Sorry, that was stupid of me.'

As he entered the room he noticed something in her hand: a small white square. Wendy caught him staring at it, and said, 'I found this on the mat.' She indicated the garden. 'What were you doing?'

He struggled to focus on her question. 'The gate was open, banging in the wind.'

'Didn't you shut it earlier?'

'I thought I had.' He couldn't take his eyes off the envelope. 'We'd better open that.'

Wendy looked down as if she'd forgotten what she was holding. His tone had probably betrayed that he knew what it was, but she said nothing as she took out a slip of paper. She read the message and handed it to Rob. As with yesterday's, it was short and to the point:

YOU KILLED HIM

Rob was frozen for a minute: he couldn't move, or speak, or think.

Wendy snapped him out of it: 'What is this?'

'Hold on.' He put the cricket bat down and fetched the other note. Wendy seemed to tremble as she studied it.

'When were you going to tell me about this?'

'I found it last night, but I didn't want to—'

'*What?* Why haven't you given it to the police?'

'I didn't think it would achieve anything.'

'It's not just your decision to make.' She hadn't raised her voice, but there were tears in her eyes. 'I live here, too, Rob.'

For now. The words almost slipped out, and thank God he managed to stop himself. But Wendy was glaring at him, her eyes narrow with suspicion.

'Do you know who sent them?'

'Of course not! How could I?' He was genuinely offended by the question, and that acted to take the sting out of the conversation.

'I don't know.' Restlessly, she thrust the note back at him. 'We have to do something. They're accusing us of killing him.'

Rob's mind was in such turmoil that he could only mutter: 'Who?'

'The man on Sunday.' She gave him a look. 'Who else would it be?'

'No, yeah, sorry.' He scratched his head, then yawned. 'Let's go back to bed, talk about this in the morning.'

First he tapped a code into the alarm control, activating the room sensors. Even a false alarm would be better than getting caught unawares, he thought.

Not a word was spoken as he got into bed. Wendy immediately turned her back on him. Lying awake, Rob was conscious of the debilitating fear, slowly increasing its grip on his thought processes. If there was an enemy out there, then a Rob Turner at twenty, thirty – even at forty – would have liked his chances in a fair fight against anyone. But with fifty just around the corner, perhaps it was natural that he wouldn't have the same level of confidence, or bravado.

As he lay there in the dark, he was forced to contemplate that his strength and courage might be ebbing away, leaving him ill-prepared to defend his family.

FOURTEEN

The second challenge was more ambitious. It was outside, this time, at a location that offered no real cover. You were exposed to the risks of being seen, challenged, chased away.

You accepted those risks. By now you were committed. Devoted. Compelled to do whatever you were asked.

The tools required on this occasion were easy to source: a strong pair of gloves and a concrete paving slab, the latter favoured for its greater density over the original suggestion of a cement block.

You formed a plan. Roles were assigned, escape routes plotted and memorised.

The location was a busy stretch of motorway, close to Southampton. The precise site for the attack depended on a number of factors. First, there had to be a bridge crossing the motorway. The traffic volumes had to be high, but also moving fast: there was far less satisfaction to be gained from a bottleneck.

You had been instructed to produce a high-speed impact. Lots of noise and chaos.

You chose a late afternoon in winter. Fading light. Fast traffic. The rush hour.

You made the necessary calculations, carried out experiments, deployed a stopwatch and drew up plans.

Which I approved.

The vehicles below you were travelling at seventy, eighty miles per hour, some even faster than that. It came down to milliseconds, just as life, survival, so often does. A near miss or a tragedy: milliseconds.

The block almost landed on a windscreen, but the car seemed to veer slightly; perhaps the driver was spooked by a hint of movement on the bridge. The block glanced off the roof and ricocheted into another car, striking the side panels, shattering the windows and bursting into fragments. A noisy, fabulous detonation.

In truth, it was mostly harmless. But the shock of the impact had done its work, causing both of those first vehicles to lose control. One of them spun in the carriageway and came to rest sideways on to the approaching traffic. The other collided with the central reservation and formed a similar obstruction.

Two lanes out of three, blocked, impassable. In milliseconds.

There were fourteen cars, two vans and a truck involved in the crash. Nearly all contained just one person – an indictment of the wastefulness of modern travel. From this pile-up came eleven casualties: two serious injuries, including the loss of a limb, and five moderate injuries. A handful of the occupants made it out completely unscathed, even though the news footage showed significant damage to their vehicles. The triumph of modern engineering, or just sheer good luck.

In terms of the human cost, this was far more serious than the fire, and yet it received only a fraction of the attention. The local papers and TV got excited for a week or more, but it attracted almost no interest from the national media. It seems the road network is the one sphere of life where we routinely accept carnage on a scale that would be unthinkable anywhere else.

But for you, my Brood, this represented a major advance. You had caused untold pain. Blood was spilled, albeit somewhat remotely.

The next challenge had to be on a more intimate scale. Personal. Visceral. You had to cut the flesh, draw the blood, expose the meat of another human being.

I told you what I wanted.

You had to find me a victim.

FIFTEEN

Tuesday began with a strained discussion about the notes. Wendy insisted that the police had to be informed, and in the end Rob capitulated. 'If that's what you think is best.'

'I have no idea what's best. But if something else were to happen, and we haven't mentioned it. . .' She shuddered. 'Think of the trouble we could be in.'

Not much Rob could say to that. Once he got to work he texted Jason Dennehy again, saying they needed to meet. Dennehy replied but didn't ask why, which struck Rob as suspicious. The groundworker could only spare a few minutes tomorrow at midday, but Rob would have to come to Bosham, a village south of Chichester.

Then came an encounter with the tabloid press, in the form of a snide little man who'd talked his way into the office building and buttonholed Rob in the communal kitchen area. The resulting altercation was witnessed by half a dozen staff from the accountancy firm, as well as Cerys and a couple of his own guys, who at least made themselves useful by ejecting the journalist from the building. Afterwards it was Cerys who had discreetly explained what the intruder wanted, saving Rob the trouble of having to go through it again. But it meant the cat was well and truly out of the bag.

During a break for lunch, Rob did an online search for news and soon wished he hadn't. A couple of papers were running stories of the man having been 'ritually abused'. Claiming to have inside knowledge from an officer on the enquiry, his wounds were compared to previous victims of satanic cults, dredging up various grisly examples, mostly from America, including Gerald Cruz, Son of Sam and Charles Manson.

That evening Rob was able to confirm with Dawn Avery that it was only lurid speculation. 'No one on DI Powell's team would dare leak anything, I can tell you that.'

'But he was tortured, though?' Rob asked. 'So could it have been some kind of ritual?'

After a significant hesitation, and an apologetic glance at Wendy, Dawn said, 'There's no specific evidence, but of course we can't rule it out at this stage.'

The detective had called in at Wendy's request, and wanted to know how she could help. At the sight of the notes, she was briefly aghast.

'When did you get these? Have you both been handling them?'

Rob and Wendy dropped their heads like a couple of schoolkids called to the front of the class. Wendy meekly apologised, while Rob tried to convey the confusion and uncertainty that had led him to say nothing about the first note.

Dawn looked decidedly dubious. She asked Wendy to put the notes inside an envelope. 'God only knows if we'll get anything from these. Fortunately, I suspect they weren't sent by anyone involved in the crime. It's more likely to be some troublemaker who lives close by and heard what happened.'

'We were due to go away on Saturday,' Wendy told her, 'but now I'm not sure if we should.'

'It'll be fine.' Dawn forced a smile. 'Tim and I can keep an eye on the house, if you like.'

She diverted them from their anxieties with some small talk about their destination – a house on the north coast of Norfolk, which had once belonged to Wendy's aunt; she had specified in her will that it should be used as a retreat for all her family and friends.

'Sounds perfect.' Dawn spoke with real longing. 'And just think: no one up there will know anything about this.'

Once she'd gone, Rob admitted to feeling slightly less worried about the notes. Some malicious neighbour had been trying to torment them, that was all.

They passed a quiet evening together, gently multi-tasking: half an eye on the TV while Wendy played *Bejeweled* on her phone and Rob read up on ground source heat pumps. The sort of pleasantly low-key evening they had shared countless times – marred only, perhaps, by the knowledge that he'd taken far too many of them for granted.

Later, in bed, the fears came creeping back. He thought of the news reports he'd read online, the comparisons to Charles Manson and the like. You tortured to extract information, surely? Or had it been for fun, a matter of sadistic pleasure?

He thought about tomorrow. Looking Jason in the eye, and wondering if his darkest fears would be confirmed.

The worst thing was, Rob only had himself to blame.

The truth about Iain Kelly had come out at the worst possible time. Faced with the banks' refusal to tide them over, Rob had approached Jason Dennehy to see if he could borrow money from some less orthodox sources.

He couldn't say he was unaware of the risks. He'd played poker with a few of the characters from Jason's lawless days and had a pretty good idea of how they earned their money. But with a lot of cash sloshing around, he thought that investing some of it in a solid, reliable business might be an attractive proposition for them.

So it proved. The firm got a much needed injection of capital, and Rob was confident that he would be able to repay the loans in time. Then Kelly did a runner, and the full story came to light:

not only had Iain undermined the business, but he'd also borrowed money from Jason and some of his associates.

Understandably, there was a lot of anger, not a little of it directed at Rob. To stave off demands for immediate repayment, Rob had ended up offering three of the lenders a share in the business itself. The deal was done in Jason's name alone, with his fellow investors preferring to take a low profile.

The agreement was that Rob would strive to make the business consistently profitable – which he had more or less achieved – and then either buy them out, or perhaps sell up and take a less stressful role in the years leading to his retirement. As far as Rob was concerned that was still the plan, but he knew Jason wasn't renowned for his patience – or his temper. And if someone had started spreading rumours that Rob wasn't as innocent as he'd made out. . .

Then there was the matter of Iain Kelly's death. Rob had no reason to doubt it had been anything but an accident, but he couldn't completely dismiss the possibility that Kelly had been murdered, perhaps by one of the many people he'd swindled.

And was Rob now in their sights?

On Wednesday, he woke refreshed after a surprisingly good night's sleep. Wendy brought him a cup of tea, along with the news that there was no sign of another note. Unfortunately, anxiety about today's meeting prevented him from feeling much relief.

To his eternal shame, Rob had never told Wendy about his deal with Jason. At the time he'd convinced himself that he was sparing her the worry, and that within a few years the debts would be quietly settled, and then forgotten. He'd had to take Cerys into his confidence, however, since he relied on her to put together the financial records needed by his accountant.

His first stop of the day was at the site of a new eight-bedroom mansion near Amesbury, where he had to review progress on the installation of a ground source heat pump – hence last night's reading matter. The job had been assigned to two of his most experienced engineers, and a long and detailed meeting with the project's architect confirmed that everything was on track.

All good – except that the architect had turned up an hour late. Now Rob faced a frustrating journey to Bosham, which included what felt like half a lifetime stuck behind a tractor. Never the calmest of drivers, he was in a steaming temper by the time he reached the village, twenty minutes later than planned.

A familiar Iveco flatbed was parked outside a large, secluded house with a mini-excavator and a half-filled skip on the drive. Pulling up behind the truck, Rob sent a text to say he was here. The reply came back at once: '*Meet by the water*'

Rob got out of the car, still in a foul mood but also a little uneasy. It was a cool, windy day of squally showers, and there wasn't a soul to be seen.

He wondered if Jason might have lured him out here, and thought, belligerently: *Bring it on*. Pumped up, his hands curled into fists as he walked the fifty yards or so to the end of the lane, where a gentle slope led down to a shallow waterway. Bosham was situated on a tidal inlet that formed part of a vast natural harbour, so the ground was flat and soggy, and you were never far from some muddy creek.

There were a few sailing boats off to his left, and a fisherman on the other side of the creek. *Potential witnesses*, Rob thought, just as a voice shouted: 'Hey!'

He turned to see Jason Dennehy striding out from what must have been the back garden of the property he was working on. Despite the inclement weather, he was wearing dirt-encrusted cut-down jeans and a black muscle vest that showed off his huge biceps. There was a hunched, aggressive look to his posture, his bald head glistening with rain or sweat, his brow furrowed with what Rob took to be anger. His tattoos had never looked more like warpaint than they did now.

'What's this about, then?' Jason demanded.

Rob felt his stomach shift: a fight or flight response kicking in. 'That's what *I* want to know.'

Jason frowned as he closed the distance between them. Then came a slightly mocking smile. 'You don't look yourself, Rob. Something on your mind?'

He knew. Rob suddenly felt sure of it. His instincts had been correct, and his only chance now to avoid a beating was to get in first. Without warning he threw himself forward, slamming into Jason's body with enough force to send them both sprawling on the ground.

SIXTEEN

Rob came to his senses almost from the moment they collided. Even with the element of surprise he would be no match for Jason. But he was committed now, and had no choice but to pin the other man to the ground for long enough to explain.

Fine in theory. But the earth beneath them was slick from a recent shower, and Jason was too agile to be restrained for long. Rob tried to bring his knee up to press on the man's stomach while also keeping his face out of range of a head butt. As they grappled, he managed to say, 'Are you trying to destroy me?'

'What are you—' Jason groaned as Rob landed a punch to his stomach. But it was a tactical error: with his own hand free, Jason clawed at Rob's face, his palm slamming against Rob's nose. 'Fucking maniac.'

Rob twisted away, felt blood running into his mouth. 'Couldn't wait for your money, so you—'

'What the fuck're you talking about?' With frightening strength, Jason bucked his body as if having a convulsion, catapulting Rob into the soft, sticky mud.

'A dying man.' Rob threw up his arms to shield himself from the assault that was bound to follow. 'You sent him into our garden, Sunday afternoon. . .'

Belatedly he realised that Jason had frozen, half-sitting up. 'I dunno what you're on about.'

Panting for breath, Rob lowered his arms and wiped blood from his face. 'Those cronies of yours, then. Collins, and Bernie something.'

'Bernie's not around any more.'

'Dead?'

'He's in Thailand, you muppet. And Col wouldn't have a go at you. I know some of my mates are dodgy, but they're not the fucking Mafia.'

'Just tell me you don't know anything about the guy on Sunday.'

Jason exhaled. *What. Fucking. Guy?*

'There was a man found tortured, in Petersfield.' He studied Jason's face for any giveaway signs of recognition, but saw none. 'In our garden.'

'You're kidding?' Dennehy sat back and issued a rueful laugh. 'Well, fuck me!'

Somehow, Rob also managed a grin. He'd forgotten that groundworkers swore more than any other trade, except perhaps for his own.

Jason rose, then thrust out a hand and helped Rob to his feet. Across the creek, the fisherman was staring, transfixed. Jason blew him a sarcastic kiss.

'There's a hosepipe at the house, if you wanna clean up?'

'Yeah. I better had.' Rob touched his nose, gingerly. The bleeding seemed to have stopped, but his face was a mess, and his clothes were filthy.

'Bloody hell, Rob.' Jason was shaking his head in bewilderment. 'Lucky for you I'm in a good mood, otherwise you'd be in fucking hospital.'

Rob didn't think he was joking. They trudged up the slope and on to an immaculate lawn. The foundations were being dug for a huge extension at the rear – a snooker room, according to Jason. 'Got a kid they think's gonna be the next Ronnie O'Sullivan. He's six years old.'

While Rob used the hosepipe to wash his face, Jason fetched a roll of kitchen towels and they both wiped off the worst of the mud. Rob noticed that the tattooed sleeve on Jason's left arm was nearly complete – a tangle of vines and black roses, swirling around his favourite motorcycle, sports car and dog. There was a new image, too, on his stomach: a vivid and wickedly accurate caricature of his partner.

Somewhat belatedly, Rob asked, 'So, why the good mood?'

'What? Oh, Dean's asked us to marry him.'

'Yeah? Congratulations.'

'Not sure if it's my thing, to be honest. But nice to be asked, innit?'

Jason rustled up seats by the simple method of flipping a couple of wheelbarrows. The sky had gone dark and another shower looked imminent, but the air felt slightly warmer.

'So,' Rob began, 'Sunday afternoon, we're having a family barbecue in the garden when this guy knocks against the fence. . .'

He recounted the incident in detail. Jason listened patiently until Rob talked of giving a statement to the police. 'D'you say anything about me?'

'Of course not. I had no reason to.'

'So why lay into me like I'm the enemy?'

'That was stupid. Rush of blood to the head, or something.' Rob heaved up a sigh. 'It was me who suggested the music led him to us, and the police feel it was almost certainly a random choice. And yet. . .'

'You think it wasn't?'

'I don't know. But I have to rule it out, don't I?'

Jason had produced some cigarettes from somewhere. He lit up, then offered the box to Rob, who'd never smoked in his life but felt sorely tempted to try one now.

'Since Sunday, there have been a couple of other things.' He described the letters, the gate found open in the middle of the night, and the feeling he'd had at times that he was being watched. 'That's only just occurred to me, while I'm telling you this.'

'All right. I can see why you're looking for a reason, even if there isn't one.' Jason sucked on the cigarette, then expelled the smoke in a rush. 'But why would I be in the frame?'

Rob fought an urge to look away. 'Iain Kelly,' he said simply.

Jason's face darkened. He took out the cigarette and held it at arm's length, lips pursed as if to spit. 'What about him?'

'A lot of people still think I must have known what he was doing. And I don't blame them – I should have woken up to it sooner.' He paused, but all he got was a non-committal shrug from Jason. 'You and some of the guys from poker lost a lot of money.'

'Yeah, but that's our problem. And I don't blame you – 'cos it was me that decided to lend it to him: no one else.'

'But he was trading on the business reputation the whole time, the reputation that he and I had as partners.'

Jason shook his head. 'Nah, it was a private loan. *I* cocked up, not you. Thought the wanker wouldn't dare try to rob me.' A final puff on the cigarette, then he flicked it into the mud. 'Anyway, you offered to pay some of it back.'

'Because I felt guilty. He swindled a lot of people that I knew and liked.'

'Yeah, well, that offer still counts in your favour. . . just about.' A wry smile. 'If anything else happens, and you need some help, give me a shout, yeah?'

'I will. Thanks.'

Rob felt his phone bleep, checked the display and found a re-minder from Cerys. 'Shit. I'm meant to be interviewing some-one at two.'

'Not like that, you aren't.' Jason pointed to his mud-splattered shirt and jeans.

Rob sighed. He might just make it home in time to shower, but it would be a close-run thing. 'Bloody traffic's horrendous. That's what got me in such a bad mood.'

'You need to chill a bit, mate.' Jason gestured lazily at the water. 'You live in one of the most beautiful places in the world. Of course it's gonna be busy.'

'Words of wisdom,' Rob murmured.

'Too right, and here's some more.' Jason reached for another cigarette. In a very different tone, quiet and gritty, he said, 'I wouldn't go talking to anyone about Iain Kelly, and especially not the cops, yeah? Might make life a lot harder for all of us.'

There was a beat of silence, a long moment of intense eye contact, and then Rob broke away and nodded. He wetted his lips before speaking.

'Understood.'

SEVENTEEN

Georgia didn't quite believe it. Not that she was desperate to be 'besties' or anything – not with the stars of BitchWorld like Amber, Chloe or Paige. But it was better than having them as enemies, especially as most of her year group would be attending the same sixth-form college in September.

In BitchWorld it was all or nothing. Ignore them and they'd do everything they could to make your life hell. The only other option was to worship them, and no way did Georgia want to do that. Now, thanks to some poor dead guy, it looked like she might not have to.

She'd decided it was probably worth the risk she'd taken in telling the other kids what had happened on Sunday – her dad would go ballistic if he knew, but to her mind, if the word was already out there, it couldn't really hurt to fill in some of the details.

On Monday she'd hung out in the park at Heath Pond with a big group from her year, all still hyper from having finished their GCSEs. It had gone okay: most of the girls preferred talking to listening, so Georgia was quickly able to fade into the background.

Yesterday, after surviving the sleepover, she hadn't been in the mood to do it again, so she'd gone for a walk and lied to Wendy that she'd been with her friends. She knew her mum worried if she didn't mix with people, but the trouble was that Wendy didn't have a clue what it was like to be in Georgia's skin.

Wendy and Rob's upbringing had been normal, cosy, safe – never any shortage of love or money – and so they both seemed convinced that Georgia's experience must have left her weighed down with all kinds of trauma and stress and psychological pain, even though she maintained that it hadn't.

Half the time she couldn't even work out whether she thought of her as Mum, or as Wendy. There was no question that the woman loved Georgia to bits, but did she love her, really and truly, as a *daughter*?

Georgia didn't know. Maybe she never would.

Rob, though, was definitely getting cooler towards her. In his eyes, she was going the same way as Josh: someone who spoke back, who wouldn't play by 'Dad's' rules. Pretty soon it would only be Evan who mattered to him.

Oh God, Evan. . .

Another problem.

Amber and Paige had messaged to see if she wanted to meet up. *Not really*, was the honest answer. But she had nothing better to do.

Once she was safely out of sight from home, she took out the cigarettes and lighter she kept stashed in her room. She wasn't that fussed about smoking, but knew it helped her fit in. On Monday nearly everyone had been passing smokes around, and some of them shared a joint. Georgia had so far steered clear of drugs, for reasons she couldn't have explained to anyone from school.

Her past life, prior to adoption, was a closely guarded secret. Georgia had always feared the reaction from BitchWorld, if they knew the truth, but seeing how impressed they were when she described the man dying in the garden, she had begun to reconsider. Her own story was just as dramatic as that – maybe more so.

The centre of Petersfield was quiet, probably because of the rain showers. She'd once heard it said that the main square looked like something out of Charles Dickens. For most kids her age that meant deadly dull, but Georgia secretly thought it was lovely. Compared to where she came from, it was paradise.

Amber and Paige were waiting by the big statue, both staring down at their phones. They wore the same type of outfits as her, black leggings and sleeveless tops, but to Georgia's eye they looked far better in them. Wendy was always insisting that Georgia was slim – and in the eyes of a middle-aged woman she probably was – but put her next to these two and she looked wide and lumpy, misshapen.

Georgia saw the instant they spotted her, but pretended they hadn't. Something was said, and sly glances exchanged. Georgia felt her insides knotting up.

In one sense she understood how stupid it was to worry what these clueless bitches thought – and physically she had no fear of them at all. The problem was the influence they had over Georgia's social status. Ridiculous that these things mattered, but they did. They really did.

Their greetings were friendly enough, though Georgia stayed wary. The sleepover had gone okay, but only because Paige hadn't been there. Put her together with Amber and you got a kind of chemical reaction: two basically safe substances suddenly became dangerous.

Paige suggested they go to the bakery café across the road. Georgia offered the half-finished cigarette round but they wrinkled their noses, like it would be unclean to share anything of hers.

The café was busy, but they managed to find a table against the side wall. Georgia's stomach rumbled at the sight of cakes and pastries. She wanted a doughnut but knew the other two would be straight on their phones, Instagramming pictures of Georgia 'pigging out'. They ordered skinny lattes, so Georgia did the same.

'Are the cops still at your house?' Paige asked, and Georgia thought: *Here we go*.

'Not really,' she said. 'It was only ever a bit of the garden that he was in.'

'Do they know who he is yet?'

Georgia shrugged. 'Don't think so.'

Amber said, 'He was all sliced up, that's what my sister reckons. By devil worshippers. They were cutting pieces off him and everything.'

'I wonder if they ate them?' Paige said, just as the waitress brought the drinks.

'Ugh, gross!' Amber said, but she was giggling, too.

'There was a case like that in Germany.' Georgia felt she had to contribute. 'This guy had a fantasy about being killed and eaten. He found someone who agreed to do it, only first they both ate bits of him before he was de—' She broke off. 'What?'

With a shudder of distaste, Paige said, 'TMI, Georgia.'

'*Way* too much.' Amber took a sip of coffee and used her tongue to remove the foam moustache. 'So, imagine if it's, like, someone *you know* that did it. Because it could be.'

Georgia sat back. 'It's nothing to do with—'

'Devil worshippers, though!'

'But it probably isn't true. There's always stupid rumours—'

'Are you calling her sister a liar?' Paige snapped.

'You'd better not.' Amber's eyes were cold. 'She got it from a *news*paper, okay? There was a thing like it a few years ago. Some people got hold of this girl – I think she was special needs or something – and they like knew her a bit, enough to get her to trust them.' She glanced at Paige, and they gave a matching snort of laughter. 'So they took her prisoner, and just. . . did what they wanted to her.'

'You're kidding! Like, what sort of. . .?'

'Anything,' Amber said. '*Every*thing.'

'Ooh.' Paige shivered, wriggling her whole body with excitement.

*

Some passing boys provided a welcome interruption. Georgia didn't care who they were or whether they noticed her. She drank her coffee, grimacing with every swallow, and then became aware of a familiar, creeping discomfort.

She was being stared at.

She checked over her shoulder; Amber and Paige had decided to play it cool, so the boys were tapping on the glass to get their attention. But that wasn't it.

Turning back, she realised that someone was using the reflections in the mirror beside her. It was a woman sitting at the table behind Amber and Paige; she averted her eyes as soon as Georgia looked that way, but there was no doubt she'd been studying her.

Georgia gave it a minute, then glanced back. The woman was concentrating on her phone in a way that seemed fake, somehow. Sure enough, she took a quick peek to see if Georgia was still watching, then went back to her phone.

She was quite old, perhaps thirty or more, with a thin face and short, spiky brown hair. Not pretty, but not ugly, either – she had fine cheekbones and clear, pale skin. She was wearing a dark blue t-shirt, and she had a half-sleeve tattoo on her left arm: some kind of dark, dense Celtic pattern that Georgia couldn't help envying a little. You don't mess with a woman who's done that to her body.

So why is she spying on me?

As she tuned back into the conversation, Amber was saying, '. . . the tiniest dick in the world', and Paige burst out laughing, but Georgia couldn't join in.

Shit, is the woman a reporter?

Amber had asked a question; Georgia registered the word 'brother' but that was all. Then Paige said, 'Oh yeah, she *so* fancies him.'

'What?' Georgia asked. The woman in the mirror looked up again.

'You do, don't you?' Amber clasped her hands over her chest and sang, lightly, *Oh, Evan, my beautiful brother, Evan!*

'Shut up,' Georgia growled, but that only made it worse.

'She wants to fuck him,' Paige declared, and Amber nodded, still singing: *Evan, take my cherry – 'cos no one else is gonna want it!*

Georgia just glared at the table top, waiting for them to get bored.

'Be honest,' Paige said softly. 'You did admit it. Hannah told me.'

Georgia's head snapped up. Hannah was supposed to be a real friend; she was always saying how fake and two-faced Paige was. . .

Amber twisted the knife: 'You told her he's the hottest guy you know.'

'That is *so* disgusting,' Paige declared. 'Your own brother.'

'I didn't say that,' Georgia shouted, 'and if Hannah said I did, then she's lying, and anyway he's not even my brother, so shut up!'

That brought silence. Frowns. Confusion.

Georgia felt the blood drain from her face. Her skin crawled. It felt like the whole café was listening.

'What do you mean?' Paige asked quietly.

'Nothing.' Georgia jumped up, almost knocking her chair over. 'You're fucking bitches and I hate you!'

Customers and staff alike were staring at her as she stormed out, among them the woman with the spiky hair. The expression on her face was hard to read, but it might have been amusement: probably gloating at her misery.

Georgia hurried away, feeling sick to her stomach as she thought about what she'd said.

He's not even my brother. Oh, jeez.

How could she have been so stupid?

EIGHTEEN

Rob didn't get home till gone seven. After leaving the office, he'd decided to take a stroll around the town centre to get his thoughts in order. Of course it had never really made sense that Jason would send a dying man into his garden; but having ruled out the involvement of Dennehy or his associates, where did Rob go next in search of an answer?

He had no clue. And his melancholy deepened when he learned that a tabloid journalist had infiltrated the offices of the charity in Winchester, speaking to several of Wendy's colleagues before her motive was rumbled.

'She was after information on *me*, that's the thing. Trying to dig up the dirt.'

'It's bloody disgraceful. I don't know why you're not furious about it.'

'Because you're angry enough for both of us – as usual.' Wendy gave him a pensive smile. 'And because I realised that she wasn't going to get anything juicy. It made me appreciate what a lovely group of people I work with. We should be grateful that our jobs don't require having to stoop to such levels.'

Rob grunted a sort of agreement. After all, he could hardly claim moral superiority over anyone right now. But he was pleased to hear that she intended to work from home tomorrow afternoon.

'I have a report to finish in the evening, but it means I can do the big shop on my way home, then pack for the holiday without you under my feet.'

She wanted to know about his day, but of course he couldn't mention the encounter with Dennehy, or his mad race to clean up and change clothes before going to the office. There was a small bruise to the side of his nose, but he claimed to have bumped it on the car door.

'The interview was okay. He seemed to know his stuff, but he was just so desperate. I'm the boss of a small plumbing firm, being made to feel like I'm Simon bloody Cowell.'

Wendy dragged out the silence, before saying, in a passable imitation: 'You're through.'

'Don't joke. I know you see it even more than I do, how tough it is out there. But this guy today gave me a sob story about one of his kids. The implication was: reject me and you're punishing my children.'

'So what are you going to do?'

'Sleep on it – and then probably employ him.'

For dinner, Evan volunteered to cook a chilli; Livvy had already made a key lime pie for dessert. They were talking about food when Georgia stomped into the kitchen, ignoring them all, and helped herself to a Diet Coke from the fridge.

'Chilli for dinner, courtesy of Evan,' Rob told her.

'Not hungry.'

'But you must be—'

'Don't want it.' She popped the can and turned to leave; still no eye contact with anyone.

'Georgia, wait. . .' Wendy began, and Evan darted into his sister's path, hands raised and bobbing on his feet as if playing basketball.

'You're going nowhere, buddy, not after insulting the chef—'

'Stop it,' Georgia cried. Evan moved in for an embrace but she wheeled away, slopping Coke on to the floor. 'Get off me!'

'C'mon, give your brother a hug.'

He tried again and this time she shoved him hard in the chest. 'Leave me alone, I'm not a pervert.'

Evan reeled back as Georgia stormed out and slammed the door behind her.

'You could see she wasn't in the mood,' Livvy scolded him. To Rob and Wendy: 'I think something may have happened in town.'

'It's those bloody so-called "friends" of hers,' Wendy fumed.

'Teenage girls,' Livvy said with a mock shudder. 'I tell you, it's such a relief to grow up.'

After that, dinner was just the four of them. Only when he'd cleared his plate did Rob steel himself to ask if anyone had heard from Josh. Prompted by a nudge from Livvy, Evan said, 'Uh, yeah. This project of his isn't quite finished, so he's saying he'll make his own way up there, Sunday night or Monday.'

'Oh, well I suppose that's not—' Wendy began, but Rob's temper erupted.

'It's bollocks! On Sunday there'll be another excuse, and by then we're in Norfolk and it'll be too late.' He slammed a hand on the table. 'Just once, why can't he do what he bloody well agreed?'

His outburst was met with silence. Livvy was blushing, while Evan looked disgusted. *Nice one, Rob*, he thought to himself. *Alienate your whole family.*

It was left to Wendy to enquire, calmly, of Evan: 'How would he get there?'

'He was a bit vague about that. Train and then a bus, maybe.'

'He won't. It's the middle of nowhere.' Rob knew he was overreacting, and yet still couldn't stop himself. 'And how come he rang you? Why won't he ever speak to me or your mum?'

At this, Livvy let slip a smile. She turned away to hide her reaction, but it was enough to restore some sanity.

Rob snorted a laugh. 'Okay, no one needs to answer that.'

'Despite what you might think,' Evan said, 'all that stuff about psychic connections between twins doesn't really exist. I've tried to find out what he's up to, but he basically said I wouldn't understand. I'm Evan the Thicko, remember?'

Rob shook his head. They'd all had a taste of Josh's dismissive tone over the years, although he continually insisted that he didn't mean to cause offence.

'Right,' he said. 'We're collecting him on Saturday morning, and I don't care if we have to pick him up and throw him in the boot.'

He was prepared for opposition, but none came. All Evan said was, 'Shall I tell him?'

'No, better if we just turn up. Don't give him a chance to wriggle out of it.'

Before bed, Rob patrolled the house just as he had done the previous night, checking all the doors and windows – even testing the garden gate to ensure it was bolted.

In the bedroom, Wendy had a Robert Goddard novel open on her lap. She'd recently started wearing glasses for reading, and while she was mortified by the need for them, Rob thought they looked great on her.

'Flaunting yourself, in those specs,' he said. Wendy chuckled, but didn't take up the invitation to flirt.

Slipping into bed beside her, Rob stretched out and sighed. 'What are we going to do about Georgia?'

'Leave her be. Evan said he'll try and find out what's up, once the dust has settled.'

'Great! So now he's the go-between for *both* our other kids! What a ringing endorsement of our parenting skills!' He stared morosely at the ceiling. 'Makes me think we bit off more than we could chew.'

Wendy inhaled sharply. 'That's a dreadful thing to say. She's no more of a challenge than any other fifteen-year-old.'

'No, but if we'd known the kind of grief we'd be getting from the twins – or Josh, anyway – I doubt if we'd gone ahead with the adop— *ow*!' Without warning, she had prodded him in the stomach.

'That's unfair. If people knew the stress that teenagers cause, no one would have children at all. And if you remember, we went on trying for more after the twins were born.'

Rob grunted. 'So?'

'Well, would you still make a comment like that if Georgia was the daughter we'd *conceived*, rather the daughter we adopted?'

'Right at this minute? I think I would.'

There must have been enough feeling in his voice that she didn't berate him, which he expected – and probably deserved. He turned over, assuming it was better to leave it there. Then, to his amazement, Wendy shuffled closer and he felt her breath tickling the back of his neck.

At first his body tensed; from the shock of it, maybe. And because he was still grouchy and fed up. 'Isn't that a bit unfair?' he said.

'What do you mean?' She shifted, as if preparing to break apart.

'One minute you don't want me anywhere near you, because you're gearing up for. . . when it's all finished. The next minute you're coming on to me.'

He heard a little intake of breath; then she tutted, sadly, and moved away from him. 'I'm sorry. I was just trying to offer some comfort.'

Stupid, Rob.

He was searching for an appropriate response when she said, 'I'm a mess, at the moment. I'm so confused. So worried.'

'Me too,' he said quietly.

'Then tell me that. Talk to me about it.'

'I do.'

'No, you don't. And that's what it comes down to, the reason I said what I said.'

He waited out another silence, wanting a fuller explanation, while also dreading one.

'You're never really here, Rob, and you haven't been for years. I feel like I've only ever got about sixty per cent of your attention – and I can't live like that any more.'

'I don't. . .' He cleared his throat. 'I don't think that's very fair.' It was the only response he could muster, and it sounded lame even to him.

'Do you know something about this?'

The question made him jump; literally, the bed shook a little. 'What?'

'Sunday. The notes. If I hadn't found the second one, I doubt if you'd have owned up to them. Are you hiding something from me?'

'No. Of course not.'

Wendy sniffed in a way that seemed to express both satisfaction and regret: *I have my answer – and it's the opposite of what you've just said.*

NINETEEN

Your next challenge was on a smaller scale, yet more ambitious. You travelled to London, cruising the streets around Kings Cross and Euston. You drove a dirty, anonymous van, bearing number plates stolen from a similar vehicle. The search was harder than expected, but eventually you found the perfect victim – not in the centre of the city but in Twickenham, on the embankment overlooking Eel Pie Island.

He was a homeless, hopeless, shambolic specimen, so incapacitated that he offered no resistance. He could barely walk. His speech was unintelligible. Later, when he had dried out, you learned that he had once attended a good school – albeit in some godforsaken northern town – and then a polytechnic. He claimed to have had some musical talent, an ambition to play keyboards and sing.

It hadn't worked out. He'd discovered drink at the age of fourteen, and it had held far more allure than music, more than women or even drugs (the drugs came later). He'd held down a few ordinary jobs, but he'd also worked, finally, in the music business, as a roadie. He claimed to have tales to tell of those days, wild tales, but few of them made sense.

He called himself Baz. We didn't get his full name: he no longer seemed to know it, having lived on the streets for many years.

He'd had a family once. A wife, and a child, but something had happened: he couldn't remember what. He had blocked it out, though at night he would often scream for the child, and rage about the doctors that couldn't save her.

Without the booze he was noisy and disruptive, so he had to be medicated, kept in a stupor until liveliness was required.

He had many tattoos, acquired during his time on the road. From his mumblings it became apparent that the road crew would get wasted in some far-off corner of the world, and compete to have the most obscene image etched on to their bodies. Baz had female genitals at the base of his spine. He had a prominent politician of the eighties fellating his equally prominent opponent. He had a limbless baby with the face of a young woman who presumably meant something to him. Offensive images, which had to be removed.

I required you to engage with him, to form a bond but at the same time have no feelings. That was important, for what was to follow.

It is no easy task to inflict pain, calmly and methodically, on another human being. Because of that, you were led to it gradually. Everything was discussed: the variety of methods, and the devices – the tools – that you might wish to use. And the pace of the torture, the *progression* of it, was crucial to get right.

I recommended frequent pauses, to assess the effect of your work; recovery time was also important, for you as well as him. You were fighting against years of learned behaviour, overcoming the natural resistance to cause harm.

I encouraged you to think yourselves into the part, the way actors do – drawing on real life experiences, channelling the emotions produced by those memories to act without inhibition, to punch and kick, peel and puncture, to stab and slice.

But not kill. I was saving that, because I knew how rapidly the extraordinary becomes ordinary.

Even then, my thoughts were moving beyond this one victim.

For you – my followers, my Brood – mass murder was the ultimate goal.

TWENTY

Wendy spent a dizzying morning in the office on Thursday, conducting a final debrief with the case workers on her team, then calling round to their partners in social services and the NHS. She wanted to be sure that everyone knew the status of the two dozen clients she was currently supporting.

On the way home she stopped at the supermarket. The aisles were pleasantly cool and quiet, and she had plenty of time to reflect on last night's painful conversation with Rob. Perhaps it was mean of her to be so blunt, especially at the moment when they were both under pressure. But equally she would struggle to retract the accusations she'd made – because her instincts said that Rob was keeping something from her.

What did she think it was? She knew that the revelation of his former partner's duplicity had nearly destroyed him. But Iain Kelly had been so charming, so energetic and seemingly committed to the business that neither she nor Rob had ever doubted his loyalty. Wendy despaired of the fact that Rob was working himself into an early grave to restore his reputation, when for some people – especially in a small town like this – there would be no shaking off the idea that he'd been in on it, or had known and done nothing.

It had occurred to her that some of Kelly's creditors were pretty unsavoury people, particularly those linked to Jason Dennehy, whose friendship with Rob had been compromised by the crisis. Did Rob now fear some kind of reprisal?

She drove the short distance from the supermarket on autopilot, appalled by her own theory. Surely there was nothing in their past that could bring about, even indirectly, the kind of savagery they'd witnessed on Sunday?

The thought that came next stunned her so profoundly that she stalled the car while turning into Russell Drive, and was lucky to avoid a side-on collision. Raising a hand in apology to the driver who'd been forced to make an emergency stop, she spluttered forward and pulled up on the drive, her hand visibly trembling as she took the key from the ignition.

What if this wasn't linked to Iain Kelly?

What if the connection was to Georgia's past life?

No, it couldn't be. Wendy opened the front door and called out for a hand with the bags. Evan and Livvy had agreed to help Livvy's parents decorate their dining room, but Georgia was supposed to be home, and Wendy was hoping to find out why she'd reacted so aggressively to Evan's humour.

Georgia adored her brothers, but for Evan she reserved a particular type of hero-worship, carefully concealed beneath a veneer of sarcasm. Thankfully, the arrival of his first serious girlfriend hadn't disrupted the relationship: Livvy had treated her as an equal from the beginning, and the two found common cause in mocking Evan's obsession with sport. Last night's spat had been quite out of character.

After bringing in a couple of bags, Wendy shouted again, but the house felt empty. A quick search confirmed it. As well as leaving her bedroom in disarray, Georgia had failed to set the burglar alarm or double-lock the door.

Feeling disappointed rather than worried, Wendy sent a text: '*Where r u?*'

The house was stuffy, so she opened a few windows, then unlocked the terrace doors and stepped outside. After yesterday's showers, today was humid and still; Wendy basked in the warmth for a minute, then sorted out the groceries and moved on to the spare bedroom, where she had set out the suitcases and several piles of freshly laundered clothes. When the doorbell rang, her first thought was: *Georgia's forgotten her key again. . .*

There was a frosted glass panel in the door; the shape beyond it was female, but not Georgia. Cop, nosy neighbour – or worse?

The woman on the step was unfamiliar, a pretty, waif-like blonde who bore a vague resemblance to a young Sienna Miller.

'Hi! You must be Mrs Turner?' Her accent was English, well-spoken with a hint of a lisp. 'Can I see Evan?'

'He's not here.'

'Oh. Are you sure?'

Wendy started to look over her shoulder, then checked herself. 'Who are you?'

'Oh God, sorry! I'm Lara, from college – that's how I know Evan. We sort of lost touch – I took a gap year, went travelling, met a guy, you know?' She giggled, fluttering her eyelashes, but Wendy wasn't quite buying the ditzy routine. 'Anyway, I saw Ev at Mish's party last week, oh God that was *such* a great ni—'

'Mish?' Wendy cut in.

'Misha Watson? The party was at her house in Romsey, her parents are *lovely* people, well, I'm sure you know that!'

Wendy gave a weak smile. Even if this wasn't a journalist, another worrying possibility had occurred to her.

'He's out with Livvy,' she said, adding pointedly: 'His girlfriend.'

Lara was unfazed. 'I know Livvy, I'm in one of the group selfies with her – you know where Mish is holding that big inflatable. . .' Blushing slightly, she mimed a phallus.

Wendy smiled, and couldn't help but relax. 'I'm sorry you've had a wasted journey.' As she spoke, there was a waft of air through the house, and what might have been a quiet clunking sound.

'It's *so* weird.' Lara studied her phone, chewing absently on her bottom lip. 'I was sure it was today they said to come round. . .'

'You'd arranged to meet?'

'Mm, I've got a place at Warwick, doing History of Art – I know Liv's at Manchester, and it's not exactly the same as her course, but still I was hoping to get an idea of what to expect. . .'

Wendy nodded automatically, but her mind was on that draught. If she hadn't shut the terrace doors properly, they were likely to swing open, and Rob was always griping about the stress on the hinges. . .

'I have to—' she began, but the girl suddenly burst out coughing, doubled over and hacking up her lungs like a sixty-a-day smoker. When she looked up, her face was bright red, eyes streaming.

'G-God, so sorry. Can I use your bathroom?'

Wendy could hardly refuse, but she was uneasy. This felt too much like a ruse to gain entry to the house – exactly the kind of subterfuge a sly tabloid hack might employ.

She showed Lara to the toilet in the hallway, and caught a frown as the door shut. It must have seemed peculiar that Wendy was virtually standing guard outside.

'I couldn't have a glass of water, could I?' she called.

Wendy said yes, but listened for the click of the lock as she went into the kitchen. She lingered awkwardly in the doorway until she heard the toilet flush, then moved out as Lara emerged. The girl took the water with a grateful smile but took only tiny sips, as if in no hurry to leave.

'Sorry you had a wasted journey,' Wendy said, reaching for the glass as soon as it was lowered.

'Yes, such a shame. When's Ev due back?'

'Not till later tonight – if at all. He often stays over.'

'At Livvy's? Whereabouts is that again?'

'Hambledon.' Wendy narrowed her eyes. 'I don't have the address.'

Lara shrugged, backing slowly along the hall. When she cast a fretful glance at the stairs, Wendy thought: *Does she think Evan's hiding in his room?*

But all the girl said was, 'Thanks, Mrs Turner. I'll message Evan, and hopefully we can meet up soon.'

'Oh, we—' In her relief, Wendy had been about to mention the holiday, but she stopped herself in time. 'I will,' she said, smiling inanely. She didn't want this stranger knowing the house would be empty.

She opened the front door and Lara stepped out, gave her one more slightly quizzical look and then, mercifully, was gone. Wendy shut the door and almost laughed at her own foolishness. How could the presence of a young girl have made her feel so apprehensive? It was completely irrational.

She sniffed. *Pull yourself together!* Then she hurried into the study, curious to see if Lara got into a car, but the girl was nowhere to be seen. Odd.

Wendy returned the water glass to the kitchen and was heading for the stairs when she sniffed again. There was a funny smell in the air. Not the girl's perfume, but something else. Something sour and nasty.

She trudged up the stairs, unable to shake off a conviction that the girl had come here with an ulterior motive.

She stopped on the landing. The smell had drifted up here, too. But it wasn't as bad in the spare room, so she was able to put it from her mind while she packed. It occurred to her that Lara could be both a genuine friend of Evan's but *also* on the hunt for gossip. Well, she hadn't succeeded, that was—

A loud clatter from downstairs made her cry out.

Wendy froze. Her heart was in her throat. It sounded as though someone had thumped on one of the windows at the back.

She straightened up, her roving gaze unable to find what she was looking for. A phone was her first priority, but the bedroom extension had broken years ago, and they hadn't bothered to replace it. No point, when everyone had mobiles.

But her phone was in the kitchen.

She was out of the room and hurtling down the stairs before it occurred to her that she'd made a dangerous assumption. She'd visualised the sound as coming from outside, but what if it wasn't?

What if it was someone *inside* the house?

She dashed into the kitchen, registering on her way past that the living room seemed empty. Grabbing her phone, she keyed in three 9s, thumb poised to hit the *Call* button while she lifted a long-bladed knife from the magnetic rack on the wall.

Then into the living room – and it *was* empty. The terrace doors were shut, and there was no sign of anyone in the garden. She let out a shuddering breath. Now she thought about it, the likeliest explanation was that a bird had flown into one of the doors. It had happened once before, and scared the life out of her on that occasion, too.

She took a closer look. No smears or marks on the glass, and no feathers on the terrace, but it was still a good theory.

To demonstrate that her nerves were under control, she went outside and made sure the gate at the bottom of the garden was bolted. There was a solitary crow on the roof, and she wanted to think it was nursing the mother of all headaches.

After checking the side gate, Wendy returned to the terrace and noticed that one of the doors was further open than she'd left it. Could it have blown open, when there was only the lightest of breezes to stir the soupy air?

Now the house loomed over her, the door waiting like an open mouth. Her *home*.

'There's no one in the garden.' She said it aloud, to show how confident she was. Then she marched inside, and was almost at the hall when the front door slammed shut.

She had to choke back a scream. But it was only Georgia; at first scowling, then worried. 'Mum?'

Wendy staggered backwards, laughing with relief. 'Sorry, you gave me a fright. And *I* gave you a fright, probably.'

Georgia was still frowning, so Wendy said, 'First time on my own here since Sunday, and I've been a bit jumpy. Haven't you felt like that?'

'Nope.' As usual, Georgia's body language was closed and defensive. But she didn't turn away or run to her room, and for once Wendy was able to assess her properly. *She's unhappy, so unhappy.*

Then came a memory of the theory that had struck her earlier, and she felt hollowed out with tenderness and concern. Moving closer, fearing rejection, she gingerly rested her hands on Georgia's shoulders. 'You know Dad and I are worried—'

'You don't have to be, I've told you.'

'Not just about you, but Evan, Livvy, all of you. A man died in our home—'

'Our garden.'

'All right, but it's still a terrible thing.'

'Yeah.' Georgia's tone was flat, almost indifferent. 'But we didn't know him.'

Maybe she was trying to reassure Wendy that she wasn't affected by the tragedy, but in doing so she seemed callous, which in itself was a cause for worry.

She can't win, Wendy thought, *and neither can I.*

'Please, Georgia. We care so much about you.' She realised she couldn't explain herself; not without blubbing, at least.

'I know.' A sniff. 'Gonna have some toast.' Georgia eased free of the embrace, made for the kitchen but turned back, wrinkling her nose. 'Who's got BO?'

TWENTY-ONE

That evening Rob arrived home, not to the cold beer and relaxing night in front of the TV that he'd anticipated, but to a heated discussion about body odour.

'I'm not trying to be difficult,' he said yet again. 'I just can't smell it.'

'That's because it's faded by now,' said Wendy, but Georgia sniffed and said, 'It's still there, just about.'

Wendy looked grateful for the support. 'You do believe me, don't you?' she asked Rob.

'Of course I do. The question is, how did it get here?'

They were standing in the hall. Rob had driven home, nervously awaiting another confrontation like the one last night – *Are you hiding something from me*? – and instead he'd listened to a confusing account of an unwanted visitor, followed by various strange noises and then the discovery of a sour meaty smell that might or might not have been body odour.

'Are you sure no one's cooked anything unpleasant?' he asked. 'Evan would boil up a rat if he was hungry enough.'

'No, I checked with him.'

'And this girl, Lara?'

'He's fairly sure he doesn't know her, and neither of them met anyone like that at Misha's party.'

'So how did she know all about it?'

'Maybe she was there, but just watching him from afar.'

'Or Facebook,' Georgia muttered, and they both turned to look at her. 'Not everyone bothers with their privacy settings. There'll be loads of pictures, and if people are tagged it's easy to find out more about them.'

Wendy shuddered. 'That makes a lot of sense.'

'All right, let's accept that she came here under false pretences. What did it achieve?' Rob winced. 'Hold on – was Livvy with Evan when you called him?'

'I expect so,' Wendy said. 'They've spent the day painting.'

'What I'm wondering. . .' His gaze flicked from Wendy to Georgia and back. 'Well, maybe Evan *does* know her, but couldn't say so in front of. . .'

'Two-timing Livvy?' Wendy sounded incredulous, while Georgia looked appalled.

'Evan wouldn't cheat on her. That's. . . *ugh*, no! He just wouldn't.'

Rob was immediately contrite. 'I'm sorry. I'm just trying to find something that explains this. . . weirdness.'

There *was* another possibility, which Rob kept to himself until Georgia had gone upstairs and he and Wendy were in the kitchen, making coffee. First, though, Wendy admitted that his suggestion made sense.

'Evan's only human – and he's a man. I think sometimes we expect him to be a saint, if only because. . .'

'Josh isn't,' Rob finished for her. 'So maybe this Lara bumped into Evan at the party. They have a chat, then he forgets all about it, but she doesn't. After all, he has inherited his dad's animal magnetism. . .'

Wendy's laughter contained a strong note of ridicule. Rob poured fresh coffee from the cafetiere, glad of an aroma to savour rather than worry about, then said, 'My other theory is a lot less amusing. Could the girl have been a decoy?'

'A decoy?' Wendy looked baffled.

'So that someone else could get in.'

'Oh, God!' Her hand flew to her mouth. 'The doors were unlocked, so maybe that was the noise?'

'I'm thinking, that might explain the smell – though it's just a theory, remember.'

'Should we call DS Husein?' Wendy seemed to direct the question at herself. 'But what do I say? He'll just think I'm neurotic.'

'No, he won't,' said Rob, but he was thinking: *Actually, he might.*

Wendy put her coffee mug down. 'We ought to see if there's anything missing, at least.'

It took them only a minute to go through the ground floor rooms. All their electronic devices were accounted for, and there was nothing absent from any of their shelves or cupboards. Thinking of the impact Wendy had heard, Rob examined the carpet in front of the French windows and pointed to some smudges of dirt.

'That could easily have been me,' Wendy said. 'I didn't take my shoes off.'

'Let's hope this is just our overactive imagination, eh?'

Rob was making for the stairs when Wendy called him back. 'I don't think anyone could have got up there. I was either here in the hall, or up in the spare room.'

Above them, a door opened; Wendy ushered Rob back to the kitchen, and they were innocently drinking coffee when Georgia slouched in. 'Evan's shoes,' she said.

'Sorry, darling?' Wendy said.

'This morning, he was looking under the stairs for an old pair of trainers, to wear for painting. Maybe that caused the smell?'

Rob nodded, and once she was gone he said, 'Sounds plausible to me.'

'Oh, I hope that's it.' Wendy ran a hand through her hair. 'Otherwise, the thought of leaving the house empty for ten days. . .'

'We'll hide the valuables, set the alarm. And we can give Dawn a key.'

'You know she's bound to have a snoop around?'

'So what? My porn collection is long gone.' He winked. 'And as far as I know, we don't have any heroin stashed behind the bath!'

But he didn't feel quite so light-hearted when he went up for a shower. He had a niggling feeling that there was a bigger picture here, something which he and Wendy were simply failing to see, perhaps because they couldn't step back far enough.

He took the opportunity to check the floor safe in the bathroom. It was concealed beneath a removable tile, and contained their passports, various legal documents, Wendy's best jewellery and a couple of thousand pounds, saved up from the occasional cash jobs that he did for close friends and family.

It was a quiet evening. As a thank-you for the painting, Livvy's parents were taking her and Evan out to dinner, and then they were staying over. Georgia only toyed with her meal, vanishing to her room as soon as she was allowed. Wendy had a pile of ironing, and Rob said he needed to sort out some paperwork.

In truth, it amounted to little more than half a dozen quotes to review and send off; a couple of orders to approve. Once that was done he searched online for news stories about Sunday, but found nothing in any of today's papers – at least not in their electronic form.

The story was dying down, it seemed, for lack of fuel. He considered telling Wendy, but decided it was better not to raise the subject at all. He didn't want another interrogation like last night's, though on the question of Jason he was beginning to feel a little more reassured. Sunday's incident was completely random, he had decided, and the notes were from some local troll.

Before bed they played a couple of card games – speed and piquet – to get into the holiday mood. The house in Norfolk was well stocked with cards, board games and even a table tennis table. In past years they'd organised family competitions across a range of activities, complete with homemade medals for the winners.

This year's victors might as well be crowned all-time champions, Rob reflected, for it was unlikely they would ever hold such competitions again.

'I'm going to enjoy subjecting Josh to the torture of physical exercise,' he joked to Wendy, but it prompted only a wan smile.

'I keep wondering if we should make more effort to get in touch, find out why he needs to delay. . .'

'He'll be terminally vague, like he always is. Look at that party for your mum's seventieth. He knew all the details, swore blind he'd be there on time, and what happened?'

'That was four years ago—'

'He'd have missed my dad's funeral if I hadn't driven like a maniac to fetch him. I still find that hard to forgive.' Conscious that he sounded too aggressive, Rob lifted a hand in conciliation. 'All I'm saying is that "reliability" is not his middle name.'

'Then perhaps we ought to accept that.'

'Let him stay in Canterbury, you mean?'

'We should go and see him. But if he's adamant that he doesn't want to come, I don't think we should pressure him.'

'But what about. . . our news?'

She shook her head, as if unwilling to be plagued with minor details. 'We'll have to tell him separately, or something. I can't think about that now.'

'We don't have to do it at all,' he reminded her, as gently as he could. But she had picked up a book and was staring at it with fierce concentration: the discussion was at an end, and he could only recall, sadly, what she had said to him last night. *You're never really here, Rob.*

He couldn't completely dispute that, of course. But maybe she just didn't notice him the way she used to.

TWENTY-TWO

Baz was with us for weeks. He was our pet, our plaything. It was fascinating to observe your interaction with him. I made note of your contrasts, your strengths and weaknesses; I assessed your loyalty and your potential use to me.

The time for his death was drawing close when he escaped. My plans were left in disarray, thanks to the carelessness of one of you.

As a result, there was punishment; that was only right. Order has to be maintained within the Brood, you all accept that.

In truth, the escape served us well. I could see you were tiring of him. You needed the kill, and then a greater challenge.

Inadvertently, Baz led us directly to that challenge.

Our next victims.

A family.

TWENTY-THREE

Wendy had planned out her Friday in advance: finish packing, a bit of baking for Norfolk, then a thorough round of housework, indulging her irrational belief that she would relish the holiday all the more if she left the house clean and tidy.

'By the time we come back it'll be dusty again,' Evan pointed out, when he caught her polishing the dining room table at eight in the morning. He and Livvy had called in on their way to Portsmouth for a day of shopping. Although she'd been invited to Norfolk, Livvy had received the counter offer of a week in Cyprus with three female friends.

'No contest, eh? Holed up with me in rainy Norfolk, or sun-worshipping with her mates in Ayia Napa. . .' Evan joked about it, but Wendy knew how much he was going to miss her.

He also had a reasonable point about the dust, though that wasn't why Wendy had already decided to forego most of the housework. She'd said nothing to Rob, either, partly because her decision had been prompted by a dream – a vivid and particularly unpleasant dream – that had woken her in a panic in the early hours. As she lay and recovered, she decided that yesterday's unwelcome theory had to be tested out, one way or the other. And that meant a trip to Lyndhurst.

She was ready to depart by nine, but Georgia was still fast asleep. Wendy stood by her bed, reluctant to disturb her but also concerned about the girl waking to find her gone. She knew that teenage biorhythms meant Georgia favoured late nights and later mornings, and her justification for lying in bed was that she'd finished her GCSEs but couldn't get a part-time job until her sixteenth birthday, another month away.

'Georgia,' she whispered. 'Darling?'

There was a spasm of movement and a disgruntled face appeared. 'Uh?'

'I've just got to pop out for a couple of hours, okay?'

'Gnth.'

'Try not to waste the whole day. Is there anyone you can meet up with?'

'*No.*'

Wendy frowned. 'All right, don't bite my head off.' She gestured at the room. 'Make sure you clear up in here, at least. I've been asking you all week.'

'I'll do it later. Go away!' Georgia turned over and pulled the covers up, leaving Wendy standing there, frustrated.

I'm doing this for you, she wanted to snap. She was still fretting over Georgia's slightly cold reaction to the death on Sunday. She hadn't mentioned it to Rob, as he might see it as confirmation of his worst fears about the effects of the trauma she'd suffered in her childhood.

And did Rob truly regret the adoption? Wendy couldn't bear to believe that, even though, right now, she had to agree that Georgia didn't always make it easy for them.

The girl had been born into a chaotic household in Portsmouth to an unknown father, a mother addicted to heroin and a violent drug dealer for a stepfather. Having heard of the case via a colleague, Wendy and Rob had fostered the girl a couple of times until her mother successfully kicked the habit. This period of stability ended in tragedy when Georgia was ten. A new partner, Mark Burroughs, stabbed her mother to death in a drunken fight, only to realise there was a witness to his crime. In a psychotic rage he'd chased the girl upstairs, slashing at her legs, and Georgia only escaped by leaping from a first floor window.

By this time the twins were into their teens. Wendy and Rob had long since given up on having more children, but Wendy, after nearly two decades in adult social care, had come to despair of her ability to provide genuine, constructive help. The daily battle against budgetary constraints and political pressure – not to mention the constant criticism and belittling of the profession in the media – had left her feeling burned out. As she'd exclaimed to Rob: 'If everyone who feels like I do reached out to just one person, we'd hardly need social services any more.'

His response was simple enough: 'Well, let's do that, then.' And who better to help than the girl they'd already fostered?

Little had they realised that they were on the brink of disaster themselves, courtesy of Iain Kelly. Soon Rob was working eighteen-hour days to keep the business afloat, the house was mortgaged to the hilt once more, and Wendy, who'd gone part-time in order to be at home for Georgia, was forced to return to full-time work.

From the outset, Wendy had been careful to ensure that Rob understood the range of emotional issues that the girl was facing as she dealt with her grief, and the difficulty she would have in forming attachments to her new parents – while also navigating a way through all the normal challenges of adolescence.

Nevertheless, Wendy was proud of the stability they'd been able to provide, which was why she feared that Sunday's incident could set Georgia back years. And even though she knew it was completely wrong to regard an adopted child in such terms – as though she were a project to be completed – Wendy found it hard to shake off a correlation between Georgia's happiness and her own success or failure as a mother.

Hence her decision to drive across Hampshire on the basis of an instinct that she hoped, fervently, was wrong.

*

The journey took a little over an hour, heading south-west into the heart of the New Forest – a wild and often beautiful landscape that was neither new nor entirely forested. Unlike Rob, she was a calm, patient driver, and as much as possible she tried to focus on nothing more than the road ahead. She didn't want to dwell on yesterday's visitor, or the mess she was making of her thirty-year relationship.

The place she sought was a pub, The Britannia, a couple of miles south of Lyndhurst. Unlike many of the establishments she'd passed, it wasn't quaint or rustic, with hanging baskets and Tudor beams. Set back from the road in an area of scrubby heathland, it was a 1960s single-storey, flat-roofed timber-clad box, a strange and undesirable blend of log cabin and transport café, plastered with VOTE LEAVE posters and the flag of St George.

There was a generous car park, empty but for two cars. One was a battered old Jaguar with cherished plates, which Wendy noted with a grim smile.

She parked alongside it, checked her appearance in the mirror and then took a moment to compose herself. This was something she'd done throughout her career, a way of assuming the right persona for a potentially difficult encounter. She had to be friendly but professional, sympathetic but practical: crucially, she had to be authoritative. *They don't have to like you, but they* must *respect you*. That was the maxim, and it would apply here as much as it ever did at work.

She shut her eyes, but flashbacks from the dream intruded on her meditation. She was at home when someone knocked on the door. It was Mark Burroughs, released early from prison. He shouldered past her, yelling out Georgia's name. A DNA test had established that he was her natural father, and now he was taking custody of what was his. 'You can't stop me, bitch,' he snarled at Wendy. 'She ain't safe here, in this madhouse. You've failed her.'

That, Wendy felt, was clearly her own subconscious talking. She doubted whether Mark Burroughs regarded Georgia with anything other than resentment or hatred, and he was certainly in no position to judge Wendy's abilities as a parent.

All the same, she had a battle to convince herself that there was no truth to the allegation.

TWENTY-FOUR

Georgia hadn't been nearly as sleepy as she'd made out to Wendy. In fact, she'd been awake on and off for hours, curled up and crying, steeling herself to check the latest hateful updates on social media.

She's a sicko
A fucking freak
She tries to pretend he's not her brother! #deluded #headcase
Did SHE kill the guy in the garden? U gotta wonder. . .

It took off after someone got hold of separate pictures of Georgia and Evan and used Photoshop to make it look like they were kissing. The result was posted on Instagram, and now half her year group were adding insults and jokes. A whole shitstorm of abuse, and there was nothing Georgia could do. She just had to ride it out.

This morning she'd tried retreating into her most cherished fantasy – the one where her real father suddenly turned up, whisking her away from her troubles. She'd obsessed over his identity for years – not so much when she was first adopted, because she could see that Rob and Wendy were trying their best. But the longing to be rescued came back when Rob's business partner screwed them over. They'd tried to pretend everything was fine, but Georgia had picked up on the tension; so many nights when she'd lain awake and listened to them arguing, terrified of what might come next: a punch, a scream, one of them grabbing a knife. . .

It had never come to that, and up till the past few months things hadn't seemed too bad. But she could sense it slipping away again, an uneasy truce starting to break, and what happened on Sunday seemed to have made things worse.

The trouble was, deep down Georgia knew her real dad was never going to turn up; and if he did he wouldn't fit the fairytale profile of a rich, kind, handsome prince. More likely he'd be just another doped-up loser.

Wendy got out of the car. The sky was clearing, allowing a little sunshine through, and the air was agreeably warm, with a hint of wood smoke and more than a hint of diesel fumes.

The interior of the pub looked dark and gloomy. It was ten fifteen, so presumably not long till opening time. As she approached the building she heard dogs barking inside. Undeterred, she pushed against one of the double doors and was surprised when it swung open. She called out a greeting and heard, over the whine of a vacuum cleaner, the dogs silenced by a shout.

Wendy took a step inside, holding the door in case a quick exit was necessary. There was a large dining area to her left, and a smaller lounge to her right. The bar was directly ahead, with an open door behind it. A woman strode out and said curtly, in an Eastern European accent, 'Closed now.'

She was in her thirties, Wendy thought, slim and attractive but very much off-duty: no make-up, hair tied back, and dressed in a cheap grey tracksuit.

Wendy said, 'I wanted to see Kevin, if he's around?'

She regretted the intonation – framing it as a question gave the woman an opportunity to deny his presence – but after a vaguely hostile appraisal she nodded. 'Wait.'

There was a brief, muffled exchange in the back room, before the vacuum cleaner started up again and Kevin Burroughs strode into the bar. Wendy had last seen him on a TV news bulletin, leading a group of the accused's supporters away from the cameras after the verdict had been announced. He was an overweight man in his sixties, with thinning red hair and a bulbous nose. He wore a grubby white vest and jogging pants with holes at the knees. A pair of Rottweilers accompanied him into the bar, silent now and studying Wendy with mild interest, as if she could only ever represent a side dish rather than a main course.

'You from the council?' Burroughs said, and frowned when she shook her head. 'So how do I know you?'

'I'm Wendy Turner. My husband and I adopted—'

'Georgia.' Burroughs gave a bitter snort, then moved towards a low table in the lounge area and dragged a stool out with his foot. The Rottweilers lumbered alongside, never more than inches from his legs. Like him, they were carrying too much weight, but Wendy guessed they were more than capable of maintaining order if things got rowdy.

Remembering her training, Wendy held her head up and tried to appear confident as she strode to the table. She wasn't afraid of dogs in general, but this pair made her nervous – or, rather, it was their owner who gave her reason to be wary.

Staying in bed didn't help her mood, and Georgia felt a spark of anger at the idea that she was lying low at home. Better to get out there and show everyone she wasn't bothered by the taunts.

Knowing there was likely to be a crowd at Heath Pond, she took a detour towards town, then doubled back along a smart residential road called The Avenue. A couple of times she had the feeling that she was being followed, or watched, but she didn't see anyone.

The road was elevated above the park, and it came to a dead end with pedestrian access down a set of walled-in steps. Either side of the steps there was a bench with views across the lake. One of the benches was occupied by an old couple with a little dog. Georgia sat down on the other one, shielded her eyes with her hand and scanned the kids' playground. No sign of Paige, but Amber was there, along with a fair few of the BitchWorld crowd, including some who'd put comments on Instagram.

Georgia took out her cigarettes, went to light up and thought: *Nah.* She didn't really enjoy smoking, so why do it? Who cared about being seen as cool? It was bullshit.

She reminded herself that none of this came close to the trauma she'd gone through with her mum's murder – or months later, having to deal with the humiliation of the trial, when the barrister who represented Burroughs tried to make it seem like *she* was the one who'd caused the violence, bringing in evidence from a local shopkeeper who claimed Georgia was a 'feral' child, completely out of control.

A savage, he had called her, in front of a court full of people. Georgia would never forget how she had felt in that moment; the damage she'd have done if she'd had the chance.

You can't prove them wrong, so better to prove them right.

It was like with Mark Burroughs. She knew Wendy was petrified of the day he got released from prison. Georgia wasn't. She wanted Burroughs to see how she lived now. In her fantasy he would stand miserably on the pavement, begging for a handout like the whiny little loser he was; meanwhile Georgia would sneak behind the wheel of Rob's Land Rover and run him down. Squash the fucker flat!

She grinned, just as one of the boys noticed her and drew the others into a huddle. Georgia pretended to read something on her phone. She heard scornful laughter but ignored it. There were little kids in the park, running and screaming, and a dog was barking somewhere. Then came the wet clatter of geese taking off from the water, something she loved to watch, so she risked a look and saw the group ambling across the playground in her direction. They were all grinning, giggling, ready to have some fun at her expense.

Well, let them try. She'd take them on, if she had to.

Directly below her, a young man was crossing the lower road that ran alongside the park. He trotted up the steps and then stopped, peering at her over the wall. When he smiled, there was such a light in his eyes that for a moment Georgia was dazzled by it.

He nodded at the bench. 'Mind if I sit there for a minute?'

Wendy took a seat opposite Burroughs, and decided there was no point being coy. 'How is Mark doing?'

He scowled. 'Like you care.'

'Do you visit him very often?'

'Not really,' he admitted, before adding, sourly, 'His choice.'

'Well, I'm sorry about that – from your point of view, I mean.'

'Yeah, you don't have no sympathy for Mark.'

Wendy was genuinely taken aback. 'Do you think I should? For a man who murdered his partner?'

Burroughs shifted unhappily, the stool scraping against the laminate floor. 'They fought all the time, those two. Drank like fishes, and couldn't handle their booze.' He flinched, as if embarrassed to make such an admission on licensed premises. 'Get her in one of her rages and she'd smack the hell out of him – I saw the bruises, more than once.'

'That doesn't excuse what he did. And what about chasing Georgia through the house? Slashing at a ten-year-old girl with a knife? He'd have killed her, too, if she hadn't got away from him.'

This time Burroughs looked sorrowful. 'The madness was on him by then, I reckon. But yeah, it was wrong. He had to serve his time for that, and he is.'

There was a moment of silence. Just as Wendy was about to speak, Burroughs said, 'But that relationship weren't so straightforward, not by a long chalk.'

Wendy gasped. 'What?'

'Georgia and my lad. She'd wind him up something rotten. Not scared of a bit of blackmail, either. Threatening to tell people he'd done stuff to her, unless he gave her money, or let her stay out late.'

'I don't believe that.'

'Why not? You think little girls are all sweetness and light?'

'Of course not.' Wendy added some steel to her voice. 'I was a social worker, Mr Burroughs. I've dealt with all manner of human beings.'

He caught the disdain in her voice, and knew that he was supposed to. 'Bloody meddlers,' he said. 'So what d'you want?'

'A guarantee that he'll leave her alone.'

'He's serving a life sentence, for Christ's sake! And so are we.' He jabbed a finger at her. 'If something's happened to Georgia, it's nothing to do with my lad, so don't you go dragging his name through the mud.'

The dogs had begun to growl at such a low pitch that the floor almost vibrated. Wendy felt cold sweat on her back.

'I care about my daughter.' She stood up, clutching her bag to stop her hands from shaking. 'I'll do anything to protect her. *Anything*. And I want that message passed on.'

Burroughs studied her intently. One of the dogs started to rise but he nudged it with his foot. 'You got other kids, yeah?'

'Yes.' Wendy braced herself for some kind of threat, but Burroughs had a reflective look in his eyes.

'You probably think I'm making excuses for my boy, but it's only 'cause I can't give up on him. It ain't easy, accepting your own kids have done terrible things. It hurts more than you can believe.' He looked her in the eye. 'I pray you never find out how that feels.'

TWENTY-FIVE

Georgia cringed a little as the man sat down and threw one arm along the back of the bench. She wasn't sure why she'd nodded, rather than saying no. In the park, Amber and the others were staring in disbelief.

They think this is my brother – and the gossip is true.

Then she remembered the faked picture they'd all been sharing. This guy next to her was nothing like Evan: he was shorter, heavier, with dark wavy hair and a rounder face. Quite cute, as well, though not as fit as he'd looked from a distance—

Amber's seeing him at a distance!

The thought thrilled her. Maybe they'd get the impression that he was interested in her, making the rumours about Evan easier to shrug off.

He was wearing good clothes, too: Levi's, a Jack Wills t-shirt and black Timberlands. After a couple of casual remarks about the weather, which she thought wise to ignore, he said, 'Not much going on.'

'Nah.' *Play it cool, Georgia.*

'Pretty dead, this town.'

'It's *sooo* boring,' she agreed, and before she knew it they were chatting away like best buddies. His name was Milo, and he was starting uni at Winchester in a couple of months. In answer to her question, he said he was nineteen, though he looked a year or two older than that.

Then came the dreaded question: 'Do you have a boyfriend right now?'

Georgia shook her head, inwardly furious that an image of Evan had flashed through her mind. Her feelings for him were so complicated, so painful that most of the time she buried them deep and tried to focus instead on Livvy, on imagining how it would be to live inside Livvy's skin.

Anything but another day as Georgia the Savage.

Milo brought his left leg over his right, his knee gently bumping against her thigh. 'You must get asked a lot.'

She shrugged, aware that she was blushing but unable to control it. Milo's eyes were blue and bright, though there were dark crescents beneath them. He looked tired but also strangely energised, and she wondered if he was on something.

'Boys around here are lame, I bet that's what it is. Boys your own age, I mean.' His dirty little laugh felt like it had poked his fingers through her eyes and opened up her brain.

Did he know about Evan?

'Hey, what's wrong?'

Georgia gave a flick of her head: crazy thoughts. 'I'm fine.'

'Probably coming on too strong. Sorry.' He smiled, holding eye contact, and said, 'But you really are gorgeous, you know?'

She snorted. She didn't believe it, but the compliment sent a warm glow through her all the same.

She found herself staring straight at Amber, and couldn't resist a quick sarcastic grin. Looking in the same direction, Milo said, 'Friends of yours?'

'Not really.' His phone buzzed, and with his attention on a text, it was easier to confess: 'That girl with the blonde hair, she pretends to be my friend, but she's an evil two-faced bitch.'

Milo grunted. 'A couple of boys at my school once invited me to smoke weed in the local park. When I got there, they stole my phone and kicked me so hard in the balls I couldn't move for about an hour!'

'Oh no.' Wincing, Georgia instinctively reached over and patted his leg.

'After that, I was very careful who I made friends with.' Milo gestured at the BitchWorld crowd. 'You have to be the same.'

'Yeah, I will, don't worry.'

'Good to hear it.' He gave her a soft, affectionate slap on the arm. 'So what are you doing tomorrow night?'

'Tomorrow night?' Repeating his question bought Georgia some time. 'Why?'

He grinned. 'Because I might be asking you out, that's why.'

'Yeah, right.' Her heart was hammering away. *Stay cool.*

'Nothing serious, just a drink somewhere.'

Then she remembered where she'd be tomorrow, but decided to play along. 'Don't have ID.'

'We'll go to Portsmouth. Plenty of pubs down there that don't give a toss about ID.'

'Nah, not Pompey.' She shuddered. 'Anyway, how would we get there?'

'Drive, of course. Or take a cab.'

She rolled her eyes. 'That'll cost a fortune.'

'So what? I've got a fortune.'

'Yeah, right.'

'It's true. My dad's a millionaire.' It didn't come out as a boast, but as a simple fact, like saying, *My eyes are blue.*

'Lucky you,' she muttered, because her instinct was to believe him. *Shit: could this be any more perfect. . .?* 'I can't, tomorrow. I'm going away.'

'Really. Where to?'

Georgia said nothing. Maybe it was just her imagination, but Milo didn't seem very surprised. A sudden terrible thought occurred to her: *he knows.*

*

She felt sick, dizzy. Didn't want to face him, but she had to.

'Is this a set-up?'

For a second Milo looked worried – no, he looked absolutely shit scared – and Georgia knew she had guessed right.

'You're with them, aren't you?'

'Wh-what do you mean?'

'You know.' Georgia gestured angrily at the group in the park. 'Fucking Amber and Paige. Are you related to one of them, is that it?'

Because wouldn't that be perfect, from their point of view – for Georgia to be humiliated all over again by someone's *brother*?

Milo had leaned over to look her right in the face. Now he slapped his hands on his knees and let out a spluttering laugh. 'Why would you think that? I've never seen any of them in my life.'

She said nothing, glowering at Amber until the girl felt the attention, whereupon Georgia gave her the finger.

'Listen,' Milo said, 'I have no idea what the problem is between you and that girl, but I swear it's nothing to do with me.'

She ignored him. Amber's retaliation was to start play-hugging one of the boys, pressing her tits against him for Georgia to see. Pathetic.

After a moment Milo put his hand on her shoulder. 'Sorry if I made you think—'

'Doesn't matter.' She checked her phone. 'I've gotta go, anyway.'

'Will you give me your number?' He waited for her to respond, his hand still in place. 'How long are you away for?'

'Ten days.' She wriggled to let him know he should remove his hand. 'Give me your number, then I'll decide if I want to get in touch.'

He chuckled. 'Good idea.' He read off his number then pushed again, in a friendly way, to get hers, but Georgia wouldn't budge.

They stood up at the same time, and she didn't protest when he leaned in and kissed her, softly, on the cheek.

'Enjoy that holiday. Where is it, again?'

'Norfolk, near a village called Branham.'

'A hotel?'

'No, a house. My mum's aunt used to live there. It's right by the sea, though you can't really go on the beach where we are. It's all, like, marshes and stuff.'

'Nice place to chill out, then.'

'Yeah, I suppose.' She glanced at the park, saw the whole gang were watching once again. She prayed that they'd seen the kiss.

'Well, it was lovely to meet you,' Milo said.

'You, too.' She stepped forward, landed a peck on the cheek then danced out of reach as he went to embrace her. 'Text you next week, maybe.'

'Please do,' he said, and then called out, 'See you again?'

Hurrying away, Georgia nodded but didn't look back; in the hours that followed she kept replaying that line in her head, and each time it seemed less and less like a question.

TWENTY-SIX

Rob made it home by five on Friday afternoon. There had been a spike in emergency call-outs, unusual for the summer, but not to the extent that Rob had to don overalls and pick up a toolbox himself. Cerys was on top of the paperwork and, he suspected, actively relishing an opportunity to manage the office without having him peering over her shoulder.

Their farewell was a formal handshake, but then she threw her arms around him. 'Try to relax. After all this, you really deserve a break.'

Rob had felt unexpectedly emotional, and could do nothing more than nod and smile.

At home, Wendy was vacuuming the stairs. She seemed surprised to see him, but also, he thought, slightly irritated. Joining him in the kitchen, she reported that Evan was in Portsmouth, helping Livvy buy clothes for her own holiday.

'What, like a burka?' he joked.

'Oh, come on. He isn't the jealous type.'

'No, but it's not easy, seeing your girlfriend go on that sort of holiday. Meanwhile he's stuck with us, playing Scrabble while the rain hammers down.'

When Georgia wandered in, Rob braced himself for a confrontation. But she was in an uncharacteristically cheerful mood, a lightness in her movements as she fetched a glass of water.

'Good for my skin,' she said, when Rob teased her about healthy living.

'Your skin's lovely,' Wendy said.

'It can always be better,' Georgia replied, and skipped out.

'Who swapped our daughter for a human being?' Rob asked in disbelief.

'No idea. She came back from town like that, but wouldn't tell me a thing.'

'Wow. All we need now is for Josh to greet us in the same civil manner, his bag all packed and ready to go, and I'll be willing to believe in miracles.'

'I was going to phone him earlier, but it slipped my mind.' Wendy looked pensive, preoccupied by something. *As if I'm not*, Rob thought.

'Don't worry. We'll be seeing him tomorrow.'

When he suggested a drink, she said, 'You haven't forgotten that Tim and Dawn are popping round in a bit?'

'Bugger, I had. I might as well take a shower, then.'

'While you're up there, have a quick scoot through the wardrobe, see if there's anything else you want.'

Perhaps it was an illusion, but Rob felt he was beginning to relax as he stood in the shower. There had been no media contact today, and nothing new when he searched online. No more of those silly notes, no unwanted visitors or nasty smells.

Although there were sound reasons to dread this holiday, he focused instead on the positives. Earlier he'd checked the forecast for Norfolk, and there was a lot of fine weather expected for next week, with only light breezes. If true, that should give everyone's mood a boost – the winds off the North Sea could make the most glorious day feel like mid-winter.

This reminded him that he hadn't sorted an old sweater, something to wear if they took the rowing boat out. Then he promptly forgot about it until he was on the way downstairs. Sighing at his own mental frailty, he returned to the bedroom.

The right-hand side of the wardrobe was where they stashed old clothes to use for DIY and other messy activities. He reached for a baggy woollen jumper, then spotted a grey fleece that would be even better. To get it he had to kneel down and shift a pile of clothes, taking care not to dislodge several boxes of Wendy's footwear.

And then he saw the trainer.

He recognised it at once. The understanding came as a lightning-fast progression of simple statements: That's a man's trainer – It's not my trainer – I've seen it before – Or I've seen one just like it before – I saw it on Sunday. . .

On the foot of a dying man.

He reared back as if it might jump out and attack him. For a long time he just stared, hoping it might transform into one of Evan's tatty trainers or an old football boot: something that wasn't going to turn his world upside down.

A twinge of cramp brought him back to his senses. He shifted position, then lifted the few remaining clothes and shoeboxes in case the trainer's twin was concealed close by.

While he was searching he remembered that the dying man had been wearing only one trainer. He shut his eyes and pictured him collapsing to the ground. . . the right foot had been bare, he thought. And this was the shoe for the right foot.

Another memory: Dawn or DS Husein expressing disappointment about the results of the search, saying something like, *He was missing a shoe, and we haven't even found that.*

Well, now they had.

Then he amended the thought: Not quite.

I've found the shoe. No one else knows about it yet.

He tried to get his thoughts in order. A man had died in their garden, his assailants unknown. The family had been routinely considered as suspects but quickly discounted. . . and now the man's missing footwear had been discovered inside their bedroom.

Then add the anonymous notes – didn't this discovery make it more likely that they'd come from whoever had killed the man? And instead of reporting the first note straight away, Rob had held on to it. How would it look now if he revealed the victim's shoe?

He pictured the likely sequence of events. The police would take the trainer away for forensic examination, and then question Rob closely about how he came to find it. Wendy, too, would face a pretty tough interview – and perhaps the rest of the family as well? Anyone, in fact, who'd had access to the bedroom over the past five days.

Lara. Although Wendy had been adamant that the girl hadn't gone upstairs, she'd also mentioned hearing a noise, and had been afraid that someone had sneaked into the house while the terrace doors were unlocked. That smell of body odour must have been from whoever hid the shoe.

A door opened on the landing and Rob's heart nearly stopped. He heard urgent footsteps on the stairs, but they were running down, not up.

Georgia. Just Georgia.

He let out a breath, and went back to the police angle. He could explain all this, but how much of it could he substantiate? Not a thing.

It was a theory – and to the police it might seem like nothing more than a feeble attempt to deny his own guilt.

The forensic tests were bound to find blood from the victim, but what if there was no DNA from anyone else? Worse still, what if there was DNA from him or Wendy? Could something have come off the other clothes and shoes in the wardrobe – flakes of skin or something?

Oh, Christ. Rob balled his fists and pressed them against his temples. This was insane. Someone was trying to frame them for murder. Jason had mocked Rob's attitude towards his associates: *They're not the fucking Mafia.* But what if one of them had gone rogue, without Jason knowing?

Or could Josh have—?

He had no idea where the thought came from. More insanity: he shut it down at once. Josh was in Canterbury, for Christ's sake. And Josh wasn't a killer.

Evan? Evan wouldn't be mixed up in anything; or Georgia—

From downstairs, he heard Wendy calling his name. She must be wondering what he was doing up here.

'Just a second!' he shouted, his voice dry and broken. He needed to think: if he was going to report this, he'd have to get his head round the idea that the police would view him as a suspect.

He remembered Jason's warning yesterday, and wondered to what extent the police would go trawling through Rob's past. If Iain Kelly's name came up, Rob could hardly refuse to talk about him. . .

A chiming sound from downstairs barely registered. His attention had snagged on something there, and he had to back up to work out what it was.

If.

If he was going to report this. . .

'Rob!' Wendy's shout contained an unmissable hint of *Get a bloody move on!*

He stood up on shaky legs. If he admitted to the discovery, he'd have to leave the shoe in place, take his chances that it didn't have any of the family's DNA on it.

That *if* again: sneaky little bugger. Then came another call from Wendy, and he understood that the chiming sound must have been the doorbell, because what she said this time was: 'Rob! Tim and Dawn are here!'

Tim and Dawn. His old mate Tim, and Tim's second wife, Dawn.

Detective Sergeant Dawn Avery.

TWENTY-SEVEN

It should have been a pleasant enough experience, Wendy thought, socialising with friends on the eve of a holiday. Instead she was still brooding over the visit to Kevin Burroughs. Even though she'd ruled out a connection between Mark Burroughs and Sunday's incident, she now had to consider the accusation that Georgia had tried to manipulate her birth mother's boyfriend. Wendy's heart said it wasn't true, but her head didn't readily agree.

She'd decided there was no point mentioning any of it to Rob. He'd come in from work in a remarkably cheerful mood, all things considered, and she wanted to preserve that for as long as possible. Looking ahead to tomorrow, she was starting to worry about Josh, and his likely reaction when they turned up on his doorstep. Although she saw why Rob favoured the surprise tactic, she feared it could cause yet more animosity.

The problem was that neither he nor Josh could see how alike they were; both stubborn, and single-minded to a degree that bordered on selfishness.

Busy preparing drinks, she heard the door open but didn't look up until Tim exclaimed: 'Bloody hell, mate. You look wiped out.'

Now she glanced round. Rob was almost staggering into the kitchen, his face blanched of colour. He gave a comically theatrical shrug, then greeted six-year-old Leo, who was perched on a stool, excitedly showing Georgia a new game on his mum's iPad.

It was Dawn who offered some understanding: 'This has been such a tough week for you all. The holiday couldn't have come at a better time.'

'Yeah. I feel shattered, actually.' Turning back to them, Rob caught Wendy's enquiring gaze and looked away with what, to her, seemed like guilty haste.

Tim wanted to know if Rob intended to take his bike – in his view, holidaying somewhere like Norfolk could only be justified if you were going to make use of the mild climate and flat terrain. 'Otherwise you ought to be in Greece, or Italy, or Florida. What's wrong with you, man?!'

Rob took the ribbing in good spirit, and started to look a little more normal. Drinks and snacks were carried out to the terrace, though Georgia and Leo went no further than the living room, where they stopped to watch TV. That seemed like another sign that Wendy had to be candid, even if it meant making an idiot of herself.

'We had a visitor yesterday,' she said as she sat down. 'A young woman, claiming to be a friend of Evan's.'

Tim made a guttural noise in his throat – 'Oh ho' – which earned him a sharp look from Dawn. Wendy ran through her encounter with Lara, fighting the conviction that she must sound like a paranoid fool.

Dawn listened impassively, then said, 'And she's definitely not a friend of Evan's?'

'Not even a "special" friend?' Tim joked, twiddling his fingers to indicate the inverted commas, and reminding Wendy why she'd never really warmed to him.

Tactfully, she said, 'It's a fair question. Rob and I wondered that, too. But he's adamant that he doesn't know her, and we believe him.' She raised her glass of wine, then paused with it close to her lips. 'Do you think we're being ridiculous?'

*

To Rob's ears, the question sounded slightly harsh, though Dawn took it calmly enough. Rob was just grateful that the conversation required little input from him. His thoughts were fuzzy and confused; he was terrified of blurting out something that would bring this friendly gathering to an abrupt halt. He imagined Dawn having to call DS Husein, or perhaps DI Powell, then the humiliation of being cautioned, and taken to a police station for formal questioning.

And what about Wendy? What about Georgia?

He made a supreme effort to dial back in. Dawn was saying, '. . . probably a reasonable explanation.'

Wendy said, 'Like someone outside of Evan's circle, trying to get the gossip for reasons of her own?'

'Exactly. For some people it's all about the kudos of being in the know.'

'That's encouraging. But while the girl was here, I kept getting the feeling she was stalling. And once she'd gone, there was a horrible smell in the air. Body odour. Georgia came home soon after and noticed it right away.' Wendy sent Rob a sharp glance, as if he'd failed to support her then, or ought to have been doing more now. He could only give a helpless shrug as she went on: 'Oh, and before that there was a loud noise, like something hitting the glass.'

Confused, Dawn said, 'The smell wasn't from the girl?'

'Absolutely not.'

'And the noise? Did you see or hear anyone else in the house?'

'No. My first thought was that a bird had flown into the window – which has happened before, admittedly.'

At that, Wendy seemed to flounder. Rob somehow found the wherewithal to ask Dawn if anything had been done with the notes.

'I decided to get them checked, because it occurred to me that they should have been sent to us.'

She sounded so severe that Rob said, 'I know, I'm sorry—'

'Not that.' She gave him an odd look. 'I mean, if someone suspected you of a crime, they'd send anonymous notes to the police, wouldn't they? Not to you.'

'Oh.' Rob felt himself blushing, certain that he'd just made himself seem even guiltier. 'I suppose so.'

'Still just a crank, though?' Wendy asked.

'Probably. But a careful one. There were no fingerprints on them, other than yours.'

'Getting dodgy letters, as well?' Tim marvelled. 'What'd you do to deserve this?'

'Nothing.' Dawn made a praying gesture with her hands, pressed them against her lips, and said, 'Look, the main issue here is that you two are worn out. And when your nerves are stretched, it's natural that every little event takes on sinister con-notations – which isn't a criticism,' she added hastily. 'In your place, Tim and I would be just the same.'

'Too right,' Tim agreed. 'It would put me off barbecues for life, what happened to you.'

Inwardly, Rob cringed, but Wendy ignored the wisecrack and actually looked relieved. Addressing Dawn, she said, 'We should let it go, is that what you're saying?'

'Yes. Which is why the holiday is such a good idea. It's a complete change of scene. And you don't need to worry – I'll pop in every day to make sure the house is—'

'There's no need,' Rob cut in. 'I'm not sure it's even worth leaving keys, really. It's not like we've got pets or anything. . .'

He trailed off with Wendy staring at him in confusion. She made a little huffing noise, and said, 'Well, I for one will relax a lot more if I know you're coming by.'

As she got up and went into the house, Tim sniggered. 'Just delete your internet history, mate.'

Rob produced an idiotic grin. 'I feel bad, knowing how busy you are,' he said to Dawn, 'and with the baby on the way. . .'

'Not a problem. The job takes me out and about, so calling in for a couple of minutes makes no difference.'

'Jeez, mate, will you stop worrying!' Tim exclaimed. 'If you want my advice, I'd recommend a little smoke of something to help you mellow out.'

Dawn made to cover her ears. 'I didn't hear that.'

'Hear what?' said Wendy, as she returned.

'Herbal relaxation.' Tim mimed puffing on a joint. 'Bet there's some good stuff to be had in the lawless wilds of East Anglia?'

'Not really my scene,' Rob said, still trying to stifle his panic. 'I suppose Evan might know, or Josh—'

'I don't think either of them are interested in drugs,' Wendy declared. Rob caught Tim smirking, while Dawn responded with one of the most diplomatic shrugs that Rob had ever seen. Then the conversation went off in a different direction, taking Rob further from anything he might have said about this evening's discovery, and it felt like his fate was sealed when Wendy handed Dawn a spare set of keys, along with a slip of paper on which she'd written the code for the burglar alarm.

Tim raised his bottle in a toast. 'Here's to a fantastic holiday for the Turners – and no more nasty shocks!'

'I'll drink to that,' Wendy said, and even Rob managed a sickly smile, though there was presently only one thought in his head:

Dawn's got the keys. . . and she'll snoop.

They chatted for another ten minutes, Tim draining his beer and not very subtly shaking the empty bottle. Wendy ignored the hint; it was Dawn who read the signals, intervening when Rob suggested another drink.

'Thanks, but I'm sure you need to get sorted.'

Wendy hoped she didn't look too grateful. They exchanged genuinely fond farewells – even Georgia accepted hugs from Leo and Dawn, only to disappear to her room before the front door was shut behind them.

'Thanks again for all your help this week,' Wendy said to Dawn.

'Don't mention it. Just make sure you enjoy that holiday.'

'We will.' Wendy sounded heartfelt, but it was as dishonest a statement as anything she'd said in years.

Once they'd gone, she turned to Rob, who raised his eyebrows and said, 'I think Tim could have stayed here all night.'

'I know. So why did you offer him another drink?'

'Didn't want it to feel like we were turfing them out.'

She followed him into the kitchen, and had the impression that he was almost running away from her.

'What's happened?'

She saw him blink rapidly. 'Nothing.'

'When you came down, you looked like you'd seen a ghost.'

'Did I?' He shrugged. 'Just tired. Anyway, you've been a bit off this evening. Neither of us are at our best at the moment, are we?'

It was hard to deny that, but Wendy wasn't entirely convinced. 'Why the change of heart about leaving keys with Dawn?'

'I didn't like the idea of them having a look round – Tim rummaging through your underwear drawer.' They both grimaced, and then Rob added, 'But you're right, though. At least they'll keep an eye on the place.'

TWENTY-EIGHT

She didn't believe him, Rob was sure of that, but for now he seemed to be off the hook. As Wendy busied herself grilling some chicken for their dinner, Rob slipped out and fetched a couple of plastic bags from the cupboard under the stairs, then hurried up to the bedroom.

He'd scarcely had time to think through the ramifications of what he was about to do, but he knew now that there *was* no time. In the morning they were driving to Norfolk, leaving a friend who was also a police officer with free access to the house. He had to put the trainer somewhere safe until he'd decided what to do with it.

Still the range of possibilities continued to plague him. Had Jason Dennehy given him a false reassurance? Was one of the kids mixed up in something?

Crazy thoughts, but then he remembered Dawn's expression when Wendy had denied that the twins would ever take drugs. Aren't the parents always the last to know – or the last to accept the truth? Rob knew he couldn't risk involving the police if there was even a tiny chance that one of the twins – or Georgia, even – was implicated in some way. Certainly some of Josh's past behaviour had been impossible to fathom – like the time he convinced the school cricket team to turn a maths teacher's car on to its roof, all because he'd been graded A when he felt his work deserved an A*. . .

Closing the bedroom door, Rob put his hand inside one of the bags so that he didn't have to touch the trainer directly. Another thought occurred to him: the person who'd hidden the shoe hadn't wanted it to be found – or else they'd have left it somewhere in plain sight. That must mean they were intending to tip off the police, and Rob would be caught red-handed in possession—

He heard an unmistakable creak on the landing. Panicking, he sent shoeboxes tumbling out of the wardrobe as he wrapped the trainer in a bag and shoved it under the bed.

It wasn't in Wendy's nature to be suspicious – there had been various times in recent years when she'd had serious misgivings about Rob, and the lengths he was going to in order to keep the business afloat – but always she'd relied on the belief that he would tell her if he needed to. Now, though, something about the way he'd raced upstairs just didn't feel right.

Her fears seemed to be justified when, after a couple of minutes of agonising, she decided to follow, and found that the bedroom door was shut. That made no sense.

For a second she was going to knock, but then she thought: *It's my bedroom.*

It's my husband.

She opened the door and found him, frozen in a peculiar crouch, with the wardrobe in disarray. For a moment he looked guilt-stricken, as though he'd been caught doing something shameful.

'What's going on?'

'Just looking for a sweater to wear on the boat. Sorry about. . .' He indicated her dress shoes, which had spilled on to the floor.

'Rob, are you sure there isn't something wrong?'

He'd already turned away from her, kneeling to gather up the shoes. 'I'm fine. Are *you* okay?'

She sighed, discomfited by his tactic of throwing the question back at her. The only way to combat it, she decided, was to come clean.

'Look, earlier today, I. . . Hold on.' She frowned, because Rob had lifted a pile of old clothes, trying to get at a fleece. 'Where's the laptop?'

'What?'

She moved down beside him, leaning into the wardrobe to check the next compartment. 'The old Toshiba. It was in here.'

'Was it?' Rob sounded stunned. He rested a hand on the floor, as if worried he might topple over.

Wendy tried to remember when she'd last seen it. 'I definitely backed up the photos after Christmas – and this is where I put it.'

He was shaking his head. 'Maybe one of the kids used it?'

'I can't see that.' The laptop had been Jurassic by the time they'd relegated it to a back-up device for their pictures and videos: the kids would recoil at using such primitive equipment.

'Unless you've put it somewhere else, and forgotten?'

'I suppose so.' In normal circumstances she might have greeted his remark with indignation, but now she hoped she'd been that forgetful. 'If not, it means someone has taken it – yesterday, maybe?'

'Except Dawn's just said that we're basically overwrought, and imagining things.'

'But we're not. This proves it.'

'*If* it's missing. Even then, we can't actually prove anything.'

Wendy could sense his unease, but she didn't understand it. Why would he be so reluctant to accept—?

'The main thing is that we wiped the drive, didn't we?' he said, interrupting her train of thought. 'So there's nothing of value on there.'

'Just a lifetime of photos. All our most cherished memories.' Wendy sniffed, close to tears.

'Hold on. Didn't Josh mention the laptop when he was home at Easter? Something he wanted to copy from it?'

'Did he?' Wendy didn't recollect anything. 'You think he took it with him?'

'Might have done. We can ask him tomorrow.'

Wendy sighed. 'I don't know. I'm half inclined to forget the holiday, and call the police.'

Rob felt wretched, diverting her attention on to Josh. He knew better than Wendy that the laptop had almost certainly been stolen – by same person who had left the trainer. The same person who was trying to frame them for a murder.

But the fact remained that he couldn't afford to involve the police. Not yet, at least. Maybe by the time they got back from Norfolk, he'd have a clearer idea of what he should do. . .

Then came another question that almost literally knocked him sideways.

'Is there any chance that all of this is connected to Iain Kelly?'

'Wh-what?' he asked. 'Why would you think that?'

'I don't know. But we agreed at the time what a terrible irony it was, dying the way he did.' Wendy got up, took a tissue from the box by the bed, and blew her nose. 'He made a lot of enemies, people like that Jason Dennehy. What if he was harbouring a grudge against you?'

Rob stared down at the carpet. Time to own up.

'He isn't. I spoke to him on Wednesday.'

'What?'

'The same thing occurred to me, so I went to see him. But Jason's adamant that he doesn't blame me for what Kelly did. And he was genuinely shocked when I told him about Sunday.' While Wendy digested this information, Rob added, 'I'm sorry I didn't tell you sooner. I just thought, because it didn't lead to anything. . .'

She waved away his apology, staring mournfully at her reflection in the wardrobe mirror. 'I had my own theory, too. With me it was Mark Burroughs.'

'Burroughs?' Rob felt a jolt at the name. 'Jesus, if that bastard—'

'I know, I know. But I don't think he's part of this, either.' She described how she had paid a visit to the pub owned by Burroughs senior, and with a rueful smile, said, 'I think perhaps it's time to be a bit more honest with one another.'

He nodded, because he had no choice but to stick with the lie, and said, 'I think it is.'

TWENTY-NINE

Because of the escape, it was necessary to take some precautions. Fortunately these could be employed as part of the next challenge, since again they required you to draw on a wide range of skills.

In the first stage I wanted you to follow them, research them, look into their lives – even have personal encounters with them, if you could do it safely.

I wanted the family unsettled, nervous, paranoid.

Slowly, gradually, I wanted them scared.

For our own safety, it made sense to engineer their guilt, in place of ours. I wanted a tripwire all ready to go, something to set off at any moment should the police start looking in our direction. (No reason why they would, of course.) It was also an opportunity to have enormous fun at their expense.

But then it got really interesting.

Your incursions were a great success. As well as planting the evidence that would incriminate them, you also found an old computer. From this came all manner of glorious detail, and some fascinating discrepancies – like the girl who sprang from nowhere.

We looked at their photographs.

We watched their videos.

But we also recovered their data. Information they believed had been wiped. As a result, my plans were brought forward. The ultimate aim could be achieved so much sooner than I had anticipated.

We know they leave tomorrow. We know their destination is a holiday home, a lonely cottage on a remote, secluded stretch of the Norfolk coast.

How perfect for them.

How perfect for us.

THIRTY

By Saturday morning the humidity had broken, not with a storm but with the return of a misty drizzle that clung to their skin as they loaded the bags and cases into the Land Rover.

They were underway by eight o'clock, which the kids seemed to regard as the crack of dawn. Evan shut his eyes and promptly fell asleep. Georgia declined an offer to select the in-car music, preferring the solitude of her earbuds; Rob wondered if she was listening to anything or just using them as a barrier.

Could have done with some myself, he thought. So far today he and Wendy hadn't spoken much. She'd maintained a kind of brittle cheerfulness, making a conscious effort not to dwell on the events of the past week, while he did his best to keep up the pretence that he could put it behind him.

He was in the mood to drive fast, and for the most part got his wish. When they were held up by an accident on the M25, he kept a tight lid on his temper, aware that it would alienate Josh if he turned up in a foul mood.

It was ten to ten when they came into the city through Harbledown and took a left turn towards Whitstable Road. Josh was one of five students sharing a tile-hung terraced house in Harcourt Drive, midway between the university campus and the city centre.

Parking was never easy but they managed to find a space, slightly overhanging a driveway. Wendy asked Evan and Georgia to stay in the car, and to let them know if someone needed to get past.

'I just hope we're early enough to catch him at home,' she fretted, but Rob feared the opposite: a sleepy Josh coming to the door, having completely forgotten about the holiday.

Wendy knocked on the door. Waiting beside her, Rob realised he was clenching his fists and made an effort to relax. He gazed at the soft grey sky above the houses across the road. It was cooler here than at home, but at least the drizzle had petered out.

After Wendy had knocked a second time, they heard movement inside the house. The front door was opened by a man in his late twenties with slicked-back hair and a voluminous, hipster-style beard. He was barefoot, and wrapped in a maroon dressing gown.

'Sorry if we woke you,' Wendy said. 'Is Josh up yet?'

'Josh?'

'Josh Turner.' She glanced at Rob as it struck them both that this man didn't recognise the name. 'Sorry – are you staying with someone?'

'No.' The man frowned, taking an age to gather his thoughts. 'I live here. But, uh. . . there isn't anyone called Josh.'

After going round in circles for a minute, they were invited inside. The man wasn't particularly unfriendly, but he spoke with such drawling disinterest that Rob couldn't help but get frustrated.

His name was Eric, and he was a post-grad at Kent. He shared the house with four other students, two of whom were male – Ikram and Max, names which sounded vaguely familiar to Rob.

But no Josh.

'How long have you been here?' Wendy was examining the hallway, as if trying to work out whether they'd come to the wrong address.

'Couple of months.' Eric's eyes grew distant as he trawled what was presumably the vast – or simply overloaded – database that was his memory. 'You know, uh. . . the guy before me might have been called Jack, or Josh, or. . . you know, a *J* word.'

Now he mentions it, Rob thought.

'What about. . . Miya, is it?' Wendy asked. 'Is she here?'

'Miya? Uh. . . yeah.' The man nodded but didn't move.

'Can we speak to her, please?'

'Uh. . . let me check.'

As he trudged upstairs, there was a tap on the front door and Evan came in, with Georgia trailing behind him. Evan sensed the mood at once: 'Is Josh all right?'

'He's not here,' Rob said.

'What, he's gone out?'

'No. According to the bloke we've just spoken to, he doesn't live here any more.'

'You're kidding?'

Wendy grasped Evan's arm. 'Did he ever give you any indication. . .?'

'No. Not a thing.' Evan was shaking his head in disbelief. 'Typical bloody Josh.'

Then Miya appeared, also clad in a bathrobe but with jeans underneath, tying back her long hair as she padded downstairs. She was a young Japanese woman, blinking curiously at them as though woken in a hurry. She nodded at Rob and Wendy, then saw Evan and gasped.

'Oh wow, you're the twin brother!' She had an accent that Rob thought was East Midlands. 'You really do look alike.'

'Do you know where Josh is?' Wendy asked.

Looking confused by the desperation in Wendy's voice, Miya took the last couple of stairs in slow motion. 'He moved out – weeks ago, now. I can't believe he didn't tell you.'

'Well, he didn't,' Rob said bluntly.

'Was this before the end of term, or after?' Evan asked.

'Before, I think. He was. . .' Miya shrugged, looking sombre. 'He seemed to have problems. One day he just packed up and left. He hadn't said he was going, but Ellie was home at the time, and caught him loading stuff into his car.'

'His *car*?' Wendy turned to stare at Rob. Although Josh could drive, he'd never owned a car, and surely couldn't afford one at the moment.

'Is this Ellie around?' Rob asked Miya.

'No, she left straight after her exams. You're lucky to have caught me – I'm off tomorrow for a few weeks.' A hopeless little shrug. 'I assumed Josh had gone back home. He told Ellie he was dropping out.'

'*What?*' Rob's shout made her jump, and he quickly apologised.

'Did he say what had gone wrong?' Wendy asked. 'Or anything about where he was going?'

'The way Ellie told us, it seemed like he was leaving Canterbury and we wouldn't be seeing him again.' She brightened as Evan produced his phone and slipped out of the door. 'Oh, you can call him, can't you?'

'He mostly ignores us.' Wendy sniffed, and wiped away a tear. 'So nobody has any idea where he is?'

'I'm so sorry, Mrs Turner. I wish I could help more.'

'You're sure he said he was dropping out?' Rob asked. 'Could he have got a job, maybe? Something that required him to move away?'

'I suppose so. But Ellie didn't mention it.'

'Okay.' Rob could barely disguise his frustration. As he turned away there was a hesitant cough from Miya that seemed to signal more bad news.

'After he'd gone we had people looking for him. I didn't see them, but Ellie did – and Max, I think. They came a couple of times. Two men. Ellie said they were quite. . . threatening.'

Wendy groaned. 'Did they say who they were, or why they wanted him?'

Miya shook her head. 'They just wanted to know where he was. Max nearly got into a fight, because we couldn't tell them. He had to show them Josh's old room to prove he wasn't there.'

Rob was now so anxious and confused that he couldn't come up with a single constructive question, but Wendy suggested they exchange numbers. 'Please call me if he gets in touch, or if you hear anything that could help us find him.'

'Of course.' Miya looked close to tears herself. 'We had no idea he'd actually gone missing, otherwise we would have. . .'

Wendy nodded. 'It's not your fault.'

They congregated on the pavement, waiting restlessly while Evan made another attempt to reach Josh by phone. Wendy gave Georgia a hug, staring at Rob over their daughter's shoulder. Her plaintive gaze seemed to ask for something he couldn't give, and he turned away, ashamed to be at such a complete loss.

What kind of trouble was Josh in, that he'd had to do a runner? *And could it be connected, in some way, to what had been happening at home?*

'It just rings,' Evan reported. 'No answer, no voicemail.'

'What now?' Wendy asked.

Rob shrugged. At the sound of a car door closing, he remembered the Land Rover was partially blocking a driveway. 'We could take a look on campus. Wouldn't his address be registered somewhere?'

Wendy nodded eagerly, but Evan was doubtful. 'It's the summer break, *and* it's a Saturday. I doubt if there'll be any admin staff around.'

'Still worth a try.' Rob felt a tingling at the back of his neck and absently glanced round, wondering if Miya or Eric was peeking out at them. 'Let's split up. Georgia and I can check out the university, while you and Evan have a look in town.'

Wendy turned to Evan. 'Are there any places he's mentioned, or anyone he might know around here?'

'Doubt it. He's the original hermit.' There was a bitter note of betrayal in Evan's voice. Then he said, 'Actually, there's a café he likes. Said it has a lot of interesting characters.'

Clutching at this lifeline, Wendy said, 'Let's go, then.'

'Best get something to eat while you're there.' Rob gave Georgia an encouraging smile. 'And we'll grab something at the uni.'

Closed off as usual, the girl only shrugged, prompting Wendy to offer her own consolation: 'It's all right, darling. We'll find him.'

But Georgia, with a wisdom that belied her age, said only, 'Maybe he doesn't want to be found.'

THIRTY-ONE

It wasn't something she'd be proud to admit, but Wendy felt relieved when Rob suggested they split into pairs. He was prone to fly off the handle at the best of times, and since last night he'd been irritable and withdrawn. The more he'd tried to persuade her that there was an innocent explanation for the missing laptop, the more convinced she became that he didn't actually believe it himself.

And now her beloved son was missing, and quite possibly in danger. Coming on top of Sunday's incident, this was almost too much to take.

She wasn't optimistic that the search would bear fruit: more valuable was the chance to speak to Evan without his dad breathing down his neck. 'You genuinely didn't know about this, did you?' she asked, as they started walking towards the city centre.

'No, and I'm really pissed off. I want to know he's okay, and then I want to smack him in the mouth.'

'Evan.' Wendy was repulsed by talk of physical violence. 'Let's think constructively. How long since you last heard from him?'

'Monday, wasn't it?'

'And you're absolutely sure it was him?'

'It was only a text, but. . . no, I'm sure it was – and why would an imposter—?'

'Sorry, no.' She patted his arm. 'Forget that.'

Once they'd crossed the railway line the streets became progressively more crowded. Straight ahead was the Westgate, and the picturesque remnants of the ancient city walls; another couple of minutes and they were on the main cobbled thoroughfare in the medieval heart of the city. Wendy and Rob had visited several times since Josh began his degree, and they had enthusiastically approved of his choice. Canterbury appeared to be a safe, prosperous little city – not that different to Petersfield in many ways.

But Sunday had proved them wrong about that, she thought grimly. Was the same thing going to happen here?

Thinking aloud, she said, 'Why would he ditch his degree so close to the end of the year? And why not come home? I mean, he could lie about taking his exams and we'd be none the wiser.'

'Doesn't make sense.' Evan was trying to find the café via an app on his phone. 'We need to go right, just over the bridge.'

'Unless he *has* been lying about his results, do you think?'

'Nah. He's a fricking genius. He admitted to me that he finds it too easy, sometimes. He'll sit there, surrounded by students staring at the board, puzzling over the equations and shit, and it'll hit him that no one else can make sense of what, to him, is completely simple.'

Wendy gave him a friendly nudge. 'I suspect that *equations and shit* might sum up the difference between Josh and the rest of the family when it comes to maths.'

'Yeah, Evan the Thicko.' Before she could protest, he said, 'Actually, I think it scares him. He understands what he's looking at, but he doesn't know *how* he understands it.'

To Wendy, this admission placed Josh in classic territory for a mental breakdown. Her concern was now so intense that the question of whether or not he finished his degree was irrelevant. All she wanted was to know that her son was safe and well.

The café was called the Boatman's, a short distance along Stour Street. Unlike most of the eateries in the city centre, it was neither a trendy coffee house nor a quaint touristy tearoom: just a plain and simple place to eat. There were about a dozen tables, and roughly the same number of customers, mostly male, mostly on the heavy side, mostly sporting tattoos and piercings and what Wendy would class as aggressive demeanours.

'I take it this is what he meant by "interesting characters",' she murmured.

There was a single waitress, a teenage girl, with an older woman handling the cooking duties. Wendy suggested that Evan look on his phone for a photograph of Josh, but it was hardly necessary: when the girl saw Evan she reacted just as Miya had done.

'I wonder if you can help us,' Wendy said. 'We're looking for Josh Turner.'

'My twin brother,' Evan clarified.

'Yeah, I thought you must be.' She tilted her head, studying his face. 'Not quite the same, though, are you? His ears stick out more.'

Evan couldn't help grinning; this was one of several minor differences that most people failed to spot.

'Has he been in lately?' Wendy asked.

The girl frowned at the tone of her voice. 'Not for weeks, I don't think.'

'Does anyone else know him? Any of the staff, or other customers?'

The girl dug her tongue into her cheek. 'Can't think of any. He'd always sit by himself, reading or on his phone.'

'Surfing on his phone?' Evan asked. 'Or playing games?'

'Talking, mostly. He used to get a lot of calls. Sometimes it's annoying to the customers, but he'd always speak really quietly.' She twitched a nervous smile. 'The whispering man, I used to call him.'

The café clearly had a reputation for gargantuan breakfasts, but Wendy and Evan couldn't stomach anything more than coffee and toast. They found a table by the window, and both began surveying the quiet street in the somewhat fanciful hope that Josh might come strolling past.

'This is very peculiar,' Wendy said. 'The Josh we know is allergic to phones.'

'And who would he be getting calls from? We're talking about a man who has more hats than friends – and he doesn't wear hats.'

The toast arrived, complete with little sachets of butter and jam. Wendy smiled at a memory of Josh's ineptitude: he could never open such things without them exploding over him. Perhaps, in here, he'd asked the waitress to help?

She turned sharply to hide the pain from Evan. Outside, a group of men passed by in noisy debate; lagging behind them was a round-faced young man who looked vaguely familiar. Must be someone very like him in Petersfield, Wendy thought.

Evan was back on his phone, searching for wifi. As she watched him, a treacherous question formed.

'I don't suppose you two have any sort of. . . code word? A way of letting him know there's an emergency?'

She'd expected him to be indignant, even angry, but instead there was a wry grin. 'Funny thing to ask.'

'He ignores virtually all of his messages, so it struck me that you might have cooked up a system to let him know when there's something he absolutely has to answer.'

'There is, sort of,' Evan conceded. 'I tried it back at the house, and not had anything yet.'

'But he knew about the holiday. He knew we were coming here today.'

'Dates and times don't register with him, do they? And especially not if he's in trouble.'

Or in the grip of a breakdown, Wendy thought. And alongside that was the vow she kept repeating to herself: *I won't lose him. I won't lose him. I won't lose him.*

But what if she had?

*

She bestowed her second slice of toast upon Evan, but with a warning: 'It's bribery. Eat that, and send him another *code red* or whatever it is.'

'All right. But I wouldn't hold out much hope.'

She watched him tap out a message, his face dark with tension. In the circumstances it seemed cruel to ask after Livvy, but she figured they were both in need of a distraction.

Gloomily, he said, 'She and her mates are planning to drink the island dry – and then do God knows what.'

'It's probably just talk. I'm sure she'll be missing you.' When he only shrugged, she leaned forward. 'You two are all right, aren't you?'

'Dunno really.' He gazed intently at his coffee. 'Nothing lasts forever, does it? Three years is a long time at our age.'

'You think it's run its course?'

'Not just about what *I* think, is it? Like you and Dad.'

Shocked, Wendy could only stutter: 'Wh-what is?'

He looked up, smiling gently. 'Don't panic, I'm not gonna put you on the spot. But I'm guessing that one or both of you is looking to get out. And if that's what you want. . . I mean, I know it'll be tough – for Georgia, especially – but it's better than living a lie.'

Wendy kept her face impassive, even while her insides churned. 'Do you really mean that?'

'Yeah, I do.'

She nodded slowly, seeing the truth in his eyes. 'As you've said, though, it isn't just up to me.'

Evan's phone buzzed. He checked the display and did an almost cartoonish double-take. 'Bloody hell!'

Wendy's heart began to race. 'Is it Josh?'

Evan nodded, answered quickly, and at the sound of her other son's voice on the line Wendy had to resist an urge to snatch the phone.

'You're okay, though, bruv? . . . Yeah, worried sick, of course . . . No, they're gonna have to . . . Go on, then.' He made a 'writing' gesture to Wendy, who handed over a pen and her pocket diary. Evan scribbled down an address and said, 'Yeah, soon as we can.'

For a moment he looked distracted, perhaps because the café door had just opened behind her.

'So he's all right? Where is he?'

'Not too far, apparently.' Evan's gaze flicked away again as Wendy took the diary.

'Come on. I'll ring your dad and get him to pick us. . .'

But Evan wasn't listening. She turned to track his gaze, just as the door opened and a thin, shabby-looking figure hurried out and disappeared from sight.

'That's odd,' Evan said. 'He just came in, gave me a really intense look, then left without buying anything.'

'Maybe he knows Josh. . .' Wendy let it trouble her for a nanosecond, but she preferred to concentrate on the positive news. 'We've found him, that's what matters.'

THIRTY-TWO

Fletch got out of the café sharpish when he realised the kid had noticed him. Legged it into a doorway and waited for them to come out.

What he wouldn't have given for a mobile phone right now – but with the *need* back on him he'd pawned the phone weeks ago, along with anything else that would bring in a few quid. Still, this could mean a right windfall!

Except the kid looked weird, somehow – or rather *not* weird. Made him worry he was mistaken. The woman had to be his mum. A decent-looking bird, probably the same sort of age as Fletch, though she looked a lot younger. Not much space for a skincare regime in the life Fletch had lived.

Following them gave him a proper buzz. At eight or nine he'd longed to grow up and be a private eye: Sam Spade on the trail of the bad guys. He moved in a zig-zag, using the crowds for cover – not easy when most of the well-offs gave him a wide berth. Funny to think he'd only come out for a spot of cadging by the cathedral, tapping up tourists in ten-minute bursts before the rozzers moved him on.

Kent was almost the right word for how he'd describe people round here.

Once past Westgate they turned into the road to the station, and his spirits nosedived. Fletch didn't have the cash for a ticket: he'd barely begged enough for a cup of tea. Anyway, how much was Nyman gonna pay just to learn the kid had jumped on a train?

Then they stopped without warning, milling around near the car park. Fletch found a place to loiter at the entrance to a block of flats next to Sainsbury's, though with so many pedestrians coming and going there were times when he couldn't see them at all. This Sam Spade shit was proving harder than it looked.

A lot of traffic rolled past, which he mostly ignored, but something about a silver Land Rover snagged his attention. Was it a glimpse of the lettering on the side?

He fell in behind a couple of giggly students and found it hard to take his eyes off their arses, but what really made his heart beat faster was the sight of the Land Rover drawing up at the kerb. The kid and his mum climbed in, and as it pulled away Fletch had a clear look at the sign on the bodywork: *Turner Plumbing & Heating*.

Fucking *Turner*!

Pay phones were hard to come by these days, but by a stroke of luck there was one outside the station. The man himself answered, and Fletch's voice clogged up. 'Th-that kid you're after, I think I've just seen—'

'Who is this?'

'Sorry, yeah.' He introduced himself, and Nyman grunted, like he'd prefer someone else to be bringing the good news. 'He was just in the Boatman's café, with what I reckon was his mum.'

'You sure it was him?'

'Well, at first. . .' This was where he had to be careful. 'He did look a bit different, kind of in better shape than I thought he was.'

'So maybe it wasn't him?'

'No, but they just got into a Land Rover with a sign on it – *Turner Plumbing & Heating*. So it's gotta be, ain't it?'

'And where's it gone, this Land Rover?'

'I dunno. I ain't got wheels, have I?'

'Take a walk round town. Check the car parks. And spread the word, all right?'

'Oh, I can do that, Mr Nyman.' Fletch felt his chest swelling with pride, a long-forgotten sensation. 'And will there be. . . you know. . .?'

'Call in at the Ox later. Jeb will see you right.'

The connection was cut but Fletch went on gripping the receiver, a grin on his face as he tried to figure out who would be most impressed by his new status. 'Nyman's asked me to spread the word. . .' Or: 'Nyman and I need a favour. . .'

Nah, this: 'I was chatting to *Johnny Nyman*, and he wants you looking out for an important vehicle. . .'

Busy rehearsing his lines, the day got better still when he went to cross the road and caught some gorgeous bit of stuff giving him the eye. Must have been the first time in thirty years, but there was no mistaking the way she'd clocked him. A hippy-looking blonde, real slip of a thing; couldn't have been more than nineteen or twenty.

Sam fucking Spade or what!

THIRTY-THREE

The trip to the campus proved fruitless. After twenty minutes of hurrying from building to building, Rob was hot and weary and out of ideas. The university wasn't uninhabited – there was evidence of a summer school, as well as what might have been a corporate gathering – but they had no success in locating anyone from the administrative staff.

Retreating to the Gulbenkian café in the heart of the campus, Rob took a gulp of tea and said, 'That was a good point about Josh not wanting to be found. But we do have to make sure he's all right.'

Georgia, chewing on a flapjack, gave an expressive shrug. 'What about the holiday?'

'Your mum and I discussed that. If he really doesn't want to come, we're not going to force him.'

'Right.' Georgia absorbed this news with such a preoccupied expression that Rob couldn't help grinning.

'What, d'you wish you'd been given the same deal?'

She surprised him by saying, 'No. I like it there.'

'Really? With us boring farts for company?' This was a perfect opportunity to ask about the tension between her and Evan, but Rob couldn't bring himself to do it. Instead he tutted. 'I feel like I haven't been much of a dad to you lately.'

Squirming with embarrassment that the conversation had turned personal, Georgia said only: 'You're okay.'

'Well, we worry ourselves sick about you – though I'm not sure what practical use that is to anyone.'

'Me either.' He was rewarded with a shy smile as she sipped, daintily, from her carton of Ribena and then wiped her mouth, not so daintily, with the back of her hand. 'What if we don't find Josh today? Are we still going to Norfolk?'

'I'm not sure. Do you think we should?'

'Dunno, but there's no way Wend— Mum would want to.'

'Oh, talk of the devil.' His phone had buzzed. Rob answered in a rush, and was overwhelmed by Wendy's delighted exclamation: 'He's all right! Evan's heard from him.'

'Thank God for that.' Rob gave a thumbs up to Georgia. 'Where he is?'

'Still in Canterbury. Evan has the address. It's all been a bit of a mix-up.'

Rob made the right noises in response, but he didn't see how a 'mix-up' could explain what they'd heard this morning. For Georgia's sake he maintained a positive demeanour, but his stomach was crawling with anxiety as they hurried back to the car.

The fact was, Josh had deceived them. No doubt, to his mind, there would be a sound reason for doing so, but Rob felt sure they weren't going to like that reason when they found out what it was.

Ten minutes later they pulled up outside the railway station. Georgia was in the front seat, so both Wendy and Evan got in the back. Wendy kissed the crown of her daughter's head as she climbed in, then clapped Rob on the shoulder. 'It's *such* a relief, isn't it?'

'You're sure this is for real?'

'Yes!' Wendy sounded shocked by the question. In the rear view mirror Rob sought out Evan's gaze and held it for a moment. The response was an ugly scowl.

'Mum isn't lying to you, Dad.'

'I know. I'm just not in the mood for a wild goose chase.'

A tense silence followed. Rob was disgusted with himself for snapping at them. Yes, he was frantically worried about Josh, but why could he only ever express the anger and not the fear?

He muttered something about being a bit wound-up, and hoped they would detect the note of apology in his voice. 'You've got the address?'

Evan read it out, and the satnav brought up a destination on the eastern edge of the city centre. 'Other side of the tracks,' Evan remarked as they drove beneath the railway bridge on Wincheap, then took a left into a maze of residential streets.

And he had a point, Rob thought. They were heading into an area that was very different from the clean, photogenic city familiar to its many visitors. The satnav drew them along narrow streets of redbrick terraces, the roads choked with parked cars; at one point Rob struggled to find a gap to allow an oncoming car to pass. The driver gave Rob the finger and mouthed: '*Wanker.*'

Rob exhaled slowly, and said nothing.

Finally they were at their destination, a rather drab estate of council-built homes just off Zealand Road. A lot of parked cars here, too, so they had to drive on a short distance from the address Josh had given them: No. 18, Flat 2.

'Are we all going?' he asked, casting a dubious glance at a football game in progress just along the road. A lot of unruly-looking urchins who would think nothing of kicking a few dents into the Land Rover.

'I think we should,' Wendy said, opening her door, and Evan said, 'Why don't you stay, if you're worried about the car?'

Rob didn't react, but he was stung by the venom in his son's tone. It was a reminder that, despite being a genial soul, Evan could turn vicious in defence of his mother. And that caused Rob to wonder what else they might have talked about during their time together.

He felt the bump of Wendy's arm against his as they converged on the pavement. 'Don't fly off the handle.'

'I'll do my best.' He gave it a couple of seconds, then said, 'Evan's very touchy.'

'Mm. I think he feels betrayed.'

'By me?' Rob snapped, thinking: *What had she told him?*

'No. By Josh.'

'Oh, right. I get you.'

The building was set back from the road at the top of a grassy bank. It was two storeys high, and seemed to be divided into half a dozen flats. They had to follow a path around to the side to find No. 2.

The doorbell wasn't working, so Evan knocked, and the four of them clustered around a metal framed door, all a little nervous.

He won't answer, Rob was thinking, just as a key rattled in the lock. Evan took an involuntary step back, and by the time Rob had moved to see round him, there was a man facing them in the doorway.

And Rob, in that first instant, thought: *This isn't our son.*

THIRTY-FOUR

For Wendy, the problem wasn't one of recognition – Josh's dark brown eyes were unmistakable – but she was no less disturbed by her son's appearance.

Now she understood the double-takes, the air of confusion exhibited by Miya and the waitress when they saw Evan. Because the figure before them still bore a resemblance to his twin brother, but only in the sense that the pair of them could be employed as a kind of 'Before' and 'After' – perhaps in a campaign against the perils of unhealthy living.

Whereas Evan was lean, muscular and tanned, Josh was scrawny, with a small pot belly, and pale as a ghost. He was wearing a beanie hat indoors, in summer, which puzzled Wendy until she realised she could see bare skin around his ears. Had he lost all his hair?

'Oh my God, what's happened to you?'

Josh shrugged, as if he didn't see what the fuss was about. He'd grown a raggedy beard, and wore a ring through his nose as well as two hoop earrings in each ear. This was *Josh*, Wendy had to remind herself, who'd always disdained body art and piercings, and who favoured formal, preppy clothing instead of the jeans and t-shirts worn by his fellow students. Even at Easter, when they'd last seen him, he hadn't looked anything like this.

'Bloody hell,' Evan muttered. 'Since when did you become a henchman in a Liam Neeson movie?'

That comment – and Georgia's snigger – broke the tension. Josh shyly beckoned them in. Instead of the usual hug, Evan slapped his brother's arm with a hint of real force. Georgia accepted a kiss on the cheek, wrinkling her nose when his beard tickled her face. Rob offered a handshake, somewhat reluctantly, which Josh shook with equal reluctance. And then it was Wendy's turn.

Nothing less than an embrace would do, and Josh seemed to appreciate that. She held him close, and wasn't at all repelled by the stench of ingrained sweat in his clothing; not when she could barely find room to contain all the anxiety and fear.

'You're not looking after yourself properly.'

'Laundry hasn't been a priority, I admit. Other than that, everything's fine.'

'No, Josh. You're in trouble.' She broke away in order to gauge his reaction.

'Where did you get that idea?' His eyes twinkled with a trace of his usual vitality, and she saw in them the mischievous – perhaps some would say *devious* – character that had been present in him from the beginning. Even as a toddler it was always Josh who'd pushed the boundaries, while Evan observed from a safe distance.

The others had filed through to the living room. Josh waved her on, but didn't follow until he had shut and locked the front door. Wendy passed a tiny, cluttered kitchen and two closed doors which presumably led to the bedroom and bathroom.

The living room was a fair size, made cramped by a worn leather sofa and a four-seater dining table, as well as a dozen or so boxes of books and clothes. The curtains were partially open but most of the light was blocked by a row of shirts and sweaters on hangers.

'Did you rent this furnished?' Wendy asked. 'How long have you been here?'

'Yes – and about two months,' Josh answered, then coughed harshly. His voice sounded slightly gruff, adding to her fear that he was suffering from a serious illness.

Rob nudged one of the boxes with his foot. 'It looks like you've only just moved in.'

'Haven't got round to unpacking. Been busy.'

'Oh?' Wendy said. 'Because we've just learned that you dropped out.'

He frowned. 'Why would I do that?'

'It's what you told Ellie, apparently, when you suddenly did a flit.'

'Mm. Only because it was the prudent explanation, in the circumstances.'

Rob turned on him. 'Yes or no, Josh. Have you dropped out?'

'No, I haven't.'

'Thank God,' Wendy said, and gave Rob a stern look.

'How'd your exams go?' Evan asked.

'Satisfactorily. Yours?'

'Not too bad, thanks.'

'Good. Have to call you Evan the Not-so-Thicko.'

'Yeah, all right,' Rob cut in. 'What about this project?'

'Project?'

'The one that stopped you coming home at the end of term.'

'Oh, that. It's ongoing.'

'Why would uni set you work at this time of year?' Wendy asked.

'This is more of a . . . private endeavour.' Josh had been avoiding his father's eye as he spoke; now he avoided Wendy's as well. 'Apologies if you were led to believe otherwise.'

Rob seemed ready to explode. Wendy sent him another warning glance, then said to Josh, 'Is it connected to the men who came looking for you at the other house?'

'Ah.' Josh smiled thinly. 'Pity they had to mention that.'

Rob moved so abruptly that for one terrible second Wendy thought he was about to grab Josh and throttle the explanation out of him.

'Need the toilet. Through here, is it?'

Josh nodded, rearing away as his father stomped out and slammed the door behind him. Wendy caught a sorrowful look on Georgia's face, and wondered if she had made the same assumption. It was a disturbing thought: Rob undeniably had a temper on him, but he'd never been remotely violent towards any of them.

Turning back to Josh, she said, 'What did you hope to achieve by not telling us? You knew we'd be coming here to collect you.'

He nodded quite readily. 'Thought I could sort it out somehow.'

'If there's a problem, you should have spoken to us. We might be able to help.'

A quick smile acknowledged her switch to present tense. 'Not that sort of problem, I'm afraid.' For the first time the mask of flippancy had fallen away, and the resulting glimpse of his vulnerability made for a heartrending sight.

'So what's up?' Evan asked. 'Why are you hiding out here in disguise?'

'There's a long and rather pitiful explanation, but I really don't see—'

The crash of a door startled them all, but Josh moved quicker than anyone, lunging at a spot on the floor beside the sofa, then leaping back up with a hunting knife in his hand. Georgia screamed, but Wendy hadn't even begun to react when Rob stormed into the room.

'What the hell are you playing at, all that shit in your bedroom, you stupid—'

Rob hardly seemed to notice the knife. It was only when Wendy grabbed his arm that he broke off, narrowing his eyes as if seeing Josh for the first time.

'Georgia, it's fine.' Wendy kept her voice low but firm. She jabbed a finger at the sofa. 'Rob, sit down. Josh, put that thing somewhere safe. I don't want any shouting or arguing – but I *do* want answers.'

'There's a reason all his clothes are in here,' Rob said through gritted teeth. 'It's because his bedroom is full of cigarettes and tobacco.'

'Josh, you haven't started smoking—' Wendy began, but Rob was shaking his head.

'We're talking *thousands* of cigarettes. Whole tubs of tobacco.'

'He's right,' said Josh. 'This isn't about personal consumption.'

'Then what?' Wendy asked, still mystified by the depth of Rob's fury.

'Smuggling,' he said, and Wendy almost laughed, thrown by the word's historical associations: pirates, secret passages and tales of derring-do.

'You are fricking kidding me?' Evan said, and Wendy didn't care for the hint of admiration in his voice.

'The labels are foreign,' Rob explained. 'I'm guessing our son has been importing tobacco products and selling them on, minus the small matter of paying duty.'

'Guilty as,' Josh said. 'Though it seemed a harmless enough pursuit at first. I don't approve of the high taxation levels on recreational substances, and I certainly don't agree with much of what this government spends our money on—'

'Sorry,' Rob spluttered, 'I must have missed the bit where you became a taxpayer!'

'I mean in the general sense.' Josh wasn't riled at all. 'It was in modest enough quantities to be insignificant in terms of revenue. At first I sold only to students, after careful vetting. But then a local convenience store became interested, a newsagent or two, and the operation expanded—'

'Hold up,' Rob interrupted again. 'I'm betting those guys who gave your housemates a hard time weren't from Revenue & Customs?'

'Possibly not. I wasn't there.'

'Josh, be serious,' Wendy said. 'Who were they?'

'Specifically, I can't tell you.' He looked at his watch, and then had the temerity to yawn. Wendy could see that Rob was on the brink of another outburst, and perhaps Josh spotted the danger, too, for he said, 'Look, why don't I explain it on the way?'

Wendy could hardly believe what she was hearing. 'Are you. . .?'

Josh nodded. 'I've decided I could do with a holiday after all.'

THIRTY-FIVE

He was upstairs when the visitor arrived. A taxi had been sent to get him because Fletch had no form of transport and no money.

The driver was a regular, and he tooted politely to announce their presence. John Nyman rose to his feet with the customary popping of knees and a weary, sighing breath. He was a strong man of sixty-two, but when he kept vigil in this room he felt more like ninety years old, and as weak as a sapling.

From the bed came a softer sigh; a faint, scratchy voice said, 'Someone here?'

'For me,' Nyman said. 'They won't be long.'

He hadn't realised Mary was conscious. It was becoming hard to tell the difference; increasingly she would drift in and out, here and not here, and the room was always so stifling, so heady with morphine and decay that sometimes he fell into confused waking dreams of his own, and for hours afterwards had to claw his way back to reality.

'Who?' she asked.

'No one important,' Nyman told his wife. Her hand felt as cold as stone, but her brow when he kissed it was burning; her eyes were closed and she didn't respond. Gone again: drifting in and out, in and out, but always away from him and the life they had built together.

Gary was downstairs, and he answered the door. Pausing on the landing, Nyman heard the fear in the visitor's voice as he explained who he was, and it couldn't help but prompt a smile. Gary rarely had to do anything nasty these days: his reputation did the work for him.

Nyman joined them in the kitchen. The house was just off the Margate road, high on a hill with a commanding view over the lush, rolling countryside of North Kent, and nowhere was that view better appreciated than in the spacious, triple-glazed breakfast area.

'Lovely place, Mr Nyman. Lovely.'

'Yeah.' He studied Fletch, noting the deterioration in the man over the past year or so, and experienced a flash of incandescent rage. How could it be that his Mary was barely clinging to life while this worthless little scrote continued to pump his body full of shit and still draw breath?

The bitterness must have shown in his face, for Fletch reeled back and fell into a seat. 'How's Mrs Nyman doing, only I heard sh-she. . .' He lost his nerve as Nyman glared at him. *I don't discuss my wife's health with scum like you.*

'What've you got for me?'

'Oh, it's good. Like I said on the phone—'

'What you said on the phone, pardon my French, made no fucking sense at all. So why don't you explain it to me again?'

'About the café?' Fletch didn't get it.

'Not the café,' Nyman said. 'Tell me about the woman.'

The story wasn't quite as confusing the second time around. After the initial phone call, Fletch had made sure all his contacts were on the lookout for a Land Rover with the name Turner on the side. Top priority, because it was John Nyman who wanted to know.

'Bruce Fisher came up trumps after ringing round a few pals. Someone had just seen it on Wincheap.'

That sighting was soon followed by another: the vehicle was parked on an estate near Zealand Road. Here Nyman sensed that Fletch was trying to skip over the sequence of events, and said, 'Hold on. So you could have called it in from Bruce's pub?'

'Y-yeah,' Fletch stammered. 'Benefit of hindsight and that, maybe I should've—'

'We could have had him this morning, you arsehole.' Gary's voice was a touch too loud; Nyman gave a subtle nod at the ceiling and the younger man apologised.

So did Fletch: 'I'm truly sorry. I wanted to check it out myself before I gave you duff information.'

Fletch had, by his own account, raced over there as fast as his withered legs could carry him, only to be told by a gang of kids that he'd missed the Land Rover by two or three minutes.

'And this is where the woman enters the picture?' Nyman asked.

'Yeah. I'm on the pavement when she wanders up, asks if I'm looking for someone called Turner.'

'Wanders up from where? Another house on the estate?'

Fletch thought hard, a pale tongue creeping from his mouth. 'She sort of came from behind some parked cars.'

'So she had a motor,' Gary said, 'and you didn't get the frigging number.'

Nyman held up a hand. 'Let's hear the man out.'

'I ask how she knows, and she says it's 'cos I'm standing outside his flat. Plus, she says it doesn't surprise her that he's in some kind of trouble.'

'So what's the deal with her?'

'Dunno, but I reckon there's an axe to grind. Said she'd come to see him, but he'd gone off in the motor with his family. I asked if she had a key to his flat – no luck there, but I got something just as valuable.'

'Then give it to us,' Gary growled, 'or piss off.'

Fletch coughed, turning to Nyman. 'You did say about a reward, Mr Nyman. . .'

'That I did, Fletch.' Immune to Gary's displeasure, Nyman took a roll of twenties from his pocket and peeled off two hundred pounds.

Fletch was almost slavering at the sight. With trembling hands he dug out a crumpled scrap of paper.

'Norfolk,' he said grandly. 'She's one hundred per cent that's where they're going. The whole family, like, to a posh holiday home. That's pretty good, eh?'

'Not bad, Fletch. Not bad.' Nyman tossed the notes into the air: Fletch hesitated for only a second before scrabbling on the floor to collect them up. He was on his knees, stuffing the money into his pockets, when Nyman said, 'We're gonna take a look at the flat. You're coming, too.'

Fletch lost some colour from his face. 'M-me?'

Nyman grinned. 'Beats walking home from here, doesn't it?'

'I-I could call a cab. . .'

'An ambulance, more like,' Gary muttered, and Fletch lost a bit more colour.

THIRTY-SIX

As he drove out of Canterbury, Rob reflected on the irony that he and Wendy had anticipated a ferocious battle to persuade Josh to accompany them, only for him to come willingly. The less welcome irony was that they could never have envisaged that he was in this kind of trouble.

Despite the dreary weather, Josh wore sunglasses when he left the flat. There was no mistaking his nervous, watchful air. Rob thought of the knife that his son had kept close to hand, and how he had seemed, for a moment or two, fully prepared to use it.

When they accelerated on to the slip road for the A2, Josh let out the sort of sigh you'd expect from a condemned man who has just learned of a reprieve.

'Pleased to be getting out of here, then?' Rob said.

'A change of scene does everyone good.'

'Not if you're somewhere lovely, and the change is to somewhere shit.'

This was from Georgia, and it delighted Josh. 'The starting point is relevant, that's true.' He nudged her affectionately. 'Got a boyfriend yet, Squirt?'

'*No.*'

'Girlfriend, then?'

'*No!* Shut up!'

It fell to Evan, the natural diplomat, to change the subject. 'You totally bald under that?'

Josh pulled off the cap. 'Pure cue ball.'

'A cue ball with shaving cuts,' Evan said.

'Well, there's an art to it. I hadn't realised what a bumpy skull I've got.'

'It's all those brain cells fighting to get more space.'

'Very funny, E the T.'

'E the Not-so T, remember. I reckon I'm in line for a 2:2 at least.'

'Mm, but it's a degree in football.'

'Are you gonna take the piss about my exams?' Georgia broke in. ''Cos Evan's a genius compared to me.'

'Hey, don't do yourself down,' Evan said, and simultaneously Josh said, 'I'm sure that's not true.'

Rob glanced at Wendy and they shared an almost involuntary smile; it seemed like only the blink of an eye since the most they'd had to worry about was this sort of bickering – usually over Pokémon cards, or which DVD to watch. Trivial things, though at the time Rob had often raged at them for squabbling.

Why on earth couldn't he have appreciated how lucky he was?

'It started last year, when I noticed how many students smoke roll-ups.'

They'd settled into the rhythm of a long journey, the conversation tailing off as Rob pushed the Land Rover up to a comfortable ninety in the outside lane. After cresting Blue Bell Hill, Rob had taken a moment to savour the dramatic sweep of the Medway valley before gently prompting Josh for his explanation.

'At first I went to France as a foot passenger. Then someone told me about Adinkerke, just over the border in Belgium. It's a kind of Mecca for nicotine addicts. I borrowed a car and increased the number of trips. To avoid suspicion I recruited the help of a girl called Ruby. She's a physics student who looks like a *Vogue* cover girl. Her social network is just ridiculous—'

'Everyone's social network is ridiculous, compared to yours,' Evan cut in.

'True. But the pubs and clubs in Canterbury are desperate to have girls like Ruby coming through their doors. One of her favoured proprietors put us in touch with his cousin, who owns a chain of convenience stores. This chap Arshad had been selling contraband tobacco for years, but was having problems with his regular supplier – or so I was told.'

Josh paused to cough. 'For a while we all did fantastically well from it, until the regular supplier realised that his position was being usurped.'

'Who is this supplier, exactly?' Wendy asked. 'What does he do?'

'His name is John Nyman, and he has fingers in lots of pies. He buys and sells. He steals, smuggles, extorts, defrauds.' A grim smile. 'And he hurts people.'

No one spoke for a moment, perhaps because this was so different from Josh's normal demeanour: flippant, facetious, wryly superior.

But Rob couldn't keep his frustration in check for long. 'You're a very bright individual, Josh. How come it never occurred to you that tobacco smuggling was likely to get you into trouble?'

'My speciality is numbers. The numbers I ran on this indicated that the risks were minimal, providing I kept it small and contained.'

'But you didn't,' Rob said – a point which Josh immediately conceded.

'My calculations failed to allow for greed, ambition, ego. I suspect I had an unhealthy need for Ruby's admiration. Also, I was curious to see if I could operate an illicit enterprise without resorting to violence or intimidation.'

'Josh the Cuddly Criminal,' Evan drawled.

'This is serious!' Rob snapped. 'What do you think Nyman will do when he finds you?'

'He already has.'

'*What?*' Wendy said, almost yelping the word.

'A couple of months back I was lifted off the street, taken to an old warehouse and given what I think they classed as a "light beating".' Josh sounded bizarrely matter-of-fact, though Wendy had twisted in her seat and was examining him carefully, as if he might bear scars that they had failed to notice.

'Are you all right?' Wendy asked. 'Did you go to hosp—?'

'Mum, stop fussing. It wasn't nearly as painful as I expected, actually – because of the adrenalin. It's more the terror that you're going to die.' Somehow he managed to chuckle. 'Nyman wasn't present, but on his behalf I was told that my contract with Arshad was terminated, and I was prohibited from selling tobacco products on Nyman's territory.'

Wendy, on the brink of tears, said, 'I wish you'd come to us for help.'

Josh only made a humming noise, politely dismissive. Rob understood her instinct to sympathise, but he had a question: 'If you got warned off, why wasn't that the end of it?'

Evan gave a disgusted laugh. 'Isn't it obvious? He ignored the warning.'

'It was a ludicrous proposition. Nyman decided I should pay reparations – ten thousand pounds – except I was barred from selling on his territory. Where was the money to come from? It was practically guaranteed that I'd have to get back into business.'

'Maybe Nyman planned it that way,' Rob said. 'He gets the money, as well as a good reason to punish you again.'

'God, you're a twat,' Georgia said, in an affectionate way.

'Thank you, Squirt.' Josh blew her a kiss.

'How do you know Arshad hasn't ratted you out?' Rob asked.

'Because he's equally scared of Nyman. He couldn't risk buying from me again, but he did hook me up with a relation of his in Tonbridge. That's where I offload most of the stuff at present.'

'Most?' Wendy queried.

'I'm still selling on campus. I've got to. I have overheads, like any business—'

'Tell it to Alan bloody Sugar,' Rob muttered in disgust, and Wendy shushed him.

'Ten grand isn't an impossible sum – I was hoping to reach my target within a few days.' He grinned. 'I really had intended to join you in Norfolk.'

Rob wasn't amused. 'But you're selling it again. So even if you pay the guy his "reparations", you're still going to be in trouble.'

'But Nyman believes I've left town, and with my new appearance I'm not easy to spot. I've walked past students from my course who didn't recognise me.'

Evan gave a troubled groan. 'We went looking for you in the Boatman's café. There was a bloke who came in, saw me and then left very quickly.'

'What did he look like?'

'An old guy, very thin, scruffy. A druggie, maybe.'

Checking the mirror, Rob saw a flicker of alarm in Josh's eyes, even as he said, blithely, 'Doesn't sound familiar.'

Wendy asked about his studies. Josh assured them that, once the debt to Nyman was settled, he saw no reason why he couldn't complete his degree at Canterbury. 'He'll have his money, and I'm sure he has other things to worry about besides small fry like me.'

'I hope you're right,' she said. 'But why didn't you just come home in the first place?'

'Because the problem was mine,' Josh said simply. 'I didn't want to burden you.'

'Plus you had to sell the rest of the tobacco,' Rob said, not quite buying the selfless line.

'Could've done that in Petersfield,' Evan joked. 'Little pop-up shop by Heath Pond – selling it to Georgia's mates, you'd make a fortune, eh?'

Rob didn't see it, but from the way he winced, Georgia must have prodded him.

They made good time on the M25, but once on the M11 the requests for a comfort break started up – it was two in the afternoon and the twins, as always, were hungry. Rob agreed to stop at the next motorway services, and they rolled into Birchanger Green at about two fifteen.

As he pulled into a parking space, Rob spotted something and had an idea. He studied his phone and gave a sigh of exasperation. 'Just got to make a work call.'

'It's Saturday,' Wendy said.

'The heat pump job – they're working all weekend to stay on track. You go on.'

Looking dubious, she linked arms with Josh and followed the other two across the car park. Rob put the phone to his ear, while moving behind the Land Rover and surreptitiously lifting the tailgate. This morning he'd hidden the trainer, wrapped in two layers of plastic, amongst the cases and bags for the holiday. Now he retrieved it, locked the car and dumped the trainer in a nearby waste bin, pushing it deep below a mass of fast-food cartons.

He was far from certain it was the right thing to do. But with Dawn Avery having a set of keys – and knowing that whoever was framing them could pull the trigger at any moment – he'd had no choice but to get the thing out of the house. Only then came the realisation that, by moving crucial evidence of a crime, he was automatically implicated in that crime. In which case, disposing of it was surely the only safe option?

All he could do was pray that the decision didn't come back to haunt him.

THIRTY-SEVEN

Wendy had no appetite, so she gave Evan a twenty-pound note and sent the three of them to buy some food. As she waited by the entrance, fighting off another bout of suspicion that Rob was hiding something from her, she remembered the grave warning from Kevin Burroughs: *It ain't easy, accepting your own kids have done terrible things.*

Well, now she knew how that felt – and she'd found out a lot sooner than even Burroughs might have expected.

Rob didn't spot her until, after standing aside to let an elderly couple pass, he stepped through the doorway and practically jumped out of his skin.

'Oh! What are you doing there?'

'Thought I'd wait for you.'

'There was no need.' His gaze shifted uneasily. 'Are you okay?'

'Of course I'm not.' As tempting as it was to confront him, there were more important things to discuss. 'Where did we go wrong? I mean, our son is a *criminal*, Rob.'

He pulled a face. 'Yeah – though to be fair, it's not robbing banks, or beating up old ladies.'

'Don't you dare take that line.' Years ago she'd made it clear that she would have no truck with any of the tax dodges and fiddles open to the self-employed. 'It's still illegal, and it could land him in prison. We brought them up to obey the law – not to pick and choose.'

He nodded mournfully, but again she had the feeling that this wasn't uppermost in his mind. She started to speak but choked up. She probably couldn't express it in words, but just as painful, in a way, had been the sight of Josh – thin and pale, with a shaved head – and all the terrible connotations that such an appearance had in terms of his health.

'I feel like I don't know him. My own son.'

Again, Rob only nodded, and said, 'When have we ever?'

'Do you think this is connected to last Sunday?'

The question was prompted by her frustration, a need to shock him into focusing on the conversation, and it had the desired effect. Rob looked her right in the eye for the first time.

'Josh?'

'Well, why not? These men who are searching for him – if they've beaten him up in the past, then they're obviously capable of violence.'

'I guess so.' He pondered. 'But if Sunday was supposed to send a message to Josh – or to any of us – it didn't work, did it? Because we still don't understand.'

'Do you think we should ask him?'

'Maybe, but not yet. Let's talk about it later, shall we?'

Fobbing me off, Wendy thought. Feeling unaccountably disgusted – with Rob, with Josh, with the world – she said, 'All this brutality, it's hard not to feel like we've been cursed.'

Aware that a few passersby were glancing their way, Rob gave an awkward shrug. 'I don't know. Plenty of people have it worse than us.'

'Oh, I'm not doubting that. I've spent my career trying to help *those* folk. What I mean is, there's a huge section of the population that never encounters anything remotely dangerous, and yet here we are – Sunday's incident, and the Iain Kelly business, and now Josh. . .' She pursed her lips. 'And even Georgia's experience. It's starting to feel like this family has trouble running through it like a stick of rock.'

She knew she was becoming far too emotional. Rob patted her arm, somewhat ineffectually, then splayed his fingers as if to count.

'What happened to Georgia was in her old life, before she was living with us, so that doesn't really count.' Next finger. 'With Josh, yes, he's got himself in trouble. But he did so unwittingly, because he has tunnel vision and saw an opportunity to make some cash.'

'Iain Kelly, and your mate, Jason.'

'There's nothing out-and-out criminal about Jason. And let's be honest, after thirty years in the building trade it would be a miracle if I *hadn't* fallen foul of some dodgy types at one time or another.'

'And then Sunday,' she said.

'Yep. That's the mystery, I agree. But the other things. . . in the course of a lifetime, I don't think they amount to anything unusual. It's just bad timing, I guess, to have Sunday's thing and this trouble with Josh crop up within the same week.'

At that moment the kids came over, arms laden with burgers and soft drinks. Wendy had to leave it there, and told herself that at least Rob was trying to reduce her angst, rather than contribute to it.

Josh suggested they eat on the grassy bank next to the car, and they were trooping across the car park when someone shouted, 'Hey there!'

Wendy turned, correctly sensing that the call was directed at them. It had come from a man who was ambling in their direction. He was enormous – perhaps six three or four, and probably not far off three hundred pounds. He was wearing jeans and a red polo shirt, and his clothes bulged with a combination of muscle and fat. A former wrestler, perhaps, or a rugby player gone to seed.

Not that he was old – probably no more than mid-thirties, Wendy estimated. He had a thatch of almost white blond hair, and piercing blue eyes. He was ten or fifteen feet away when he turned and said, in a curiously soft voice, 'It is, you know. It's him.'

He was speaking to a woman who stood, somewhat pensively, beside a red Nissan Qashqai. She was about thirty, tall and thin, with short brown hair brushed flat and parted at the side. She wore beige slacks and a cream blouse, buttoned tightly at the neck and wrists. There was an ill-matched pink handbag over her shoulder and she was clutching car keys in one hand, jiggling them impatiently.

Wendy thought she heard a little gasp from Georgia, but ignored it when the man continued his advance. His gaze was fixed on Rob, whose wariness turned to bewilderment when the man clapped his hands together.

'I do not believe it! Here, of all places.' He spoke with a strong American accent, pure *golly gee whiz*, and his eyes were shining with a messianic thrill. 'We are the biggest *GoT* fans in the world – literally speaking, in my case!'

Rob shook his head dismissively. Evan and Josh were still walking towards the Land Rover, while Georgia darted backwards, behind Wendy.

'Ilsa, it's him. Come and say hi.' He grinned. 'She's kinda shy. Doesn't agree with invading someone's privacy, but I know you'd be cool with that.'

'I'm sorry, you've made a mistake,' Rob said.

'Uh uh, no mistake. I watch that show for *days* without a break, my friend.'

'Show?' Wendy repeated, as confused as Rob.

'*Game of Thrones*.' The man took this as an invitation to move closer. He had extraordinarily clear blue eyes, almost mesmising in their attraction: when he glanced at her, Wendy found it impossible to look away.

'Mistaken identity, I promise you,' Rob said.

'Gabriel, leave them to their picnic.' This was from the woman, whose voice was harsher, and had a slight German accent.

But the man – Gabriel – only laughed, a strange hooting sound, complete with a phlegmy rumble that almost shook the ground. 'I don't think so. I know Lord Stark when I see him!'

Now there were sarcastic laughs from the twins. The man turned that way, grinning uncertainly as if worried he'd missed a punchline.

'That's Sean Bean,' Josh said.

'I know.' The man gestured at Rob. 'Can I get a selfie? Hey, Ilsa, come on!'

As the woman came forward, Wendy felt Georgia plucking at the back of her shirt. The girl was almost cringing, fearfully, and mouthed something that Wendy didn't quite catch. It seemed to be: '*I know her.*'

'That's our dad,' Evan was saying, 'and he isn't Sean Bean, okay?'

'He looks nothing like him,' Josh added, glaring suspiciously at the man.

'No, no, I'm good with faces,' Gabriel insisted. 'This is him. Lord Stark.'

While the debate raged, Wendy turned back to her daughter. 'What?'

'That woman,' Georgia hissed. 'I've seen her before, in town.'

A change in the tone of the conversation forced Wendy to turn away. Gabriel had drawn himself up to an intimidating height and crossed his arms. The smile had gone, and there was a look of petulant rage in his face.

'You know, I think it's pretty fucking rude to treat a respectful fan in this manner.'

The soft voice made the words seem even more threatening, somehow. Wendy moved closer to Rob, preparing to restrain him if he should suddenly decide to lunge at Gabriel, but her husband stayed remarkably calm.

'I'm not Sean Bean. I'm not an actor. Have a safe journey to wherever you're going.'

Gabriel shrugged. The woman was at his side now, draping one hand on his shoulder.

'We're going wherever you're going,' he said. 'Maybe we'll just tag along. Follow your car.'

'I wouldn't advise that,' Rob said, and now there was some aggression in his voice.

Gabriel countered with a sarcastic smile. 'It's a joke. You take things too seriously, my friend.'

Rob grunted, glanced over his shoulder to check on Georgia, then escorted her and Wendy to the car. Gabriel stayed where he was, he and the woman watching as the family climbed into the Land Rover.

'See you again,' he said, and gave a mocking little flutter of his fingers.

Wendy was struck by something odd in his voice, and she didn't work out what it was until her door was shut and Rob had started the engine.

The American accent had gone.

THIRTY-EIGHT

No one spoke until Rob had negotiated the exit road and rejoined the motorway. It was Evan, finally, who said, 'Well, that was different.'

There was a dry chuckle from Josh, but Rob had the impression they were all a bit shaken by the encounter. Rob himself had no idea what to think. Definitely something unsettling about the couple, but he wasn't inclined to dwell on them for long.

The fact that he'd ditched the trainer was of far greater significance. It was now an irrevocable decision, for better or worse. He chose to see it as a positive step: no matter that an unknown enemy was still out there, intent on setting him up for murder, Rob had just neutralised their main weapon against him. There was a sense of liberation, too, in knowing that the next ten days would be spent in a safe haven, far away from Petersfield. In their absence the house could burn to the ground for all Rob cared; they had plenty of insurance.

All he had to worry about was Josh. Upon reflection he'd struggled a little with Wendy's assessment of their son's criminality. Right now he was in no position to cast judgement on anyone.

Glancing in the mirror, his daughter's expression made him frown. 'You okay, Georgia?'

She shifted uncomfortably in her seat. 'I think I've seen her before.'

'What?'

'That woman – Ilsa, was she called? I was in a café on Wednesday, with Amber and Paige. She was at the table behind us – only her hair was spiky, and she had more earrings and stuff. And tattoos on one arm.'

Hidden by the long-sleeved blouse, Rob thought. But it seemed such a bizarre coincidence that he couldn't really give it any credence.

'It can't have been. Are you sure?'

'I-I don't know.' Georgia's voice wobbled. 'I didn't see her that clearly, I suppose. . .'

'So not a hundred per cent?' He glanced at Wendy, who shrugged: *Makes no sense to me, either.*

'Could they just be similar looking?' Wendy asked.

'I guess,' Georgia admitted.

'I think that's all it was, then,' Rob told her. 'I really wouldn't worry.'

After that, there was silence while the takeaway food was consumed. As they travelled north and east the terrain flattened out, though it remained pleasantly green and wooded, a gentle landscape beneath the mellow, cloud-filtered light of this changeable summer.

On the A11 the flow of traffic was disrupted by caravans, and cars towing boats; clusters of motorcycles buzzed through the queues like wasps. Fighting his irritation, Rob turned his attention back to Josh.

'You were saying you nearly have the ten grand that Nyman wants?'

There was a typically grudging response: 'Yes, though there's also the issue of raising funds for my living expenses next year.'

'Don't worry about that for now. I'm thinking about how to make sure Nyman doesn't see your new appearance. You'll need the anonymity when you go back.'

'I have that covered. Ruby's offered to take care of the handover.'

Wendy jerked in her seat. 'And you were going to let her? It could be dangerous.'

'Not really. Ruby's effect on people practically guarantees her immortality.'

'No one's immortal, it only feels like it at your age,' Rob growled. 'Now, let's say you arrange to meet on Monday or Tuesday. Somewhere neutral – I'd suggest a car park at a big shopping mall, like Thurrock or Lakeside.'

'But the money's in Canterbury, and I don't have my car—'

'I'm gonna drive you. We'll collect the cash and you can point Nyman out to me from a safe distance. Then I'll take care of the handover.'

'Dad, I appreciate the offer, but this is my problem—'

Wendy interrupted: 'We're your parents, Josh, and we want to help.'

'Exactly,' said Rob. 'And I intend to make sure Nyman understands that this is it now. You two are quits.'

Josh gave a laugh; when Rob checked the mirror he saw the other two were smirking.

'Very macho, Dad,' said Evan, 'but I doubt if he's going to be intimidated by a middle-class plumber from Sussex.'

'We'll see, won't we?' Rob spoke with such quiet determination that no one challenged him.

It was a valid point. What they couldn't know was that Rob planned to ask Jason Dennehy to provide back-up. The man had offered his support, after all – so what better way to see if that offer was genuine?

The last few miles were slow and frustrating. The narrow road meandered through a succession of ancient villages, where clusters of parked cars or the jutting edge of a building created choke-points, the traffic backed up for what felt like an age.

Having noticed that Evan was periodically checking the road behind them, Rob turned into the service station in Branham, explaining that it made sense to refuel now, as well as buying the fresh food they hadn't been able to bring in the car.

The other reason was to see if the red Qashqai came past, but of course there was no sign of it. He drove on, and a couple of minutes later he turned right into the imaginatively named Sea Lane. The cottage was about two hundred yards from the main road, a two-storey building of flint with patterned brick edging and a pitched roof of terracotta tiles. It stood in a slightly elevated position on a quarter-acre plot that was more meadow than garden, busy with wild flowers and framed by avenues of beech, ash and white willow trees.

The lane was barely wide enough for the Land Rover, but theirs was the only property along here, so Rob didn't expect to encounter any other vehicles. A sudden flash of movement up ahead caused him to jerk the steering wheel.

'Did you see that?'

'What?' Wendy craned to look, before turning to examine him.

'It was—' Rob wanted to laugh, it was so absurd. 'Someone just crossed the lane.'

'A cyclist, wasn't it?' said Josh.

'Wouldn't it be too marshy to ride along there?' Wendy, like Josh, sounded mystified by Rob's reaction. 'They'll be back in a minute, I expect.'

Perhaps she was right, though no one appeared as they drew up outside the cottage. Rob's mind was in turmoil but he didn't want to say why, for fear of scaring them, or sounding ridiculous. Or both.

Was he losing his mind?

*

Evan opened the gates and stood back as Rob drove in and parked on the drive. While Wendy unlocked the front door, Rob wandered out to the lane and turned towards the coast. An old farm building had once stood at the bottom of the lane; now it ended in a clump of bushes and a muddy footpath through the saltmarsh.

Did I see a cyclist? he asked himself. *Well, yes: Josh verified it.*

Could it be who I thought it was? Unconsciously, he shook his head. *Of course not.*

Inside, there were cupboards opening and closing, a kettle being filled, a burst of music as Georgia switched on the TV. Rob helped Wendy open all the windows to clear the fusty air.

The house had three double bedrooms and a bathroom upstairs; a living room and dining room downstairs, along with a good-sized kitchen and a smaller room that was alternatively an office or an extra bedroom. After carrying the cases up, Rob lingered in the back bedroom, which was the one he and Wendy tended to use. It offered a stunning view of fields and trees to left and right, reed beds and tidal marshes straight ahead, and beyond that a narrow strip of flat blue sea.

Not that Rob was admiring the scenery. He was scouring the network of inlets and paths, trying to find the cyclist amidst the palette of greens and browns.

Movement in the doorway made him jump: studying him carefully, Wendy asked, 'What's wrong?'

He snorted. 'Where do I start?'

'*Touché.*' Drifting towards him, she said, 'I just asked Josh about the missing laptop. He doesn't have it.'

'Oh. Pity.'

He sounded far too neutral, but fortunately Wendy didn't push him. Instead she changed tack: 'Going back to Jason Dennehy – does he know about this place?'

'Not as far as I can recall, no.' He turned to face her. 'Of all the things we need to worry about, I don't think Jason's one of them.'

'But what about his friends? You've always said they're a murky bunch.'

'Have I?' He shrugged, but it was a poor attempt at insouciance.

'I've been thinking. . . that time you employed the private detective—'

'Enquiry agent.'

'Whatever. Didn't he say that Iain had disguised his trail quite well, but that he still wasn't particularly hard to find, if you knew what you were doing?'

Rob nodded irritably. He'd hired the agent to trace Kelly, in the hope of taking legal action, but soon realised he was throwing good money after bad.

'So Jason – or one of the others – they could have done the same thing and tracked Iain down in Spain?'

'It's possible, but there's no evidence for that. Look, I don't think there's any link to what's happened this week, so can we just leave it?'

She flinched at his tone. 'I'm only trying to—'

'I know. But the point of coming here was to get away from all that.' A glance at the window, while the voice of his conscience said, *Don't take it out on her, just because you removed evidence of a crime; because you lied and you're lying now. . .*

Wendy regarded him with an enigmatic but disturbing expression. He waited out an awkward silence, and wasn't expecting the quiet, regretful way that she said, 'Once we've sorted out here, I think you and I should go for a walk.'

THIRTY-NINE

The Announcement, that was how Wendy had come to think of it. Leaving the house, she noticed Rob's hand trembling as he reached for the gate. Wendy felt jittery, too. After all the grisly distractions of the past week, the decision she'd made about her future was at the forefront of her mind once again.

She'd gnawed at the issue for a long time before saying a word to Rob; and ever since that first conversation she had worked on the Announcement in her head, shaping what would be the most difficult speech of her life; testing the logic of her arguments, anticipating questions and formulating responses until finally she felt confident that she could deal with any number of objections. She could handle confusion, anger, even grief.

The reaction she feared most was pain. There was no rehearsing a scenario to cope with raw, honest pain. And now the Announcement was horribly close; perhaps only a matter of hours away.

Rob had set off at a marching pace, but Wendy was determined not to speed up. Gradually he adjusted his stride until she was alongside him, their shoulders sometimes bumping as they avoided the brambles and nettles bursting from the hedgerows.

The early evening was mild rather than warm, the sky a shade of cream too subtle even for a paint catalogue. The air held the rich aromas of salt and mud, and the only sounds were the trilling of birds on land and the far-off hoot of birds over the sea; the wet trickle of water in unseen ditches and channels; the ever-singing grasses.

I'll come here again, she thought, reacting to a sudden, irrational fear that this would be her last visit.

They'd spent a couple of hours unpacking, unwinding, mostly in different parts of the house. Wendy had taken a shower, while Rob mooched round the garden and spent a suspicious amount of time at the bedroom window. Evan had gone for a run, and Josh and Georgia had taken themselves off to the garage to set up an old table tennis table. A whoop of celebration from Georgia had offered Wendy a glimmer of hope: maybe the next ten days wouldn't be so terrible after all.

We're all grown-ups now, practically. Sensible, mature people.

A thought to savour, all too briefly, as Rob turned and muttered: 'That person I saw as we turned in here. . .'

'On the bike?'

'Yep. Well, the kid riding it. . .' He blew out a breath. 'He looked just like the lad on Sunday.'

'You're not serious?'

'Same sort of hair, same build – even his clothes looked similar.' Rob waited a second, then gave a snort. 'Go on, say it.'

'Well. . .' She spread her hands. 'It can't be.'

'I know. But what if it is? That's all I have going round in my head. *It can't be – but what if it is?*'

'It was only a glimpse,' she pointed out.

'Oh yeah, fraction of a second. But sometimes you just know, don't you?'

'I suppose so.' Wendy sighed. This explained why he'd been so antsy: it wasn't the Announcement at all. But he couldn't be right. He couldn't be.

The most comfortable walking route took them to the village, about a mile away. The only person they encountered was an elderly woman wrapped up as if for winter, herding a couple of excitable terriers. She gave them a quick nod and made the indeterminate guttural noise that seemed to represent a greeting in rural Norfolk. Shortly after that, they passed through a kissing gate, climbed a low rise and fell so closely in step that Rob, in spite of the purpose of their walk, somehow reached for her hand, and Wendy somehow took it.

She said, 'You know what we discussed earlier, about how some people never experience as much as a burglary, while others run into all kinds of grief?'

'Uh huh.'

'Well, something I've noticed over the years is that when people have a lot of things going wrong at once, they seem to lose the ability to make clear decisions. It's as though, faced with an overload of stress, the brain simply shuts down. It doesn't want to know.'

'And you think that's us?'

'Isn't it? Since last Sunday, what have we really done except bury our heads in the sand?'

He seemed about to disagree, only to say, 'No, you're right.'

A kink in the path meant they had to break apart, and in the instant of separation she was reminded – *the Announcement, the Announcement* – but after threading through the gap Rob took her hand again, and said, 'God, we need a drink!'

For Rob, the bombshell had come in late December, in that endless, stultifying period between Christmas and New Year. During an innocuous stroll around Heath Pond, Wendy had revealed that she felt their relationship had run its course, and thought they should separate.

Rob had been flabbergasted. His automatic response – *Is there someone else?* – had offended her. She claimed there wasn't.

'So why break up the family just for. . . what? A fantasy of what single life might be like?'

Crossly, she'd said, 'Don't belittle the strength of my feelings.'

'All right, but it's not as though we're fighting all the time. We don't hate each other.'

'Do you want to wait till it gets that bad?'

'Who says it will? I mean, is it inevitable?'

After throwing out a few examples from among their friends and colleagues, she said, 'Even if it's not as terrible as that, the best we can probably hope for after thirty, forty years together is indifference. And as I said when we've covered this ground in the past, I don't want the final stage of my life to be notable only for indifference.'

'I know. And I've always agreed.'

'But nothing's really changed, has it? We're still not making the effort to spend more quality time together, and we don't *do* anything with the time that we have. I want to *live*, Rob. And I know this sounds selfish, but I want to be able to please *myself* – for practically the first time as an adult.'

Try as he might, he'd been unable to break her conviction that a spell of independent living would rejuvenate them both – and possibly even spark a reconciliation.

'I see us living a few miles apart, meeting up occasionally – sharing custody of Georgia, of course. And who knows, maybe one day you could ask me out on a date?'

'What if you meet someone else first? Or if I do?'

'Then I'd be glad for you, and I hope you'd be glad for me.'

The news had left him reeling, but Rob was encouraged to hear Wendy say there was no desperate hurry: seeing Georgia through her GCSEs was the absolute priority for the coming year. But after that, perhaps once their daughter was safely installed at her sixth-form college, they could begin to make the arrangements.

Then the subject was put aside, and for weeks Rob had been able to persuade himself that this was merely another mid-life wobble, rather than a full-blown crisis, and that a better solution could be found – some foreign travel, perhaps?

'No,' she said simply, when Rob floated the idea of saving up to take a few months off and see the world. 'Even if we could afford it, which I doubt, there's no way you'd be able to leave the business for that long. You'd drive us both crazy within the first week.'

'Not if we can wait till it's really thriving. . .'

'And who can say when that will be? I'm sorry, Rob. That's not the answer.' She said she wanted to tell the children well in advance. 'We should make the announcement when we're all together, somewhere we can discuss it calmly. Let's take a week in June, once all their exams are done, and go to Norfolk together.'

Here, in other words.

Now.

There were two pubs in the village; one renowned for its cuisine, the other less fashionable but a more relaxing place to drink, so that was where they went. Tonight there were several patrons who knew them well enough to exchange pleasantries. One of the bar staff had recently had a baby – delightful news, albeit something of a shock, given that the girl had enjoyed a brief summer romance with Evan just a few years before.

'They're old enough to be starting families of their own,' Wendy reflected, and Rob's mournful expression was another reminder that the Announcement was close. . . so close.

'And yet they still need us, don't they? Georgia's moody as hell, always in and out of friendships. Evan'll be pining for Livvy in a day or two, and as for Josh. . .'

Wendy nodded. 'I'm glad you suggested trying to meet this Nyman on his behalf.'

'It's got to be resolved, for *our* peace of mind as much as his – not that he seemed bothered about taking up my offer.' Rob took a sip of his dark, reddish bitter. 'It's high time he started living in the real world, and saw what a mess he's making—'

'Peas in a pod, my dear,' she said, and if he heard the fondness in her voice, his tiny shudder seemed a strange way to acknowledge it.

'Don't say that.'

'Well, you are, I'm afraid. It's why he infuriates you so much.'

Glowering at the pub's ancient hearth, cold and unused in the summer, he said, 'To be honest, I've been dreading this holiday. And I know it's probably the same for you, and you just want to get it over with, but after everything that's gone on lately, I don't think it's a good idea to say anything to them now. In a situation like this, when we've only got each other to rely on, the risk of driving a wedge into that. . .' He shrugged, and seemed furious that what was clearly a prepared speech had fizzled out rather than ending on the powerful note he must have intended.

'I'm sorry, Rob.'

'I'm not asking you to change your decision, but just to—'

'Delay, I know. But I don't think I can. I've carried it inside me for so long.' She dabbed at a tear. 'It feels like it's eating away at me, and if I put it off now. . .'

'No, all right.' He sat back heavily, like a man who has just staked everything on the very last throw of the dice – and lost.

FORTY

In Nyman's business, status was everything. If you made a threat, you had to carry it out – and more importantly be seen to carry it out. Josh Turner had been warned off, but he'd ignored that warning, and plenty of people knew it. Nyman had no choice but to take action.

He wouldn't have admitted it to anyone – and especially not to Gary – but he felt slightly reluctant. He suspected they were kindred spirits, him and this kid.

Within his own world, Josh was no doubt a smart guy. Beavering away at his degree, probably burdened with a ton of student debt, he'd spotted a chance to make some money and grabbed it with both hands. He'd rightly seen that the system was against him. Work within it and you'd be lucky to scrape five or six quid an hour at some shitty zero-hours job. Far smarter to take on the system – *beat* the system – and rake in the cash.

Josh had known there were risks, though he'd thought only in terms of being caught by the authorities. When Nyman's men had given him a slap, the kid swore he had no idea he was stepping on someone else's toes. That was his one big blunder, and again it was understandable – he probably came from a respectable, law-abiding background; didn't mix with the likes of Nyman in his everyday life.

But he'd gone too far, so he had to pay the price.

*

Nyman was a smuggler, but a proper one. He wasn't interested in sneaking past customs with his contraband hidden in a suitcase or the back of a car. Nyman's imports – chiefly marijuana, various party drugs, alcohol and tobacco – came in via a pair of fishing boats that met mid-Channel, with the stock transferred to the UK vessel and brought ashore on a quiet stretch of coast. The beach near Dungeness was his favourite spot; Nyman was rarely present at the handovers any more, but still it gave him a warm glow to think he was continuing the noble tradition of centuries: giving the finger to authority.

Earlier they'd driven into Canterbury. Ironically, Josh had been holed up on an estate where, through one route or another, a fair quantity of Nyman's merchandise was consumed. Their arrival – in a brand new BMW 7 series – caused a little flurry of excitement, denying them the opportunity of a discreet entry. Turned out the flat was protected by a good set of locks. Nyman knew people who could breeze through a door like this, but getting them here would take time. In any case, breaking in and robbing the kid wouldn't be enough to restore Nyman's status.

No, it had to be face to face.

It had to be Norfolk.

Other preparations were necessary before they could depart. Nyman had made private arrangements for his wife's care, and the agency who supplied the nurses were able to organise some extra cover – for an extortionate fee, of course.

He didn't linger over his farewell: Mary was in no state to appreciate anything he might have said, and the longer he sat there the harder it became to get up and leave. He settled for a quick press of his lips against the papery skin of her forehead, and a whisper: 'Bye, love. See you tomorrow.'

He'd packed an overnight bag, along with gloves and masks and a few tools of the trade, just in case. He hadn't yet decided how to play it with Josh: something to ponder on the journey.

As always these days when he left the house, Nyman was touched by the notion that he would not see his wife again. It was a feeling he remembered vividly from the early years, though back then it was because he didn't know if he'd make it through the day, given the perils of carving out a niche in the underworld of south-east London. So much worse, somehow, that it was Mary in this predicament.

If pressed, he might well concede that his current woes were partly down to his wife's illness. He'd been too willingly distracted, and maybe too soft. *What kind of pussy lets a university geek run rings round him?* That was the question lurking in Gary's eyes whenever Josh was discussed.

But the really niggling worry was this woman who'd been watching the Turners. Didn't sound like a girlfriend, from Fletch's description – and an unhappy girlfriend would surely just confront the kid, wouldn't she?

Handing over the address of the family's holiday home to a stranger – and not just any stranger but a filthy old scrote like Fletch. . . that was just plain odd, and it left Nyman wondering what else Josh was messed up in.

They stopped en route at a pub in Ely and took their time over an indifferent meal. Nyman drained a couple of brandies, and rested his eyes for the remainder of the journey.

They reached the village of Branham at eight p.m. and delved into a few side roads, noting the presence of a single village store, a petrol station and two pubs; grateful for the absence of a police station or any sort of civic building. Very little CCTV anywhere, which was a bonus.

The house was actually between Branham and the next village, Burnham Deepdale, accessed via a narrow lane which petered out on the salt marshes along the shore. A one-way road, effectively, with limited space to manoeuvre. On the plus side, the property was remote, and very private.

Driving on, they passed a couple of fields before spotting an almost identical route to the coast. Bumping along the track, they reached a gravel car park on the edge of a muddy, reed-infested creek. A lot of ruts in the mud close to the water, presumably from boat trailers. Luckily there was no one around this evening.

They parked up to wait for dusk. The sun had fallen out of sight and the sky was a deep shade of blue. Nyman opened his windows and breathed the salt air, listened to the hoot and squawk of sea birds and tried to experience every sensation as profoundly as Mary might have done. Mindfulness – or some such bollocksy term they had for it nowadays.

Gary paced the car park and chain-smoked like an old-time expectant father. He was a man who craved easy solutions; the Turner kid had riled him by mouthing off, and now Gary was itching to make good on the threat that the next punishment would be on a different level.

By nine the light was dimming but not gone. *About right,* Nyman thought. Too dark and they'd be on their guard, might not come to the door.

He called to Gary, who ditched the last cigarette. 'Time?'

'Yeah.'

'Brilliant.' Gary opened the back door, stretched for something beneath the seat, then moved round to the front. Settling behind the wheel, he handed Nyman a Glock semi-automatic pistol. 'Brought this, for extra persuasion.'

FORTY-ONE

They'd eaten later than planned, because Rob and Wendy had gone off to the pub. 'Thanks for inviting us,' Evan had muttered sarcastically, but Josh said, 'First-night reprieve – and we deserve it, eh, Squirt?'

Georgia had shrugged. 'Dunno. What's "reprieve"?'

Both of them were making an extra effort to be nice, which freaked her out – Evan because of all the horrible stuff this week, Josh because no one should be this chilled when they were in such big trouble.

Georgia had made the decision to stay off social media for the entire time they were up here, so she wouldn't know what was said about her in BitchWorld – and she wouldn't care. That just left the weirdness today, and the woman who seemed to be the same one from the café. In the end she decided to go with Dad's explanation that they were all feeling paranoid and stressed-out, which made a lot of sense.

He and Mum had returned in a funny mood. Georgia fled the dinner table at the first opportunity, only to be called back by Wendy: 'Where are you going?'

'Getting something,' she lied.

'All right. But come down soon, please. We agreed to spend the evening together.'

Georgia felt sick to her stomach: somehow she just knew. *They're splitting up.*

She'd been reading the signs for months, deciding it was either divorce or a terminal illness that they were keeping from her. But if it was an illness there'd be hospital appointments – and Rob and Wendy would have got on better, putting aside any differences in the time they had left.

The tears came in a rush and she threw herself down on the bed, burying her face in the duvet. Her old life had been just like this – scary, confusing, uncertain. The new life was supposed to be better.

She was getting hot, couldn't breathe. As she flipped on to her back there was a sudden flash of light through the window. Car headlights, it must be.

She got up and moved to the window, puzzled by the fact that the lights had now vanished. Had a car turned into the lane, then reversed back out again?

She opened the window and immediately heard an engine, soft and purring. She glimpsed the dark rectangle of its roof, passing between a dip in the hedgerow. It seemed to be slowing down, so perhaps that was why the lights had been switched off.

But the only house along here was theirs.

So its destination had to be. . .

'*Here*,' Georgia whispered.

Evan and Josh were washing up. Wendy and her relatives had agreed that they should do without a dishwasher here, on the basis that sharing out simple chores would help them to savour their downtime all the more. Josh regarded this as illogical, and Evan, too, made a show of protesting, though secretly he approved.

He slipped a couple of plates into the hot water. Josh, on drying duty, was methodical but painfully slow. They could hear the murmur of voices from the lounge. 'Big family conference coming up,' Josh had predicted earlier.

In the light of this morning's conversation with his mother, Evan thought he could guess what was coming, but he hadn't expected Josh to have a clue. Maybe his brother was finally learning to pay a bit more attention to the world around him – he'd certainly asked plenty of questions about last Sunday's incident, though he had no better theories than anyone else as to why it had happened.

'So tell me about this Ruby,' Evan said. 'Sounds like you've got the hots for her.'

'Absolutely. It was infatuation at first sight – on my part, that is. She barely knew I existed until the importation business got underway.' He paused, and the plate he was holding squeaked as he dried it. 'Turns out that girls really do go for the bad boys.'

'So I've heard,' Evan said. 'And you got lucky, did you?'

Josh gave an enigmatic smile. 'I can neither confirm nor deny. . .'

Before Evan could take the piss, there was a strange exclamation from his dad. Evan caught only part of Mum's response: '. . . at this time of night?'

Josh turned and said, 'What's up?'

'Dunno.' Evan saw Rob come into the hall and head towards the front door, with Wendy just behind him. 'Think we might have a visitor.'

Rob couldn't remember the last time he'd felt as nervous as this. On the way back from the pub they'd discussed the timing of the announcement, and Wendy had suggested leaving it a day or two. She'd been taken aback when Rob flatly rejected that idea.

'The kids aren't stupid – they'll soon realise something's up.'

Then she admitted that Evan had virtually said as much this morning, in the café. Wendy had avoided giving him a straight answer. 'I didn't think it was right to tell him without everyone being present.'

Rob wondered if there was a different reason – that Wendy wasn't as committed to the decision as she made out. To her it must have seemed like a pretty cheap tactic on his part, to go from pleading for more time to urging her to get it over with. Perhaps there was some truth to that, but his main desire was to avoid prolonging the agony.

His insides were churning throughout the meal. He kept expecting Wendy to say something, but found he couldn't find it in him to prompt her. Afterwards Georgia made her usual dash for freedom, and the twins agreed to wash up.

Taking refuge in the living room, Rob poured himself a brandy. *Breaking out the hard stuff* would be the usual joke here, but neither of them said it.

'Pour me a small one, would you?' Wendy said.

Rob nearly dropped the bottle when someone knocked on the door. They had no close friends up here, no neighbours to speak of. . .

'Who'd be coming round at this time of night?' Wendy asked, and they both looked at the clock on the mantelpiece. It was nine fifteen.

Rob kept hold of the bottle as he marched into the hall. The front door was solid timber but there was a pane of glass in the panel to the left, partially frosted, with just enough clarity to get an impression of the person standing on the front step.

It was a man, of medium height and build, and possibly quite old. He appeared to be alone.

'Think it's all right,' Rob said. Probably someone whose car had broken down on the main road.

His hand was on the latch when the twins burst from the kitchen. Josh started to speak but the words didn't form quickly enough, and Rob's brain simply wasn't capable of responding in time.

What he realised later – for all the good it did – was that Josh had been trying to shout: *Don't open the door.*

FORTY-TWO

Nyman had used firearms before, but he scrupulously avoided having them in his possession. It was a sure route to a prison cell. For security at home he was content to rely on baseball bats, knives and reputation.

'Got it earlier, it's clean,' Gary assured him. He was almost panting, like a dog that expected a reward.

'We won't need that here.'

'You don't know. Look how often it's the soft jobs that go tits up.' He registered Nyman's expression, then scowled. 'All right, I'll keep hold of it.'

'You will,' Nyman agreed. 'And you're staying in the car.'

'What?' Gary's face went slack with disappointment. 'That fucking kid—'

'I want a quiet chat, one on one.'

'But he didn't listen before—'

'He thought he could hide from me. This proves he can't. I'm gonna make it clear that it's his family who'll suffer from now on.' He slapped Gary on the shoulder. 'Keep a close watch on the house. Stop anyone who comes out. I'll shout if I need you.'

He sounded calm, and he genuinely was. Very little fazed him any more, and why should it? Compared to what Mary was going through, nothing mattered a damn.

He opened the gate, frowning when a security sensor bathed him in light. There was a bell, but he preferred to knock. Within seconds a shadow moved in the window beside the door. Nyman expected them to check him out, so he'd opted to wear a crisp white shirt and a dark blazer. Golf club casual: prosperous and reassuring.

Now the door was opening. *Here goes. . .*

Rob faced the man in the doorway and saw at once that this was no stranded motorist. There was an intensity to his gaze that spoke of a serious purpose, and Rob would have guessed, even without Josh's intervention, that this was John Nyman.

He was in his sixties, tall and lean, with short grey hair and green eyes. Smartly dressed, he stood with his hands loose at his sides. No sign of a weapon.

The man was giving Rob a similar appraisal, could probably see that Rob wasn't in bad shape for his age – but equally could have been better.

'I'm here for Josh,' the man said, just as Rob felt someone move alongside him.

It was Josh. The man nodded at him, then saw Evan, hovering just behind, and gave a laconic grin.

'Twins, yeah? Well, I never.' He studied Josh. 'Nice makeover.'

Rob growled, 'Are you Nyman?' just as Josh said, 'I can handle it, Dad', and Wendy yelled: 'You attacked our son!'

Nyman stood his ground; if anything, he looked faintly amused by the commotion. Rob shifted closer to block the doorway and spotted a BMW in the lane. There was a man at the wheel.

'Who's that?'

'My driver. He'll stay there, while you and I have a chat.'

He was addressing Josh, who nodded and tried to ease Rob aside. 'It's okay, Dad. Mr Nyman and I will talk out here.'

'No way,' Rob said. 'We're not leaving you alone with him.'

'I'd better come in, then.' Nyman indicated the bottle in Rob's hand. 'Courvoisier, is that? Don't mind if I do.'

Rob couldn't help himself – he lunged at Nyman but was restrained by his sons, both of them pulling him away. He was vaguely aware of Wendy moving in the other direction.

'Dad, don't interfere,' Josh shouted. 'I'm not a child. I can fight my own battles.'

Nyman smiled at that. 'There doesn't have to be any trouble,' he said quietly. 'But your boy and me, we have business to discuss.'

'We know,' Rob said, and Evan, at his shoulder, told Nyman: 'You're outnumbered here. Try anything and you'll have us all to deal with.'

'There's going to be no fighting,' Wendy declared. She held up a phone. 'Tell me why I shouldn't call the police, right now, and have you thrown in jail?'

Nyman hooked his thumbs behind his belt and rocked back on his heels as he thought about his answer.

'Because I doubt if you want your boy thrown in jail beside me. A bright lad like that, he doesn't want to be starting adult life with a criminal record.'

Wendy was shocked to hear it spelled out, but still didn't think they should be giving this man the time of day. And yet, at Josh's urging, Nyman was soon installed in their living room, sitting in the centre of one sofa while the four of them were grouped around the sofa opposite. Josh kept insisting he could speak to Nyman alone, but Rob and Wendy flatly refused.

'This it, is it?' Nyman asked, once Josh had made the introductions.

'Yes.' Wendy jumped in before anyone could contradict her. She was praying that Georgia had heard enough to stay quiet, hidden away upstairs.

Rob flinched suddenly. 'Is the back door locked?' he asked Evan.

'I'll check.' Evan was gone for a few seconds, and Wendy heard what might have been the scrape of the knife block. She tensed, horrified by the thought of a knife being used, even in self-defence. But Evan when he reappeared was empty-handed.

To draw his attention away from her sons, Wendy told Nyman, 'You're a bully. A bully and a coward. And I *will* call the police if there's any aggression whatsoever.'

Nyman regarded her as though she were no more than a tiresome pest, some harmless insect to be swatted away. He seemed so neat and placid – nothing like the image she'd formed from Josh's description – and yet there was an air of suppressed violence about him, a sense that his true nature would soon come to the fore if needed.

A hint of that menace appeared when he said, calmly, 'If I'd wanted him badly hurt, there's no way he'd be standing here now.'

Wendy gasped, and had to grab Rob's arm to keep him from launching another attack. Nyman was unperturbed.

'The punishment he had was about right for what he'd done. It was meant to scare him off, send him looking for a safer way to earn a few quid.'

Josh went to speak, but Rob got in first: 'You're demanding ten grand. How the hell he's supposed to find that sort of money, if he can't sell the tobacco?'

Nyman looked baffled. He regarded Josh, whose face, Wendy saw, had gone bright red.

'He was meant to stop once he'd paid me. I got the money a few weeks back, but then I heard he was still selling. And that, I'm afraid, is taking the piss.'

Wendy felt the shock run through Rob's body, just as it did through hers.

'You mean. . . there isn't a debt?' she asked.

'Not any more. But a lot of people know that some smartarse college kid muscled in on my operation, then ignored the warning to get out. Acting like he's untouchable. I can't have that.'

In unison they turned on Josh. Rob said, 'What the hell are you playing at?'

'I need money for next year, all right?' Josh's voice was high-pitched, defensive. 'A few more days and I'd have reached my target.'

Wendy let out a sob of frustration. 'You lied to us, Josh!'

'So what, Mum? People lie all the time.' His eyes narrowed at her, almost maliciously. 'You and Dad aren't as pure as the driven snow—'

'Don't talk to her like that,' Rob yelled, and at this Nyman jumped to his feet.

'Save the family bust-up for later,' he growled, jabbing a finger at Josh. 'Here's the deal. You're gonna give me all the merchandise you got stored at your flat, then you piss off home and never come back.'

Josh seemed calmer dealing with Nyman than with his parents. Shaking his head, he said, 'I have to complete my final year, but I am prepared—'

His attempt to negotiate was interrupted by a sudden high-pitched scream, choked off almost immediately.

Georgia.

FORTY-THREE

She had studied the man as he got out of the car. There was something about his movement, his attitude, that told her exactly who he was, why he was here, what he wanted. . . and Georgia was ten years old again, in bed, fed up and lonely and trying to sleep the day away.

It was a Tuesday in term-time – maths, science and then games – and the night before she'd exaggerated the symptoms of a headache enough to be given the next day off. Mum didn't care either way: she was pissed up on the sofa.

Mark turned up at about midday, off his head as usual. He'd had a key copied, secretly, when he realised the relationship was coming to an end. Georgia was woken by loud swearing, followed by the crash of a plate being thrown against the wall.

Then a shout which turned into a scream, the very worst sound she had ever heard. And it wasn't just meaningless noise – Georgia understood that later, in hospital, when she could finally bear to go over what had happened.

Her mum had been trying to call out a warning. Not Georgia's name, which would have revealed the girl's presence. As messed up as she was, her mum had been smart enough to try for '*GET OUT*', knowing Burroughs would assume it was directed at him.

Except it hadn't worked. Georgia's first thought was that Mum was in trouble. She needed help. Georgia couldn't just run away.

She was halfway down the stairs before she realised her mistake – it was too late. By then it wasn't even her mum any more; just a body, and that moment would be forever seared in her mind: the body, and the knife Mark Burroughs was holding; the blood on the knife and on Burroughs, and the way he had looked up and seen her frozen in place—

It couldn't happen again. She had to be quicker this time. Quieter. Smarter.

She peeked out of the window, making sure the other man had stayed in the car. Though the sky still glowed with pale light, the landscape was a mass of shadows. Easy to imagine movement in the lane and across the fields: an army of bad guys creeping up on them.

The driver would see her if she tried climbing out of her window. Besides, it was too far to fall. Better to go out through Mum and Dad's room, where she could climb on to the conservatory roof, then down into the back garden.

She heard voices from below. The man had come inside, but no one was screaming or shouting – yet. Probably they were trying to keep him calm, keep him talking. . .

Giving me time to fetch help! The thought jolted her, but also made her proud. This was her family. It was her job to save them.

She crept across the landing, shivering at a flashback of that cold, smelly house in Southsea, Burroughs yelling abuse as he tore up the stairs, Georgia nearly wetting herself when she realised he was going to stab her, was going to open her up and let the blood pour out—

Swallowing down an urge to vomit, she made it to the bedroom window, her heart hammering as she gripped the frame and climbed out. The conservatory roof was only plastic and didn't feel very strong, so she quickly eased down to the front edge, already planning what came next – finding a route through the field in the dark, out to the road and then running full speed to the village to fetch help and call the police. . .

Could have been out on a date tonight – that crazy thought came to her as she dropped to the grass and landed with a groan.

She'd been thinking about Milo a lot: a silly fantasy where she'd stayed behind in Petersfield, ten days with the whole house to herself, Milo taking her to dinner, somewhere posh with candles on the table and expensive champagne; afterwards, as he walked her home, they'd start kissing, and the kissing would lead to—

Save it for later. Georgia stood up, tested her ankles and then, wincing, took a few quick steps across the garden. . . and there he was.

Milo.

She nearly fainted. This was bad news, really bad, to be hallucinating. . .

Except it *was* him. Milo. Right there in front of her, in three dimensions. Totally real.

He was breathing fast with excitement, his eyes colder than yesterday, cold and sort of blank. Right away she knew that he hadn't come to rescue her. In any case, how could he have known—?

She opened her mouth just as he slammed into her, knocking the air from her lungs and shutting off the scream that her mum – her poor dead flesh-and-blood mum – would have regarded as pathetic. No help to anyone.

Wendy placed the sound as coming from the back of the house. Evan was closest to the kitchen, and he sped off without a word. After a second, Josh followed his brother, while Rob rounded on Nyman, lifting the brandy bottle as if to strike. 'What have you done?'

'Nothing.' But there was a trace of doubt in Nyman's face. 'If Gary's disobeyed me, I'll sort him out myself.'

His confusion sounded genuine enough, and both Wendy and Rob were too disorientated to do anything but follow him out of the room. Nyman wrestled with the unfamiliar catch on the front door, finally pulling it open, but as he stepped outside a giant shadow loomed into his path.

'What the fuck—' he managed to gasp, then fell at their feet.

Milo had one hand clamped over her mouth, the other twisting her arm painfully behind her back. He marched Georgia, tripping and stumbling, along the side of the house, a few weak moans of protest escaping from her throat.

As they reached the corner, she heard a scuffle from the lane. The view was partially hidden by her dad's Land Rover, but she could see part of the visitor's car, the man behind the wheel twisting and jerking in his seat as if being electrocuted.

Then Georgia saw why.

There was another figure crouched by the car, tall and slim and dressed in black, stabbing the driver in a frenzy of violence that made Georgia feel dizzy with shock. She shut her eyes and once again Mark Burroughs was behind her on the stairs, grabbing her ankle as she threw herself out of the window, slashing at her leg as she fell. . .

She vomited. With a cry of disgust, Milo whipped his hand away from her mouth, but clung on as she toppled forward and landed heavily on her knees. It felt like her heart had stopped. Points of dazzling light danced in her head, and she thought, *This is the end.*

Gasping and spitting, she was hauled to her feet. She heard the front door open and turned in time to see the visitor step out. But he hadn't noticed the figure lying in wait by the door, a huge man who punched him in the stomach with the force of a battering ram.

The visitor collapsed. Behind him, Mum and Dad were crowded together in the doorway, open-mouthed with shock. The attacker, she realised, was the man who'd mistaken Rob for some actor from *Game of Thrones*.

The figure by the car hurried towards them. It was the woman from this afternoon – only now her hair was spikier, her face pale and cold. Much more like it had been in the café on Wednesday.

Ilsa. A little out of breath, and splattered with the blood of the man she'd just killed, but otherwise quite happy. Pleased with herself.

'Hello, Georgia,' she said.

FORTY-FOUR

Rob saw Nyman go down and briefly thought that someone had come to their rescue. That notion survived for barely a second, until he saw the identity of Nyman's attacker.

The enormous, overbearing man from the motorway services, Gabriel, had stepped back from Nyman's body and was watching Rob carefully. A young blonde woman appeared from behind him, blocking any possible escape route across the drive. At the opposite corner, Georgia was in the clutches of a stocky, round-faced young man, while the woman who'd been with Gabriel this afternoon strode confidently towards them, holding a knife in one hand and something else, hidden by her side, in the other.

With a triumphant smile, Ilsa displayed the object for them all to see.

It was a gun.

Wendy could only stand and stare in horror. It gave her little comfort to know that Rob was equally overwhelmed, and less still when Josh burst from the house, skidding to a halt behind them.

'Are you—?' he began, then: 'Oh, fuck.'

'Where's. . .' Wendy managed to stop herself from mentioning Evan. She tried to divert their attention by confronting the man with Georgia. 'Leave my daughter alone!'

He ignored her, glancing instead at the couple who'd so unnerved them this afternoon. Gabriel and Ilsa were in charge, she guessed, and the threat they posed couldn't be clearer now the woman was pointing a gun at Rob.

Sounding remarkably unafraid, he said, 'What are you doing here?'

'You'll find out,' Gabriel replied calmly. His accent was Home Counties English, not American. Then another woman emerged from his shadow, slim and blonde, and Wendy recoiled.

'Lara?'

There was no doubt that this was the girl who'd conned her way into the house on Thursday – and Ilsa must have been in the café, just as Georgia had claimed. . .

They followed us here, Wendy thought. All of them, working together.

There was a weak moan from Nyman. He was curled in a foetal position, clutching his stomach. The sound almost obscured a noise from the side of the house; Wendy prayed they hadn't heard it, but Ilsa gave a predatory twitch.

'There's one missing.'

'Round the back,' Gabriel called, and with that Wendy dropped the pretence and screamed: 'Evan, run! Get the police!'

Gabriel snatched the gun from Ilsa as she dashed past, bringing it to bear on them just as Rob took a step forward.

'I'll shoot you now if I have to,' Gabriel said. 'But I'd rather not spoil the fun.'

After finding no sign of Georgia in the back garden, Evan and Josh realised that all the activity was taking place out front. While Josh ran through the house, Evan decided it would be quicker if he took the path round the outside.

He was hurrying that way when a wiser instinct spoke up. *Don't reveal yourself. Wait till you know what you're facing.*

He lifted the paring knife that he'd taken from the kitchen and crept up to the corner. His guess was that Nyman must have had men watching the house, who'd caught Georgia as she tried to get away. What a brave kid.

The security light was shining out front, which had the benefit of casting the sides of the house in deeper darkness. Evan thought he could risk a look without being seen, but the sight that greeted him was utterly surreal.

Georgia was just a few feet away, in the grasp of a pudgy, prosperous-looking man of about Evan's age. Josh and his parents were hemmed in by the front door, with Nyman sprawled at their feet. Of the four people who seemed to have taken control, two were the couple who'd acted so strangely at the motorway rest stop.

Evan felt sick with confusion. If Nyman had been attacked, did that mean Gabriel and the others were the good guys? And why hadn't Nyman's driver intervened?

He took the risk of leaning a little further. The driver was just visible, slumped in his seat. Dark, wet patches on his face gleamed in the brightness of the halogen light.

Blood.

Then the woman, Ilsa, barked: 'There's one missing.' Evan turned and sprinted along the path, dimly aware of his mum urging him to get away.

Reaching the lawn, he cursed as he triggered another outside light. But the bottom of the garden was a welcoming pit of darkness. He aimed for a gap in the hedge that would allow him to squeeze through to the marshland beyond, and was almost there when a shape detached itself from the mass of shadows and brought him down in a clumsy but effective tackle.

Evan hit the ground sideways, jarring his right elbow and losing the knife. He almost snapped his wrist as he tried to roll and spread the force of the impact, but his movement was impeded by his attacker, who punched Evan in the groin and sent a shockwave of agony through his body. As he lay there, gasping for breath, Evan felt the vibration of running footsteps and understood that he wasn't going to get away.

FORTY-FIVE

Keeping his family safe was the immediate priority, but at the back of Rob's mind lay a hunch that a lot of things were about to become clear.

For a start, he saw that they were facing two different threats. Gabriel and the people with him had no connection to Nyman, and judging by the look on Ilsa's face as she produced the gun, Rob guessed that she and Gabriel hadn't brought it along.

It must have been taken from Nyman's driver, who was now either dead or grievously wounded. Rob had little sorrow to spare for the man; nor was he naïve enough to think that Gabriel had done them any favours by attacking him.

Georgia was led into the house first, and they were warned that she would suffer if they tried to resist. As they filed in after her, Gabriel scooped Nyman off the ground as easily as Rob might lift a child. One by one they were frisked, and had phones, keys, money and even their belts taken away.

The gun was wielded by Lara, a young woman who looked vaguely familiar to Rob. The barrel trembled in her two-handed grip, and for a moment he was tempted to go for her. But in a confined space, even an accidental shot could be lethal.

No, he thought. Evan was their best chance. He was fast, athletic, he knew the area.

They were herded into the living room and told to sit together on one of the sofas. Gabriel dumped Nyman on the floor. Rob barely registered his howl of pain because Ilsa had appeared in the doorway with Evan, conscious but groggy, propped up between her and a small, wiry man with a mess of dark hair.

'S-sorry, guys. Ambushed.' Evan spat blood as he spoke. He sank to the floor at Wendy's feet, and now Rob had a clearer view of the man who had brought Evan in – a young man in his early twenties, perhaps, but who could easily pass for a teenager, especially when seen from a distance.

For Rob, it was like the last piece of the puzzle had dropped into place. But it was Josh who spoke first. 'Can anyone tell me what the hell is going on here?'

'You'll find out soon enough,' Gabriel said.

Nyman, lying face down, made an effort to roll over. 'You're a dead man,' he gasped through the pain.

The apple-cheeked young man who'd captured Georgia kicked out at Nyman. 'How dare you address the leader that way.'

'Milo.' Gabriel gave a shake of his head, and there was no missing the authority he wielded over the others.

'I mean it,' Nyman growled. 'You messed with the wrong feller here.'

'Really?' Amused, Gabriel permitted Nyman to turn over and climb, shakily, to his knees. At the same time he gestured to Lara, indicating that she should hide the gun from view. 'Let's hear it, then.'

Nyman was furious with Gary. Somehow he'd been rolled, sucker-punched – and yes, Gary had warned him not to go into the house alone. But the attack had actually come from outside, from this lumbering great beast of a man, which meant his enforcer had cocked up.

And where was Gary now? Why hadn't he burst in and put things right?

Desperate to restore some dignity, Nyman tried to stand but got no further than his knees. The pain in his gut was a roaring fire, melting him from the inside. No matter how often he blinked, his vision kept distorting, making it hard to get a fix on his attackers.

The ringleader was a huge man, probably twenty stone of muscle and fat, who carried himself with surprising grace. Alongside him, there seemed to be four others, two male, two female. The older of the women was tall, thin, and hard-faced: to Nyman she looked like a lifelong protestor, an anarchist or one of those dykey peace campaigners, if they still existed. The other three were little more than kids, all with that easy, sneering confidence that comes from a middle-class upbringing. A bunch of pampered, wannabe rebels, then – maybe even friends of Josh or his brother?

'I dunno what you're doing here,' Nyman told them, 'and I don't much care. Josh here owed me money, but it's all settled now.' He turned to the lad. 'Isn't that right?'

Josh shrugged. 'I suspect you're wasting your time.'

Nyman took in the family, hemmed in together on the couch: Josh, his mum and dad, his sister – and now he noticed that the other brother, the clean-cut version of Josh, wasn't so clean-cut any more, slumped with his head on his mother's knee.

They all looked shit scared, and Nyman knew that was the absolute worst thing. A situation like this, you had to bluff it out, not betray any sign of weakness.

'I've had enough,' he announced. He made an almighty effort to stand, but the big man pushed him back down. 'I'm not part of whatever—'

'Oh, you're part of it. You *chose* to be part of it.' The big guy waved to a pretty blonde girl who brought her hand out from behind her back. She was holding a gun.

'That from Gary?'

The big man nodded. 'He's dead.'

Nyman put his hands over his face and swallowed back a sob. *Mary*, he thought, instantly forgetting all that crap about showing no weakness.

'Look, please.' From somewhere he'd found a humble tone. 'This lot are nothing to do with me.'

'We know that,' the big man said, and the dykey woman said, 'They're ours, not yours.'

'I dunno what you mean.'

'It's simple,' the big man said. 'Ilsa fed this address to the man in Canterbury who was looking for Josh. We followed him to see what he did with the information, and that led us to you.'

'But. . .' Nyman faltered as it dawned on him that this guy – and all the people with him – were totally unhinged. 'Look, I don't want them. Let me go and you can do what the hell you like.'

'You'd contact the police,' the blonde girl said.

'Me? You gotta be kidding.' *No – crawl to them, remember.* 'I wouldn't, I swear.'

Christ, he hated to hear himself grovelling like this, but knew the stakes had never been higher. Then, out of nowhere, came the most unexpected support: 'Let him go.'

It was Josh. He regarded Nyman with a sad, tender gaze.

'And why should I do that?' the big man asked, curiously.

'Because his wife is dying.'

There were gasps; Nyman couldn't tell exactly who had reacted, because he was staring, dumbfounded, at Josh. 'How d'you know that?'

'Everyone knows,' Josh said. The pity in his voice tore at Nyman's heart, but he already understood far better than this kid that it wasn't going to cut any ice with the bastard standing over him.

Nyman knew exactly how it would play out now, and this was the moment when he had to accept the grim, appalling irony that he would never see his wife again, not because of *her* death – after all these long months of steeling himself to endure and survive that unimaginable loss – but because of his own.

FORTY-SIX

Wendy was astonished that Josh would speak up on Nyman's behalf, but she was also impressed by his courage. Gabriel had been an unnerving enough presence in a busy car park this afternoon; within the confines of the holiday home, he was frankly terrifying. There was a light of pure mania in his eyes, and he radiated a sense of entitlement that was almost regal in its scope.

Judging by the way they hung on his every word, the other four were delighted to play the role of devoted followers. Ilsa and Lara she had seen before, but the two men were unfamiliar. The one who'd captured Evan was referred to as Kyle, while the other was Milo. How Gabriel had managed to recruit what might otherwise have been respectable young people, Wendy had no idea – but she knew well enough that such mysteries occurred from time to time, usually with tragic consequences.

Nyman was ordered to lie face down. He started to obey, only to lash out at Ilsa before hurling himself over the empty sofa. It was futile: Milo, Ilsa and Gabriel were on him at once.

'You'll suffer for this!' Nyman raged as they forced him down on the floor. 'You fucking lunatics, you're gonna pay—'

'Be quiet,' Gabriel snapped. 'No one wants to hear it.'

'Please.' Knowing about Nyman's wife made him seem more human; Wendy felt she had to speak up on his behalf. 'Don't hurt him, please.'

With an irritated flick of his head, Gabriel said, 'Cushion.'

Rob and Josh both inhaled sharply. Wendy didn't understand why, until Ilsa took a cushion from the sofa and tossed it to Milo, who placed it against Nyman's head.

Lara made to pass the gun to Gabriel, but he shook his head. 'You do it.'

The girl reacted with surprise. Wendy pictured her on Thursday – the chatty, scatty blonde, peddling the fake bonhomie that had almost, but not quite, had Wendy fooled.

She was duplicitous, yes, but outright evil?

With an embarrassed little shrug, Lara stepped forward. Her expression was hard to read, but there seemed to be – God forbid – an element of pride.

'Lara, please,' Wendy said again. 'You'll go to prison for the rest of your life.'

Rob added: 'You should shoot *him*, for Christ's sake' – a nod at Gabriel – 'and give yourself a chance.'

Ignoring them, Lara skirted round Kyle, who was kneeling on Nyman's legs. As she crouched down, Nyman gave up his frantic writhing and lay still. Wendy heard a sigh, before he murmured, 'God bless, Mary. We'll be together soon.'

Lara grasped the cushion with her free hand and put the muzzle against it. Wendy felt the breath catch in her lungs. Surely this wasn't going to happen? Surely there were limits here?

The girl pulled the trigger. The noise was deafening, painful. They all cried out.

The body jumped, twitched a few times, and was still.

And Wendy understood. They all understood.

There were no limits.

The next half hour or so were a blur to Rob. It took a minute for his hearing to recover from the gunshot, and while the family held one another during this time, supporting each other as best they could, no one tried to speak.

Georgia moved on to Wendy's lap and buried her head against her mum's neck. Evan stayed on the floor, his hands clamped over his face. Josh sat with his head tipped back, staring up at the ceiling while gripping his mother's hand. Wendy, like Rob, was mostly gazing straight ahead, but without focusing. All of them fighting to deny the evidence of a terrible new reality.

The smell in the room was foul, a metallic stench of raw meat, blood and bodily waste. Immediately after the execution, Lara had turned to Gabriel with the expression of an eager pet, a puppy that's learned to fetch for the first time.

'You did well,' Gabriel told her. Lara had looked ecstatic at this modest praise, though Rob thought he detected subtle currents of envy and resentment from the others.

Gabriel seemed content to leave them alone while he oversaw the removal of Nyman's body. The dead man was dragged out by the ankles, leaving a hideous stain on the carpet, the blood and brain matter still wet and glistening.

Rob was aware of the front door opening and closing; he heard vehicles manoeuvring on the drive. Gabriel's acolytes came and went, but a couple of them were present at all times, and the gun stayed with whoever was posted in the room.

It took Rob a while to appreciate just how deeply shocked they all were. Wendy was right: facing overload, the human brain simply retreats into denial. *We shouldn't just be sitting here*, he thought, *numb to the danger we're in.*

But what can we do?

It was just after ten thirty when Gabriel wandered in, chewing hungrily on a Mars bar. He whispered to Lara, who passed the gun to Kyle on her way out. It was the first time the scruffy young man had held the firearm. He looked smugly pleased, but also slightly disgruntled that it had taken so long to get to his turn. He had a surly, resentful look about him, exactly the attitude that Rob had perceived from a distance on Petersfield common.

'So it's Sunday, then – what this is about?'

The rest of the family jumped when Rob spoke. Kyle seemed about to answer, before deferring to Gabriel, who nodded.

'You killed that man,' Rob continued: 'And after that, you stalked us. Followed us here.' He waited for denials which never came.

In the silence, it was Wendy who hit on the big question: 'But *why*, that's what I can't understand. Why would you do this?'

'Because you helped him,' Gabriel said.

'The man in our garden? We had no choice. Anyone would have—'

'It's for the Leader to decide. Only the Leader.' Kyle's reverential whisper chilled Rob to the core. He used the word *Leader* as though it were a title, a name, as well as a description.

'But it didn't even save him,' Rob said. 'Anyway, you were trying to frame us for the death, weren't you?'

'That was one possibility,' Gabriel agreed, 'until an even better opportunity presented itself.' He smiled. 'This one.'

FORTY-SEVEN

Gabriel surveyed the room, regarding each of them in turn before staring long and hard at one person in particular. Wendy was willing him to shift his gaze.

Not her, please. Do anything to me, but not Georgia.

Rob had picked up on the same vibe, but when he shook his head at Wendy the message was clear: Don't come out and plead on her behalf, because that was what they fed on. Give them a hint of vulnerability and they would deliberately, sadistically exploit it.

Even after Gabriel had confirmed their worst fears – that the string of bizarre incidents this week all sprang from what had happened on Sunday – still it made no sense that they would be targeted simply for offering help to a dying man.

The door opened and Milo came in. Wendy thought she'd seen him walk past the café in Canterbury this morning, and earlier an embarrassed Georgia had described how he had got chatting to her at Heath Pond yesterday afternoon.

'He asked me out, but I said I was going away. He reacted like he already knew, so I thought he might be something to do with Amber and those. . .' She blushed deeply. 'But it was this.'

Now Milo opened his fist and let Gabriel take a pill of some kind. Then he offered one to Kyle, who grinned at Wendy as he swallowed it down.

'A long night ahead,' he said, and asked Gabriel, 'Are we giving them to. . .?'

Gabriel shook his head. 'We'll keep them awake in other ways.'

He was staring at Georgia again. Wendy tensed, preparing to throw herself at his mercy, but Gabriel just muttered something and Milo dug in his pocket and came out with a handful of plastic cable ties.

Evan reacted first: 'You've got a gun. You don't need to tie us up.'

Kyle, who was nearest, immediately lashed out with an open-handed blow to Evan's face. 'Shut up!' he roared. 'You speak *only* when spoken to, understand?'

Bristling a little, Gabriel told Milo: 'Get them all securely tied.'

'*All* of them?' Milo queried, as if that wasn't the original plan.

Gabriel nodded curtly. 'For now.'

Evan and Josh were moved to the opposite sofa and made to sit with their hands tied behind them. Another tie was used to link their restraints, leaving them sitting awkwardly, back to back. Kyle won a laugh from Gabriel with a joke about conjoined twins.

Rob was ordered to stand and place his hands behind his back. He stayed put.

'I want some answers. What are you doing here?'

'You've been warned,' Gabriel murmured. A nod to Milo, who snatched Rob by his hair and pulled him to his feet. Rob swung a clumsy punch but he didn't stand a chance. As his hands were being cuffed, he regarded Wendy with a look of naked shame. Then he was shoved to the floor, and Georgia was hauled from her mother's embrace.

'How long are you intending to keep us like this?' Wendy asked. 'It's nearly eleven o'clock. What if we need the toilet?'

'Piss in your knickers, lady,' Kyle muttered as he leaned towards her. Wendy recoiled at the familiar meaty smell of body odour.

'You!' she said with a gasp. Kyle caught her meaning and blew a sarcastic kiss. This must be the intruder who'd sneaked into the house while Lara kept her distracted out front. And then, for a time, Wendy might even have been alone there with him. . .

It was a horrifying thought – until it occurred to her that if she'd been attacked or even killed on Thursday afternoon, this probably wouldn't be happening now.

The rest of her family would have been spared.

Once all five of them were secure, Gabriel hurried out of the room, followed by Milo and Lara. Only Kyle remained, and Wendy was sure she'd heard a warning from Gabriel on his way out: 'Don't fuck this up.'

With the door firmly shut, Kyle hefted the gun in his hand and regarded it with something like awe. He walked slowly around the room, examining his prisoners, all now securely bound with their arms behind them. Tied together, the twins were struggling to get comfortable on the sofa. Rob, Wendy and Georgia sat on the floor, a few feet apart. Wendy tried wriggling closer to Georgia, but Kyle barked at her to stay put.

'So what happens now?' Rob asked.

Kyle ignored him.

'Okay, blank me, just like you did on Sunday. But I don't see why you can't explain the purpose of all this.'

Rob was avoiding eye contact with Wendy, but she did her best to mouth: 'Don't goad him.'

Then Evan protested: 'We've done nothing to deserve this.'

'Forget it, Ev,' his brother said. 'Anyway, it's clear he's just the monkey.'

Glowering, Kyle sat down by the door and rested the gun in his lap, the barrel pointing in their direction. From upstairs there was a series of heavy thumps and a loud scraping noise, as if furniture was being moved. Rob asked what they were doing, but to no avail.

After a minute or two, Evan said, 'So why follow Gabriel? What do you get out of it?'

Kyle coloured slightly, and aimed his gaze at a point just above their heads.

'It's because they're weak,' Josh said. 'Inadequate personalities.'

'Anyone can see that Gabriel's a dick,' Georgia said, and this, at last, provoked a response.

'He's a visionary,' Kyle insisted. 'It's not for the likes of you to understand. You're worthless.'

'A visionary?' Rob repeated, incredulously. 'Explain that to us. Tell us what you mean.'

'He knows what's coming. The signs are everywhere, but most people are too dumb to see it.' Kyle made a noise in his throat, a little gulp of emotion. 'When the next crash happens, they'll be lambs to the slaughter.'

Rob snorted. 'So where did he find you lot? And how did he persuade you to buy into it?'

'We didn't have to be persuaded. We were proud to be chosen.'

'What Gabriel has done is simple enough,' Josh said, addressing his family as if Kyle wasn't there. 'You gather up a group of needy, pitiful outcasts and give them a sense of belonging. Once they've been suitably brainwashed, they're little more than automatons. Poor Kyle here has all the free will and initiative of a toaster.'

This was Josh at his most annoyingly supercilious, and the intention was clearly to irritate Kyle to the point where he revealed more than he should. A dangerous strategy, in Wendy's view, but for now it seemed to be working.

'There's a firestorm coming,' he told them, his tone deadly serious. 'When the next financial crisis hits, there'll be no government rescue. No banks means no money. No money and society will fall apart. Thanks to Gabriel, a few of us *will* be prepared for that. A chosen few, ready to do whatever it takes to survive.'

He stood up, his limbs jerky and restless, and took a couple of steps towards Josh, waving the gun as if he desperately wanted to use it.

'Because we'll have practised, you see? We alone will be ruthless enough to survive in the chaos.'

'So that's all we are to you, then?' Rob asked. 'A trial run?'

Wendy didn't want to go in this direction, for Georgia's sake, although it seemed ridiculous to worry about shielding the girl from the truth. Right now they had to face up to it.

She said, 'Did you steal a laptop from our house?'

Kyle nodded readily. 'That changed everything. Until then, we were playing a long game. Befriend you, if we could. Scare you. Mess with your heads. But then we learned about this place—'

'How?' Wendy shook her head in dismay. 'The hard drive was wiped.'

Kyle sniggered, and Josh tutted sadly. 'Nothing's ever deleted, Mum.'

'Ilsa recovered the data,' Kyle said. 'She found a document with passwords, including one for Hotmail. We read your emails and found this address.'

Wendy shut her eyes. She recalled sending the details to a builder, a couple of years ago, when they were getting quotes for some maintenance work.

'Let me get this right,' Rob said. 'We were. . . "chosen" for this, just because the guy went to our garden? And you followed him, right? That's why you were watching, out on the common?'

Kyle gave a surly nod, but seemed reluctant to elaborate.

'All we did was call an ambulance—' Wendy began, but Rob spoke over her.

'You didn't send him to us?' He sounded animated, as if seized by an idea.

'No,' Kyle snapped, now looking furious.

'In that case, he must have escaped.'

'You just shut up!' Kyle swung the gun in front of Rob's face, the barrel missing by less than an inch. 'Not another word, or I'll cut you wide open.'

Rob had ducked back to avoid contact, but now he thrust himself forward again, as if daring Kyle to strike.

'Go on, admit it. He escaped – because you screwed up!'

FORTY-EIGHT

Rob had no real idea what it would achieve, riling the man like this, but he couldn't resist. What kept playing on his mind was the image of Kyle last Sunday, observing from a distance, as though the dying man had been sent on a mission to destroy their lives.

Rob recalled that the police had been puzzled by the lack of physical evidence on the common. 'Did you drive him to Petersfield?' he asked now. 'Or are you staying close to our address?'

Kyle sneered. 'You think I'm going to tell you that?'

'Might as well. It's not like we can do anything with the information.'

He pretended to enjoy the young man's discomfort, though inwardly he was sick with tension. If Kyle refused to say, it implied that the family might pose a threat in future, suggesting that their fates weren't sealed. But if he answered these questions, it almost certainly meant they were destined to die here.

Rob could sense that Wendy, for the sake of their children, didn't want him spelling out the hopelessness of their situation. But Rob wasn't willing to believe it was hopeless. That was why he intended to push and probe, to open up as many cracks as he could, and Kyle seemed like one of the weakest members of the group. *The initiative of a toaster*, as Josh had put it.

'You were in Petersfield, then?' he said. Irritated, Kyle turned his back on them for a second as he walked over to the door. Wendy used that moment to shuffle closer to Rob, pressing her foot against his leg. Georgia also moved towards her brothers, all of them seeking the reassurance of physical contact.

Rob went on: 'The funny thing is, I think I nearly reversed into Milo and Lara on Monday morning.' He chuckled. 'If only I'd known, eh? I could have put my foot down.'

Kyle said nothing. He resumed his position by the door, drew up his knees and scowled into the middle distance. After a few more attempts to engage him in conversation, Rob gave up. The family sat in silence, exchanging brave smiles and encouraging nods, but Rob knew these efforts to stay cheerful would falter soon enough. The strain of sitting with their hands tied behind their backs was already painful; eventually it would be unbearable.

Wendy whispered, very quietly, 'Are you all right?'

'Yeah. You?' Both of them watched Kyle for a reaction, but he seemed to have drifted into a reverie of his own.

'Do you think he can hear us?' Wendy was barely mouthing the words, so Rob shook his head.

'I was winding him up for a reason,' he said. 'Looking for an angle.'

She shrugged, as if to say: *I understand, but there isn't an angle.*

Not one that can get us out of here, at least.

Slowly the minutes dragged by, taking them past midnight, and into Sunday. There were more loud noises from upstairs, banging and hammering, and a couple of times Rob thought he might have heard the front door closing. It was an enticing thought, that some of their captors had left the house, but what could they possibly make of that opportunity?

The tragic irony, Rob thought, was that Nyman had turned up here with a gun. Without that, the family might have been able to fight back.

As if by telepathy, Wendy whispered. 'Don't try anything stupid.' Then, apologetically: 'Reckless, I mean.'

'I won't.' He said it to reassure her, though if the chance came to do something – anything – that might get them out of here, Rob thought he would probably take it.

Evan and Josh also began to murmur to each other, both of them focused on supporting Georgia, telling her it was going to be okay. The girl looked grateful but unconvinced; she was far too pragmatic to fall for their attempts.

'At least this isn't anything to do with Burroughs,' Wendy whispered. 'Or Iain Kelly.'

Rob grimly agreed, though the comment reminded him of Jason Dennehy's offer of help. What he wouldn't do to have the big, fearless groundworker here right now – along with a few of his friends.

An hour passed, and Kyle didn't move an inch. At times his eyes were drooping a little. If the young man dozed off, Rob might be able to creep up on him, perhaps kick him hard enough to knock him out. . .

Yeah, right.

Kyle's head dropped, then jerked upright again. He scowled in their direction, waggled the gun in his hand, and settled back.

The second time it happened, Rob made the mistake of shifting position, as if to ready himself, only for Wendy to say: 'I need the toilet.'

Rob shot her a look, cross that she'd ruined his plan, and she whispered, 'It's too dangerous.'

Kyle stifled a yawn. 'You'll have to wait.'

'I need to go, too,' Evan said, and Georgia said, 'And me.'

'Tough.'

'These cuffs are cutting off our circulation,' Rob said. 'Can't we at least stand up and stretch?'

Kyle lifted the gun and shut one eye, taking aim at Rob. 'You will stay where you are.'

'Fine,' said Josh. 'We can stink the place out, but my guess is that Gabriel's likely to make *you* clean it up.'

'Josh,' Evan muttered, naturally more cautious than his brother.

'It's true. I bet Kyle is given all the menial tasks – aren't you?'

Kyle reacted, getting up on his knees. But his head was cocked, and then Rob heard the dull thunk of a car door slamming. A moment later the front door opened and the atmosphere in the house abruptly changed: all kinds of noise and bustle that made it apparent to Rob that their best chance of escape had just slipped away.

Milo came in, followed by Ilsa, Lara and, finally, Gabriel. They were carrying large paper bags. The smell of hot food was over-powering.

'Have you missed us?' Lara asked, giggling at nothing in a way that suggested she was high on something. Rob guessed the pills they'd swallowed earlier were amphetamines, but he wondered what else they might be taking.

'It's quite a night!' Gabriel said, by way of a greeting. 'Bodies to move. A car to hide. And then food – courtesy of the money we liberated from your wallet.'

Rob snorted. 'Happy to treat you. Now why not eat up and go, and we'll say no more about it?'

Gabriel smiled. 'I admire your nerve, Rob, genuinely. But no.' He shook his head, and the smile vanished. 'We're not going anywhere.'

FORTY-NINE

Now, with food to eat, Wendy felt that the tension had abated slightly. At Gabriel's command, their cuffs were removed and they were offered some lukewarm chips and a few limp slices of petrol station pizza. No one felt hungry, but Rob urged them to eat what they could. 'We might not be given anything else.'

It felt glorious to have their arms free, to be able to stretch and twist their aching limbs and then sit together on the sofa. Meanwhile, the five intruders kept their distance, sitting in a semi-circle in front of the door. Gabriel had taken the gun from Kyle and given it to Ilsa, who ate virtually nothing while the others stuffed their faces. For the most part the two groups ignored each other as they ate, but towards the end of the meal, Lara passed them a two-litre bottle of Coke.

'Drink plenty,' Wendy advised, after Georgia took only the tiniest of sips.

'But I need the loo.'

'I know. We'll see—'

'After the meal,' Gabriel interrupted, winking at Georgia.

Wendy was desperate to believe that this new, benign atmosphere was a positive sign – that Gabriel and his followers had come to their senses and were now looking for a way out of the horrific situation they'd created.

But that was ridiculous, an inner voice told her. The family were all witnesses to cold-blooded murder. How could Gabriel possibly leave them alone?

Once the food was consumed they were escorted, one by one, to the toilet on the ground floor. Wendy felt a bloom of hope. There was a small window above the cistern, which she or Georgia might be able to squeeze through.

But Evan went first, and returned with the news that the window had been nailed to the frame. 'Milo waited outside with the gun. He said that if he heard me breaking the glass, he'd shoot through the door.'

Worse still, they were being cuffed once more, their protests ignored. When Georgia was out of the room, Wendy finally gave in to a sense of helplessness. Leaning close to Rob, she said, 'We're not going to get out of here, are we?'

'Yes, we are. Don't think like that.' Rob's voice was tight with determination and anger. 'Any chance I get, I'm going for these bastards.'

Wendy, for once, couldn't admonish him. When it was her turn to be led out, she briefly considered trying to break away, perhaps run upstairs and get out through one of the bedroom windows. But what if they'd secured those, too? Besides, she had Lara holding her by the arm, and Milo following behind with the gun pointing in her direction.

I'm a coward, that's what it is. In the toilet there was a blessed minute of privacy. She hunched over, buried her face in her hands and wept until Milo thumped on the door and shouted at her to hurry.

All this for helping someone. That was what she struggled to come to terms with. She kept picturing the man's terrible wounds – wounds that had been inflicted by a group of young people who'd just casually eaten pizza in her living room. She drew some strength from Rob's defiant attitude, but knew there was a fine line between courage and recklessness – and the latter could get him killed without achieving a thing.

'Now, are we all refreshed and comfortable?' Gabriel asked, when the family were grouped together on the floor.

He had taken one of the sofas, the upholstery groaning beneath him. Milo and Lara were on the other sofa, while Ilsa and Kyle paced each end of the room.

'Let us go now, please.' Wendy decided to make her appeal before Rob could say anything. Fighting back those images of the blood-encrusted body in her garden, the stench of infection and decay: *That can't happen to us, please God don't let it happen. . .*

When no response came, Rob said, 'I'll stay here, if you let the others leave. And then we can come to an arrangement, maybe?'

'Oh?' Gabriel was amused.

'Look, I can lay my hands on a fair bit of cash.'

Wendy tried not to frown: that had to be a lie – unless Rob knew something she didn't.

'Very kind of you,' said Gabriel, with patronising courtesy, 'but this isn't about money.' He gave them another of his bright, messianic smiles, before confirming Wendy's very worst fears. 'You see, we're here to make you suffer.'

Josh spoke up: 'Don't bother trying to reason with them, Dad. This is just another component of the torture.'

'He's right,' Evan said. 'It's like a game to them.'

'You can learn a lot from games.' Gabriel went to add something, only to pause, and raise a fluttery hand to his brow.

It was Kyle who stepped into the breach: 'Challenges, not games. They form an essential part of our preparation. You have to break the boundaries that constrain normal behaviour. Not flinching from cruelty or savagery.'

'Is this more of your post-apocalyptic crap?' Rob asked.

'It isn't crap,' Gabriel said, while gently massaging his forehead. 'It's about competing for scarce resources and *winning* every time. It's about taking what you want, when you want it, with no regard for the needs of others.'

'Sociopath 101,' Josh murmured, but Gabriel refused to take the bait.

'Put it any way you want. Deride it, too, if that makes you feel better.'

Rob said, 'The man on Sunday, did you send him to our house?'

Kyle flinched at the question, just as Rob had hoped, but Gabriel answered candidly: 'No, he escaped from us. It was. . . unfortunate.' A glance at Kyle, who squirmed.

'You killed him, though,' Wendy said.

'How could we? Baz was alive when he got to your garden.'

'He was dying.' Wendy's voice rose with emotion. 'And you inflicted the wounds that led to his death.'

'We tortured him, that's true. But he was nowhere near death when he escaped; otherwise he'd never have got away, would he?'

'So you're saying someone else did it?' Rob asked.

'Why not?'

Rob only grunted, disdainfully, but Wendy said, 'What on earth could he have done to deserve that kind of treatment?'

'Who says human beings have to deserve what happens to them? Ask anyone who ever suffered a flood, an earthquake—'

'Yeah, okay, we get it.' Rob interrupted to spare Wendy, but she wasn't finished yet.

'Who was he?'

'No one. Some homeless guy we picked up one night. Lara pretended to be a volunteer from a hostel. He went like a lamb to the slaughter.'

Wendy swallowed. Rob had the sense that she was tormenting herself, almost, when she asked, 'And how long did you. . .?'

'He was with us about three weeks.' Gabriel let that sink in, then said, 'I doubt if you'll survive for that long, but we'll see.'

He yawned, as if to show how little the statement meant to him, and closed his eyes. For several long seconds, nobody moved or said a word.

Three weeks. Three weeks of unimaginable pain and fear.

Rob glanced at Wendy, and could tell she was thinking the same thing. It was almost two o'clock in the morning, but still only their first night as prisoners. . .

Then Ilsa, the most reticent of the group, cleared her throat and said, 'Leader?'

Gabriel's eyes snapped open and focused on Georgia. A chubby forefinger rose to point. 'Take her upstairs.'

FIFTY

It was what she'd known would happen. What she'd guessed from the start. It was why she'd barely said a word over the past few hours. *Don't be noticed*, that was the first rule – a rule she'd learned when Mark Burroughs had begun to look at her in a way that made her stomach curl.

The same way Gabriel was looking at her now.

After he spoke, there was chaos. Rob and Wendy were shouting and pleading, and then the twins joined in, all four of them trying to wriggle into a circle around her, like bodyguards round a pop star. For just a second Wendy's hands brushed against hers, but with the cuffs it was impossible to get a proper grip.

Milo and Lara pulled Georgia to her feet, lashing out at anyone who got in their way. Josh caught a boot on the side of his face, and Evan was winded from a kick in the stomach.

Georgia felt hot tears on her cheeks but fought back the sobs for fear of making it worse for Mum and Dad. Once out in the hallway she let her body go limp, forcing her captors to bear her weight. Lara grabbed a fistful of her hair. 'Stop pissing about, bitch! Any more of this and I'll cut your nipples off.'

She held up her other hand, showing Georgia the glinting blade of a craft knife. Milo saw it and quickly looked away.

'Come on,' he urged her. 'Don't make it worse than it is.'

'Why?' she shot back. 'You're gonna kill us whatever we do.'

It was Lara who said, 'Yes, we are. And before that, we're going to put you through a living hell.'

Been there, Georgia thought, and tried to look as though she wasn't bothered. But she didn't say a word, because she knew she couldn't sound brave. Not at the moment.

This was going to be far worse than anything Mark Burroughs might have done.

'Where are you taking her?' Wendy asked, as the door shut behind them.

'The bedroom,' Gabriel snapped, with an impatient gesture that meant, *Where else?*

Yes, it was a stupid question. Wendy knew that, but she was only trying to keep Gabriel down here. Nothing terrible would happen to Georgia until Gabriel joined her in the bedroom, that much was clear.

Gabriel was the leader. The alpha male. He would be first.

At the thought of it, Wendy made an involuntary choking noise. Fearing she was about to vomit, she turned away from Rob and dry-heaved.

'You bastard,' Rob growled at Gabriel. 'All that shit about the collapse of society, and really it's just an excuse to rape a child.'

'She's sixteen—'

'Fifteen,' Wendy corrected, but Gabriel was unfazed.

'Fine. In the world that's coming, that'll make her practically middle-aged.'

'Bullshit,' said Rob. 'Why not just have the guts to admit you're a paedophile?'

Gabriel was staring at Rob, his huge body trembling, eyes glittering with rage. Sensing a violent outburst, Wendy cried, 'Please don't do anything to her. Georgia's had a rough start in life.'

'Adopted, isn't she?' Gabriel jeered. 'We guessed from the photos – after years of the twins, this girl suddenly pops into existence.'

Wendy nodded; there was little point in denying it. 'Her birth mother was killed by an abusive partner, a man who also attacked Georgia.'

From Ilsa came a grunt of satisfaction. 'Didn't I tell you?' she said to Gabriel. 'The girl is different to the rest of them.'

'Please just bring her back. She's been through so much trauma—'

'Oh, boo hoo!' Gabriel mimed wiping tears with his fists. 'Don't you get it yet, Wendy? This is about *suffering*. The more you speak up for her, the worse it'll be.'

'Well, I'm warning you,' Rob said quietly. 'You'd better not hurt her.'

Wendy expected the threat to provoke Gabriel, but in that moment his eyes lost focus and he turned away. Kyle gave him a worried glance, then hurried out of the room. Wendy listened hard, hoping against hope that there was a good reason for the distraction – someone at the door; someone who could rescue them – but she heard nothing.

Then Gabriel's body gave a jolt, and he laughed, apparently at nothing, and drawled, 'We're not gonna hurt her, we're gonna fuck her.'

Wendy kept quiet, understanding now that any protest would only fuel his sadism.

'Milo can be next, if he asks nicely. What about you, Ilsa?'

Wendy saw the tall woman give a shrug. 'Perhaps.'

'Yeah, you will.' The door started to open as Gabriel said, 'And Kyle may or may not want to. . .'

'Want to what?' Kyle was holding a mug from the kitchen.

'Screw Georgia.'

Thrown off stride, Kyle nodded far too vigorously. 'Oh, yeah. Yeah, I do.' He handed the mug to Gabriel, along with something in his other hand: pills. 'Thought you might. . .'

'Yeah.' Gabriel gulped down the pills, drained whatever was in the mug, and said, 'Lara will, of course. Lara's hungry for experience.' He was staring at Kyle as he spoke, enjoying his discomfort and confusion.

'How will she. . .?' The young man must have realised how naïve he sounded, and quickly shut up, his face glowing red.

Gabriel let out a booming laugh. 'Do you need me to draw a diagram? No, better still, we'll take some photos.' He turned, leering at Wendy and Rob. 'Put them on Instagram, what do you think? I know how competitive it is at that age, but four or five partners in a night – that should get her noticed by her friends!'

FIFTY-ONE

They took her into the larger of the two bedrooms at the front – the one that Evan used, along with Livvy when she came with them. Georgia was thrown on to the bed, and then understood why they'd chosen this room: it wasn't just the big double bed, but the fact that the mattress sat on a metal frame.

And they'd brought handcuffs – not proper police ones, she didn't think; more like the things you saw on hen parties. They were going to chain her to the bed.

But first Milo took off her clothes, while Lara held the blade against her throat. 'Give me a reason,' she said hungrily, when Georgia tried to move.

Lara could have been so pretty; she had the sort of doll-like features and glowing skin that Georgia had always craved, but up close there was something in her eyes, something so twisted and cruel that made her probably the ugliest person Georgia had ever seen.

They left her underwear on. 'Leave that for Gabriel,' Lara told Milo. It was plain, boring M&S stuff that Georgia, in normal circumstances, would have been embarrassed about. But having Milo see her like this meant nothing compared to how she felt at his betrayal.

Everything about their conversation yesterday had been a lie; just part of a plan to get close to her and her family, and find out more about the holiday.

'All set, then.' Milo shared an uneasy look with Lara, and they stood in awkward silence for a few minutes. Milo went to the window, lifted one of the curtains and stared out at the darkness. 'Middle of nowhere,' he muttered.

'Be glad,' was all Lara said.

In daylight the views from the house were amazing, but at night the darkness was total. It always gave Georgia a delicious thrill that there were no artificial lights to be seen, like going back to a time before electricity: just fires and starlight. *A primitive state of being*, Josh had once called it.

And wasn't that perfect for Georgia the Savage?

Five or six minutes passed, then Lara said, 'Wait here', and stomped out of the room.

Milo stayed at the window. Georgia guessed he didn't have to be worried about having his back to her. She was lying flat, her arms stretched out like two points of a star, chained at the wrists to the top of the bedframe.

'I liked you,' she said – or tried to say. She'd spoken so little this evening that her tongue seemed to have swollen, and couldn't shape the words.

'What?'

'Y-yesterday.' She shivered. 'I was worried, at first, that it was part of a trick being played by those girls in my year. But when you said you weren't anything to do with them. . . I thought you actually fancied me.'

Milo half turned in her direction, then thought better of it. He scratched his head, sending strands of hair pointing in all directions.

'Well, yeah,' he muttered. 'You're not a bad looking girl.'

'So you're happy to let Gabriel have sex with me?' She made sure her gaze was burning into him. He could feel it; she knew that from his body language.

'If that's what he wants.'

She swallowed, said nothing. Milo went on staring into the dark. The way his head was almost touching the glass made it look like he wanted to dive out of the window.

A minute passed. Then another. *Try again*, she urged herself.

'I was gonna text you.'

'Yeah?' he said sadly.

'I wanted to leave it a few days, so you didn't think I was too keen. But I'd hoped we could meet up.'

'Right.' Now he spun and took a few steps towards her, much livelier all of a sudden. He indicated her position on the bed, and actually winked. 'I guess we can have our fun a lot sooner now.'

'What?' She must have shown her revulsion, because he looked pissed off; the sympathy she'd been trying to build melting away.

'The Leader will do as he pleases. But afterwards. . . he's generous, you know?'

'Generous?' Georgia couldn't believe how casually he was talking about it. 'And what if I don't want to be raped?'

'Look, I can't help—'

'Yes, you can. You can let me go.'

'What?'

'Take off the handcuffs. I'll get out through the window.'

'No, Georgia. That's not happening.'

She felt the tears coming and fought them back. 'Tell me why you're doing this.'

Impatiently, he glanced at the door. 'Gabriel's explained it.'

'He didn't make any sense.' In truth she'd been too distracted to listen: all she could think about was the trouble they were in; not *why* they were in it. 'But what did we do?'

'Christ, will you stop asking that? It's a matter of chance, that's all. Random chance.'

'Random. . .?'

'You know what *random* means, don't you? Instead of asking, *Why me?* you should be asking, *Why not me?*'

'Why would I ask that? I'm not fucking stupid.' The anger burst out of her, taking them both by surprise. 'I don't deserve to be treated like this. *No one* does. And you know that, which is why you can't look me in the eye.'

'I prefer to look at your boobs.'

'Ugh, that's lame.' Sensing she had him off balance, she said, 'What's wrong with you, Milo? You and the others, bowing down to Gabriel like you're happy to be his slaves.'

'He's a great man, he really is. I wish you could've. . .' He tailed off, lost in thought for a moment. 'He taught me how to see the world as it really is – as it's going to become, when things fall apart.'

'You can't really believe any of that crap? Huh. Instead of worrying about the end of the world, you ought to be worrying that you're going to jail for the rest of your life.'

'I won't.' He sounded genuinely confident. 'I don't have a criminal record – not a single thing. Once we're done here, we'll burn the place to the ground, getting rid of all the DNA, all the fingerprints – and there's nothing that connects us to any of you. . .'

He regarded her with pity, and there was just a hint of apology in his voice when he said, 'So we *will* get away with this, Georgia. And there's nothing you can do to stop us.'

FIFTY-TWO

There was something wrong with Gabriel, Rob decided – quite apart from the insanity that had driven him to this behaviour in the first place. The room wasn't unduly warm, but he looked pale and clammy, a sheen of sweat on his face.

Kyle and Ilsa kept casting anxious glances in his direction. Gabriel had been sitting, almost trance-like, for several minutes. When Lara returned, she looked puzzled by the fact that he hadn't moved.

'She's ready, Leader.'

'Don't do this,' Wendy pleaded. 'I'm begging you, Gabriel. . .'

Her intervention brought him sluggishly to life. With a malicious smile, he heaved himself off the sofa and padded out of the room. Kyle rubbed his hands together and said, gleefully, 'The real fun begins!'

It was a cheap attempt to provoke them, which they all ignored. Rob shuffled round, turning away from Kyle. Wendy was sitting to his left, and Evan and Josh were more or less directly opposite. Making sure they could see him well enough to lip-read, he whispered, 'Are you two okay?'

Josh wore a customary scowl, while Evan only shrugged. Kyle had wandered over to the doorway and sat on the floor: he seemed to have lost interest in them. Ilsa was closest, but she'd picked up one of their phones – Wendy's, possibly – and was staring at the display. As Rob watched, she suppressed a yawn.

'We all have to stay alert,' he said. 'I know it won't be easy, but one of us might get a chance to fight back. If that happens, we have to be ready—'

'Rob.' Wendy nudged him, but he shook his head.

'Normally I wouldn't want either of you taking big risks,' he told the boys, 'but I've got to be honest. I think we're at the point where we have nothing to lose.'

Georgia froze when she heard Gabriel on the stairs. The slow, deliberate *thud, thud, thud* made her think of fairytales and horror stories. *The monster's coming to get you!*

And that was true, wasn't it?

Lara entered the room first, gesturing at Milo, who quickly hurried out. He had to dodge round Gabriel, who'd stepped over the threshold and then stopped, rocking back and forth like a huge tree on the point of collapse.

Georgia wondered if he was drunk, or high. Earlier they'd been taking pills: speed or something. Maybe it was a bad batch, and he was having a reaction to it.

Lara sat down on the bed and slapped Georgia's stomach, hard enough to make her body convulse. She laughed at the reaction, and gently trailed her fingertips over Georgia's bra.

'I'm going to get you warmed up,' she said, her gaze fixed on Georgia, drinking in the fear. After a few seconds she turned to Gabriel, as if expecting him to react, but his eyes were shut. He was wiping his face with both hands, while breathing in ragged sighs.

One evening last summer Georgia had joined a load of kids in the park and got drunk on a bizarre cocktail of vodka, gin, Pernod and various other spirits that they'd sneaked out of home. It had all tasted foul but she'd swigged down her fair share, not wanting to be the one that couldn't take it. How she had felt the next day was just how Gabriel looked now: like he might pass out at any second. Or throw up.

Passing out would be great news for Georgia, but the idea of him vomiting over her was nearly as bad as the thought of him doing. . . the other stuff.

Her skin crawled as Lara leaned over, licked a path across her cheek and then suddenly nipped at her earlobe. Ignoring the cry of pain, she grabbed Georgia's face and pinched her lips into a pout. She moved in, as if to kiss her, but instead spat on her mouth.

Georgia recoiled, screeching in disgust, and Gabriel said, 'That's enough.'

He advanced, looking a bit healthier. Lara's hand moved down, pushing between Georgia's legs. 'I can make her wet for you.'

'No.'

'But you said—'

'Later.'

Sulking, Lara withdrew her hand and gave Georgia an evil glare. It reminded her of Paige in one of her moods, and that thought gave her strength. Lara wasn't much older than her; just a spoilt, immature little girl.

And totally fake: Georgia watched how Lara made her face go all sweet and girly before turning to Gabriel. Stretching on tiptoe to kiss his cheek, her arms moving round his enormous waist.

'Are you all right, Leader? I'll stay if you want. . .'

He shook his head. There was a moment when Lara might have pushed it, but she spotted something in Gabriel's eyes – Georgia saw it, too – and quickly bowed her head.

'Leave the door,' he said as she made her way out.

'Oh, I will,' Lara said. 'I want to hear her scream.'

Wendy couldn't bring herself to encourage the twins to risk their lives, but neither could she contradict what Rob had said.

All the fears she'd harboured about her inadequacy as a mother seemed to be borne out by her failure to protect Georgia. Sitting here, helpless, while the girl was subjected to rape: she would never forgive herself for that.

But did 'never' have any real meaning, given that she, and Georgia – the whole family – were likely to be dead within a matter of hours or days?

After a few minutes Lara flounced in, followed by a morose-looking Milo. The four disciples eyed one another uneasily, but said nothing.

The door remained open. Wendy realised it was deliberate: either they wanted to hear what was happening, or they wanted the family to hear.

She thought back to Thursday, and how she'd never quite fallen for Lara's act. If only she'd had a better idea then of just how depraved this girl really was. But she shouldn't have been particularly surprised – her career had supplied many examples of the evil that sometimes lurks behind an innocent façade. She'd once been charmed by a meek, softly spoken young man who, it turned out, was systematically torturing his girlfriend with burning cigarette ends.

She wondered what, if anything, had warped Lara's personality. Perhaps, if her life had taken a slightly different path, she might have become a genuine friend and classmate of Evan's, rather than this devious imposter.

That led her to reflect on the criminal enterprise that had brought Nyman to their door. If Josh had been caught and prosecuted, no doubt plenty of people would have mused on the wrong turns in *his* life, that he'd resorted to smuggling tobacco. . .

And throughout these attempts at distraction, it was Georgia's fate that kept tearing at her conscience. *Is she okay? What's he doing to her? Please let her come through this without too much pain, too much trauma.*

Please let her survive.

*

Georgia had to think fast. Physically there was nothing she could do to stop Gabriel raping her. She was handcuffed, helpless; he was twice her size and immensely strong.

If he went ahead and abused her, she knew it would be just the start. After him, the others would follow.

So she had to use her brain. And, strangely, although she was half-naked, chained to the bed and separated from her family, she felt more confident than at any time since Gabriel and his gang had burst in on them. Perhaps being on her own was an advantage, not having to worry if her behaviour matched up to what Rob and Wendy expected of her.

Also, the glimpse she'd had of Lara's childishness, and Gabriel's struggles with his hangover or whatever it was, had made her appreciate that they were human beings, too. As strong as their position was right now, it didn't mean they were unbeatable. They had weaknesses, just like with Mark Burroughs.

Georgia could have been killed that day, but she'd been prepared to do whatever it took – leaping through an upstairs window – to save her life. She had to remember that.

'It's my period,' she said, as Gabriel started to unbuckle his belt.

'Really?'

'Started yesterday. It's *really* not nice.'

Without a word, he shoved his trousers down. His thighs were huge and soft, white as chalk, and almost hairless. He was wearing boxer shorts, and with one hand he rubbed at a distinctly small bulge. He looked pissed off rather than turned on, so maybe her tactics were working.

'And I've got diseases. STIs.'

'Oh?'

'I've shagged loads of boys at school, and never used condoms. Sleep with me and you'll catch something.'

He grunted, sounding bored. Slumping down on the bed, he kept his back to her and rested his left hand on her boobs, pawing at them while his right hand worked inside the boxer shorts.

Georgia held her breath. Her stomach was cramping, and she felt faint with nausea. She knew he didn't believe a word of it, but she wasn't going to give up.

'It'll be so gross, because I smell, too. Didn't have a shower today.'

Ignoring her, he took his hand away and hunched over. The blond hair at the nape of his neck was wet with sweat, and there were patches of it beneath his armpits. He was playing with himself but at the same time growling with frustration.

Finally he stood up, pulled off his shirt and threw it over his shoulder. His chest and belly were as pale and smooth as his legs, his torso the shape of a barrel, quivering as he panted for breath.

Next he dropped the boxer shorts. Naked, he turned towards her, still unable to work up an erection. Georgia tried to imagine Livvy in this situation: what would cool, clever Livvy have to say?

Call that a dick!

No. She'd seen too much of Gabriel's temper, his ego, to risk that kind of taunt.

'Why don't we just pretend it happened?'

He stopped. 'What?'

'It's too soft.'

'You're gonna make it hard.'

'No.'

He took a step closer. Close enough to smell the sour, oniony smell from his groin. She clamped her mouth shut, trying not to gag.

'Put it in.'

'If that goes in my mouth, I'll bite it off.' As if to prove it, she bared her teeth at him.

Gabriel stared at her in disbelief. Most people were terrified of him, she realised. But she didn't seem to be – and he couldn't deal with that.

His hand had stopped working and instead he was cupping himself, as if for protection. His face twisted up and went red; he looked like a gigantic, monstrous baby on the brink of a tantrum. Then he sucked in a breath and let it out in a furious roar, dropping to his knees with an impact that shook the floor; pounding his fists on the carpet as if, with just a fraction less self-control, it would have been Georgia on the receiving end of this violence.

FIFTY-THREE

From the living room, it sounded as though the ceiling had caved in. They heard the colossal crash, along with a bellowing cry of rage that could only have come from Gabriel.

Rob, who'd been steeling himself to cope with his daughter's cries, had no idea what to make of this outburst. Among the followers, there was similar confusion. Ilsa gave a disgusted sigh, while Milo rolled his eyes. Lara had her back to them, hiding her reaction, and Kyle, who'd been ogling her body, turned away to hide a smirk.

'He's a madman, you know that,' Rob said. 'This is your chance to stop him.'

Kyle went to respond but Ilsa snapped, 'Say nothing.'

From upstairs, they heard Gabriel shout, 'Do it!'

'Please,' Wendy groaned. 'We're begging you. Don't let him hurt her.'

'Impossible,' Milo said, and Ilsa added, 'The Leader does what he pleases.'

'Four against one, but you're scared of him,' Evan muttered, and for this he received a vicious, swiping kick from Kyle.

Then came more shouting from overhead. This time it wasn't just Gabriel. The family shared grim smiles at the sound of Georgia's voice; they knew that stroppy tone very well indeed. Rob felt a rush of pride that she was arguing back, though it was tinged with fear that she might push Gabriel too far.

Ilsa murmured to Lara: 'We should get some rest, continue this tomorrow.'

'I'll stop when Gabriel wants to stop,' Lara said coldly. 'If you can't handle it, maybe *you* should get some rest.'

Ilsa looked furious. Conscious of the family listening, she leaned closer and hissed what sounded like: 'This is not going to plan.'

'Don't worry,' Lara gloated. 'She'll be screaming her head off soon enough.'

But instead, there was only an ominous silence. After a couple of minutes, Lara made a huffing sound and marched out. Milo went to follow but Kyle grabbed his arm. 'Let me go with her.'

When they were gone, Rob caught Ilsa's eye and said, 'You're a lot smarter than your friends. I think you could bring this to an end, right now, if you wanted.'

Ilsa met his gaze, her expression merely cool, rather than hostile, and said, 'It is not in my hands.'

For all his size and power, and the way he bossed everyone around, Gabriel had just reacted like a toddler, throwing the toys out of his pram.

Afterwards, he seemed exhausted by it. He sat on the floor beside the bed, took half a dozen deep breaths, and then snarled at her: 'Bitch.'

'Wanker.'

'This is a privilege, to spend time with me.'

'Fuck off, is it? You're a pig.'

Suddenly they were raging at each other, but it was more like an argument between siblings, neither of them moving, neither of them putting their words into action. Georgia had a good excuse – she was tied up – but Gabriel's reluctance was harder to understand.

Except that he looked like shit.

'I hope you've got Ebola,' she taunted. 'You're gonna die with blood coming out of your eyes.'

It all stopped when they heard footsteps on the stairs. Gabriel climbed to his feet, jabbed a finger at her and said, 'You shut up now.'

She wasn't completely sure what he meant by that until Lara entered the room. She examined Georgia carefully, and can't have missed the fact that her underwear was still in place. 'Did you do it?'

He only made a noise – 'Mmm' – that could have meant anything.

'Was she good?'

'Not really.'

Lara pulled a face, like pretend disappointment; Georgia thought she looked secretly pleased. 'Is it my turn now?'

'No. I'm not done with her yet.'

Lara gently pulled Gabriel away from the bed and embraced him, burying her head in his stomach. 'What's wrong, Leader?'

Before he said anything, one of the others came in. It was Kyle, who reminded Georgia of a really snide boy at school – the type that caused trouble but always managed to blame someone else.

'Everything okay?' he asked.

Gabriel seemed to be in a daze, so Lara said, 'We don't need you here.'

Kyle ignored her, coming up to the bed and studying Georgia with a mixture of curiosity and lust.

'If you want the family to suffer, they have to hear her screaming.'

Lara let go of Gabriel, and waited for him to respond. He looked as though he didn't much care any more, but finally nodded.

'I can make her scream,' Lara said. 'It'll be a pleasure.'

From the way Kyle grinned, Georgia could see that he and Lara – even if they didn't like each other much – were a bigger threat to her than Gabriel. The tricks she'd used on him weren't going to work with these two.

But she couldn't make things worse for Mum and Dad, or the twins. That mattered to her more than anything.

Kyle ran his greasy fingers across her stomach. 'How much this hurts depends on you.'

'I won't do it.'

'You will. You'll howl with pain.'

'No – *ahhh*.' She let out a whispered groan as Lara grabbed her hair and pulled so savagely that a clump of it came out at the roots. It was agony. Georgia bit her lip until she realised she was drawing blood, then opened her mouth and gasped for air.

But she hadn't screamed.

Lara wiped the hair from her hands and spat in Georgia's face. Then she raked Georgia's thigh with her fingernails, drawing blood in several places. Across the bed, Kyle made a noise in his throat; hungry, and desperate.

'I want to have her now.'

'No. Gabriel said not yet.' Lara looked to him for confirmation, but Gabriel had wandered towards the doorway, and wasn't listening.

'I can touch her, though.' Without waiting for an answer, Kyle thrust his hand between her legs. Georgia tried to make her muscles go rigid. She couldn't help but express the shock and pain, but kept it to a low-pitched whine that wouldn't travel far.

'*Scream*, you little bitch!' Lara went for Georgia's mouth, just as she'd done earlier, but she wasn't paying enough attention – Georgia whipped her head forward and managed to catch Lara's forefinger between her teeth, biting down hard until she felt solid bone.

Now it was Lara who let out an earsplitting cry, falling back as blood spurted from the wound. Georgia braced herself for retaliation but Lara just ran out of the room, bawling her eyes out.

Pathetic, Georgia thought, then became aware that Kyle was staring at her in horror. She tasted the coppery flavour on her tongue, touched her lips together and realised there was blood all round her mouth.

Georgia the Savage.

After some crashing in the bathroom, Lara returned with her finger wrapped in a tissue. 'Can't find disinfectant,' she said, weeping in a self-pitying way.

'Probably downstairs,' Kyle said.

Cradling her hand, Lara whined, 'She hurt me, Gabriel. We have to make her pay.'

'I know.'

'I want to be the one. When it's time.'

He grunted. 'All right.'

'It was going to be Milo,' Kyle reminded them.

Gabriel shrugged. 'Let's go down, do something else.'

'But what about her punishment?' Lara insisted.

'Yeah, we'll force her to listen instead.'

It took Lara a second to get his meaning. Then her eyes lit up. 'The twins?' she asked excitedly.

Gabriel nodded.

FIFTY-FOUR

Rob could get nothing else out of Ilsa. As they waited to see what would happen next, the boys shifted closer to their mum and dad. Rob murmured something about Georgia's strength, and Wendy knew he was encouraging them all to think positively. But it wasn't enough to drown out the voice in her head, warning her to prepare for the end.

A screech of pain seemed to confirm her worst fears, but even as Wendy reacted she caught a frown from Rob and understood why he looked confused.

'That's not Georgia,' Evan whispered, and Josh said, 'It's the overbred hippy chick.'

Sure enough, Milo muttered something to Ilsa, who merely shrugged, as if nothing more could surprise her tonight. From upstairs there were creaks and thumps, but no other raised voices. They could only wait, and hope; Rob and Josh immobile, Wendy and Evan rocking slightly, unconsciously working some of the tension from their bodies.

Then came a heavy tread on the stairs. Gabriel entered the room, still pale and bleary-eyed but a little more alert than earlier. Lara was with him, red-faced and gripping her forefinger, which was swathed in tissues.

'Where's your medical kit?' she demanded. 'Your *animal* of a daughter bit me.'

Good, Wendy thought. But all she said was, 'Look in the kitchen.'

'You'd better not have hurt her,' Rob said, and Wendy threw in another plea for the girl to be brought back down.

Gabriel shook his head. 'I've not finished with her yet.'

Wendy kept her face impassive, but inside she was rejoicing that he'd confirmed one thing, at least.

She was alive. Whatever else had happened, Georgia was alive.

They heard sounds from the kitchen, and a minute later Kyle came in with a tray of drinks. 'Black coffee,' he told Gabriel. 'This'll help.'

Gabriel drank gratefully, and directed Milo and Ilsa to move the sofas to the far sides of the room, depositing Wendy on one and Rob on the other. Milo had the gun now, and he sat next to Rob. Ilsa stood between Wendy and the twins, who remained on the floor.

Once Lara had returned, her finger crudely bandaged, Gabriel gave the order to proceed. Kyle took out a vicious, narrow-bladed knife and knelt down behind Josh. As he cut the plastic ties, Josh groaned with relief and threw out his arms, causing Kyle to dodge back.

'Stay still,' Gabriel warned, as Kyle moved round and released Evan. But any thoughts of resistance ended when Milo jammed the gun into Rob's side. 'It'll take a fraction of a second to pull the trigger,' Gabriel added. 'Remember that.'

Sighing, Wendy asked, 'What do you want from us now?'

Gabriel glanced at Lara, content for her to reply on his behalf.

'Entertainment,' Lara said, with a gleeful smile. 'Your boys are going to fight.'

What they required was an old-fashioned boxing match. A bare knuckle fight.

The twins were permitted to stand up and restore the circulation to their arms and legs. Gabriel, Lara and Kyle formed a loose perimeter at one end of the room, armed with knives.

'A proper contest,' Gabriel instructed them. 'With real aggression.'

'Impossible,' said Rob. 'They don't hate each other.'

'Neither do most boxers. It's a question of incentives.' Gabriel smiled at the twins. 'To start with, how about. . . the loser gets his arm broken?'

Evan and Josh turned to Rob, plaintively appealing to their dad for answers in a way that neither of them had done for years. It shamed him to the core that he had nothing to offer, no advice to give. Whatever they did, it would mean punishment and pain.

'Do it!' Gabriel snapped.

With weary disdain, Josh removed the rings from his nose and ears and dropped them on the floor. Then he stuck out his chin and said, 'You first.'

'Wait!' Lara cried, and Rob let out a sigh. Had they only been bluffing?

Then she said: 'Take off your shirts.'

Reluctantly, they obeyed. As their audience settled down to watch, Rob felt Milo relax slightly; maybe, if his concentration wavered, Rob might get a chance to disarm him.

Evan finally swung a well-telegraphed punch, which Josh didn't bother to parry. It caught him in the chest and he took a step back, not badly hurt but exaggerating.

'Harder than that.' Gabriel drained his mug of coffee and perched on the sofa, close to Wendy.

Josh went next, a slow one-two to the stomach which Evan instinctively tried to block, responding with a little flurry of his own. Both of them were still flat-footed, breathing normally, and Rob could see it wasn't going to impress Gabriel or Lara.

'It's nearly half three in the morning,' he said. 'Why don't we all just get some sleep?'

For a moment it looked as though Gabriel had some sympathy for the idea. Ilsa certainly did – she was yawning constantly, sipping at her coffee as if it were the only thing keeping her awake – but Lara glared at him. 'They're going to fight.'

'It's okay, Dad,' Evan muttered. He and Josh exchanged a few more blows, and Rob saw the guilt, the silent apologies when one of them caught the other a little too forcefully.

'They're just playing,' Kyle complained, and Gabriel agreed. 'Raise the stakes,' he said.

'We're fighting, aren't we?' Evan paused to rub his sore knuckles. Josh had a faint abrasion on his cheek, and his eyes were watering from a blow to the nose.

'It's not enough.' Lara darted past them, grabbed Wendy around the neck and put the knife to her cheek. Pressing till the skin turned white beneath the blade, she marked a slow trail down to Wendy's jaw, not quite drawing blood but close to it. . . so close.

The twins watched in horror, and Gabriel gave a nod of approval.

'A proper fight,' he said. 'It's either your blood – or hers.'

Now it was Georgia's turn to be eaten up with fear. Instead of celebrating the fact that she'd been left alone, her imagination was tormenting her with all kinds of ideas about what might be happening to her brothers.

Anything suggested by Lara had to be bad. With the exception of Gabriel, maybe, she thought that Lara was probably the nastiest of them – an evil witch, hiding behind the blonde hair and the blue eyes. Georgia hoped the bite wound went septic.

But there were other things to think about. She'd survived Gabriel's first attempt to rape her. Next time she might not be so lucky. And being left alone was really important. It meant she had the best chance of any of them to escape.

'Oh yeah,' she muttered to herself. 'Easy peasy. . .'

She stared at the ceiling and tried to think about it rationally. The handcuffs were too strong to snap or pull apart, and she'd tried yanking her hands out of them and couldn't do it. Was she brave enough to break some bones, if that was the only option?

No. Not yet, anyway.

So, what else? How far could she move? The cuffs fed through the gap between the mattress and the headboard, and were connected to the bedframe. Georgia couldn't move more than a few inches to one side or the other. She couldn't move down the bed, and she couldn't sit up. Hopeless.

Not quite.

'I can go up.' She said it out loud, wanting the idea to sound more positive than it felt inside her head.

Digging her heels into the mattress, she lifted her body and pushed backwards until her head was almost touching the headboard. That was metal, like the frame, but with leather padding on the front. Georgia rested, thinking hard, trying to imagine this was a puzzle. Like something from one of those maths lessons she'd hated so much.

She lifted her head and pushed again until she was beginning to sit up. It was painful, tipping her head forward, but now her arms were bent at the elbows, her hands level with her shoulders, and the handcuff chains were loose enough to allow for some movement.

Ignoring the burning pain in her neck, she wriggled on to her right side so at least she could see what she was doing. The cuff on her left hand was now pulled taut, but it meant she could push her right hand beneath the headboard. By twisting her wrist until it hurt, her fingertips were just able to brush against the frame.

The muscles in her neck and arms were screaming; to ease them she brought her hand up and gripped the bottom of the headboard, taking some of the weight off her upper back. But it wasn't enough: gasping, she withdrew her hand, wriggled down and lay flat, having to accept that it was useless. She was at totally the wrong angle to reach the bedframe – and even if she could get hold of it, what good would that do?

One of her fingers was still throbbing; she looked and saw a trickle of blood. Must have caught it on a rough edge at the back of the headboard. *Great.*

It was a silly, niggling pain. Couldn't clean it or dress it, couldn't do anything about it – and wouldn't it be bloody typical if *she* was the one that got blood poisoning, not Lara?

This worry occupied her for a minute or two, until another thought slowly wormed its way in. Caught it on what?

She took a few deep breaths, lifted and pushed, turned on her side and stuck her hand through the gap. This time the angle of her wrists made it easier to go up rather than down. Cautiously she patted her fingers against the back of the headboard until she found what had cut her finger.

It wasn't a rough edge. It was something on one of the upright metal posts that fixed the headboard to the frame. A screw, by the feel of it, protruding slightly from the post.

The pain in her back was burning again, but she lived with it for a few more seconds. Pressed her fingers against the screw until she could visualise it, then pushed a little more. . .

And it moved.

FIFTY-FIVE

They were hurting one another properly now. The sight of her sons, her beloved boys, pitched against each other took Wendy back to the night of their birth, and the excruciating physical pain which she had borne, quite willingly, on a rush of adrenalin-fuelled desire to bring them into the world quickly, and safely, and well.

After a difficult labour, it had been the most indescribable relief when first Josh and then Evan was parcelled up and placed in her arms, to be held close and loved and protected from that moment on. Seeing them now, and hearing the punches, the grisly wet smack of bone on skin, the groans and gasps – most of all, the sheer horror in their eyes that they had to do this to each other – made it the most sickening thing that Wendy had ever witnessed. The tears streamed from her eyes and she sobbed, hopelessly, and felt every blow as if it were landing on her.

Josh's face was mostly intact, because Evan was concentrating on body punches. Rather than use his left hand as a guard, Josh was cradling his stomach, and from his laboured breathing Wendy thought he might have a couple of cracked ribs. His own blows, while inexpertly thrown, had several times caught Evan in the face. Evan had a bleeding nose as well as dark, swollen bruises around both eye sockets. There were splatters of blood on the carpet where he kept having to spit, and his tongue worried at a loose tooth.

And to know that they were doing this for her, to keep her safe from these knife-wielding sociopaths. . .

Utter barbarity. And then it got worse.

Gabriel and his followers had become increasingly animated, with Milo rueing that they hadn't thought to place bets. There were whoops of admiration when Evan landed a punch to the chest that made Josh stumble, then drop to his knees, and suddenly Lara yelled, 'Get them naked!'

'What?' Gabriel snapped.

'I want to see if it turns them on.' She giggled. 'It turns me on.'

Wendy caught a scathing look from Ilsa, and distaste from Milo and Kyle. But the only reaction that mattered was Gabriel's, and although his chuckle sounded a bit forced, he nodded wearily.

'Go on.'

Evan and Josh were too dazed to offer much protest. Evan slipped off his shorts and Josh struggled to his feet, then slowly unbuttoned his jeans. Wendy looked away. Rob was glaring at Lara as if he could kill her with his bare hands.

Ilsa, who had positioned herself behind Lara, caught Gabriel's eye and slowly shook her head. Without acknowledging her, he barked, 'That's enough.'

'What?' Lara was indignant. 'They're still in their underwear.'

'I don't want to see a lot of dicks swinging round,' Gabriel said, and Milo, with a fake laugh, said, 'Me either!'

Suddenly irritable, Gabriel told him to check on Georgia. 'And make sure you lock her in.'

'Leader—' Lara began as Milo hurried away, but Gabriel cut her off.

'The birds are chirping out there. We're getting some rest.'

Unseen by Lara, Ilsa gave a victorious smile. Wendy filed it away, thinking of that line: *My enemy's enemy. . .*

Lara was still whinging: 'But it's just begun to get interesting.'

'A few hours' sleep and you can do what you like.' Gabriel motioned casually at the twins. 'Get them to fuck each other if you want.'

Lara gaped at him, then clapped her hands and squealed: 'Oh my God, *yes!*'

*

The noise from downstairs was becoming more and more frightening. It sounded like Evan and Josh were being beaten up. Georgia drowned it out by concentrating on the pain in her back and arms, and once that became too much to bear she switched her focus back to the cries from her brothers, and the awful cheering from Gabriel and his followers.

If only she could get free. . .

But she was having no luck. What she'd thought was movement must have been an illusion – her fingers slipping because they were greasy with sweat. She couldn't grip the screw tightly enough to make it turn. She'd even tried wedging it beneath her fingernail, and that hadn't worked.

Eventually she collapsed back, aching and exhausted. She wanted to cry but wouldn't give in to it. Rest, and try again: that was all she could do.

She realised it had gone quiet downstairs. The dread tore at her heart. Were the twins okay? The image of Nyman's body came back to her, the way he had jerked as the gun was fired, his limbs twitching as the life drained from him. . .

She shifted back up the bed, wiped her fingers dry and pushed her hand behind the headboard, only to hear someone coming up the stairs.

Shit.

She scraped her hand again, pulling it back, and realised the sheet was all rucked up where she'd been moving up and down. But there was nothing she could do to hide it: just had to hope they didn't notice.

As the footsteps came closer, she found herself thinking of the past week, all the time and energy she'd wasted, obsessing over Amber and Paige, with never a clue that the real enemies had been edging closer and closer. She pictured Ilsa, in the café, a witness to her humiliation, and then Milo, Milo and his clumsy attempts to hit on her, which Georgia – because she was lonely, and mostly unliked – had wanted so much to believe were genuine. . .

It was Milo who came in now, averting his eyes from her body in a way that he hadn't done before.

'What's happening down there?' she asked. 'What are you doing to them?'

'Your brothers were fighting.'

'What?' That made no sense. 'Fighting each other?'

'Yeah. It took some persuading, but they really went at it.'

'You mean you forced them. . .?' Georgia swallowed. 'Are they all right?'

'I suppose.'

He was so casual, so uncaring, that Georgia longed to punch him in the mouth. But that wasn't the plan. In a gentle voice, she said, 'This isn't you, Milo.'

'Not true.' He didn't sound cross with her; just bored. 'We're turning in for a while. Gonna leave you here, okay?'

'No, it's not okay.' She grinned, to lighten the tone, and rattled the handcuffs. 'It's agony like this. I won't sleep at all.'

'I'm sorry.'

'Couldn't you take one of them off? Just one. It's not like I can get my hand out.' She tugged on the cuffs to prove it. 'And I still can't go anywhere, can I?'

He put his hands on his hips, frowning down at her like a doctor with a difficult patient.

'And there's a key for that door,' she reminded him. 'So you'll lock me in, as well.' She waited out a tense silence, then went for Plan B. 'Let me sleep for a bit, and then you could come back and. . .' She nodded down at her body, prompting Milo to sneak a glance at her boobs. He looked shocked – but tempted.

'I can't. Not till Gabriel. . .'

'He doesn't have to find out, does he? This can be between us.'

Milo turned slowly, examining the room, and Georgia knew she'd won him over.

'All right, I'll free your left hand. But don't try anything stupid. Gabriel thinks up punishments like you wouldn't believe.'

'I won't. It's just to help me sleep.'

He fished out the keys and unlocked the handcuff from her left wrist. The relief was indescribable, but she held back from stretching out or making it too obvious how good it felt. She wanted him to think she was still weak, trapped: the hopeless victim.

'Be back in a few hours,' he said, moving towards the door.

'Wait!' she called. 'There's one more thing.'

He turned, looking sour. 'No.'

'Just a tissue, that's all.' She twitched her nose. 'So I can clean my face.'

Without a word, Milo left the room and returned with a long strip of toilet paper. Perfect. Now she needed him to leave her alone. But after taking a few steps towards the door, he hesitated, turning back.

'You have to understand, it's not personal, any of this. It's just something we have to do.'

'That's not true—'

'No, please,' he interrupted. 'I wanted to let you know, so it won't come as a shock.' Agitated, he pushed a hand through his hair. 'How it ends, I mean.'

Georgia struggled to keep her expression calm. All she could manage was one word, which came out like a cough: 'How?'

'There's five of us, right? And five of you. So, what we – Gabriel – decided is that we'd each take one of you and, you know, finish it. Ilsa wanted you but I said. . .' he cleared his throat. 'I said, I think *I* should do it.'

Georgia nodded. Felt she had to say something, but she couldn't. Her throat had closed up. She ought to be asking *when*. . . but did she really want to know?

'One kill each, you see?' Milo said. And then: 'I can't promise that it won't hurt, but I'll try to make it quick.'

Perverse as it sounded, Rob knew they probably had to feel grateful for the position they were in. It could have been so much worse.

They were all alive, at least, and physically in one piece – though the fear of what might have been done to Georgia continued to plague them all. And now there was to be a temporary respite.

Their wounds went untreated, but Evan and Josh were allowed to dress, at least, and given a little water. They could barely make eye contact with one another, or with their parents. Then all four of them were marched upstairs, docile as sheep as they followed their jailors, the twins wincing with every step. It was only when they had to walk that Rob understood just how exhausted they were, the normal fatigue heightened by hours of emotional stress.

They were placed in Rob and Wendy's room at the back of the house. This was one of two bedrooms that still had working locks. They were warned not to attempt communication with Georgia, or Lara would go to work on the girl with a knife. Despite that threat, Wendy almost succumbed, issuing a tiny cry as they reached the landing.

The bedroom had been cleared of furniture, except for the bed, and the windows had been crudely nailed shut. Rob took this as a sign that their cuffs might be removed, but there was no such luck. The only concession was that their hands were bound from the front rather than the back, but as an extra precaution Kyle used a length of nylon rope to bind their ankles together, leaving them sitting in the shape of a cross, with no more than a few inches' play in the rope around their feet.

'What about Georgia?' Wendy asked. 'Can't she be with us?'

'She's fine where she is.' This was from Gabriel, who filled the doorway, sometimes resting his head against the frame as he watched Kyle at work. The gun was back in his possession, and Rob didn't like the way he kept glancing at it.

Still he persisted: 'Surely it's easier for you if we're all in one place.'

Gabriel stared at him for a long moment, as if unsure how to respond to Rob's insolence. Then he turned and left. The door was shut, and locked, and there was silence.

Rob studied the rope and saw straight away that the knots would be a struggle to reach, let alone untie. He was sitting furthest from the bed, with Evan to his left, Wendy to his right and Josh directly opposite. It was a horrible, forced intimacy, at the end of a night when the twins were clearly desperate for some solitude and privacy in which to work through their shame.

'I just hope she's all right,' Wendy fretted.

'I think she is,' Rob said, uncomfortably aware that he had nothing on which to base that opinion. He'd never felt more impotent or disgusted with himself. Not only had he failed them – as a father, as a husband – but he had deceived them, too.

If he had been honest with Wendy from the start – if he'd owned up to the discovery of the trainer, and brought in the police right away – then perhaps all this would have been avoided. Even before that, it was his fear of a link to Jason Dennehy that had blinded him to the real danger; if only he'd read the signs correctly, and seen the progression of tiny steps that had led them to this terrible predicament. . .

But would Dawn or DS Husein have acted on their concerns, and given them sufficient protection? Rob guessed he would never find out.

'Evan, Josh,' he said quietly. 'What they made you do tonight was inhuman. I'm very, very proud of the way you both handled it.'

'Me too.' Wendy was crying quietly as she nodded her agreement. Evan and Josh looked no less embarrassed, but after a minute Evan forced a reluctant half-smile when his brother quipped: 'A lifetime of expensive counselling ahead, if we make it out of here.'

'We're going to,' Rob said, with all the vehemence he could muster. It was the only way he could make amends – to maintain a positive attitude even when he felt anything but positive – and it meant leaving unspoken what he was really thinking.

What's going to happen to us?

How will it end?

FIFTY-SIX

Kyle snapped awake and was instantly alert. No confusion at all about where he was, or what was happening.

He'd decided to sleep downstairs, away from the others. He was on the floor in a small, fusty room that might once have been a parlour, then a study, and was now a neglected sitting room with a couple of mismatched armchairs and an antique writing desk. He'd found a pillow and a blanket, pulled the cushions off the armchairs and made himself a half-decent bed.

He checked his phone for the time: a little after ten. He'd expected to wake sooner than this, but of course he'd been up till around four a.m. Exhaustion had forced them to call a halt to the night's entertainment, and it explained why the house was still so quiet.

He sat up, feeling achy and yet refreshed, then rested back again. Why not enjoy the downtime while he had the chance? Lie and daydream for a while.

There was a lot to reflect upon, after all. Amazing to think that only a week ago they'd been happy with a single victim, and now they had five. . .

Kyle was twenty-two, and just like the others, he had come to regard the Brood as his only family. His mother and his stepfather had rejected him completely, and he knew he would never see them again. He could still recall every word of the last conversation with his mother, nearly three years ago, her voice dripping with scorn as if she loathed everything about him.

'You were an accident. A mistake. I was nineteen, and you were the result of a. . . well, not a one-night stand, exactly, but not much more than that. I can't remember if they'd had the morning-after pill in those days, but if they did I wish to God I'd known about them. Would have made my life a darn sight easier.'

And mine, Kyle had often thought since.

His early childhood had been chaotic. The few settled spells had been at his grandmother's rural home in Hampshire, but she and his mum would invariably fall out over something, and then Mum would drag him off to some dingy bedsit at the other end of the country, usually chasing jobs, men, or both. Each relocation meant different schools, different faces and fashions, different taunts in different accents – but the humiliation, the pain, hardly varied at all.

Then, when Kyle was nine, his mother was rescued by a wealthy Canadian man a decade her senior. Off they trooped to Forest Hill, an upscale suburb of Toronto, to start anew. Kyle quite liked the city, and the climate – and, of course, the affluence – but in this new home he was only ever tolerated at best. Soon he learned to carve out a life of his own: solitary, silent, invisible.

His mum disgorged three kids in quick succession, and with each one it couldn't have been clearer that Kyle was taking up space better occupied by the *real* family. After a final showdown – when Kyle had perhaps said and done a few things he shouldn't – he had returned to Britain and gone to live with his grandmother while studying for his A levels.

That had worked out okay for a while, but his grandma was already ill by then, grouchy as hell and happy to treat Kyle as her personal slave. Within a few months he'd found a place to crash through some colleagues at the DIY store where he worked part-time. They introduced him to the party scene around Portsmouth, and before long he'd been fired from the job and kicked out of college. He'd bummed around for a while, sofa-surfing and living on his wits, borrowing from his gran when she agreed to it; stealing from her when she didn't. . . and then he met Gabriel at a party.

The Leader was only a budding prophet at that stage, though the messiah complex had been immediately evident. He was already in a loose relationship with Ilsa, the estranged daughter of an Anglo-German actress and a Belgian diplomat. A few months later, Kyle introduced Milo, who he'd known at college, and Milo brought along his friend, confidante and unrequited sex object, Lara. Gabriel wanted Lara from the moment he saw her, and she was dazzled by his interest: it was a fait accompli which both Milo and Ilsa accepted without a word of protest.

And with that, the Brood was complete, though it would be another year or more before they embarked on their present journey. Gabriel's plans only crystallised once they had found a place to live together – and for that they had Kyle to thank. For the past eight months their base had been the remote, rundown bungalow belonging to Kyle's late grandmother. His aunt, who lived in Scotland, had allowed him to stay there rent-free, partly to keep an eye on the place and partly to spite Kyle's mum, who she despised.

Without a doubt, all four of them had been lost – emotionally, spiritually and any other which way – when they became sucked into Gabriel's orbit: all susceptible to a commanding figure who could offer some purpose to their lives.

Kyle had come to regard the Armageddon stuff as Gabriel's schtick, while also recognising that it was entirely plausible. Certainly the man's formula for survival chimed with Kyle's deeply felt antipathy towards the rest of humanity, so he'd willingly gone along with the indoctrination. Who wouldn't want the sense of absolute power that Gabriel could bestow? It still made him hard when he pictured the moment he'd released that paving slab into the path of a speeding car on the M27; harder still when he thought of how he'd sneaked into the Turners' house last Thursday.

Lara had provided the distraction, while his mission had been to hide the dead man's trainer. Finding the laptop had been an amazing thrill, but nothing like the feeling he got from being alone in the house with Wendy: that moment when she'd come upstairs to pack, and he had been hiding in the main bedroom; knowing that if she walked in and saw him, he'd have to *do* something, right there and then. . .

Kill her – or maybe more than that.

He thought about it at length while he masturbated, running through an alternative scenario where Milo hadn't sneaked into the garden and thumped on the terrace door, creating the distraction that enabled Kyle to leave the house without being seen.

He was riding out the vague sense of self-loathing that always followed an orgasm when he heard creaking from the ceiling above. He tracked the tiny sounds along the landing and down the stairs. Someone was taking care not to wake anyone else.

Then a tapping at the door, and the handle turned; Lara's cute little nose poked into the room, her eyes big and frightened: the proverbial rabbit in headlights, except that she was also holding the gun.

'It's Gabriel,' she said, her voice a husky whisper of panic. 'I can't wake him.'

FIFTY-SEVEN

Wendy wrestled her way out of a long, traumatic dream, only for the details to vanish upon waking, leaving her nothing but a feeling of the most profound sorrow.

Then she opened her eyes and understood why.

Is Georgia all right? – that was her first clear thought. *Had they left her alone during the night?*

Somehow the four of them had managed to sleep, lying back with their hands resting in their laps and their feet bound together. The little twitches and kicks from the others had disturbed her sleep and influenced her nightmares: now she recalled how at one point she'd been deep underwater, her legs trapped in a discarded fishing net.

The room was unusually gloomy, even though Wendy had a sense that it was quite late. The birdsong was muted, whereas normally she would wake to hear them in full voice. On a fine day she liked to creep downstairs and step barefoot on to the lawn, the cool grass sparkling with dew beneath the rising sun, the whisper of the sea like a soothing chant. . .

All just a daydream now, a hopeless fantasy.

She wondered why they'd been left undisturbed for so long. Gabriel and his followers were surely running on adrenalin, enhanced by whatever artificial stimulants they were taking. So why weren't they up and about?

Something's happened. Wendy had no idea where the conviction came from, but once lodged in her mind it wouldn't be argued away.

Around her lay the three other points of their awkward, poignant cross. Josh had managed to roll on to his side with his hands tight beneath his chin, just as he used to sleep as a child. Wendy felt a wave of tender concern as she studied the bruises, the dried blood that marked his and Evan's faces.

I want revenge, she thought with uncharacteristic venom. *I want the people who did this to suffer.*

Rob was snoring, but Wendy tuned it out and listened with all her might; after hearing nothing for five, ten minutes, she dared to wonder: had they gone? Was it possible that these monsters had lost their nerve and chosen to sneak away, never to be seen again?

Oh, please.

And then she heard it: a voice from the next room. It was female – Lara, probably. Not words, but a yelp. A cry of alarm.

Something's happened.

Kyle didn't move at first. He wanted to make the most of this opportunity to study her face. Usually Lara hated it when he leered at her, but right now she had other things on her mind.

'What do you mean?' he asked.

'He won't wake up. I've tried listening for his heart but I can't, because of how he is. . .' She choked back a sob. 'I don't think he's breathing.'

Kyle frowned. 'Where's Ilsa?'

'I-I don't know. She might have gone outside.'

His frown deepened. He didn't like it that Ilsa could have moved through the house without him hearing. What was she up to?

'Milo?' he asked.

'I didn't want to wake him yet.' Lara looked embarrassed. 'I thought he might panic.'

Whereas I won't. Kyle swelled a little at that. Even though Lara hated his guts, it was him she'd come to for help.

Following her upstairs was another rare treat. Her bare legs were long and tanned. She wore only a baggy white t-shirt and possibly a thong, possibly not; a tantalising thought that carried him to the landing, where she turned and made a shushing gesture. Milo was curled up on the floor outside Georgia's room, like a faithful family dog.

The bedroom Gabriel had chosen for himself was the daughter's room, judging by the personal effects. The bed was a large single, up against the wall, and Gabriel was lying with his back to them, no more than a beached whale beneath a thin duvet.

That explained her doubts; apologetically, she said, 'I couldn't move him.'

'All right.' First they needed more light. Kyle swept the curtains open and experienced a moment of utter confusion.

The world had vanished.

Then he registered the droplets of water on the glass, the sense of a shifting mass, and realised what it was. A dense sea fog had descended during the night.

'Jeez.' He turned, knelt on the edge of the bed and placed one hand on Gabriel's thigh, another on his spine. The Leader didn't stir.

'Oh my God.' Lara issued a long, quiet moan.

'Gabriel?' Pressing harder now, Kyle half stood, pulling on Gabriel's shoulder until eventually the giant mass moved and he flopped on to his back. Kyle stumbled off the bed but just managed to avoid falling to the floor.

Gabriel's face was visible now. Lara edged closer to Kyle, her body actually nudging against his as she stared, horrified, at what had become of the man she worshipped.

Kyle glanced at the blank sheet of mist beyond the window, and for a moment it was as though they had all been transported – as a consequence of their crimes, perhaps – to a kind of netherworld; a purgatory.

'I don't believe it.' He looked and sounded genuinely stunned. 'This is. . .'

Perfect, he thought, but could not say.

Rob woke to a nightmare, his whole body stiff and aching. His first impulse was to turn and stretch, but neither his arms nor his legs would properly obey. Opening his eyes, he found Wendy regarding him with a sad smile.

'I wish I could say it was a bad dream.'

'Uh?' He lifted his head, winced, and saw the twins were stirring. 'You okay?' he asked Wendy.

'About as well as expected.'

'Any idea if Georgia. . .?'

She shook her head. The anxiety was worn deep into her face. Rob felt his stomach lurch as it hit home all over again: the desperate trouble they were in.

'Do you think we should call out?' he asked, but Wendy gave a start, turning towards the wall. There were voices coming from the next bedroom.

They listened carefully, heard a door open, then creaks on the stairs. Wendy said, 'I think something's gone wrong.'

'What do you mean?'

'Just listen.'

So he did – sceptically at first; but then, as he heard more movement, more hushed voices, he began to think Wendy was right.

Gabriel was stone dead; the dullness of his eyes made that clear. But still Kyle went through the motions of trying to find a pulse, listening for a breath, watching for the telltale rise and fall of his chest.

Nothing, on all scores.

'What do we do?' Lara asked.

Lost in thought, Kyle didn't respond at first. 'I suppose he didn't look well – last night, I mean.'

'He wasn't,' Lara agreed. The tears had started to flow. 'He s-said to leave him but I w-was worried. So I s-slept here. . .' She pointed to a thin, crumpled duvet on the floor, then was overcome, dropping to her knees and sobbing into her hands.

Kyle watched for a moment, before kneeling down and drawing her into an embrace. To his astonishment, Lara didn't resist. Didn't even wrinkle her nose at the smell of him, or flinch as his hands roamed over her back and – very nearly – her tight little butt. He felt himself getting aroused, but knew there were other priorities.

She'd placed the gun on the floor beside her; Kyle could easily have taken it, but didn't want to poison the mood. Gently, he said, 'We need to discuss this. I'll wake Milo. Can you go and look for Ilsa?'

On the landing he paused to listen for any sounds coming from their prisoners. Lara started down the stairs, just as Ilsa strolled into sight from the kitchen.

'Awake at last!' she said, with her usual snooty disapproval. There was a whole hotchpotch of different nationalities in her DNA, but Kyle had only ever thought of her as a Nazi.

'Where were you?' he demanded.

'Taking a walk in the garden.'

Kyle snorted, as if he didn't believe her, then prodded Milo with his foot. 'Come on, sleeping beauty.'

Milo stirred, rubbed his eyes and sat up, then realised that the four of them were clustered on the narrow landing. 'Where's Gabriel?'

This could have been Lara's moment, but her nervous hesitation gave Kyle his chance.

'He's dead.'

FIFTY-EIGHT

Their first reaction, not unnaturally, was disbelief, so Kyle strode into the bedroom and waited as they filed in after him.

'Until we've decided how to play this, we don't want the family knowing.'

It was advice that Ilsa immediately disregarded. 'What has happened to him?' she asked in a strident voice.

'Ssh!' Kyle hissed. 'I have no idea. I was downstairs, asleep.'

'Gabriel wasn't well,' Lara said. 'I offered to stay with him, but the bed isn't. . .' Her voice cracked. 'Wasn't big enough. I slept on the floor.'

'Didn't he. . . I don't know. . . cry out or something?' Milo asked, staring incredulously at the body.

'I didn't hear a thing. I kind of slept really heavily, I suppose.' She looked stricken with guilt. 'This morning, I tried to wake him and. . . and—'

'Came to alert me,' Kyle finished, then turned to Ilsa. 'You were nowhere to be found.'

'I was in the garden.' Ilsa sounded defensive – and they all noticed it.

'So wh-what happened to him?' Milo sniffed; he too had started to cry.

'The likeliest explanation is a heart attack,' Kyle offered. 'He was a big man, carrying all that weight – and under a lot of stress.'

'Oh, God,' Lara cried, and threw herself into Milo's arms.

Kyle frowned at her choice. 'It's very sad, but we have to think about us, and what we do next. . .'

'Oh yes?' Ilsa snorted. 'And who made you the leader?'

'I did,' Kyle said lightly. The other two were blubbing, and probably couldn't care less who led the group, but Ilsa planted her feet in a way that signalled wholehearted opposition.

'I disagree. In Gabriel's absence, I was the one to take charge.'

'Maybe you were. But this time Gabriel's absence is permanent, which changes everything.' Kyle took out his phone and tapped in the passcode. 'And this changes it even more.'

'What are you doing?' Ilsa asked. Milo and Lara caught her tone and broke apart.

'Calling 999.'

'You—' Milo made a clumsy attempt to snatch the phone but Kyle dodged away, laughing.

'That was a *joke*, you moron.' He tapped on the gallery and held the phone out. The other three crowded together to look.

Mouths fell open.

Lara studied the screen and said, 'That's Ilsa. . . and Milo.'

'Correct. But you don't miss out.' Kyle deftly swiped the screen, displaying image after image, and waited for the truth to hit home.

Milo looked as though he'd been punched in the stomach. 'You took photographs of us with Baz?'

'Lots of them. Hidden cameras are exceptionally good value nowadays.' Kyle chuckled. 'Oh, and the originals are stored elsewhere, so doing away with my phone – or with me – isn't going to help you at all. Just in case that was on your mind.'

'You traitorous little worm,' Milo growled, his grief apparently forgotten.

'Dirty, *pervy* sneak—' Lara added, but Kyle raised a hand.

'Save it. We have things to discuss.'

'Like the terms of your blackmail?' Ilsa's gaze shifted to something Lara was trying to show her.

'Not really,' Kyle said. 'This is more about *my* protection, given that I'm outnumbered. I have no intention of using these pictures – in fact, *I'*m in some of them. I did this to bind us together, so that we all understand what's at stake, and no one gets any ideas about going it alone.'

At this he eyed Ilsa. He'd anticipated that she would have the greatest difficulty in accepting his authority, in part because he'd so skilfully played the role of weakling and loser for so long. And if he hadn't been certain that she'd detested him before this, he was left in no doubt about it now.

'What do you want?' she asked, after exchanging another sly glance with Lara.

'A discussion. Let's face it, the Brood is finished. What we have to decide on now is an exit strategy.'

'And you have something to propose?'

Kyle nodded. 'The family must die, there's no doubt about that. But forget all the ritual crap. We have a gun – and when the time comes, we use it.' He mimed the act of shooting at close range. 'Five bullets. Four executions. . .'

'Four?' Ilsa frowned.

'And one suicide.'

One kill each.

The phrase Milo had used played in her mind almost constantly – that and his apologetic offer to make it quick, if he could. As if that was any consolation.

Georgia knew she must have slept a little, but it hadn't really felt like it. Trying to remove the screw was unbearably painful. Her wrist burned from the way she was stretching against the cuff. Her fingers throbbed as badly as when she'd once caught them in a cupboard door; all the skin had been rubbed from the pads during the hours she'd spent trying to grip the screw tightly enough to turn it.

But it was nearly there; another half turn, perhaps two, and it would be loose enough to remove easily. . .

In between work on the screw, she'd rested, and tried to stretch and move around as much as the handcuff allowed. She'd lost all track of time, but thought it was around seven or eight in the morning when the need to pee became unbearable. To avoid wetting the bed, she managed to twist her body far enough to urinate on the floor, and afterwards wiped herself with a corner of the sheet. She felt horribly ashamed of herself, and the smell was rank, but this was still better than lying in a pool of it.

Working on the screw was so hard, but so boring, that she managed to tune it out and let her mind drift off. She fantasised about nice things – her own bed at home, a big roast dinner, playing on her *Sims* games – while trying to block out a regular pulse of fear.

One kill each. One kill each.

The toilet paper she'd got from Milo had helped to create a drier, firmer grip, but it had quickly shredded, the fragments dissolved by her sweat. That didn't matter so much now; neither did the pain, because she could feel she was getting somewhere.

She was close, but was she close enough? For hours it had been silent, but now she could hear movement in the house.

Time was running out.

'Georgia?' Unusually, it was Milo who got it first.

Kyle nodded. 'Adopted kid, troubled past – she goes crazy and kills the family, then takes her own life.'

Lara looked sceptical. 'What about the gun?'

'Belonged to Dad. Not impossible.'

Ilsa had a wry smile. 'And the fire, to remove our DNA?'

'That still happens. Before she tops herself, she sets the house alight.'

Milo shrugged, and so did Lara; even Ilsa looked to be warming to the idea. She leaned over and murmured to Lara, before addressing Kyle: 'What does this mean, "When the time comes"?'

'There's also the question of our future. I'm certain that Rob's got a stash of money hidden from the taxman.'

'But you didn't find it when you searched the house.'

'There wasn't time then.' Kyle glowered at her. 'Anyway, we get hold of that, share it between us and then we're free to move on with our lives.'

'What reason does he have to tell us where it's hidden?' Lara asked, and Milo winced.

'That's a good point. They know they're not getting out of here alive.'

Kyle said, 'Trust me, I reckon I can convince him to co-operate.'

Nodding thoughtfully, Ilsa said, 'Perhaps we will go with your ideas, Kyle, but this does not mean you have the same authority as Gabriel.' As she spoke, she was reaching behind Milo, taking something from Lara. 'You are not the true leader, and never will be.'

Kyle humbly bowed his head. 'That's understood.'

'I hope so. If you are tempted to deceive us, please remember that we have this. . .'

Both she and Lara were smiling triumphantly as Ilsa brought the gun into view. Kyle slumped his shoulders, as if conceding defeat, only to thrust his hand into his pocket and bring it back out in a fist.

'Nice try.' He opened his fingers and let them see the cartridges. 'No good without ammo, I'm afraid.'

Ilsa went pale, her grand revolution snuffed out at birth. Milo gazed dumbly at Kyle, as if he'd witnessed magic, and said, 'You emptied the magazine?'

Kyle nodded. 'Last night, when it was my turn to guard the family.' He stepped forward and casually took the gun from Ilsa. 'Best if I take it, don't you think?'

That was the moment of capitulation. While he had their full attention, he held up a hand. 'Now, let's spare a moment for the elephant in the room. . .'

He thought it a clever pun but Lara, when she realised what he meant, burst into tears again. Ilsa, though, seemed willing to take a pragmatic view.

'We have to do something with Gabriel,' she said.

'Exactly. A burial at sea would be the best option.'

Milo snapped his fingers. 'Yes!' he said excitedly. 'I think they've got a boat.'

'It'll have to wait until dark,' Kyle said. 'We'll dispose of Gabriel, then back here to deal with the family. Agreed?'

With his plan grudgingly approved, Kyle concluded the meeting. Ilsa opened the door, ushered the other two out of the room, then barred his path.

'I am suspicious about your reaction to Gabriel's death,' she told him. 'For the rest of us, the pain is clear to see. But you. . . there is no grief. No shock.'

Kyle knew exactly what she was implying, and of course Ilsa knew that he knew. So he settled on a sombre, dignified expression, and said, 'Gabriel's ethos was all about adapting to change, quickly and ruthlessly. I guess I just learned that lesson better than you did.'

FIFTY-NINE

Wendy strained to hear the discussion on the other side of the wall. Rob and the twins were listening equally hard, and every now and then someone whispered a stray word or phrase that they claimed to have picked out, but for the most part it was guesswork.

What did come through, however, was the *tone* of the conversation. Their captors were very concerned about something – panicked, almost.

'Perhaps someone's come to the door,' Evan suggested, but his brother dismissed that idea.

'We'd have heard it. The locals knock loudly – and they all have dogs. A whiff of the blood and fear in this house and they'd. . .' He didn't bother to complete the sentence, but a shake of the head conveyed his meaning.

Both he and Evan had suffered a terrible ordeal last night; today their faces were an unsightly patchwork of abrasions and yellow and purple bruises. One of Evan's eyes was half-closed, the flesh around the socket inflated to the size of an apple. Both winced and groaned with every movement, but at least the pall of shame seemed to have cleared. Perhaps it was the fact that they had all survived the night—

They had all survived. . . Wendy felt guilty even for thinking in such terms, because it wasn't true – it could not be considered true – until she knew that Georgia was safe.

There was a sudden flurry of movement on the landing. The door opened and Kyle walked in. He was still grimy, and he stank of body odour, but there was a change in his bearing. A little more upright; strutting, almost, while behind him Lara and Ilsa sidled up like reluctant handmaidens.

'Where's Georgia? Is she all right? Can we see her, please?' The questions spilled out, but Kyle ignored them. After examining their bonds, he stepped aside for Ilsa to get past. She was holding a knife.

'We want to see our daughter,' Rob insisted.

'You don't get to make demands.' Kyle delved into the pocket of his shorts and brought out the gun. He kept it trained on them as Ilsa cut the rope from their feet and ordered Rob to stand up.

'What's happening?' Wendy asked in alarm. 'Where are you taking him?'

'It's okay,' Rob told her, but he couldn't quite keep the uncertainty from his voice.

They were about to lead him out when a question from Josh stopped them in their tracks. 'Where's Gabriel?'

Lara let out a sudden sob. Her eyes, Wendy noticed now, were red-rimmed and raw with pain. Wendy had thought last night that the enormity of what they were doing was starting to affect them, but now she wondered if it was something more.

Kyle gave Lara a furious look, then roughly propelled Rob through the doorway. While they were preoccupied, Wendy saw her chance and yelled out: 'Georgia, darling, are you okay?'

'*Mum!*' The answering scream set her heart racing, and for a moment the relief was enough to eclipse the fear that she might never see her husband again.

The activity in the house was increasing; more voices, talking in angry whispers. Georgia tried not to think about what might be going on, just hoped her family were okay. She wondered if they were being kept together, or separate like she was.

A sudden shout from Wendy gave her a jolt: 'Georgia, darling, are you okay?'

'*Mum!*' The cry took so much out of her that she couldn't manage another word. Then a door slammed, and there were heavy thuds along the hall and on the stairs.

I've failed, Georgia thought. *Time's run out.*

But still no one came in. Frantic now, she got back to work, pressing the head of the screw deep into the flesh of her thumb and forefinger, pushing and turning, the tendons in her wrist grinding against the handcuff, a burning agony she could only endure for two, three, four seconds—

And the screw came loose. She felt the difference at once, easily rolling it out. She'd done it! She'd only bloody done it!

As the screw came away, the key rattled in the door. Flinching, Georgia's hand jerked open and lost the screw: she felt it bump against her wrist and pictured it, as if in slow motion, lazily turning end over end; in a mad panic she clawed and snatched and by some miracle managed to catch it in mid-air, yanking her hand out from behind the headboard with the screw clamped in her fist just as the door opened. . .

Milo shuffled in and stopped abruptly, as if he'd sensed the echoes of her movement. Georgia stared straight at him, needing to hold eye contact while she subtly wriggled into a more natural position. But she couldn't relax her body too much, or it would make the clenched fist more obvious.

'What are you doing?' His voice sounded weak, nervous, which made it easier for her to grin at him.

'What's it look like, Einstein? I'm chained to the bed. And I had to pee on the floor.'

She said this to shock him, and it seemed to work. He recoiled, wrinkling his nose at the smell. 'Why didn't you call?'

'It was hurting so much, I just had to let go.' She couldn't tell him the truth: *I don't want you or anyone else coming near me.*

'But I was right outside,' he grumbled.

'I didn't know that, did I?'

'I hope you got some sleep?' he asked, with what sounded like genuine concern.

'A bit.' Stupidly she tugged on the handcuff as she spoke; his gaze moved that way and stayed there.

He was staring right at her fist.

Panic made her cheeky: 'So am I getting some breakfast, then? Cranberry juice and toast, please. Marmite or just butter will be fine.'

At first Milo looked more amused than angry. No, scrub that – his smile had a sadness to it that made her guts shrivel like burning paper. *Was this it?* she wondered. Was he coming for the reward she'd promised him last night?

But then he said, 'You own a boat, yes?'

'It's not ours. It's for anyone who stays here.'

'Where is it moored?'

She shrugged, playing dumb.

'You don't know?' A nastier look came into his eyes. 'Don't play games, Georg—'

'I know where it is, but there's no, like, address or anything. It's on one of the inlets. I could take you there?' she added, innocently.

'You might have to,' he said, just as the door banged open and Ilsa came in, looking furious.

'What are you doing, Milo?'

'Nothing!' He squirmed, as if he'd been caught naked. 'Why?'

Ilsa's gaze swept across the bed, but if she noticed Georgia had only the one handcuff, she didn't say anything. 'Leave her,' she ordered. 'We don't need her yet.'

*

Rob's legs nearly buckled as he was taken from the room. He told himself it was a result of the hours he'd spent on the floor, not because of the fear that he was being led to his death.

He couldn't bear the idea that he might die without knowing his family were safe. His failure to protect them was far more painful than the prospect of his own death.

He didn't go far: just across the landing to the bathroom. Lara and Ilsa saw him into the room, then moved on towards the stairs. Kyle ordered him to sit on the floor, next to the bath. He shut the door and rested against it, holding the gun at his side. He looked calm enough, but there had been an unmistakable tension between him and his fellow disciples.

If there was some sort of power struggle underway, Rob had to try and use it to his advantage.

'I'm here to discuss the terms of your release,' Kyle said. 'Of course, it will come at a cost.'

'You want money?' Rob snorted, unsure if he believed it. 'How much?'

'I'm glad you haven't denied that little nest egg – or, rather, not so little.' He smirked at Rob's confusion. 'We all know how tradesmen operate. And I've seen inside your house, remember? There's a safe, filled with cash.'

'No, there isn't—'

'If you lie to me, Rob, you can go back and sweat for a while, and I'll have some fun and games with Georgia. Or maybe we'll go with Lara's idea, of getting Evan and Josh to fu—'

'No, all right.' Rob breathed out slowly. 'I do have a safe. There's a couple of grand in cash, along with our passports, birth certificates, but that's it.'

'Do you take me for a fool, Robert? A business like yours – the turnover's got to be, what, in the millions?'

'Nowhere near. Anyway, turnover isn't profit – there's the overheads, wages and vehicles, the cost of renting an office—'

'That's crap. You're a wealthy man. You'll have tens of thousands salted away, and probably other valuables – gold, for instance.'

'I wish!' Rob said sarcastically. 'The last thing I want is the Revenue breathing down my neck, so I pay my VAT, and I pay my tax. Christ, the business nearly went under a few years ago. First the banking crash, and then my partner robbed me. Iain Kelly, heard of him?'

'Why would I?'

Rob held his gaze. 'You tell me.'

Kyle shook his head. The gun came up. 'What's the combination?'

'Let my wife and children go, and I'll gladly give it to you.'

'Be serious here, Robert.'

'I am. Let them go and you can have what's in the safe. But if I just hand it over, you're gonna kill me.' He sat up straight, projecting a confidence he didn't feel. 'So fuck off, Kyle – you're not getting it.'

'No?' Kyle tutted. 'Looks like poor Georgia's in for a busy day.'

'And is Gabriel happy with that?' Rob made a show of cocking his head to listen. 'Why isn't he the one talking to me?'

'He's downstairs.' Kyle's face had flushed; he was rattled.

'I don't think so, matey. There's no disguising a guy of his size walking round an old house. He was next door to us during the night, and I think he's still in there – the room where you were all whispering earlier.'

Kyle took a step towards him, thought better of it and kicked at the bath panel, hard enough to split the plastic. 'For fuck's sake!' he yelled, then, through gritted teeth, he hissed: 'Can't you see that I'm on your side here?'

'Bullshit.'

'It's true.' He gestured wildly at the floor. 'You have to give me something to take back to them, otherwise it'll be so much worse for you.'

'Bollocks. Do you think I was born yesterday?'

'Do you think *I* was?' Something changed in Kyle as he snapped the question back; a smug air of superiority. 'You don't recognise me, do you?'

'What?' Rob was thrown by the question. 'Before last Sunday, I'd never set eyes on you in my life.'

'True. You hadn't.' Kyle slowly brought the gun up and took aim at Rob's head. 'Get in the bath. If you won't co-operate, we might as well finish this now.'

SIXTY

Wendy faintly heard shouting – from both Kyle and Rob – but the impression she had was of a heated argument, rather than a physical battle. For that reason she offered encouraging smiles to Evan and Josh, who had dropped the pretence that they were brave, mature adults and were instead appealing to her for comfort in a way that they hadn't done since childhood.

After their father had been taken out, Evan groaned, 'This is my fault. If I hadn't been playing music in the garden, that guy might not have come our way.'

'You can't look at it like that,' Wendy said. 'No one has to answer for these actions except the people directly responsible – Gabriel and his horrible little tribe.'

'I thought the mess *I* landed us in was bad enough,' Josh said ruefully.

Evan grunted. 'Except they probably got that gun from Nyman.'

Wendy could have reminded them that lots of innocent people become the victims of horrific crimes – a man glassed while drinking in a busy pub; a woman struck with a hammer as she hurries home on a winter's night; a child snatched from her bike by a predator in the playground. Such tragedies were both the stuff of our worst nightmares as well as the staple of our everyday headlines. If we get unlucky, we get unlucky: it was a pointless waste of energy to debate the unfairness of it.

But before she could say so, the door opened and Rob stumbled into the room, white-faced and trembling with shock. Behind him, Kyle stood in the doorway, gun in hand.

'One hour to decide,' he said.

*

Kyle wasn't proud of what he'd just done, and knew he'd probably made it harder to win the man's trust. But his overreaction had been provoked by Rob's own attitude: the man was a blinkered, boorish oaf, obstinate to the point of insanity. No one could have been more reasonable than Kyle was in there, and yet Rob had refused to acknowledge it.

'Well, fuck him,' Kyle muttered under his breath. 'Fuck them all.'

The problem was that they still didn't realise what he was capable of. *Maybe it's time to enlighten them*, he thought.

Baz's death, for example. Kyle had rightly been blamed for the escape, since he'd been left to guard the man while the others were out. It had caused panic among the Brood, because of the possibility that Baz had lived long enough to reveal their location. Kyle had served up a blend of truth, lies and pure fantasy to explain how their prisoner had made it to Petersfield, only to die shortly afterwards, apparently without saying a word.

In fact, Kyle had cloaked the man's head before driving him there, ensuring that Baz still had no idea where he'd been held over the past few weeks. After kicking him half to death, Kyle had propelled him across the field at the back of the Turners' property, laying the ground for the selection of their next victims.

The whole operation had been carried off with consummate skill, and yet Kyle, to the others, was an object of derision and contempt. They all believed they were superior to him, when in truth they weren't fit to lick his boots.

Touching the gun in his pocket for reassurance, he descended the stairs and crept towards the kitchen. He could smell sausages on the grill: even now they were more interested in filling their bellies than saving their lives.

As he reached the doorway he caught Milo saying, '. . . don't see we have any choice', and Lara added, 'He's got the gun. With that and the blackmail. . .'

Stepping into view, Kyle said, 'It's a strong position, you're right.'

They didn't even have the good sense to look guilty. Ilsa turned on him, asking bluntly, 'What do you have?'

'He's admitted to the safe. He hasn't yet told me how much cash it holds, or what else is in there. I've laid it out for him, what's going to happen to Georgia if he doesn't come up with the goods. He's got an hour to think about it.'

Ilsa wasn't impressed. 'You have nothing of value, then?'

'I have plenty,' Kyle snapped. He headed to the back door, suddenly desperate for fresh air. 'Oh, and I want them brought down to the lounge, where we can keep an eye on them.'

'Georgia as well?' This was from Milo, who seemed to blush a little.

'What's the matter – haven't got your rocks off yet?' Kyle sniggered. 'No, leave her there. Never know when we might want some playtime.'

And with that he left them to it, thanking his excellent judgment that he'd rendered the gun harmless until it was back in his possession. What a perfect twist of fate it had been, that this man Nyman had turned up with such a weapon. Kyle had thought the material on the phone would be sufficient to maintain control, but clearly that had been overly optimistic. A gun was so much better.

A gun solved all his problems.

Rob felt embarrassed by Wendy's concern. It meant that he had revealed too much of the pain he was feeling.

After ordering him to crouch face down in the bath, Kyle had placed a towel over his head and pressed the gun against it. Then he started to count down from five.

A mock execution. In hindsight it was a crude, predictable way of scaring him, but by God it was effective. Even though it had lasted only ten, fifteen seconds, it was an experience Rob was never likely to forget. He had believed utterly that he was about to die.

Afterwards, Kyle had thrown back his head and laughed, then insisted that it had only ever been a joke. 'You have an hour. I want to know how much you can offer in cash, jewellery and other valuables.'

'But I've told you—'

'You're lying.' Kyle refused to discuss it, and Rob was frankly so relieved to be alive that he didn't protest any further.

Within minutes of returning to the bedroom, Ilsa came in, along with Milo and Lara, all three of them stony-faced and uncommunicative. The family were allowed to use the toilet, before being moved back downstairs.

'Some painkillers would be nice,' Evan had muttered, and Josh said, 'I'd settle for black coffee.'

No luck there, but once in the living room they were each given a couple of mouthfuls of water from a plastic bottle. The cuffs stayed on their hands, but being bound at the front wasn't nearly as uncomfortable.

Wendy pleaded with them to bring Georgia down, to no avail. Once they were settled on the floor between the sofas, Ilsa took herself off, leaving Milo and Lara to watch them from the far end of the room.

Now at least Rob had a chance to talk quietly to Wendy. He relayed his conversation with Kyle, omitting only the details of the mock execution, as well as that odd comment: *You don't recognise me, do you?* That was something he needed to mull over before he mentioned it to anyone.

'I asked about Gabriel. Kyle tried to claim he was downstairs, but he got really uptight when I challenged him. I wonder if there's been a coup or something.'

'Coup?' Evan asked.

'A change of management,' Josh explained, 'possibly against his will.'

Wendy said, 'Or perhaps he ran off in the night and left them to it?'

Rob shrugged. 'Either way, Gabriel was the lynchpin here, so his absence is going to make a big difference.'

Josh agreed. 'If nothing else, it's now five of us against four of them.'

'Exactly.' Rob glanced at Wendy and knew she was thinking about Georgia. At least the scream this morning had proved their daughter was alive; beyond that, they knew nothing about her condition. 'It could make things more volatile, but it might also give us an opportunity.'

When Milo wandered over to check on them, it occurred to Rob that whoever was on guard duty usually had the gun, but there was no sign of it. If Kyle was keeping it to himself, that too suggested a shift in the balance of power.

His thoughts drifted back to that question. Should he know Kyle from somewhere? Was there a link to Iain Kelly, after all – or was the connection with Jason Dennehy?

Of course, it might be that Kyle had said it precisely to add to his torment. And hadn't Rob – hadn't they all – spent enough time chasing their worries in pointless circles? The same questions, over and over again.

What's going to happen to us?

How will it end?

SIXTY-ONE

The garden was lost in the fog, and morbidly still. No birdsong, no traffic, just the constant trickle of water. The air was warm but with a chilly edge; Kyle could taste the moisture with every breath.

The light had a soft ivory sheen to it, as though the sun might have broken through the clouds, far above them. But he could barely make out the boundaries of the property; just vague shadows and shapes that resembled trees and hedges. It was now almost one in the afternoon. If the fog was going to lift, it probably would have done so by now.

That might count in their favour. There were unlikely to be many people on the coast or out at sea in this weather. Kyle was eager to dump Gabriel's body, and entertained fantasies about watching the rest of the Brood follow their leader over the side.

Couldn't do that until the Turners had been dealt with, one way or the other.

That was where Gabriel had got it wrong, he thought. People had been predicting the end of the world for millennia. Every generation felt that *they* happened to live in the most dangerous era in human history; and yet, day after day, year after year, the world kept turning. Societies wobbled and shook, but stayed intact – so why wait for the end times to pursue a ruthlessly selfish agenda?

Kyle preferred to put the skills he'd learned to good use right now, and he liked to think that Gabriel would be proud, in a way, of what he had already achieved. The pupil learns from the master, and one day surpasses him. It was a time-honoured story and yet Gabriel, for all his great power and insight, hadn't appeared to see it coming.

He ran a hand through his hair and it came away damp. He imagined the scruffy curls laden with droplets, like dewy grass. It was wonderful to think that soon he could clean himself properly for the first time in years. He'd deliberately neglected his personal hygiene as a way of lowering his status, because people who smell aren't perceived as a threat. They're assumed to be stupid, ignorant, lazy.

Kyle had spent a lot of time weighing up his fellow disciples, mulling over their strengths and weaknesses. Ilsa remained the greatest threat, though she at least should be astute enough to appreciate that he held all the cards. She'd joined the Brood with a track record of political activism, having dabbled with the anarchist movement after years of involvement with a group of animal rights protestors, and often hinted at the serious crimes she'd committed.

Compared to her, the other two were soft and stupid. Milo's background was similar to Gabriel's: a privileged upbringing in the Surrey commuter belt, an overbearing father and a record of disruptive behaviour that saw him expelled from several private schools. Lara was the troubled daughter of a wannabe actress and *It* girl, her father a music business executive with illegitimate offspring in every corner of the world. She'd made some money as a child model, only to develop a crippling cocaine habit by the age of fourteen. In one of Gabriel's interminable group meetings, she'd admitted to losing her virginity at eleven – and claimed to have loved the experience. *What more did you need to know?* he thought.

But when they understood the full extent to which Kyle had deceived them, they would be baying for his blood. By then, he hoped, it would be too late for them.

As for the family, well, Rob had one more chance.

If he didn't take it, Kyle thought sadly, then everyone inside the house would have to die.

Georgia couldn't believe her luck when Milo scurried out after Ilsa, locking the door behind him. Not only had he left her alone, but he hadn't noticed she was hiding something.

There seemed to be a different vibe today; both Milo and Ilsa had looked jumpy, on edge. It got her wondering what had happened during the night, but she quickly shut those thoughts down. Didn't want to go there.

Once the house had gone quiet, she transferred the screw to her left hand and turned on to her stomach, putting up with the pain in her wrist while she examined the handcuffs. They looked quite cheaply made, in which case the lock shouldn't be too complicated, should it?

The screw was about two inches long and quite thin – she thought it would fit into the lock, and it did. *Result*.

Georgia watched a lot of TV; in her favourite crime dramas the hero only had to jiggle around with a bit of metal, and a couple of seconds later the lock would pop open.

Not in real life, of course, and it didn't help that the best position to work on it meant a lot of pressure on her right arm and wrist, a lot of pain. After a few tries, with little breaks to rest, she realised that she had to do it ultra slowly, really *feel* the inside of the lock, mapping it out with tiny movements, tapping and pushing until something—

Suddenly, with a beautiful, satisfying click, the two half-circles broke apart, revealing an ugly red welt beneath the smears of blood on her wrist.

Half disbelieving, Georgia eased her hand out and knelt on the bed, looking around the room as if seeing it for the first time.

Holy shit.

She was out of the handcuffs.

Now she had to get out of the bedroom.

Back indoors, Kyle was amused to find that Lara had made him a sandwich, evidently deciding it was prudent to stay on his good side. Maybe later he'd find out what else she was willing to do for him.

But now it was time. He arranged for Rob to be escorted back to the bedroom where the family had spent the night.

'Should I look in on Georgia?' Milo asked. 'Just to check—'

'No,' Kyle barked. 'Go downstairs.'

He wanted Milo gone. Wanted a moment to find some clarity. It was in his hands to save or destroy, and now he had to decide which it should be.

Both. Both at the same time. But that was impossible. . .

Rob was sitting on the floor, looking tense but not particularly uncomfortable or afraid. Kyle sat down on the bed, resting the gun in his lap, and said, 'Well?'

'The safe is set into the bathroom floor, beneath one of the tiles. It's got about three thousand in cash, along with some jewellery worth another couple of grand. I have a few investments, which I can sign over to you, but not until Wendy and the—'

'Yeah, yeah, I know.' Kyle made a dismissive gesture. 'Tell me about this boat.'

'Boat? What boat?'

'We know you have one. I need it to dispose of a body.'

Rob blanched. 'And you think I'm going to help—'

'It's *Gabriel's* body.'

That had the desired effect: Rob gaped at him, lost for words.

Kyle said, 'Lara found him this morning. Heart attack in his sleep – at least that's what it looks like. So now there's a lot of confusion, as you can imagine. Different opinions on the best course of action.'

He paused, but Rob only gave a quick, cautious nod for Kyle to go on.

'Ilsa, for instance, is pushing for a wipeout – quick and simple executions – before we loot the place and get out of here. I'm afraid it won't take much for Milo and Lara to agree, which is why, for your sake, I'm trying to come up with an alternative.'

'And why would you do that?'

Kyle regarded him coolly; he'd steered the conversation in this direction for a reason, but now that the moment had come, he felt extremely nervous.

He dealt with it by stoking up some resentment. 'You don't get it, do you?'

'Get what?' Rob looked at him with contempt. 'And what did you mean earlier, asking whether I recognised you? We've never met, you said it yourself.'

'I was referring to a family resemblance.'

Silence – then Rob spluttered with laughter. Not the reaction Kyle had anticipated, all the many times he'd pictured this moment.

'Say that again?'

'A family resemblance.' Kyle's voice was an octave too high, and he had to press his hands down hard on his legs to stop them from shaking. 'Because I'm your son.'

SIXTY-TWO

Insanity. That was Rob's first and only thought. *This is pure insanity.*

But Kyle wasn't just a very sick and deluded individual. He was a man with a gun, and right now he held the power of life or death over Rob and his family.

That was a very good reason to stay calm, and at least pretend to consider the merits of his claim. Whether Rob could manage it, he didn't know.

He was silent for so long that Kyle finally said, 'It's a shock, I understand.'

'I can't. . . I mean, what makes you. . .?'

'Julie Jacques. She was about twenty, twenty-one. Lived in Chichester. She said you went out a few times, but you were seeing someone else as well, or separated, maybe. . .' He shrugged. 'I'm not totally sure, and I don't think she was, either.'

'Julie. . . Jacques?' Rob had one of those moments when a name sounds familiar, simply because the other person expects it to be. 'When was this?'

'Summer of 1993.' Kyle gave a tight little grin. 'I was born in March '94.'

'Summer of '93,' Rob muttered. That was the year he and Wendy had split for a few months, after the pressure of trying to conceive had fractured the marriage. Rob had gone out with a couple of women in that time; brief, casual relationships which he had regretted almost immediately, and perhaps blanked from his memory as a result.

He was no lothario, had never really slept around. This had been the era of AIDS, after all – and if you had sex outside of a long-term relationship, condoms were regarded as essential. A lifesaver.

With Kyle bristling at his silence, Rob said, 'Is this what your mum told you?'

'Rob Turner. She remembered your name, even if you've forgotten hers.'

His ghastly smile gave Rob an insight: *He's scared. This, for him, is more nerve-wracking than when he was committing cold-blooded torture.*

'I don't want to suggest that's wrong, but perhaps I knew her some other way? Friend of a friend, or maybe I chatted her up in a pub and nothing came of it.' Rob shrugged. 'If she thought I was the father, why didn't she get in touch when she found out she was pregnant?'

'She said she had her reasons. Another relationship, or something.'

He sounded evasive, and Rob guessed why. If his mother had had more than one partner around the same time, then that created doubt. In normal circumstances, this would be the moment to suggest a DNA test, but right now the very idea of giving credence to the claim was revolting.

'So you joined up to Gabriel's cult,' Rob said quietly. 'You abducted and tortured an innocent man, and when he was heading in our direction, you did nothing to stop him?'

'It was too late. I wanted to help, but I was scared.'

'No, I don't buy that. The guy didn't just randomly head for the house belonging to a man you claim is your father. You sent him that way on purpose.'

'No. No, I—'

'Yes, you did.' Rob saw the truth in his face, in the way that he squirmed. 'It was you who persuaded Gabriel to make us the next target. You've been an active part of this whole thing. Sneaking into our house – you were boasting about that yesterday. You tried to set us up, hiding the dead man's trainer, so don't give me any crap about being on our side.'

'But I am.' It came out as a childish whine. Kyle dropped his gaze, snuffling as he fought back self-righteous tears. 'I admit I did a lot that was wrong. I was so angry. For years I blamed you for my shitty life, my shitty stepdad in Canada – even when I didn't know who you were. Then, when I came back to the UK and saw the life you'd given your other kids. . .' He wiped his eyes. 'I wanted you to be punished.'

Somehow, Rob stayed calm. 'No son of mine would do what you've done to us.'

Suddenly enraged, Kyle jumped to his feet. 'Oh yeah? We're a product of our environment, not just our DNA. Who knows how the twins might have turned out living somewhere else, being treated differently? Look at Josh, for instance – he's not whiter than white – and as for Georgia.' He spat the words. 'She's trailer trash, yet you took her in, gave her a far better life than I'd ever had—'

'Because you didn't exist, as far as I was concerned. And you still don't.'

Kyle waved the gun in Rob's face and yelled: 'What the *fuck* do you mean by that?'

Rob was shaken; push it too far and he might well die right now. But Kyle's temper had ignited his own, and he wasn't going to be silenced.

'I think you or your mum has made a mistake. I don't believe you're my son, and if by some terrible twist of fate you are, then I'm disowning you, right here and now, for the crimes you've committed against my family.' Rob heard Kyle groan, as if he'd been physically assaulted, but he pressed on: 'And if you really are in charge here, your best bet would be to round up the others and get the hell out of this house.'

*

Kill him. It's all gone wrong. Just shoot him. End it.

Kyle listened to the voice in his head, while the gun turned hot and slippery in the sweat of his palm. *Save or destroy*, the twin impulses that always raged when he thought about his real father, his real family, and still he had no idea which one to favour. Whenever he'd rehearsed this conversation in his mind, Rob had invariably accepted the truth – not always readily, for sure – but Kyle had never imagined him just flat out denying it.

Or rejecting Kyle, *even if it was true.*

Could it be a mistake? He didn't want to be reminded of his mother's vagueness on the subject of her sexual past, or the fact that over the years she'd thrown out several names as possible contenders: Kyle had ignored that and listened to his gut instinct. He'd been so convinced that Rob was his dad – he even thought there was some similarity in their features, and in Josh and Evan's, but what did that mean, really? Lots of people look alike.

'I-I was brainwashed,' he said, his voice trembling. 'We all were. You saw what Gabriel was like. I couldn't stop him. I admit that I put you in his sights, and that was wrong. But I had this. . . this idea that if you were all in danger, and then I came along and saved you. . .'

'Yeah.' Rob wasn't buying a word of it. 'But you haven't saved us. You're pointing a gun at me right now—'

'I killed Gabriel,' Kyle snapped.

'You. . .' Rob looked incredulous.

'With poison. I realised it had gone too far, but I couldn't do anything until now. Without me, you'd all be looking at day after day of torture. I've saved you from that.'

'Okay. So let us loose, and call 999.'

'I can't.'

'Exactly. Because it's not true. If you have even a scrap of real humanity, you'd do what I said. Round up your collaborators at gunpoint and call the police.'

'You. . . you keep. . .' Kyle could barely speak. It was some kind of miracle that he didn't open fire right then. 'I offered you a lifeline,' he said. 'But you don't want it. Is that because of the guilt – you failed to protect your family? Or is it the shame? Can't have darling Wendy knowing all your dirty little secrets?' He saw Rob's face change and that was the breakthrough – that was the lightbulb moment for him.

Wendy.

Georgia was more scared now than when she'd been cuffed to the bed. Every noise within the house made her want to curl up and cry; it was the thought of the door opening, and one of them finding her like this. . .

But that was stupid. And it wasn't even the real reason.

Getting dressed helped a bit. Made her feel more like herself, more in control.

The window, though. If she was honest, that was the real issue. There was no hope of sneaking past Milo and the others; the only option was to escape through the window – only she'd done that once before, and the thought of doing it again. . .

The other problem was that not only had they locked the window, they'd also nailed the sash to the frame. Some of the nails were protruding, but after what she'd gone through already, she didn't think she could work them free. Her hands were too sore, too weak.

And she needed a weapon. The only furniture in the room was a wardrobe, and at first glance it was empty. She was shutting the door when her brain lit up like a warning light: *Take another look.*

It was empty of clothes, yes, but there were about a dozen hangers, all mismatched from years of visitors taking and leaving different ones each time. Most were plastic, but a couple were wooden, and there was a single one made from wire.

A noise from the landing sent her scurrying back to the bed. As she lay there, terrified, she realised she might be able to fool them. Lie back and put the cuff around her wrist – the fact that she was now dressed might confuse them for a second or two, and she could dodge past them and run out. . .

Nice idea, but no one came in. That had to be Plan B, she decided. In the meantime, back to Plan A.

But I don't want to go out the window, I don't—

'Shut up,' she whispered to herself. It was different this time. She wasn't being chased. She could do it slowly, carefully.

Back to the window, then. She decided it might be possible to work the metal hanger into the gap at the bottom of the frame. Push it back and forth, and maybe the sash would come loose. Had to be worth a try, but if it didn't work she'd have to smash the window and jump.

I can't jump I can't I can't—

'I have to,' she said. But it couldn't be done slowly. Once she'd broken the glass, the noise would bring them all running.

She had just moved to the window when she heard shouting – Kyle's voice, and then her dad's. She froze, listening hard but unable to make out what they were saying.

Then the voices faded away, and Georgia knew she had to get on with it. She picked up the hanger, the dread clawing at her heart. Either she was going to run out of time and get caught. . . or she was going to succeed and have to do it: jump out of the window.

Both options seemed equally terrifying.

SIXTY-THREE

They were gone a long time, or so it seemed. Wendy and the boys didn't talk much as they waited it out. There was a new and dangerous uncertainty in the air. Milo and Lara kept whispering between themselves, then one or the other would go over and confer with Ilsa.

Evan was suffering physically, trying to stretch his aching limbs. He and Josh quietly debated what Kyle might be discussing with their father.

'It's a negotiation,' Evan said. 'Got to be money.'

'In exchange for what? They aren't letting us go.'

Evan was shocked by his brother's blunt tone. 'We've got to hope. . .'

'Maybe.' Josh shrugged. 'I think there's more to it than that.'

A burst of muffled shouting was followed by the thump of footsteps, then Kyle manhandled Rob into the room and shoved him to the floor. He waved the gun at his colleagues. 'Get out of here.'

'Why?' Ilsa asked.

'I need five minutes. Now go!'

Gone was the pretence that they were working together. Wendy sent Rob a mystified look, and he started to say, 'Gabriel's dead. Kyle—'

'Shut up!' Kyle kicked him in the back and Rob cried out, falling to his side, his face contorted with pain.

Once the others had left the room, Kyle said, 'I've been trying to help you, but Daddy here isn't playing ball.'

'He k—' Rob groaned in agony. 'Killed Gab—'

'Never mind that,' Kyle hissed, with an uneasy glance at the door. 'Are you gonna tell them, Rob? Or shall I?'

Still trying to recover, Rob shook his head in disgust. 'Kyle claims that I'm. . . his father. Says his mum had a fling with me, got pregnant and said nothing. It's nonsense.'

'Is it?' Kyle challenged him, then turned to Wendy. 'Do *you* think it's nonsense?'

Quashing her horror at the revelation, she said, 'When. . . when was this?'

'Summer of 1993. Julie Jacques, from Chichester. She dated Rob a few times. He said something to her about breaking up with his partner, but I guess that could have been a lie. Men'll say anything to get some action, isn't that right?' He glanced at Evan and Josh, both of whom were rigid with shock.

Gasping, Rob said, 'What matters is Kyle. . . Kyle pointed Gabriel at us in the first place, and now wants thanks for saving us.'

As dismissive as he sounded, Wendy pounced on that final phrase. 'Is that true?' she demanded of Kyle. 'Are you going to let us go?'

He looked taken aback, as if he'd expected her to focus on his bizarre claim, but Wendy was nothing if not pragmatic. All that mattered was getting her family out of here.

'If I can, I will,' he said, 'but it won't be easy. And I need something, you know, something to offer, because it isn't just me. . .'

All bluster, Wendy thought, and it almost broke her heart.

He was lying.

Georgia hated herself. She was an idiot. A coward.

She'd worked at the window until the sweat poured out of her, but it was hopeless. The metal hanger wasn't nearly strong enough to shift the sash, and the gap wasn't big enough for the wooden hanger. If she had half a brain, she'd give up trying and go for the only option available to her.

But she didn't. She chickened out. She went on poking and prodding with the hanger, haunting herself with the thought that she might turn and see Mark Burroughs behind her, the knife in his hand, all ready to finish her off. . .

She knew she wasn't thinking straight. Her head was pounding and her mouth felt like she'd swallowed a sock. At times she had to pause and shut her eyes, taking big gulps of air to stop herself from flaking out. And still she wouldn't accept what it was she had to do.

Finally the exhaustion overcame her, and she sank to the floor. She was wasting time, precious seconds that might mean the difference between life and death – not just for her, but for Mum and Dad, for her brothers.

They needed her. And wasn't that idea enough to give her a little more energy, a little more courage?

She still hadn't sorted out a weapon. Staring at the coat hanger gave her an idea. She got to her feet and used the lower part of the sash like a vice, jamming the neck of the hanger into the gap and then twisting it until the wire poked straight out. By the same method she was able to fold the triangular part in two, forming a more compact handle. Now she could wield it like a dagger.

But there was still the decision she had to make. Instead, some cruel part of her mind kept taking her back to Nyman, and the way he had died. Was it too quick to feel pain, or was there a moment of absolute agony, when you felt your skull bursting apart?

Georgia knew exactly why she was torturing herself like this. It was still preferable to thinking about what she had to do next. What she had to do but couldn't.

You have *to do it.*

But I can't.

*

Rob was struggling to concentrate. The kick had struck close to one of his kidneys, and it hurt more than anything he had ever known. Waves of nausea and dizziness were shuddering through him; at times it was too painful to breathe, let alone speak.

Josh caught Kyle's attention and said, 'How much are you hoping to screw out of us?'

Then Wendy intervened, in a more amenable tone: 'I can't begin to imagine how traumatic this has been for you,' she told Kyle. 'Why didn't you approach us sooner?'

Looking stunned, he said, 'I-I only found out. . . well, it was a few years ago. But I was in a bad way then. I met Gabriel, got caught up in all his. . .'

'Manipulation?' Wendy offered, with a nod of regret. 'We've all seen what he's capable of. The control he can exert over others.'

Rob was amazed by her manner; they might have been social worker and client, chatting in the safety of some bland meeting space.

'It warped us,' Kyle said, with a self-pitying sniff. 'We grew to believe that treating people like this was. . . normal. *Desirable*. It was expected of us.'

Wendy tutted. 'And all through that ordeal, you knew there was a *real* family out there, your father and your half-brothers and sister. People who could have given you genuine support, genuine love. . .'

Rob had assumed she was just playing along, faking the sympathy, but after seeing her pause, as if about to choke up, he wasn't so sure. When she said, 'You're his victim, too', it was all Rob could do not to shout out an objection.

Kyle, Lara and the others were every bit as warped as Gabriel. They had to take responsibility for their actions.

She said, 'Fortunately, with Gabriel's spell broken, you have a chance to move on. You can – and you must – bring this to a peaceful conclusion, Kyle.'

'I want to. But what about me? What happens once I. . .' He gestured with the gun, as if fearing Wendy was going to take it off him.

'We're all witnesses to your courage, I promise.' She looked quickly at the twins, then gave Rob another, more loaded glance. 'We will speak up in your favour, and say you withstood intolerable pressure and did the right—'

A noise from upstairs broke her flow, just when she could see her approach was having an effect.

'Did the right thing,' she finished, desperately trying to work out what she'd heard.

Kyle had caught it too, so there was no sense in pretending otherwise. But perhaps this would get him out of the room and give them a chance to plan their next move. She'd been so worried that Rob would object to the sympathy she was offering Kyle.

Then came the loud, unmistakable crash of shattering glass. Kyle wrenched the door open, and they saw Milo running for the stairs.

'Go that way!' Kyle shouted to someone in the hall – Ilsa or Lara – and pointed towards the kitchen. 'In case she's got out.'

Oh, yes! The thought of it made Wendy almost delirious with hope. Could Georgia really have found a way to escape? She glanced at Rob, who was trying to haul himself on to his knees. He looked dreadful.

'You stay here,' Kyle was saying. 'It might be a trap.'

It was Lara who nervously stepped into sight as Kyle turned his attention back to the family. Another couple of seconds, Wendy thought later, and Rob's attack might have worked.

The cuffs hampered him, and the blow to his kidney had clearly taken its toll, but still he put everything into the attempt, launching himself at Kyle with furious determination. But the younger man reacted quickly, bringing the gun round and letting off a shot. The bullet struck the floor about six inches from Rob's feet. Wendy gave a horrified shriek as he threw himself to one side, then staggered back. She managed to grab him by the leg and he slumped to the floor, crying out in frustration.

'It's too dangerous.' Wendy leaned against him, trying to offer what comfort she could. But she felt his despair just as keenly, because it meant that Georgia was on her own.

There was nothing they could do to help her.

SIXTY-FOUR

At last Georgia accepted the truth. If she wanted to live – if she wanted her family to live – then she had to do it. She had to break the window.

The problem was how. If she could remove all the glass from the frame, then she might be able to hang by her arms, reducing the distance that she had to fall. But that meant breaking the window quietly – and how could she do that?

She tried using the sharp point of the coat hanger to score the glass, but it made a horrible squeaking noise and barely scratched the window. Then she got a pillow off the bed, pressed it to the glass and punched, gently, with the side of her fist. That did nothing at first, so she tried again, hitting harder.

There was a cracking sound, which seemed loud enough to be heard throughout the house. She froze; a few seconds later there was movement downstairs.

Shit. No time to do it slowly. Placing the pillow in the centre of the window, she drove her fist through it. The glass was weaker than in a modern window and shattered easily, falling to the ground in large fragments.

Then, at the sound of footsteps running up the stairs, Georgia lost her mind.

Mark Burroughs, with a knife.

She snatched the wire coat hanger, rested the pillow on the ledge and climbed up, putting one leg out, then the other. While she was facing back into the room, the door handle moved. Bracing her feet against the wall, she straightened her arms, then propelled herself outwards, trying to land clear of the broken glass, arms and legs windmilling as she dropped; glancing down to see, in the foggy gloom, the grass rushing up to meet her.

At the first hint of contact with the ground she threw herself sideways, screaming as her ankles absorbed her weight, but then she was falling, rolling, and the pain wasn't quite as severe and at least she hadn't felt a *snap*.

If nothing was broken she could run. She could get away.

The grass was cool, and soaking wet. It felt soothing, after all the hard work, and the stale air of the bedroom; she wanted just to lie here and nurse her wounds. But she knew they'd heard her, knew they were chasing—

It's Mark Burroughs, with a knife.

She grabbed the hanger, which she'd dropped in the fall, and got to her feet. But her ankles refused to hold her up, and her knees wouldn't lock. She stumbled, took a few wavering steps like a newborn foal, the pain so intense that she thought she might pass out.

She heard a gunshot, and for one terrifying moment thought it had been aimed at her. But at least that wiped the pain from her mind. She sped up, unaware that she was yelping with every step, trying to dodge a little and keep her head low, in case of another bullet. She thought of Nyman, and how he must have felt just like this – so gloriously alive and so unbelievably scared – as he waited for the end. . .

But there were no more shots. Deep in her mind she understood that the gun had been fired not at her, but at something inside the house. Something or someone.

One of her family, maybe.

She had reached the gap in the hedge when she heard the back door opening. Although it must have been well into the afternoon by now, the mist lay thick and heavy, reducing the world around her to a collection of grey, ghostly shapes – and hopefully that would make her harder to spot.

She pushed through the hedge, her ankles hurting even more as they swelled up. Limping along the path to her left, she made for the tall grasses of the reed beds. Running far wasn't an option; if they were coming after her, she would have to hide.

She wondered about calling for help, but knew that would draw her pursuers. And not much point if there wasn't anyone around. It was eerily quiet and still, which meant her own noise, as she tramped through the grass, would be easy to hear.

No chance of anyone reacting to the gunshot, either, she realised. Up here people were always out shooting rabbits, pheasants and God knows what else.

She slowed, searching for a clump of grass away from the path, thick enough to conceal her. The ground was starting to soften, and she could make out the gleam of water puddling in little hollows. Suddenly worried that she might be leaving footprints, she looked down and saw it was worse than that.

She'd left a blood trail. Must have caught her foot on the broken glass—

Without warning she was knocked flat: someone crashed into her with the full force of their body weight. Georgia sprawled forward, felt a hand pressing her head into the earth, another grappling for the coat hanger, hot breath on her neck; all the air was crushed out of her lungs and the panic, the terror, filled her whole world.

No one could have followed her so silently – *it's Burroughs, marching out of her nightmares.* Georgia's stomach heaved as she wriggled; it felt like her lungs had been pulled inside out. She was going to suffocate, and her flailing hands lost the stupid coat hanger, and the killer on her back was speaking but she couldn't understand the words; she remembered the slash of the blade, that first time: how it hadn't felt like anything much until she'd turned, practically in mid-air, and seen the stream of blood pouring from her leg—

She fought to get on her knees, managed to drag one leg up a little, and there were more words dancing around her ears, kept out by the dull whoosh of the blood pumping through her head. She thought of Ilsa, the new star of BitchWorld; Lara, who could make Amber and Paige look like rookies when it came to cruelty, and Milo, so heartbreakingly cute when he'd joined her on the bench: it was all betrayal, a lot of lies and bullshit designed to cause her pain, and now she was losing it, could feel the world turning black because there still wasn't air. . . Ilsa's eyes suddenly vivid in her memory, glittering with scorn at Georgia's tantrum in the café, and she clawed at the killer's side, her fingers brushing something solid – metal or plastic, and more dancing words, now – and with her last few seconds she grabbed it and hit out, hit out, found some air, enough to hit again, and now the weight was coming off and she could move—

Georgia, no, I'm with you don't do this. . .

Words that registered, but far too late; the killer now falling to one side and Georgia moving over and up, still hitting with all the strength she could find, all the strength and all the *fury*, an endless well of fury; and something hot splashed over her arm but she kept on hitting, punching, *stabbing*; because the thing in her hand was a knife, and the killer wasn't Burroughs, it was Ilsa, and now the blood was bubbling on the woman's lips and the light was fading from her eyes, and it was done.

A look on Ilsa's face like. . . regret?

'They're my family.' She felt it was important to explain. 'And you were gonna kill them.'

And I'm Georgia the Savage. Don't forget that.

SIXTY-FIVE

Milo was back within seconds, and told Kyle, 'She broke the window.'

'She was meant to be cuffed to the bed!'

'I know. I don't underst—'

'Get out there and find her.'

Milo went, leaving Kyle and Lara to guard the family. Wendy knew this was by far the most dangerous point of their captivity. Kyle looked skittish, unfocused, aware that his plans were falling apart and yet unable to accept it.

Anything could set him off now, but Wendy still felt she must speak. 'Please don't let them hurt Georgia.'

'Forget it,' he said coldly. 'Her choice to escape.'

'But she's your family, remember?'

It was a mistake. Kyle rounded on her, shouting, 'She's a fucking interloper. She had the life I should have had. So whatever happens to her now, it's her own tough luck.'

Kneeling on the mud, Georgia was hidden by the tall grass. Above and around her, the mist drifted in from the sea; it was damper than before, like a drizzle, soaking through her t-shirt. A lonely bird sang from somewhere far away.

It's only you and me, Georgia wanted to tell the bird. *There's no one else in the world.*

She tried not to look down, but at some point it had to be done. Carefully, cautiously. Choosing what she saw, and what she didn't.

She might be alone now, but there was a chance of someone coming along. If they saw her, she couldn't imagine what they'd think—

No, that was a lie. She *did* know. She knew all too well.

After this, the whole world would see her for what she was. Council estate scum, brought into a world she didn't deserve, that was never rightfully hers. . .

Only one place to put Georgia the Savage, and that was a prison cell.

She picked up the knife, wondering if it would be better to kill herself. But within a few seconds she knew she wasn't capable of it. Not brave enough.

And there was her family to think about. She had to save them, or this had all been for nothing.

She couldn't phone the police. The nearest house was too far away. Her ankles hurt – her whole body hurt – and she could hardly turn up on someone's doorstep looking like this.

She stood up, with difficulty, and started back towards the garden. Almost immediately she heard loud, ragged breathing, and ducked into the cover of the long grass.

'Ilsa!' a voice hissed. 'Ilsa, where are you?'

It was Milo. He came towards her, calling out in a way that made her think he didn't actually want to be heard. Crouched in the grass, she could see the tracks she'd left in the mud, and even a few bright drops of blood. Any moment now he was going to spot them.

She tightened her grip on the knife. Milo took a couple more steps, then let out a juddering sigh. He was very close, close enough to attack.

Then she heard him whisper: 'Fuck this.' He turned and strode back towards the garden. Once he was through the hedge, Georgia crept on to the path and followed him.

*

Rob stretched, gingerly, and decided that the pain in his back was receding. He didn't feel quite as sick any more. Leaning close to Wendy, he whispered, 'We've got to pray she gets away.'

'Don't,' Wendy moaned. 'I can't bear to think about it.'

'She's a smart kid. She'll do it.' He nodded towards Kyle. 'That was amazing, how you dealt with him. I couldn't have done it.'

'He's horribly insecure. Confronting him wouldn't have achieved a thing.'

'But do you buy any of the. . .' he felt awkward, suddenly '. . . what he's claiming to be?'

She shrugged. 'Well, I suppose it's not impossible. But it's a conversation for another time.'

She was right. At that moment, someone came trudging through the kitchen. Kyle leaned into the hall and said, 'Have you found her?'

They heard Milo's response: 'Neither of them.'

'Where's Ilsa, then?' Lara approached the door. 'Don't say she's run off? That witch could do more damage than Georgia.'

Milo joined them in a huddle around the doorway. 'If we stay much longer, we're in deep shit.'

Lara agreed. 'We can't leave any witnesses.' They were discussing their predicament as though Kyle wasn't present. Only now did Lara include him: 'We've got to do it, Kyle. Kill them, and get out of here.'

Georgia caught the tail end of the conversation. She'd followed Milo back to the house and crept into the kitchen. From there she heard Lara's suggestion, and then Kyle said, 'Come in here.'

She risked a glance and saw Kyle leading the other two across to the dining room. It was basically suicidal to go any further, but Georgia put that thought aside and moved along the hall. Kyle was only just inside the dining room, keeping an eye on the hall, so it was almost certain that she'd be seen. And the knife she'd taken from Ilsa was no match for a gun.

The instant that Kyle turned his head away from the hall, Georgia sped up and entered the lounge. She'd seen or heard nothing of Gabriel, which struck her as very odd, so she half expected to walk in on him now. Instead, she nearly fainted with relief to find her family sitting together on the floor. The twins looked battered, but no one appeared to be badly injured. Her mum's face lit up, but Rob was staring at her with a strange expression that immediately reminded her of what she had done. The evidence was there in the blood all down her front.

Now Wendy was registering the same thing, as Georgia crouched and held out the knife. 'Are you hurt?' her mum asked.

'Just my ankles. I'm okay.'

'But you're covered—'

'It's mud, a lot of it.' Georgia slipped the blade into the gap between her mum's wrists and applied some upward pressure, the knife jerking dangerously as it cut through the plastic.

'Careful,' Rob said. She turned to him next, heard him whisper, 'Well done, darling.'

Wendy was already moving aside so that Georgia could reach the twins, and Rob had torn the cuffs away from his wrists when a voice called out from behind her: 'Hey!'

Kyle was in the doorway. The sight of Georgia, splattered with blood and holding a knife, seemed to throw him off balance. That gave her another precious second. As she cut Evan free, Wendy moved in front of her daughter, in case Kyle tried to shoot, while Rob was pushing himself unsteadily to his feet.

'Get away from them!' Kyle advanced on Georgia. 'Drop the knife!'

She ignored him. Wendy heard a gasp as Evan was cut free. Kyle raised the gun, aiming for what he could see of Georgia, but

Wendy was the easier target. Fighting an instinct to shut her eyes, she froze, just as Milo and Lara came in and spotted Georgia.

For a brief moment Kyle was distracted, his gaze shifting away from the family. Rob must have seen a chance to redeem himself, breaking away from Wendy, but he had barely moved when he was pushed aside by someone faster and more determined.

Josh.

He was the only one whose hands were still bound, and yet he sprang forward with incredible speed, head down, hands thrust out with the palms open, like a fielder preparing to catch a fast ball. Kyle sensed the blur of movement but had no time to react before Josh struck him. He fell back and Josh went with him, his cuffed hands grappling with the barrel of the gun. Milo and Lara jumped back in alarm, while Rob moved to support his son. But before he had a chance to pile in, Josh tried to wrench the gun from Kyle's grasp, and there was a sudden explosion of noise.

The gun fell away as a spray of blood hit the floor. Josh screamed, his body jerking as Kyle rolled him aside and jumped up. Rob lunged but Josh was in the way, blood pouring from a wound to his leg. At the sight of it, Rob faltered, and that was all the chance Kyle needed to turn and run.

'Help Josh!' Wendy yelled, knowing that Kyle would have to be forgotten for now. The imminent danger came from Lara, as the gun was lying practically at her feet. Wendy was able to kick the gun out of reach, even as she saw that Lara's focus was on a quick escape. The girl managed a couple of steps before Wendy grabbed her by the neck and pulled her to the floor.

Rob was at Josh's side, so Evan and Georgia advanced on Milo, who took one look at the knife in Georgia's hand and meekly surrendered. Evan found the cable ties and used them to cuff Milo and Lara. Wendy then rushed over to Josh, who was in pain, but still conscious.

'Where did it hit?'

'Caught the outer thigh. I don't think the bullet penetrated.'

Rob had removed his shirt and was pressing it against the wound. Wendy ran to the kitchen, found the medical kit and a pair of scissors.

'It's nothing,' Josh said when she returned. 'Just a graze. Don't make a fuss.'

'I think it looks worse than it is,' Rob agreed.

'I hope you're right,' Wendy said. 'But it still needs to be disinfected.'

'Are you okay to take over?' Rob asked her. 'Evan can help.'

'Of course. Why?'

There was a look in his eyes that made her shiver. 'I'm going after him.'

'Rob, no—' she began, but even as she spoke she knew it was futile.

He was gone.

SIXTY-SIX

As he ran out of the house, Rob had to tell himself that pursuing Kyle made sense, that it wasn't just a salve for his bruised ego.

He felt humbled by Josh's bravery, but also ashamed that he hadn't been quick enough to tackle Kyle. If Josh's injury had been any more severe, Rob doubted if he would ever have been able to forgive himself.

The back door was open, and it seemed logical that Kyle had taken this route. Rob crept through the garden, alert to any movement. The mist that had clung all day was turning to rain. Hearing the distant whine of an outboard motor, he was struck by the parallels with last Sunday. Almost exactly a week ago, he had left Wendy giving first aid to an injured man while he ran out, alone, in search of the man's assailants.

On that occasion it might have been wiser to leave it to the police, and perhaps that was the case here, too. He hoped that by now one of the others had called the emergency services.

A sudden bolt of pain over his kidney made him gasp. Stopping for a second, he heard the unmistakable clunk of a car door.

It had come from the lane. Kyle must have run out here, then sneaked along the side of the house. Rob followed, the pain made worse by every movement. He was expecting to hear a car start up and roar away, but the silence held.

Rob crossed the drive and went out through the gates. There was a Mini hatchback in the lane, facing away from him. No sign of anyone inside.

Then, from behind, came the scrape of feet on concrete, and a blow to the head that knocked him out.

The bullet had cut a thin groove across Josh's thigh. Appalled but intrigued, Georgia had leaned in for a closer look, then immediately regretted it. Feeling slightly faint, she turned away and kept her eye on their prisoners instead. Milo and Lara were sitting in a miserable silence.

And then another shock: Gabriel was dead. Something to do with Kyle, apparently, but her mum hadn't been able to explain properly. She and Evan cleaned out Josh's wound and applied a dressing, then wrapped a bandage around his leg and taped it up tightly. Georgia could tell from his breathing that Josh was really hurting, though he insisted he wasn't. A sip of water, a couple of ibuprofen and he'd be fine.

'Rubbish,' Wendy said. 'You're going to a hospital. In fact, I daresay we all need some medical attention.' A worried look at Georgia here, as though she assumed terrible things had been done to her. 'Find the phone, will you?'

'They ditched the landline,' Evan said. 'One of them told me last night.'

Wendy sighed. 'Mobiles are useless out here – even if we knew where they were.'

'Use one of theirs,' Josh suggested, indicating Milo and Lara.

'I can run to the end of the lane,' Evan said. 'Should be able to—'

'I'll do it,' Georgia cut in. They all stared at her, and Josh snorted.

'Bloody hell, Squirt. Volunteer for nothing – that's the rule.'

'Yeah, well. . .' She shrugged, while inside she was shrivelling up with guilt. 'Need some fresh air.'

Wendy looked dubious. 'I don't know. It's bad enough that your dad's gone out there. . .'

'It'll be all right,' Evan assured her. 'Look at what she's already achieved.'

Georgia was in no state to accept compliments. She focused on searching Milo, who was too scared even to meet her gaze. Having found a phone, she picked up her knife and hurried out before Wendy changed her mind. The fact was, Mum and Evan had enough to do, looking after Josh and watching the prisoners. Much better that Georgia be the one to make the call.

Or *pretend* to make the call.

Rob swam back to consciousness. He didn't think he'd been out for more than a few seconds, but he couldn't move. He was lying face down in the lane, the concrete cold and damp beneath his bare chest.

Someone was kneeling on his back. A familiar voice spoke very close to his ear. 'What a shame. Thought I'd killed you.'

As Rob bucked, letting out an incoherent growl, Kyle took a fistful of his hair and pulled his head back, exposing his throat. Rob felt a knife sliding beneath his chin, coming to rest against his neck.

'Got this from the car.' Kyle chuckled. 'Could be fun to use it now, but I'm not going to.'

Again Rob tried to speak, but the words wouldn't form.

'The thing is,' Kyle went on, 'you've got under my skin, and I'm going to get under yours.' He smacked his lips together, moving so close that his mouth was almost touching Rob's cheek. 'I'll come back for you all, that's a promise. It might be Georgia first, it might be Wendy, or one of the twins. Who knows?'

The blade was pressing harder.

'It could be weeks, months, years,' Kyle said. 'And all you'll know is that it's going to happen one day, but you'll never know when.'

The blade moved and Rob gasped, every muscle tensing as he imagined a jet of blood hitting the road; then the pressure lifted from his back and Kyle was up and running; too fast for Rob, who tried to rise but was overcome by a wave of dizziness.

He retched, spat, then slowly got up on his hands and knees, feeling weak and very old. As the car started, there was a cry of alarm. Georgia rushed over and again he tried to stand, wanting to reassure her; but the world was spinning, his vision a mass of exploding stars.

'Dad!'

'I'm okay. Honestly.'

'You're bleeding, at the back of your head.'

'Am I?' He dabbed at it, felt the blood sticky in his hair. 'Doesn't feel too bad.'

'What happened?'

Rob gestured to the lane; time must have slipped, somehow, because the car had gone.

'Kyle got away.' Dazed he might be, but Rob had already decided not to mention Kyle's threat. 'In one of those Mini hatchbacks. Did you see it?'

'Uh, yeah. A red one.' She winced, guiltily. 'I didn't get the number, though.'

'Don't worry. Neither did I.' Deciding that he felt a little better, he made it to his feet, but wasn't too proud to let Georgia take his arm. 'Why are you out here?'

'The landline's down.' With a knife already in her hand, she had to let go of him to take a mobile phone from her pocket. 'Mum said to call 999 from the main road.'

'Okay. Well, I can do that.' He took a step, stayed upright, and grinned.

But Georgia, looking stricken, said, 'Dad, I'm sorry. . . I don't think we can.'

'What do you mean? We have to.'

Georgia looked unhappier than he had ever seen her. 'It's Ilsa,' she mumbled.

'Ilsa?' Rob realised he'd barely given the woman a thought. 'What about her?'

SIXTY-SEVEN

This was almost worse than being kept prisoner, Georgia thought as she led Rob through the garden. Worse than the attacks, or jumping out of that window. Because this was when the people who had taken her in, the family that loved her – the family that *she* loved – would see what she really was.

And they couldn't fail to reject her.

She felt so sick that she had to stop, once they were through the hedge, doubled over and sucking in the cool, wet air, trying not to throw up, or faint, or both. Rob held her, rubbed her back, but didn't hassle her with questions.

Maybe he's guessed, she thought, but even then he couldn't possibly know how bad it was.

They set off along the path, Georgia glad of the rain on her face. It was coming down harder now, washing away her blood trail. Even the footprints she'd left were becoming difficult to make out.

'Over here, I think.'

She stepped carefully through the long grass, letting out a moan when she spotted the woman's leg. She turned to Rob and pointed. She couldn't go any closer.

Rob was trying not to anticipate what he would see. Maybe it was because he felt sick and groggy himself; not thinking straight. But Georgia was in a bad way, that much was clear. If she had fought with Ilsa and come off best, well, so what? She had nothing to feel guilty about.

Then he saw the body.

Georgia hung back, a few feet away. After he'd been there for perhaps twenty, thirty seconds, just staring, she covered her face with her hands and began to sob, her shoulders heaving up and down in a rhythm of pure heartbreak.

Rob's duty was to offer comfort, but first he had to compose himself. Find some clarity of thought in the midst of this. . . horror.

Ilsa had been stabbed multiple times, mainly to her torso, but also to her arms, her neck, even her face. Rob didn't try to count the wounds; he didn't need to.

Now he understood Georgia's reaction. There wasn't a hope in hell of passing this off as self-defence. It was more like a frenzied attack, a sustained act of revenge.

That explained the state she was in; the blood all over her arms, her t-shirt. Had Milo or Lara noticed? To be fair, he thought, a lot of the dark stains looked like mud – and some probably *were* mud.

A bird hooted nearby, and in shock he jerked away from the body. He was aware of time pressing on them, the possibility that witnesses could materialise on the path at any moment. But Georgia was on the brink of an emotional meltdown, so first he had to take her in his arms and hold her tight. With her face buried in his chest, she made an attempt to explain herself.

'I dunno how. . . In my head it was Mark Burroughs, and he was going to kill me, and I had, I had to—'

'It's okay. You don't have to justify yourself to me.' When there was no response, he added, gently, 'I'd have done the same thing, I think.'

She broke away from him, met his gaze at last, but looked sceptical.

'I mean it,' he said, thinking of that dangerous rush of temper in Bosham, when he'd launched himself at Jason Dennehy. 'She deserved what she got. You mustn't feel guilty about it.'

'But the police. . .' Georgia swallowed back another sob. 'I'll go to prison, won't I?'

Rob blew out a sigh. In his heart, he didn't think that possibility could be dismissed. Even with the strong mitigating circumstances in her favour, it was unlikely that a court could overlook an attack of this ferocity. At the very least Georgia would be referred for psychiatric reports, and might end up undergoing years of treatment.

In some quarters she would be regarded as a monster. A freak. The simplistic explanation would be that she had unleashed the demons in her head, and no one who met her would ever forget that.

'Okay.' He hugged her again, kissed the top of her head, and said, 'Here's what we do.'

By the time Georgia reappeared, Wendy was frantic. She'd been gone at least ten or fifteen minutes, and she was wet, muddy and bedraggled.

'Did you call them? Where's your dad?'

'He's okay. He's making the call.'

'What happened? Where have you been?'

Georgia shrugged, unwilling to explain. 'Dad got hurt trying to stop Kyle,' she admitted, quickly adding, 'He's all right, though.'

'You mean Kyle's still here?'

'He was, but he got away. I helped Dad up. He was feeling dizzy, so I didn't want to hurry him. When he felt better, he went off to make the phone call and I came back here.'

To Wendy's ear, Georgia's words bore the tone of a pre-prepared statement, but Evan said, 'They're both okay, that's what matters.'

From the corner of the room, Milo grumbled, 'Typical of Kyle to get away. He caused all this, you know? Him and Gabriel. We hardly did anything.'

He'd been arguing in this vein for the past ten minutes, backed up by Lara, who now glared at Wendy and said, 'You've got no proof that us two hurt anyone. It's our word against yours.'

'We'll take that chance,' Josh said. 'I think the DNA, the fingerprints, the injuries will tell their own story, don't you?'

Lara had no comeback, but Milo frowned. 'Where's Ilsa?'

With a quick look at Georgia, who was visibly shivering, Wendy said, 'I assume she escaped with Kyle.'

'I doubt that,' Milo said scornfully, and Lara said, 'More likely he's killed her. He hated her guts.'

'He hated all of us.' Milo winced and made another appeal to Wendy. 'These are too tight. They're hurting my wrists.'

'Won't be long,' Wendy said. 'I'm sure the police can replace them with something better.'

As they continued to protest, she pondered the way Georgia's body had almost crumpled during this exchange. She pushed it from her mind when Josh called Georgia over and clasped her hand in his, reassuring her that his wound had stopped bleeding.

'I'm fine – and it's thanks to you, Squirt.'

Evan was next in line with the congratulations: 'You're a fricking hero, Georgie.'

Wendy said, 'Hey, I don't want to miss out on this.' She'd hoped for a full embrace, but Georgia resisted; even so, Wendy could feel how cold her skin was, her t-shirt soaked through with muddy water. 'You need some towels.'

Georgia wrinkled her nose. 'Gonna have a shower.'

'Oh, I don't know. . . It might be better to wait for the police.'

'Nah, it's disgusting. I've gotta get clean.' Seeing her mum's concern, Georgia leaned close and whispered, 'They didn't do anything to me, so don't worry about that.'

Wendy was hugely relieved to hear it, though she couldn't shake off the feeling that her daughter was hiding something.

She faced down more complaints from Milo and Lara, while Evan had the bright idea of making tea. For a minute or two, Wendy was alone with her thoughts, her fears; it was hard not to look around this room, once such a sanctuary from the world outside, without feeling that it had been irrevocably tainted by this ordeal. Could they ever be comfortable here again? she wondered.

Could they ever feel safe anywhere?

From upstairs, Wendy heard the pulse of the shower and felt an odd but disturbing premonition of doom. It must have shown in her face, for Josh offered an encouraging smile.

'Stop fretting, Mum. She's a survivor.'

Wendy nodded, but said quietly, 'It's what she had to do to survive that worries me.'

'Whatever it was, it's better than the alternative. I'd say be grateful for that.'

It was probably good advice. The door opened and Rob came in, grim-faced and as drenched and grubby as Georgia had been. He hugged them both, but with a strangely distant air. At Wendy's urging he wrapped himself in a bath towel, then sat on the floor and allowed her to clean a nasty cut on the back of his head. His description of recent events was practically identical to Georgia's.

'You could be concussed, you realise that?' Wendy told him. 'Not to mention kidney damage from that kick.'

He snorted. 'Trying to cheer me up?'

'I'm just warning you. When the ambulance arrives, I don't want any nonsense about not needing treatment. You're going to a hospital and that's my final word on the matter.'

Rob chuckled, but was serious when he pointed out the flaw in her argument. 'It won't be up to you – or me – where I go. When the police get here, their priority will be to sort out who did what to whom, and that's likely to take a while.'

As he said it, he glanced at Georgia, who had just rejoined them, now scrubbed clean and dressed in jogging pants and a sweatshirt. Wendy couldn't rid herself of the feeling that the two of them were engaged in a conspiracy of sorts, but she reflected on Josh's wisdom and knew that he was right: *be grateful*. It was going to be hard enough to move on with their lives as it was.

Moving on – though perhaps in different directions.

SIXTY-EIGHT

For the next few days they were at the mercy of officialdom. It was a blur of hospitals and hotel rooms, news bulletins and intrusive questions shouted through half-open windows. Long, weary interviews and painful rehabilitation, tearful reassurances for family and friends, and a growing aversion to contact with the outside world.

News crews had swarmed around the hospital; more than were present in the village of Branham. Footage of the luridly tagged 'torture house' was nowhere near as prized as even the shakiest long-range glimpse of the victims themselves.

Interest from the media proved too great for them to return home until the following weekend: instead they sought refuge in a Winchester hotel. Even here they were not immune, for images of the family had been plucked from Facebook and spread over the pages of tabloids and broadsheets alike. It was a taste of celebrity which none of them was eager to repeat.

Throughout this period, the police acted as their bodyguards, their protectors, their confidants and counsellors – but always there was an edge, another side to their voracious appetite for information.

Wendy and Evan had been first to endure a long bout of questioning, because the other three required immediate medical treatment. Rob showed signs of concussion, requiring that he be kept under observation overnight. He also underwent an ultrasound scan, after a urine test found evidence of slight renal trauma. Josh's gunshot wound required over a dozen stitches; and when Georgia passed out shortly after the first officers arrived at the house, she was judged to be severely dehydrated and suffering from exhaustion.

Rob knew differently there, but he wasn't going to say a word. Anything that delayed the point at which she would have to make a statement was good with him.

Before the police arrived at the cottage, Rob had to explain about the shoe that had been planted in their home. Although it wouldn't show him in a good light, he agreed with Wendy that he would have to come clean, whereupon Josh pointed out that he faced a similar predicament. The murders of John Nyman and his driver could not be described without explaining the context for their visit: the smuggling.

'Of course, I fully intend to play down the scale of what I was up to,' he said with a grin, 'but I can't leave it out altogether.'

Rob's other concern was Kyle's paternity claim, the sort of detail that had the potential to get the tabloids frothing at the mouth. Wendy tried to allay his fears.

'Whatever the truth of the allegations, you don't bear any responsibility for what he did.'

'They won't care about the truth – just the fact that Kyle *believed* there was a connection will be more than enough.' But he agreed that it had to be divulged.

As the investigation got underway, Kyle and Ilsa were still missing and would, in the words of the police, be urgently sought in connection with the enquiry.

'Do you really think they escaped together?' Wendy asked Rob.

With a non-committal shrug, he said. 'I only saw Kyle in the car, but I suppose she could have been crouched on the back seat or something.'

'Perhaps,' Wendy said, with a delicacy that suggested she didn't believe a word of it.

It was a relief when the conversation moved on, safely away from the other aspect of his encounter with Kyle that he was still keeping to himself: the moment when he'd put the knife to Rob's throat, and his gleeful warning.

I'll come back for you all, that's a promise.

Events moved so quickly that it wasn't until Tuesday that Rob was interviewed by two officers from the Norfolk and Suffolk Major Investigation Team. DS Husein was also present, along with a detective from Kent police called McIlroy. The location was a small, stuffy waiting room at the hospital, commandeered for the purpose. Rob was informed that he was not under arrest and could leave at any time, or seek legal advice if he thought it necessary.

He declined. 'I'm happy to help in any way I can,' he said.

As well as asking questions, the police had much to tell him. It seemed that Milo and Lara had been competing to spill the beans, blaming everyone but themselves for what had happened. Their base had been in a village close to Petersfield, where their first victim, a homeless man of unknown identity, had been subjected to weeks of torture. A forensic team was now scouring the house, which had belonged to Kyle's late grandmother.

'There's some kind of family feud between his mum and his aunt,' Husein said, 'but both are adamant they have no idea where Kyle might have gone. The aunt says she didn't have a clue that Gabriel and the others were living there.'

'But we'll catch him,' said the detective inspector, a narrow-featured, placid-looking man called Toner. 'Be in no doubt about that.'

DC Driscoll, a tall woman with a slightly flustered air, admitted that there had been no sightings to date, but explained that traffic cameras with ANPR – automatic number plate recognition – were being deployed nationwide to locate the vehicle in which he had escaped.

At that point she became slightly reticent, and moved on to the discovery of a 7 series BMW, found abandoned near the coast at Hunstanton. Inside were the bodies of John Nyman and his associate, both extremely well known to the Kent detective, McIlroy, who was bald, cheerful and reeked of aftershave.

'Losing them two will knock the crime rate down by twenty points on my patch,' he drawled. 'At least till some other scrote fills the gap.'

That provoked a taut smile from DI Toner, who changed the tone completely when he said, 'And then there's Ilsa.'

There was silence, prompting Rob to ask, finally, 'What about her?'

'It turns out she didn't leave with Kyle,' Driscoll said.

'Oh.' Rob wasn't sure if he'd ever achieved an expression as blank as the one he attempted now.

'We found her body, late yesterday afternoon.' Toner had a commanding presence, and a quiet, deliberate way of speaking that would have been intimidating even if Rob had been able to tell the whole truth. 'She'd been murdered, then dragged into the marshes. Hidden away.'

'And in water,' Driscoll added. 'Which isn't good for us, evidence-wise.'

'That's a pity,' Rob said, 'but if you're expecting sympathy for her, you won't get it from me.'

'Understandable,' Husein said gently, perhaps responding to a new air of tension in the room. 'But regardless of what she's done, her death has to be investigated.'

Toner said, 'We'll be speaking to Georgia, too, you're aware of that?'

'Of course,' said Rob. 'We all have to be interviewed.'

'Good.' Driscoll brushed a stray hair from her eyes. 'What we need from you is a clearer idea of the sequence of events, from when your daughter managed to escape. . .'

'And the timings, in particular,' Toner added.

Rob shrugged: on this point he was genuinely vague. 'It all seemed to happen very quickly. After we heard the crash, a couple of them went to investigate. I think Ilsa went out through the kitchen, then Milo followed her. He was gone for. . . a few minutes, I suppose. Then he came back, and Georgia managed to sneak past them and set us free.'

'A brave girl,' Husein remarked, with what might have been a pointed look at Toner.

'Quite,' the DI agreed. 'And when she reappeared, what sort of state was she in?'

'Jesus Christ! What sort of state do you *think* she was in?'

He was so vehement that Husein placed a cautionary hand on his arm. Unmoved by the outburst, Toner said, 'Was she upset, in floods of tears? Was she angry, scared. . .?'

Rob swallowed. 'She was very shaken, as you'd expect, but keeping it together.'

'What about her physical appearance?' Driscoll asked. 'I imagine she was in quite a mess?'

Remembering that Milo and Lara had seen her come in, he said, 'Yeah. She'd been hiding out in the fields, so she was filthy, and soaking wet.'

'Any blood on her?' Toner asked.

'I think there was some, from when she'd been assaulted by Gabriel and *Lara.*'

Driscoll caught his emphasis. 'Don't worry. Lara won't be wriggling out of responsibility for her crimes.'

Toner moved briskly on: 'You say you went after Kyle, but he jumped out on you, then drove away. Correct?'

'Yes. I was hit on the head. It was Georgia who found me.'

'And was this before or after she took a shower?'

'Shower. . .?' Thrown off stride, Rob suspected he had a look in his eyes like a cornered animal. 'Uh, before, I think. I sent her back inside, then went to the main road to get a signal and call you. That took, I don't know, maybe ten minutes.'

Driscoll: 'Why is it, do you think, that Kyle stayed around, rather than just get away?'

'No idea. Maybe he wanted a chance to deal with Ilsa?' He stopped there, conscious that he mustn't say too much. He knew Wendy had reported a conversation where Lara suggested that Kyle might well have killed Ilsa.

'So why the attack on you?' This was from McIlroy.

'Because I was standing between him and the car. I was in the way – simple as that.'

'Did he say anything to you, during the attack?' Toner was now watching him very closely. 'Any reference to Ilsa?'

Rob shrugged. 'Not that I can recall.'

'No? That's a little odd, then.'

Another excruciating silence. Fuming slightly, Rob said, 'Why?'

'Because you don't seem very surprised about her death.'

'After the past week, nothing much surprises me any more.' It was a glib response, but it gave him time to think; he'd been working so hard to keep a lid on his temper, but maybe that wasn't the natural reaction to this sort of pressure.

After a few more routine questions, Toner returned to Georgia's actions. 'It's regrettable, I have to say – not only taking that shower before we arrived, but also her clothes going missing.'

'I don't know what happened there.' Rob sat up straight, his heart beating fast, and set his face in a defiant expression.

'You have to admit,' Driscoll said carefully, 'it's quite hard to see how they could have been accidentally mislaid.'

'Not really. It was chaos once you and the ambulances got there.' The anger was coursing through him now, and this time he let it run. 'Jesus, to be fixing on that after what the poor kid went through – she did so well to escape, and then come back and set us free. If it weren't for her, you'd have been rolling up days later to find a house full of rotting corpses. So if she felt. . . *soiled* by the experience, and chose to try and hide her embarrassment, you won't hear a word of criticism from me. I'm proud of her, all right? I'm *more* than proud.'

As he sat back, crossing his arms, there was a murmur from Husein: 'Hear hear.'

Toner gave a little frown of displeasure, and said, 'I think we can leave it there for now.'

SIXTY-NINE

It took Wendy a long time to get her feelings in order. Along with the relief, the elation at having survived, there was a seething maelstrom of anger, pain, anxiety and grief. And although she'd spent a lot of time reassuring their family, friends and colleagues that they had suffered no lasting damage, she wasn't completely sure it was true. She was all too aware of the potential for psychological trauma, the effects of which might take months or years to become apparent.

But for now, all things considered, they were doing remarkably well. Despite an array of colourful bruises, Evan's normally buoyant mood had been restored almost immediately, thanks to Livvy's decision to curtail her holiday in Cyprus. She was back home by Wednesday, and the two of them were soon holed up in the media-free sanctuary of her parents' home.

After a brief infection scare, Josh was released from hospital on Tuesday morning and spent most of the week resting his bruised ribs and injured leg, playing on the Xbox that they'd brought from home. He seemed blithely untroubled by the fear of prosecution, helped perhaps by the fact that his friend Ruby had cleared his flat of any contraband. She paid Josh a visit on Thursday afternoon, and the door to his hotel room stayed resolutely shut for several hours.

On the following day came confirmation that no action would be taken against him, though DS McIlroy warned that the police would take a very dim view if he were to be found smuggling in future.

'My criminal career is behind me,' Josh was able to promise the detective, with a later aside to his parents: 'Unless I get a job in the City, of course.'

Georgia, who heeded their advice to stay offline, developed a fondness for the hotel's modest gym, and spent hours shedding calories on the cross-trainer. The exercise seemed to have a beneficial effect on her mood, though whenever Wendy attempted to talk through the events of the previous weekend, she reverted to the sullen, quick-tempered teenager that they knew so well.

Between them, Wendy and Rob agreed that this was simply her way of dealing with it. When the family liaison officer from Hampshire police suggested that they should persuade her to consider counselling, Wendy said, 'We won't rule it out, but right now it's far more important that we give her a strong, supportive home environment.'

And yes, she'd thought when she caught Rob raising his eyebrows, *I am aware of the irony in that statement.*

The matter of their relationship was another subject for a later date. Several times Wendy had felt certain Rob was about to broach it, only for him to back away. In many of their conversations they tiptoed around the issue, causing her to wonder if Rob had sensed what was different.

Could he tell that Wendy had changed her mind?

More importantly, why was she so reluctant to admit it?

While staying in Winchester they had a visit from DI Powell, as well as an emotional reunion with Dawn Avery. Dawn hugged them so closely that they could feel the baby moving, and tearfully lamented the fact that she hadn't acted on their concerns.

'The girl, Lara, talking her way into the house, and the smell of BO – and I basically said it was your imagination.'

'None of us knew the significance at the time,' Rob pointed out. 'I'm the one who's to blame, for not telling you about the trainer.'

He was still wracked with guilt about that, Wendy knew, so she couldn't bring herself to criticise him, as painful as it was to know he'd kept it secret from her.

'I panicked,' he admitted to Dawn. 'I'd only just found it when you turned up, and ridiculous as it sounds now, I was scared it might put me in the frame for the man's death.'

Ultimately, however, they were agreed that nothing they'd done – or had failed to do – would have made much difference. Gabriel and his followers might simply have waited out a short, fruitless investigation, then launched their attack on another occasion.

Thanks to the testimony from Milo and Lara, a picture was emerging of life within Gabriel's vicious little sect, which the media had gleefully likened to the cults led by Charles Manson, David Koresh and others.

'The methods he used are straight out of the Twisted Messiah's Handbook,' Powell said. 'Build 'em up and knock 'em down. Keep them insecure, play one off against another. All four of them were outcasts in some form or another, all nursing grudges against families, workmates – or just humanity in general.'

Rob said, 'I can't get my head round the idea that he managed to take basically law-abiding people and turn them into torturers and killers.'

Powell shrugged. 'In the right conditions you can manipulate people into doing just about anything – plenty of psychological experiments have proved that.'

Wendy had to agree. 'I've known of pleasant but vulnerable young mums who'd meet a new boyfriend, and within a few months they're turning a blind eye to all manner of neglect and abuse of their child.'

DI Powell also had advice on handling the media. 'You have a choice. Option one is to accept the intrusion, speak to the papers, appear on TV and radio. If you come over well – and I'm sure you would – you'll have agents fighting to sign you up, there'll be publishers offering book deals, and from then on it's life in the goldfish bowl. . .'

'We're not the bloody Kardashians,' Rob muttered.

'How did I know you'd say that?' Her eyes twinkled. 'Option two is say nothing. Refuse every request. Ignore every tiny thing they print, every online comment, no matter how scurrilous or unfair. Just *ignore, ignore, ignore.*' Punching her open palm three times to make the point. 'It won't be easy, and it might take a while, but in time they *will* go away.'

So that was what they had done, and at last there were signs that it was working – thanks in part to the competing distraction of the upcoming EU referendum, coverage of which was growing increasingly hysterical.

One aspect of the public reaction that Wendy found both touching and unsettling was the number of strangers who sent cards, as well as gifts ranging from pot plants and bouquets to various religious tracts and, bizarrely, a tin of sweetcorn. Among the messages there was one from Kevin Burroughs, passing on his son's condolences. Wendy had no idea whether Mark Burroughs had genuinely spoken to his father on the matter, but either way she decided that Georgia didn't need to be troubled with this information.

On Saturday Wendy decided to make her first excursion into town, for a little shopping. She'd built it up in her mind to be some kind of epic ordeal, but the reality was gloriously mundane. Those who knew her nodded and said hello: some looked faintly embarrassed as they did so, others more sympathetic; but no one accosted her, no one asked awkward questions or pressed for details.

Could it really be, she thought as she walked home, that life was returning to normal?

Maybe that was a little premature. At some point there would still be a trial to endure, and there was no telling what impact that could have. As yet, the matter of Kyle's parentage had not come to light, and they continued to live on tenterhooks that his claim would reach the media.

Rob had insisted that, as far as he could recall, he had dated very sparingly during their brief separation, and probably not at all in the June, when Kyle was likely to have been conceived.

'My heart wasn't in it, I realised that quite early on.'

She took his hand. 'Listen, you don't have to justify anything. It was a mutual decision to take a break, and when we got back together we agreed not to dwell upon what had happened in that time. As far as I'm concerned, that still applies.'

It didn't matter that there was a small, doubting voice in her head – *Can you completely rule out the possibility that Kyle is his son?* – because Wendy had no choice but to avoid taking the conversation too far along this route.

She was impressed that Rob had never asked who, if anyone, *she* had seen during their time apart, and thank goodness he hadn't. Wendy thought it might destroy her to admit to the stupid, drunken one-night stand that she'd had with Rob's older brother, Paul – or the fact that it had led to the most agonising dilemma of her life. Although they'd used a condom, her next period had been two weeks late, and Wendy had experienced many of the tiny, innocuous symptoms which later – with the twins – she recognised as the signs of pregnancy.

Having split up from Rob precisely because of the failure to conceive, every minute of those two weeks had been the most exquisite form of torture imaginable – on a scale that even sadists like Kyle or Gabriel couldn't have matched.

In the years after, she had sometimes wondered if the decision to adopt Georgia hadn't been some misguided act of contrition on her part. Wendy knew that was deeply unfair to Georgia herself, and just one of the reasons why she had never dared to breathe a word of it to anyone.

Turning into Russell Drive, she was glad to put such thoughts aside, though the sight of Dawn Avery's car sparked a twinge of unease. That, perhaps, was a minor example of the lasting damage – that Dawn was no longer just a friend stopping by for coffee and a chat.

SEVENTY

By the weekend, Rob was itching to get life back on track. Physically, he wasn't completely recovered, but after another urine test, which had found no trace of blood, he was pronounced to be on the mend. The severe headaches had subsided, too, and although he still felt more tired than usual, he suspected that was partly due to inactivity and stodgy hotel food.

It was a relief to get back home, even if the house felt oddly unfamiliar at first. Rob put that down to the subtle rearrangement of furniture by the forensics team, who had searched the house for evidence of Kyle's intrusion.

On Saturday afternoon Rob was trawling through his emails when Dawn Avery turned up. Tim was cycling around Hayling Island, she said. 'But I wouldn't have wanted him here, to be honest – he'd only say something inappropriate.'

Rob grinned, nervously. 'Wendy's in town. She shouldn't be too long.'

'Fine. Though you might prefer to discuss this on your own.'

'Oh?' He gave a fake little laugh at her ominous tone, and ushered her into the study.

'Back to the grind already, on a day like this?' she remarked.

'Afraid so.' He was about to throw in that corny line – *No rest for the wicked* – but changed his mind.

It was a beautiful day. Evan and Livvy had gone to the beach at West Wittering, while Josh and Georgia were in the garden, Josh reading something for next year's course, Georgia watching a Netflix show on her iPad.

Dawn told him how she'd been assigned the task of researching Kyle's background in the hope of unearthing clues as to his present whereabouts. 'I've been liaising with Toronto police, and I've spoken to his mother, Julie Jacques – Julie Bridger, as she is now.'

Rob felt as though his lungs were being compressed by an unseen force. 'Find anything useful?'

'Not really. There's a watch on the ports and airports, but his mum's certain that he won't try returning to Canada.' She hesitated. 'On the matter of Kyle's allegations, she completely denied having identified you, though I suspect she was worried about being implicated in anything. After all, something must have set him off in your direction. . .'

Invited to agree, Rob only shrugged. 'Maybe.' If pressed, he would argue that they were probably selected at random, with the reason fabricated by Kyle after the fact.

'What she has admitted is that she went out with several men during the summer that Kyle was conceived, and says she honestly doesn't know – or care – which one was the father.' Dawn regarded him for a moment, her tongue prodding beneath her upper lip, as if to dislodge something. 'Then I asked about you. She said she'd seen your photographs online and didn't recognise you at all.'

Rob nodded, cautiously. 'Good.'

'It is. Except the vibe I was getting from her. . . I hate to ask this, but do you think you could. . .?' She rummaged in her handbag and brought out her phone. 'Just take a look at these photos and tell me if you recognise her?'

'This is Julie Jacques?'

Dawn nodded. 'Bear in mind she'll be twenty years older here than when you knew her – *if* this is the girl you dated. She claims she hasn't kept any photos from that time.'

'Might be true,' Rob said, and found himself thinking of Georgia. 'Not everyone wants to be reminded of their past.'

The front door opened as he took the phone and he jumped, almost dropping it.

'In here,' he called, and was glad that Dawn's attention was diverted for a moment while he studied the pictures. *Just in case*, he thought, because his hands were visibly trembling.

Wendy opened the front door and was called into the study by Rob. He was leaning against his desk, holding a phone, while Dawn stood a couple of feet away, one hand resting on her baby bump. As she greeted Dawn, she heard Rob saying, 'Doesn't look familiar.'

'What's this?' Wendy asked, and while Dawn explained the background to her visit, Rob was swiping the screen back and forth.

Finally he shook his head, passed the phone to Wendy and said, 'Nope, don't know her.'

Wendy studied the pictures, which had been taken by a lake somewhere. Kyle's mother was an attractive, well-groomed woman who'd clearly stayed in shape, and therefore probably hadn't changed a great deal over the years. If Rob had gone out with her – and Wendy could see why he'd have wanted to – he would surely recognise her.

But Dawn couldn't quite disguise a hint of scepticism. Turning her gaze from Wendy to Rob, she said, 'I take it you do remember what your previous girlfriends looked like?'

'The serious ones, yes. But not necessarily girls I only saw once or twice.'

'Really? I think I'd still recognise the boy I kissed when I was twelve.'

With a broad smile, Wendy cut in: 'We'd all like to think that, but it's scary just how much you forget. There are holidays from my teens that I can't recall at all, school friends who've popped up on Facebook just this week and I have no recollection of them.'

Rob looked grateful for her intervention. 'It's because you're a lot younger than us, Dawn. Just wait till the brain cells start dying off, and you'll see what we mean.'

On learning that Rob hadn't offered refreshments, Wendy suggested they move to the kitchen. Dawn accepted a cup of tea, and updated them on some other developments.

'The toxicology reports made for an interesting read. Turns out Kyle wasn't lying about that, at least.'

'What?' Wendy asked.

'Gabriel had a heart attack, but it was induced. With poison.'

She explained that the cult leader had been injected with a lethal dose of potassium chloride – the very chemical used to carry out the death penalty in the United States. There were signs that other drugs had been used over a period of months, increasing his heart rate and blood pressure, pushing him into a more vulnerable state.

'Of course, he may have taken those himself, voluntarily,' Dawn pointed out. On the Saturday night, the group had been passing round what Milo and Lara believed to be amphetamines, sourced by Kyle. But tests had revealed that the pills could have contained only small amounts of the stimulant, whereas the hot drinks Kyle had made in the early hours had been laced with sedatives.

'That's why they woke so late on Sunday?' Wendy asked.

Dawn nodded. 'He wanted them all out cold, so he could deal with Gabriel, then pretend to be none the wiser when Lara raised the alarm.'

'Jesus,' Rob muttered. 'So clearly Gabriel's mind control stuff didn't work on Kyle.'

'Well, we may never know if he was genuinely in thrall to Gabriel at the start, or if he just faked it. But it's clear from what Milo and Lara have said that there's no way Kyle could have attracted his own followers. It was, you have to say, a brilliantly devious strategy on his part to join Gabriel's group, then gradually steer them towards his own objectives.'

Destroying us, Rob thought, and he was reminded that a man as driven as Kyle was unlikely to let it go now.

Having blushed slightly at her use of the word 'brilliant' to describe Kyle, Dawn said, 'This sounds so counter intuitive, but Shahid and I were discussing it, and we realised that what probably kept you all alive was the fact that they'd got hold of a firearm.'

'What?' Wendy exclaimed, and Rob said, 'How do you work that out?'

'Their plan was to keep control by separating Georgia from the rest of you, and threaten her with violence if anyone misbehaved. We know they were armed with other weapons, but nothing that carries the absolute power of a gun. . .'

Rob was nodding now. 'You think we'd have taken them on?'

'That, or tried to escape. Either way, you might have paid a very heavy price. We know they wouldn't have hesitated to use knives – Kyle in particular.' Dawn shivered. 'One look at Ilsa's body and you can see exactly what he's capable of.'

As she spoke, Rob felt Wendy's gaze shift in his direction, and he said quickly, 'I don't think it does any good to dwell on that, do you?'

Dawn raised her hands in apology. 'No, I'm sorry.' She grinned. 'Who needs Tim, when I keep putting my foot in it?'

Once she had gone, and Wendy had said a quick hello to Georgia and Josh, she asked Rob if they could return to the study to talk. 'I need to know what's wrong.'

'What do you mean?'

She made sure the door was shut, then said, 'I don't want to play games, and it might well be that you've been saying nothing for my benefit. But I think something happened, when you went after Kyle.'

She could tell at once that she was on the right track. She held his gaze until he nodded, reluctantly, and said, 'He threatened me. Said that one day he'll come back and target us.'

'Did you tell the police?'

'There's nothing they can do about it—'

'But it's more lies, Rob!' She hadn't meant to shout, or get upset. 'After all the problems it caused us last time.'

'Look, it won't help anyone, and I didn't want word getting back to you and the kids.'

'But they're at risk, they need to know—'

'Why? So they end up living in fear all their lives? I bet that's exactly why he said it, not because he has any intention of carrying it out.'

She brooded on that, and had to admit he was probably right. 'So you haven't warned Georgia, then?'

He responded with a pantomime frown. 'No. Why?'

'I'm sure I've noticed a sort of. . . secretive atmosphere lately.'

'Really? I wouldn't say that – but I could warn her, if you think that's best?'

Wendy smiled. He'd been given the perfect opportunity to come clean, and yet he was determined to say nothing. Without quite knowing why, she found herself backing away from a confrontation.

'Not yet,' she said. 'Let's have a think about it first.'

That night the six of them – Livvy was here with Evan – enjoyed a delicious takeaway curry and watched a movie together, exactly as they had done on so many occasions in the innocent world of their pre-Kyle existence. Wendy had only a couple of glasses of wine, but by eleven o'clock she was struggling to keep her eyes open.

Often Rob stayed up later at the weekends, but this evening he climbed the stairs just a few minutes after Wendy. 'I've been looking forward to this,' he murmured – and then, as if he thought she'd misinterpreted, he added: 'Compared to that hotel bed, I mean.'

'Absolutely,' she said.

It was a warm night, barely requiring a duvet, but Wendy snuggled beneath it all the same. She lay on her back, suddenly uneasy, not wanting to turn away but unable to face him. *Why is this so difficult?* she wondered.

During the meal they'd all started talking about a holiday – 'a proper holiday,' as Evan put it; going abroad to somewhere hot and relaxing and anonymous, a place where no one knew who they were or what they had been through.

'We probably should look into it,' Rob said now. 'But not for a couple of weeks, till I've got sorted at work.'

Wendy smiled. How many times had she heard that?

'I'll see how the rota looks at my place,' she said.

He grunted agreement, then lay in silence for a minute.

'So,' he said at last, 'we never did carry on with that conversation up in Norfolk.'

'No. We didn't.'

'Well. . .' He sighed. 'If we're getting back to normal. . . that means doing it soon.'

'Mm.' Her head was a mess of conflicting emotions. She knew that Rob was keeping something from her, and that made it harder to be truthful with him, to admit that she wanted to put the decision on hold.

Then, in an act of daring rebellion, he reached for her hand, his fingertips brushing against her stomach. Wendy gasped and turned towards him, silencing his tiny exclamation with a kiss, and another kiss, and then a whisper: 'No more talking.'

The announcement could wait.

The decision could wait.

The future could wait.

SEVENTY-ONE

Monday morning dawned, warm and fragrant, with a brilliant blue sky and a gauzy layer of mist slowly clearing from the lake. The sort of weather that could only herald a new beginning.

Yesterday had been almost bizarre in its ordinariness, a shocking contrast to the Sunday before, when they had fought their way free, and two Sundays ago, when the dying man had stumbled into their garden. Rob had noticed how they were all prone to sudden flashbacks: one of them might drift out of a conversation mid-sentence, or stop with a task half-complete and stare at nothing for a few seconds; usually a little touch or a few words of support was sufficient to shake off the grip of unwanted memories.

On Saturday night Rob and Wendy had made love with a passion, an intensity that was virtually unprecedented, certainly in the last decade or so. They'd clung to one another, kissing and clawing and writhing as if it were *right now* that their lives hung in the balance. After a night of restful sleep, Rob had troubled over the conversation that had preceded it – the sense he'd had that Wendy wanted to tell him something, but also that she was afraid; afraid of whatever it was that he was keeping from her.

He knew he couldn't say – not even if it risked the marriage. There was too much at stake for her; even more for Georgia.

* * *

Rob was a little nervous at first, going into the office, but Cerys had visited him at home last week, and passed on the message that he didn't want a lot of fuss.

Once he'd got through the initial greetings and sent the engineers on their way, he could relax and enjoy the mundane demands of his job. He was reviewing a quote for a heating system at a new leisure centre near Southampton when Cerys answered the phone, then cleared her throat.

'Personal call for you. Says he's "Julie's boy"?'

For Rob there was a microsecond of confusion, then he shut down his reaction, nodded casually and picked up his own handset. 'Give me a second, could you?'

Cerys jumped to her feet. 'I'll do us a coffee.'

He introduced himself, and heard Kyle take a breath. 'I said I'd come back.'

'So you did. Where are you?'

A disgusted snort. 'The plan's changed, Rob. I'm leaving this shitty country for good.'

'Glad to hear it.'

'But I need money. Fifty grand in cash and I'll leave you alone.'

Rob started to laugh. 'Don't be stupid—'

'It's doable, Rob – and you *will* do it, or else I'll tell the cops about Ilsa.'

Rob swallowed. 'What?'

'You know I didn't kill Ilsa. Georgia did.'

'Bullshit.'

'Then why do you sound so worried? Without money, I won't last long – and if I'm caught, that's what I'm going to tell them.'

'The police will never believe it. You've got no proof.'

'How do you know I haven't?' A quick, taunting laugh. 'Anyway, I don't have to prove it. If I'm caught, I'll admit to everything I did – all of it – but I'll go on insisting that Ilsa was murdered by Georgia. And you know what. . . *someone* out there will believe it. If not the cops, then a crusading lawyer, or a blogger, a schoolmate of Georgia's. . .'

Rob knew he was right. Evidence didn't matter a jot these days, not in the court of public opinion. Even if the police didn't believe Kyle – and Rob thought DI Toner might well be persuaded – the rumours and gossip alone would be enough to destroy Georgia's life.

'Fifty grand.' Taking the silence for victory, Kyle was quietly gloating. 'It's a small price to pay for peace of mind. . . isn't it, *Dad*?'

Rob felt sick. But he remembered how that instinct for self-preservation had worked for him before; now it was needed again.

'Where do we meet?' he said.

The handover was set for Wednesday, after Rob argued that he needed time to get the cash together. Kyle wanted to meet at five a.m., but the location wouldn't be revealed until Rob was underway. Leave Petersfield at four thirty, he was told, and head towards the town of Arundel, in the neighbouring county of West Sussex. Rob gave his mobile number but didn't get a number in return.

He wasn't surprised. The fear of such a move had lain at the back of his mind ever since he'd set eyes on Ilsa's mutilated corpse. While Georgia kept watch on the path, Rob had dragged the body deep into the reeds, staggering barefoot through the muddy water until he found a place where it could be submerged. He'd taken the knife that Georgia had used and buried it deep in the mud, more than fifty yards away, promising his daughter that the salt water, the mud and the rain would obliterate any evidence that might incriminate her.

'Without proof, there's nothing the police can do. You just have to stick to the story.'

'But isn't it wrong, to lie about this?'

The question had pleased him – a reassuring sign that Georgia *did* have a moral compass, despite what she'd done. Rob told her, quite sincerely, that he had no qualms about Ilsa's death, and neither should she. The woman had posed a lethal threat to them all. And the same was true of Kyle – given the nature of the man, it would hardly be a miscarriage of justice if he went to prison for Ilsa's murder.

After coming under some pressure during his own police interview, he'd been terrified that Georgia wouldn't survive a similar ordeal. But with DS Husein particularly vocal in his support of the family, it had turned out to be a relatively easy-going conversation. As she later described it to Rob, whenever the interview threatened to stray into dangerous territory, Georgia had broken down in tears, reinforcing her status as a victim.

Now Rob's plan was threatened by the one man who knew for sure that he and Georgia had lied. He was up against a formidable adversary, someone who'd succeeded in the past precisely because he had been underestimated.

Rob couldn't afford to make that mistake himself.

SEVENTY-TWO

On Tuesday Josh decided to return to Canterbury for a couple of days. Evan was driving him, and would stay to help sort out the flat. With a shyness that amused his parents, Josh muttered something about possibly bringing Ruby back for the weekend – 'If that's all right with you guys?'

For Rob, their absence was a stroke of luck. That night he lay in bed, fidgeting, until Wendy stirred, at which point he said, 'Too restless, sorry. I'll sleep in Josh's room.'

'You don't have to,' she said as he climbed out.

'No, you were sound. It's not fair.'

Sleeping alone meant he could set his alarm for three forty-five and not have to worry about waking her, or being asked where he was going. If he had to provide an explanation, he'd prefer to do it *after* he'd gone out, rather than before.

He didn't expect to sleep at all, but at some time around one he zonked out and woke to the vibration of the phone. Less than three hours, yet he felt wide awake and refreshed. He gazed around the room that Josh had repopulated with books and clothes, wet towels and chocolate wrappers; papers from his degree course that were as baffling to Rob as hieroglyphs on a tomb. *Even so*, he thought. . .

'We're more alike than I ever knew, you and I,' he murmured, and was overcome by a wave of the most intense and fragile love for his son – for both his sons, and for his daughter – and he wondered if it was the result of a premonition; a gut instinct that he would never see them again.

No. Couldn't think like that.

*

Dressing in jeans, t-shirt and fleece, he crept downstairs, collected the bag from its hiding place in the study and slipped out of the house at just after four. The day was cool but dry and very still, the midsummer twilight a luminous shade of grey.

Rob left the driver's door ajar until he was on the road, then shut it firmly and picked up speed, praying that Wendy hadn't been woken by the noise. His phone was beside him on the passenger seat, but he'd switched it off. The bag was in the footwell: not all of the money that Kyle had demanded, but a substantial amount.

Arundel was about twenty-five miles away. He'd visited the town often as a child – though never the famous castle, as the entry charges were considered exorbitant by his dad. He and Wendy had brought their own kids here a few times, and it was a favourite location for the two of them to mooch round the antique shops before enjoying a pub lunch.

This early in the morning Rob was able to take the Land Rover up to sixty or seventy, even on the narrow country roads, swinging it around the bends with what in other circumstances would have been a joyous exhilaration. He was on the A27 within twenty minutes, well ahead of schedule.

Rob doubted that Arundel would be the location for the handover. It was far too public, even at this early hour, and Kyle's image had been plastered over newspapers and TV for the past week and a half. Just yesterday there had been some minor hysteria on Sky News when a man who vaguely resembled him had been tackled while shopping in Wakefield.

By meeting Rob at all, Kyle was taking a considerable risk. Was that courage on his part, or stupidity?

More likely desperation, Rob decided. Then came a thunderbolt of an idea: *Was this a trap?* Kyle might have handed himself in to the police, then negotiated a deal whereby he would help them to incriminate Rob – and, by extension, Georgia – in return for a lighter sentence.

Oh, Christ. His hands felt clammy on the steering wheel. Since Monday he'd thought of little else but this meeting, so how was this possibility only now occurring to him?

He took a few deep breaths and decided that he was too committed to call it off at this stage. If he was caught, he would confess at once to Ilsa's murder. Unless they had solid evidence to the contrary, they would have to prosecute him, rather than Georgia.

He reached the outskirts of the town, went left at the round-about into Maltravers Street and rolled to a halt at the kerb, wondering if his fate had already been sealed.

It was four thirty when he switched on his phone. No messages yet, so he sat and waited. A fox emerged from a garden and gave him an imperious glance. A racing bike flew past, the rider almost as thin and tubular as his bike, which made Rob think of Tim, and then Dawn, and then the big, big trouble he might be in. . .

His phone buzzed with a message: *Castle car park*

Rob started the engine. If Kyle had texted it must mean he was already in place. But it still seemed like an odd location to him.

He was there a couple of minutes later. As he'd expected, it was quiet but not completely deserted. Rob spotted two elderly women in hiking gear, studying a map; there was a man walking his dog towards the river path, and presumably a couple of people getting friendly in a car with steamed-up windows, parked in the corner on its own.

After pulling in, Rob picked up his phone again. He felt self-conscious, exposed, and there was no better prop than a phone.

He waited ten minutes. Three young men staggered back to their car, laughing and singing after what must have been a long and enjoyable night. No other movement at all; and then, at ten to five, his phone buzzed.

'*Dover Lane. Go 1 mile, watch for overturned bird feeder, then right along track*'

While he was reading it, another text came in:

'*Tell no one. I am WATCHING you*'

His instinct was to look around, which he suppressed for a second, and then thought: why shouldn't he? There was no one in sight, but lots of places to hide: parked cars, trees, the museum building. Was Kyle here, right now, or was it a bluff?

Suddenly irritated, he called the number from the texts and put the phone to his ear, still checking the car park for movement. The phone rang six, seven times, and he imagined Kyle's frustration. But what was he going to do?

The ringing stopped. Silence, then a harsh voice: 'Follow instructions.'

'Where the fuck is Dover Lane? I've never heard of it.'

'On the A27. Go east past the station. It's not far after that, a turning on the left.'

'A27, east past the station, left turn soon after. Got it. And it's a bird feeder I'm looking for?'

'Ten minutes. If you're not there, I have a statement ready for the cops.'

'I'll be there. Right along the track after the bird feeder, yeah?' Rob chuckled. 'Hey – if you're watching me now, why not pop over here and I'll give you a lift?'

An angry exclamation. 'Ten minutes.' And the connection was cut.

SEVENTY-THREE

It was full daylight now, but muted by low cloud. Rob pulled back on to the main road, which even at this time of the morning wasn't particularly quiet. He wondered how well Kyle had thought out his plans. Presumably he had his own transport, or he wouldn't be able to reach the rendezvous in time. Unless he had been bluffing about being in the car park?

Too many questions, all pointless. Rob drove past the town's railway station and then slowed, searching for the junction. It was mostly trees on his left, and open farmland to his right. He also kept an eye on his mirror, in case Kyle was coming up behind him.

After making the turn, he found himself on a narrow lane heading north, with grass verges on each side and a few large properties set well back behind high hedges. Then into more woodland, and finally he spotted a bird table, presumably lifted from a nearby garden, lying just off the road at the opening to a path through the trees.

It was a dirt track, only just wide enough for the Land Rover. The ground was firm, rutted with previous tyre marks, but nothing that looked particularly recent. Rob eased his way along at about five miles an hour, alert to a possible ambush from the side.

He'd gone a couple of hundred yards when he spotted something coming towards him. It was a motorbike, small and low-powered. The rider was wearing long shorts, a dark quilted jacket and a white helmet. He slowed, raised a hand and gestured at Rob to pull in.

Rob did so, coming to a stop with perhaps thirty or forty yards between them. The rider, a slight figure who could only be Kyle, jabbed a hand to his right. Rob considered shouting out but decided just to follow instructions for now.

Stuffing the phone into his pocket, he picked up the bag and set off through the trees, with Kyle moving on a parallel course. The earth beneath him was sometimes firm, sometimes soft and mulchy. The ground rose a little, then fell away, and Rob saw a clearing up ahead.

Kyle angled his route towards Rob, only now removing the helmet. With some twenty feet between them he ordered Rob to stop, then turned a slow circle before taking a few more paces.

'Just you and me,' Rob said.

'Good. You've got the money?'

Rob hefted the bag, which Kyle eyed suspiciously. Now they were closer he could see that Kyle's clothes were filthy, and he looked half-crazed with exhaustion, his face white, eyes bloodshot. His hair was lank and unwashed, and there was a rash of angry spots on his neck. Rob guessed he'd been living rough.

'I could have dropped this off at the car park.' Rob's voice was calm enough, but there was a slight tremor in one of his legs.

'I want to count it.' Kyle took another step, dropping the helmet to the ground.

'I'll save you the time. There's fifteen thousand.'

Kyle's mouth dropped open. 'You're taking the piss?'

'It's a lot of money.'

'I said fifty.' Kyle took another step forward.

'It's the most I could lay my hands on in the time. I'll write you a cheque for the rest, if you want?'

Kyle let out an incoherent snarl, then gestured angrily at the bag. 'Open it.'

'Okay.' As Rob started to kneel down, he sensed Kyle's movement, one hand reaching behind him and drawing a knife, and now he understood why the young man was taking such a risk.

Kyle wanted money *and* revenge.

Rob straightened up, dodging sideways as Kyle lunged with the knife. His first swipe missed and before he could raise the weapon again Rob threw himself at Kyle and managed to get hold of his wrist, squeezing it with all his strength. Kyle tried to break free but Rob wouldn't let go; it meant Kyle couldn't use the knife, but he didn't drop it, either. Both men wrestled and swore, then fell to the ground, Rob conscious all the time that the blade was only inches from his face. He kneed Kyle in the stomach and Kyle retaliated with a head butt that missed its target but still caught Rob painfully on his jaw. Then, somehow, Kyle pivoted on the ground and found a way to get up; he wrenched one hand free and used his knuckles to club at Rob's head.

For a second Rob was disorientated, and Kyle was too fast, too desperate. Rob shut his eyes, almost giving up, almost accepting that his carefully thought-out plan had turned into what the Americans called a *clusterfuck*—

And then he thought: *No.* Kyle was leaning back to get more weight and momentum into a thrust of the knife. Rob let his body go limp, and when the knife came slicing down he bucked and twisted in one big violent motion that tipped Kyle sideways, the blade gouging out a divot of earth as Kyle lost his grip on the handle and fell; with a surge of energy and hope, Rob threw himself on to the younger, lighter man, who was now disarmed and off-balance.

Rob slammed his forearm down on Kyle's neck, the impact hard and heavy. He felt the sickening, sinewy pop of something rupturing. Kyle's eyes bulged and snot burst from his nose. He let out a long and terrible hiss of pain. His teeth, when he bared them, were slicked with blood.

'You would have killed me,' Rob growled, pressing harder still, riding out a few feeble blows of protest, ignoring a spasm of Kyle's knee that caught him in the groin. 'That's why I'm doing this, and I'm sorry, truly. Because I lied to you.'

Kyle's eyes seemed to widen further, and the tiny veins inside them were bursting. His tongue came out, bleeding where he'd bitten it in the struggle, and a noise issued from his throat, the air straining through his crushed windpipe; sounds that were possibly intended as speech, but could never form words that anyone would understand.

Rob decided it was a question, if it was anything. So he answered.

'I don't know. . . if you're my son, or not. . .' Gasping himself, because of the effort it required, not to let up the pressure. 'But I *did* recognise your mum's picture, and I *did* go out with her.'

There were other things he could have said – like the fact that Kyle might possibly be his own flesh and blood, but when it came down to it Rob cared much, much more for Georgia than he did for this stranger who had tried to destroy them all.

Because of that, Rob was prepared to lie to his wife, to his kids, to the police; even, if necessary, to himself.

Kyle went on staring at him, but he wasn't seeing anything, and for a time neither was Rob. What brought him back was the sound of his heart, like a jackhammer, and when he raised his head the world around him seemed to be rocking back and forth, the trees blurring in and out of focus. Two strange shadows came bobbing towards him: a hallucination, he thought, until one of them said, 'Rob?' and then: 'Shit, are you all right?'

He didn't have time to react before they were on him, immensely strong hands lifting him away from the body. He tried to stand but was urged instead to sit, to put his head between his knees and take deep breaths.

'You've had a shock,' Jason said. 'Hell of a fucking shock, by the look of it.'

Rob followed the advice, and was vaguely aware of some muttering between Jason and the other man, whom he recognised from the poker nights as his silent investor, the reclusive Collins.

After a couple of minutes, when he felt a little better, Jason came over and crouched down, gave him a wry appraisal and said, 'Looks like you did the job.'

Rob nodded, swallowing back an urge to vomit. 'He had a knife. Went for me.'

'Did he? Shit.'

'Thought you weren't going to make it.'

'Nah, wasn't easy, finding our way here.' Jason looked apologetic. 'Still, got the right result, eh?'

With that, he glanced at Kyle. Rob followed his gaze and the knowledge struck him, for the first time, that the young man was dead.

'We should be getting on.' This was Collins, a squat, dangerous-looking man in his forties. He was standing over the body, but keeping a watchful eye on their surroundings.

'He's right,' Jason said. 'Don't wanna push our luck.'

Rob stood up, brushing off mud and leaves. Jason tapped the bag with his foot. 'This the cash?'

'Yeah. All yours.'

'Expenses only,' Jason said, as if he'd been accused of overcharging. He nodded towards his colleague. 'A drink or two for this one.'

'Dirty work, disposal,' Collins said, and then chuckled. 'Well, sometimes.'

Rob wasn't sure if he'd heard correctly. His ears were ringing, a sort of feedback whine. Both men were surveying the woods, and Rob felt a quiver of fear. If they decided he couldn't be trusted, they might kill him now, and take the money. . .

Jason pointed. 'Truck's over that way. Oh, and I'd better have the phone back.'

'Of course.' Rob took out the cheap phone Jason had supplied him. They'd had an open connection when he rang Kyle from the car park, enabling him to pass on details of the rendezvous. All Jason's idea.

The two men had put gloves on and were standing each side of the body, preparing to lift it. They had an efficient, professional air which nagged at Rob.

'What do you mean, the disposal is *sometimes* dirty work?'

'This one's gonna vanish, and never be seen again,' Jason said. 'That's all you need to know.'

Rob understood that, but he couldn't help pushing. 'The method is different, though, sometimes?' Which was more diplomatic than asking, *How often have you done this?*

Jason made a clicking noise, like a friendly warning, but Collins was already saying, 'Water's easiest.'

'Water?' Rob turned on him, ignoring the fact that Jason had hauled Kyle's body up and thrown it over his shoulder as though it were a bag of cement.

'Yeah. Nothing cleaner than an accident at sea, you know?' Collins sniggered. 'Swimming. Scuba diving. Water-skiing.'

SEVENTY-FOUR

Rob felt his spine turn to ice. He said nothing; just concentrated hard on the tasks at hand. Jason had the body, and Collins picked up the motorcycle helmet and the bag of cash. Rob followed them through the trees, focusing on each simple breath, on putting one foot in front of the other.

It took four or five minutes to reach the truck, which Jason had bumped on to a grass verge on a lane adjacent to the one where Rob had parked. The body was placed in the back and covered with a tarpaulin, weighed down with several bags of sand.

The three men climbed into the cab and drove the short distance to the other vehicles. The motorbike was lifted aboard and laid alongside the body. Rob had no idea what they were going to do with either, and he didn't want to know.

Once Collins had climbed back into the truck, Rob shook hands with Jason. As he tried to pull away, Jason tightened his grip. 'Don't ever get cold feet about this.'

'I won't.' Rob was indignant, as well as scared. 'Why do you say that?'

'The look on your face when Col mentioned water-skiing.' Jason let go of his hand, only to jab a finger at him. 'Just remember, you're on shaky ground. We did what you wanted, the way you wanted it.' He nodded towards the truck. 'Same with this.'

It was like being punched in the gut. Rob clutched his stomach. 'Wh-what are you saying?' he stammered. 'We didn't ever. . .'

'Is that what you told yourself?' Jason gave him a scathing look. 'You might have put it out of your head, but I ain't forgotten a word. You wanted Kelly dead, you made that totally clear.'

'I probably did – as a figure of speech. He'd just ruined my life.'

'It weren't no figure of speech, Rob. You gave me the address of his villa. Told me how you'd tracked him down and found out it was bought in his girlfriend's name. You even said that, the year before, he'd been boasting to you about his water-skiing lessons. "Hope the bastard drowns", you said to me.'

'Yeah, but that's—' Rob broke off, because Jason had a murderous look in his eyes.

'We're done here, mate. You just get that business into profit nice and quick.' Jason winked. 'I'm thinking I might buy you out, once you're ready for the pipe and slippers.'

He slapped Rob on the shoulder, nearly flooring him, then got into the truck and drove away. Rob stumbled back to his car, dropped the keys, bumped his head on the wing mirror as he bent to pick them up, then collapsed into the driver's seat.

He was a mess.

It was a good twenty minutes before he felt safe to drive back. Even then he was on autopilot, brooding over Jason's version of their shared history. It was true that for a time he had despised Iain Kelly, and probably had wished him dead on various occasions, sometimes in front of witnesses. But that didn't mean he had gone about arranging that death.

Oddly, what sprang to mind was a vague memory of a history lesson from school: something about a king in conflict with. . . an archbishop, was it? A famous quote: *Will no one rid me of this troublesome priest?*

Had Rob issued a similar instruction? Had he really passed on what he'd learned from the enquiry agent about Iain's new home in Spain? He genuinely had no recollection of that. What he did know was that he had felt truly shocked when he heard of Kelly's death, and he hadn't seriously challenged the assumption that it was an accident.

It wasn't yet seven o'clock when he pulled up at home. Russell Drive was quiet, though he caught Phil Denning peering out from his bedroom window. Rob gave him the finger, then let himself into the house.

He listened for activity, heard none, and crept upstairs. He inspected himself in the bathroom mirror and realised a shower was necessary. While he stood under the hot water, he thought about who he was and what he'd done.

And he thought about Julie Jacques. The fact that he'd slept with her didn't make it a certainty that Kyle was his son: far from it. He thought the dates were probably off by a few weeks, at least, though he was aware that at some stage Dawn Avery might turn up with news that Kyle's DNA showed a familial match.

But either way, he knew Wendy would never accept that it was right to kill Kyle rather than hand him over to the police. And that, he thought, made his next decision somewhat easier.

After drying off, he eased the bedroom door open. Wendy was a silent form beneath the duvet, and didn't stir until he'd climbed into bed beside her.

'Spoon,' she said, so he moved on to his side and cuddled up against her.

She breathed deeply. 'You smell nice.'

'Really?'

'Shower gel.' She breathed again. 'And. . . soil, is that? Sort of loamy.'

'Of course not.' He chuckled. 'Alarm's due any time now.'

'It already went, didn't you hear it?'

'I slept in Josh's room.'

Now it was her turn to laugh. Rob held her tight, nuzzling against the back of her head, and somehow he knew she was smiling, in a fond way, as if his idiosyncrasies could never fail to amuse her, even while they drove her quietly mad.

'This announcement,' he said, and felt her flinch.

'Don't, Rob. We don't need to—'

'We do. I think I should be the one to leave, and we should tell the kids that I was the reason.'

Silence. A long silence.

And then she said, 'I've changed my mind.'

'What? When?'

'I couldn't even say, for sure. The past few weeks, maybe.'

'But isn't that just a reaction to the trauma? Because the reasons you gave me at Christmas made perfect sense, and they still do. I'm too selfish, too bound up in work, and I'm—'

He stopped. *Could he say this?*

'I'm not a good person, Wendy. Whereas you are.'

'What are you trying to tell me?' She only waited a second before adding, 'That you've done things you shouldn't? Things you regret – or things you *ought* to regret? That you're keeping secrets from me?' She sniffed, rubbed her nose, then broke from his embrace to turn and look at him. 'Well, guess what, Robert Turner? Same here. And I doubt if it makes *your* life a misery, fretting over whatever it is that *I* might be ashamed of. . . does it?'

He grunted, his way of only half-conceding. 'I'm just worried you might regret not doing it. You seemed to feel so strongly that separation is the right thing for you.'

'Perhaps I did – and who knows, perhaps I will again. But not now.'

'Honestly?'

'Honestly.' She held his hand. 'Right now I want us to be together. For better, for worse – like the man told us, all those years ago.'

But I'm a killer. Just for a moment – the merest fraction of a second – Rob thought he'd said the words out loud. But no, Wendy's expression hadn't changed. She continued to regard him with a degree of affection, tolerance and love that he didn't deserve, and never would deserve, and he understood that telling her outright would be the cruellest thing he'd ever done.

But how could he live with Wendy when he could barely live with himself?

'Well?' she said, with a sleepy half-smile. 'What do you have to say?'

There was an enigmatic look in her eye, and it occurred to Rob that she knew, somehow; that she knew – or suspected, at least – and on the matter of protecting their family, had decided that she could condone almost anything.

'For better, for worse?' he said.

She nodded. 'That's the deal. One day at a time – expiry unknown, and hopefully a long way off. . .'

He grinned; he couldn't not.

'In that case,' he said, 'I'd have to be a fool to say no.'

LETTER FROM TOM

The writing of *All Fall Down* took place during a turbulent but exciting period in my life. After several years of uncertainty and a number of setbacks, my deal with Bookouture represented the chance of a fresh start. At the point when the contract was signed, of course, there was no way of knowing whether the first book in the deal, *See How They Run*, would be a success. If it wasn't, then I knew I would probably have to put writing aside and find a new career.

Often when I'm writing one novel, I discover elements or themes that I want to expand upon in the next book – and so it was with *All Fall Down*, which takes from my previous book the idea of a family in jeopardy. In *See How They Run*, my protagonists were a young couple with a baby; here I decided on a mature couple with grown-up children. Instead of threatening intruders appearing in the middle of the night, I wanted an idyllic scene – a summer barbecue – interrupted by a man in desperate need of help.

For my antagonists, I'd long had it in mind to write about a group of people who together are capable of crimes that they would scarcely consider if they were alone. As well as the real-life examples of Charles Manson and the other cult leaders referenced in the book, there's also a lot of fascinating scientific research – such as the famous Milgram experiment – that demonstrates just how easily a commanding personality can persuade others to commit acts of extreme violence.

Although the most high-profile examples tend to come from the USA, Gabriel and his followers were actually influenced by a news story in the UK that has stayed with me for many years, and concerned a vulnerable young woman who was lured into friendship by a group of her peers. Over several days she was subjected to horrific torture and finally murdered. The savagery of the crime was shocking enough, but what haunted me about it was the deceit, the betrayal. And while most of us can just about understand how someone might kill for revenge, or greed, or passion, it's extremely difficult to accept the idea of tormenting and killing purely for fun, as part of a twisted game or 'challenge'. With that in mind I created a group that has progressed, quite calmly and methodically, towards the ultimate goal of mass murder.

Secrets of one type or another lie at the heart of this story – indeed, the working title for the book was *The Secrets* – and with older protagonists, I had the chance to create characters who were perhaps a little more compromised, and not quite the straightforward 'good guys' that a younger couple might have been. Rob and Wendy also have to contend with the difficult realisation that their grown-up children have lives as messy and complicated as their own.

As it turned out, the success of *See How They Run* far exceeded my wildest dreams, and introduced my work to a huge number of readers, many of whom were kind enough to leave reviews at Goodreads and elsewhere.. If you have read and enjoyed *All Fall Down*, I would be extremely grateful if you could add a review to the site or sites of your choice – and please do also get in touch to let me know what you think of the book.

You can contact me or find out more about my books via the links below, and receive news of my new releases by signing up to my email list:

www.bookouture.com/tom-bale

 @t0mbale
tombalewriter
www.tombale.net

ACKNOWLEDGEMENTS

Thanks firstly to Oliver Rhodes and the marvellous team at Bookouture. I am extremely grateful to my editor, Keshini Naidoo, who went way beyond the call of duty in her efforts to whip this book into shape on a rather demanding schedule. Equally, Kim Nash has been an extraordinary whirlwind of activity in support of my books. Thanks also to Natasha Hodgson, Rhian McKay and Claire Rushbrook.

At Darley Anderson I want to thank Camilla Wray, Naomi Perry, Mary Darby, Emma Winter and Rosanna Bellingham for their ongoing help and support.

For advice, feedback and general support I'm indebted to Ian and Heidi Vinall, and to Stuart and Karen Marsom. After thanking the old geezers in my previous book, this time round I want to give a shout out to Dawn, Karen, Heidi, Jacqui and Maria for decades of friendship. And as ever, the biggest debt of gratitude is owed to my first and most put-upon reader: my wife, Niki.

To my fellow Bookouture writers, thank you for the camaraderie and the warm welcome to this lovely online community. Thanks to Demetra Saltmarsh and Renee White for keeping me in physical shape to write.

Finally, can I say a huge thank you to all the many bloggers and reviewers who took my last book to their hearts and did so much to contribute to its success. I've been absolutely astonished by the response to *See How They Run*, and I want to thank everyone who has taken the time to post a review or contact me via email, Facebook or Twitter.